THE
SHAAR
PRESS

THE JUDAICA IMPRINT
FOR THOUGHTFUL PEOPLE

IN THE

by
Chaim Eliav

translated by
Miriam Zakon

THE
SHAAR
PRESS

SPIDER'S WEB

Decades after the War,
a Jew is enmeshed in
international Nazi intrigue

Published by **SHAAR PRESS**
Distributed by MESORAH PUBLICATIONS, LTD.
4401 Second Avenue / Brooklyn, N.Y 11232 / (718) 921-9000

Distributed in Israel by SIFRIATI / A. GITLER BOOKS
10 Hashomer Street / Bnei Brak 51361

Distributed in Europe by J. LEHMANN HEBREW BOOKSELLERS
20 Cambridge Terrace / Gateshead, Tyne and Wear / England NE8 1RP

Distributed in Australia and New Zealand by GOLD'S BOOK & GIFT SHOP
36 William Street / Balaclava 3183, Vic., Australia

Distributed in South Africa by KOLLEL BOOKSHOP
Shop 8A Norwood Hypermarket / Norwood 2196 / Johannesburg, South Africa

ISBN: 1-57819-250-1

Produced in the United States of America by Noble Book Press Corp.

Where can I go from Your spirit?

And where can I flee from Your Presence? ...

Were I to take up wings of dawn,

were I to dwell in the distant west —

there, too, Your hand would guide me,

and Your right hand would grasp me.

— Psalms

ACKNOWLEDGMENTS

With appreciation to the many friends in Brazil from whom I heard the stories and events that form the background for this book.

With thanks to the members of the intelligence services who work in Brazil, far from home and without recognition. We never spoke, but we always knew they were there. From time to time intimations passed between us — but saying even this is too much.

I am obliged to the editors of *Mishpachah*, the magazine which serialized this work. Their forbearance with me and the story for over a year enabled this book to become a reality.

I am indebted to Miriam Zakon, my talented translator, who gave this story life and drama in its new language.

And above all, with overwhelming gratitude to The One Above, Who weaves the tapestry of destiny and leads each of us by the hand, so that none are ever truly lost.

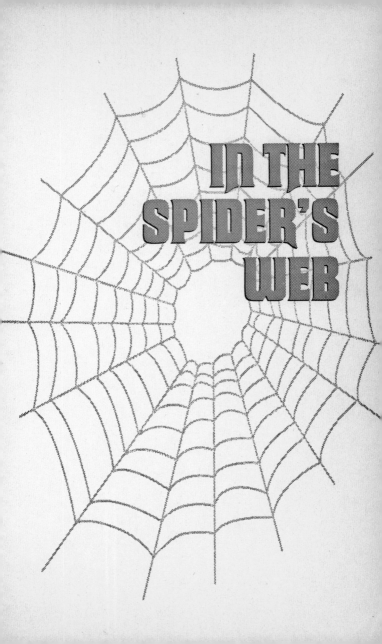

IN THE SPIDER'S WEB

The phone call came at 5:30, and changed the deal completely.

At 5 o'clock Jairo Silverman was peacefully lighting up a cigarette; he had all the time in the world. He inhaled deeply and leaned back in his new recliner. His eyes drifted upward towards the beautifully paneled ceiling, and his thoughts roamed free and unfettered. From outside the window of his office, located on the 33rd floor of one of downtown's largest and most luxurious buildings, came the muted sound of thousands of automobiles roaring past on the highways. The shadowy echo sounded like the waves pounding the surf of Santos, the city he would be visiting in a few hours, as he did each weekend.

The office was closed to the public. His two partners in the law firm had left to their homes in the suburbs. Only Claudia, their faithful secretary, remained in the next room, the sound of her clacking typewriter keys mingling with his thoughts.

Jairo Silverman gave a satisfied glance at the smoke rings lazily drifting upwards. Up, up they wandered, vanishing soundlessly as they reached the ceiling. At that hour he was still quite pleased with himself. And with good reason: In his hand he held a draft of the contract between his firm and the German Automotive Company, GAC, whose factories, the largest in the world, were being built at the outskirts of Sao Paulo. The sheaf of papers grasped in his hand represented the fruits of two years of patient effort. His office had invested huge sums in the venture, in the payment of bribes in the right places, to the right people. Interesting that his close friend, Alberto Hunkes, one of GAC's top executives, had refused to accept anything. Jairo tried to understand why. A fine man, Hunkes had been one of the prime movers in the deal. It was Hunkes who'd presented it to the factory's board of directors, giving his warm personal recommendation. He'd done so much behind the scenes. By rights, he deserved an "agent's fee" from the law firm of Silverman, Machado and Chilo. Alberto's refusal had been a stubborn move on his part, Jairo thought, unheard of in Brazil, where every business deal was entwined with bribery as a matter of course, where graft was almost legal.

Jairo bent down towards his desk. It couldn't hurt to read through the contract one more time. By its terms their office would represent GAC in all legal matters, both in Brazil and throughout the world. Jairo gave a satisfied smile. This business would bring them money, a lot of money. Even more important, it would be a tremendous source of prestige. He could already see the long lines of well-known companies standing in his waiting room, asking his firm to represent them.

Just an hour ago, immediately before their departure from the office, he and his partners, Francisco Machado and Paulo Chilo, had decided that somehow they must repay Alberto Hunkes for the incredible service he'd done them. At the same time, Jairo had decided to personally show his gratitude. After all, Alberto had actually done this for him. Hunkes hardly knew his partners; his help in this matter had come from their deep personal friendship that had its roots in a fascinating chapter that began many years ago.

Jairo finished reading through the draft, making small changes here and there. Basically, the document looked fine. He took one last look and bellowed, "Claudia!"

The door flew open. "*Si, senhor?*"

Jairo handed her the draft. "Take this, *por favor*. Put aside whatever you're doing and take care of this contract. I need four copies as quickly as possible. *Ta serto?*"

"*Si, senhor,*" she answered politely.

"Thank you," Jairo added, with a broad smile.

After a moment Jairo once again heard typewriter keys clicking energetically. The monotonous rhythm was like a song to his ears.

It was then that the telephone rang.

The jarring sound of the phone rudely broke the peaceful silence of the office. With a weary and impatient gesture, Jairo lifted the receiver. Clients who insisted on telephoning after office hours always infuriated him. And yet his natural curiosity, his desire to know who was calling so late, always overcame his anger. He answered the phone.

"Hello?"

His studied indifference as he sat in his leather armchair slowly disappeared, to be replaced by an increasingly serious and concerned mien. His eyes dashed nervously to and fro. He sat erect, emitting only one short word over and over throughout the conversation: "*Si … si … si … si ….*"

His hand, wrapped around the receiver, suddenly felt heavy. Before replacing it slowly on the phone he asked one question: "When did it happen?"

The voice at the other end of the line whispered something. Jairo did not answer, merely shook his head in a motion of anguish. When he'd replaced the receiver, he held his head between his hands. After a moment, he dialed his wife, already waiting for him in Santos.

"Paulina, it's me, Jairo. There's been a change in plans. I'm not coming tonight. I must remain in Sao Paulo. I'll be there tomorrow … yes … yes … not now … I'll explain everything tomorrow … tomorrow … when I arrive … In the meantime, go without me. Watch the children. *Chau.*"

The next call was to his partner, Francisco Machado.

"Hello, Francisco, *amigo*, cancel your weekend plans, at least until tomorrow afternoon. Bad news! Alberto Hunkes is dead. Yes, yes — dead. They don't know yet from what. Sudden death. Paulo called and told me. I don't know how he heard. The funeral, tomorrow, at ten. At the Catholic cemetery in Villa Mariana. What about the contract? How should I know? After the funeral we'll return to the office and see what must be done. *Chau.*"

Jerusalem, Israel
1 Iyar 5727 (1967)

With a final roar of its engine the Egged bus arriving from Tel Aviv came to a halt in Jerusalem's Central Bus Station. The hot, dry air of the holy city enveloped the few passengers who descended, one by one, during this afternoon hour. Yitzchak Austerlitz was the last one off. He stood on the platform for one minute, straightened his black hat and, giving his Chumash a gentle kiss, jammed the *sefer* into his slightly shabby attache. He hurried past the many city bus stops without pausing; his feet already recognized "his" stop. His heart churned with the emotions he always felt when entering Jerusalem. For almost a year he'd been making these weekly trips, arriving every Thursday and traveling to Bayit Vegan, to the yeshiva where his son Yaakov Yehoshua learned.

Yaakov Yehoshua! Just repeating his son's name made his heart beat faster. This weekly visit had become a necessity, one he couldn't miss. And yet he realized, without a doubt, that he'd had to send his only son away from home to learn. In this way, his son would fulfill the obligation, "Exile yourself to a place of Torah." But how the father suffered from the decision! Only when his young son, 14-year-old Yaakov Yehoshua, was near him, only when he saw him, did the fears that were with him constantly, day after day, recede somewhat.

"Yankele, your father's waiting for you outside!"

Yaakov Yehoshua's young friends had become accustomed to these regular visits, so different from those of their parents.

The father gave him a warm kiss. "What's new?"

"*Baruch Hashem*, fine," answered the son.

"Imma sent you the cake that you like."

Yaakov Yehoshua took the proferred cake, smiled at his father, and said, "Thanks a lot. Tell Imma it's a party for my friends when she sends us her treats."

The father gently touched his cheek. "How's the learning?"

"*Baruch Hashem*, good."

"And what about a *d'var Torah*?"

Yaakov Yehoshua knew that for the weekly visit he must prepare a *d'var Torah* based on the *gemara* he was learning. It was something his father expected of him, and he couldn't refuse. His father had actually learned in Yeshivas Chachmei Lublin, with the revered Rav Meir Shapiro *z"l*, in the years before its destruction. And yet, at this moment Yaakov Yehoshua wondered if his father, standing beside the stairs at the yeshiva's entrance, heard a word that he'd said. He was telling him a *chiddush* on the *sugya*, but his father's thoughts were clearly elsewhere. As always, when the boy had finished, he earned his father's kiss, a kiss accompanied by a deep sigh.

Afterwards, Yitzchak Austerlitz made the rounds of the *maggidei shiur*, and exchanged a few words with the *mashgiach*. Usually, this day did him a lot of good. His son's teachers were generous in their praise of him, his diligence, his excellent character, the fear of G-d that underlay his every action. What more could a Jewish father ask for?

Whenever this thought passed through Yitzchak Austerlitz's mind he would give still another deep sigh, as a quiet voice coming from deep within him whispered: *What more could a Jewish father ask for? There is something more for which to ask.*

As always, Yitzchak gave his son a long farewell hug, warm and strong, though he knew that it made Yaakov Yehoshua uncomfortable. It was embarrassing, to have all his friends see his father's feelings for him. Yaakov Yehoshua tried to pull away, but gently.

But this time, for whatever reason, his father seemed more emotional at their parting, and the hug was even stronger than usual. Yitzchak Austerlitz felt that he couldn't control himself. Tears fell from his eyes.

Perhaps he felt this way because today was the day he'd finally found the courage. Today he would visit Yad Vashem.

2

Sao Paulo, Brazil
May 12, 1967

Dawn was just beginning to touch the city's
horizon when Jairo awoke. Usually when he
was alone in his home he would sleep late,
but tonight for some reason he'd slept poorly.
Without wasting any time he opened the door of his
apartment, as he did each morning, and found the
Estado de Sao Paulo, Brazil's largest and most respected daily newspaper, lying in the hallway, placed
there by his reliable *zelador,* the apartment house's security guard, Arnaldo. Jairo bent to pick it up, feeling
his tension in the trembling of the fingers that
grasped the paper.

He closed the door behind him and turned towards
the kitchen. No wonder, he thought, that he was a bit
nervous. He still hadn't calmed down from the news
of his friend's sudden death. Not that there was
anything mysterious in Alberto's unexpected passing.

No, this would not be the first friend of his who had died so, suddenly and without warning, in his prime. That was life, Jairo knew, and no man could quite understand this deep and awesome phenomenon. And yet, though he couldn't explain it, something was bothering him. The fact that the hefty contract with GAC hadn't yet been finalized, and might now actually be invalidated, did not explain the feeling of ill omen that he felt this morning.

He entered the kitchen. The maid had accompanied his wife and children to the seaside city of Santos. He would have to make his own cup of coffee before traveling to the city, to the funeral. He opened the news-paper and began to indifferently skim through the day's headlines, moving from page to page as he always did. Suddenly — he knew. He felt his heart all but come to a stop. His eyes gazed at the headline on one of the last pages. News of Alberto's death.

GAC Executive Dies — Murder Suspected
by Rodriguez Aventura

SAO PAULO (May 12) — *Yesterday Mr. Alberto Hunkes, one of the top executives of GAC, collapsed suddenly in his home in the city's Hygienopolis neighborhood. He was brought unconscious to Samaritan Hospital and died shortly thereafter, surrounded by his wife, Regina, and his son, Eduardo. He was 55 years old.*

At the request of the widow the police performed an autopsy on the body. The results of the post-mortem indicated a large quantity of deadly poison in the deceased's stomach. The police have opened an investigation based on the suspicion of foul play. The police have placed a news blackout on the investigation, which is following several

> leads. Our reporter has discovered, from reliable
> sources, that the authorities are searching for an
> unknown man, a tourist who arrived three days
> ago from Europe, who was seen with the deceased
> in one of the city's most luxurious restaurants not
> long before his collapse.
>
> GAC has issued an official death notice,
> mourning a man who helped bring about a signif-
> icant rise in its sales in recent years, contributing
> to the firm's growing position in South America.
> The firm, the notice concludes, joins the family in
> mourning and will respectfully escort the deceased
> to his final resting place.

Shocked, Jairo put the newspaper down, his
hands shaking. He could feel his heart pounding
ceaselessly in his chest, like a sledgehammer.

"What is this?" he said aloud to himself.
"Suspected murder! It can't be! Who would want to
murder Alberto?"

The spacious kitchen suddenly seemed much too
small for him. He abandoned it for the apartment's
largest room and began to pace restlessly back and
forth. Could there be some connection with the contract that was to bind together his office and GAC?
Jairo well knew that there were some within the company who strongly opposed the deal. Hunkes had
never revealed the true reason behind the opposition,
though Jairo had a hazy notion.

His thoughts flew to the widow, Regina. In addition to her grief for the sudden death of her devoted
husband, she must be suffering from the police force's
terrible suspicion. He felt a sudden urgent desire to
call her, to encourage her, so that she know that her
good friends hadn't deserted her in time of trouble.

His hand grabbed for the telephone.

"Hello, *Senhora* Hunkes."

"*Si.*"

"This is Jairo, Jairo Silverman. I was shocked by yesterday's news. I am so grieved at Alberto's death. He was a close friend, like a brother. I share your sorrow."

"*Si.*"

The single word stabbed at Jairo's heart. The widow's voice was cold, distant. Jairo felt her chilly reaction immediately, and tried to understand what lay behind it.

"Now that I've read the newspaper," he continued, "I'm even more shocked. I'm stunned. Is there really a suspicion of murder? It's hard to believe! How could it be?"

"*Si,*" the dry, formal voice answered.

"Who?" Jairo cried into the telephone receiver. "Who in the world could want to kill him, such a wonderful man? Do the police, or do you, have any suspects?"

"*Si,*" the woman responded, never raising her voice, clearly impatient.

Jairo heard himself cry into the phone: "Who do you think wanted him dead?"

There was a short silence on the other end of the line. Then came the blow, aimed squarely at Jairo: "Your Jews, perhaps."

Jairo wanted to say something, but the words coming to his lips seemed to freeze in space. His mouth was open, but his brain seemed paralyzed. His head began to pound; he could feel the blood pressing againsthis forehead. His free hand reached for the nearest chair and pulled it towards him. Still clutching the receiver, he sat down. Even through the telephone he could feel the cold hatred that underlay those incredible words.

How could it be? What had happened to her? Could this possibly be Regina?

When he spoke, his tone had changed, was no longer full of grief. "May I understand, madam," he said in almost a whisper, "do I understand that it is not desired that I attend the funeral this morning?"

The widow's voice suddenly sounded different.

"On the contrary," she said, "you must come. I hope you will come. I am waiting for you."

Jairo was confused. What was this change in tone? What could lay behind it? Why did she so want him to take part in the funeral service? A terrifying thought passed through his brain; a thought that warned him of a possible trap, a pitfall he could not even guess at. In his heart at that moment he vowed to behave with the utmost caution and alertness. The death of his friend suddenly ceased to grieve him as it had up to now; the mystery of Alberto's passing took up all his attention. All Jairo knew now was that he understood less and less of what was happening around him.

"I understand," he said, after a short silence. With difficulty he managed to utter a final *"Chau"* before putting the receiver back on the hook.

Jerusalem
1 Iyar 5727 (1967)

Yitzchak Austerlitz didn't walk — he ran. Rather, he was pushed.

He found himself walking alone on the sidewalk that led from Herzl Boulevard to Yad Vashem. The terrifying voices that burst forth from his heart and assaulted his brain propelled him forward with a mighty, unstoppable force. For months he'd dreamed of this moment, when he would find the courage to do what he now planned on doing. Months? Truthfully, years! From the day of the Eichmann trial, which reopened the terrible wounds that had so painfully begun healing, the tremendous desire had grown. From that time, it had given him no rest.

As he approached Yad Vashem he felt his knees buckle. How he longed to flee, to escape from this place. And yet those voices, those terrible voices overpowered him and would not allow him to turn away. It was as if they had grabbed him and were leading him, as one is led to the scaffold, step after step, to the horrifying end. Yitzchak Austerlitz could not remember when he had last felt such terror as he did during these minutes, as he walked through the entrance gate and approached the buildings themselves. He felt the restless trembling that seized his entire being. Would his strength see him through during the time of trial?

Yitzchak passed by the information booth, not sparing a glance for the man within. He ignored the group of Japanese tourists who walked near him with indifferent and closed faces, their cameras flashing at the pictures of concentration camps and ghettos.

He stood before the memorial candle, his eyes hastily skimming the names of the destroyed communities that were inscribed on the floor in the silent dimness. His burning eyes could not find what he sought. Was his community forgotten, then, and not included among the others for eternal remembrance? Yitzchak could not be certain; the names inscribed in stone danced before his eyes. He could not read them clearly: The letters, seen through a haze of tears, seemed to waver, turning into terrifying images.

He did not spend much time there. This was not his goal. He reached the display room and silently glanced at picture after picture of catastrophe that was hung upon the walls. This was the first time since he'd come to Israel in 5705 (1945) that he had returned to the inferno.

Eyes filled with despair, he searched for images he could recognize. The name of his town in Galicia, the town where he'd been born, where he'd lived, and where he'd lost all that he possessed, did not appear in the captions. And yet each picture brought out of his searing memory horrifying images of those accursed years.

Yitzchak wandered among the photographs, not knowing how much time had passed as he traveled again through the darkness of the past. He did not feel the presence of others in the hall, did not pay attention to that which was happening around him. He did not know if anyone was near or if he was alone, wandering once again through the horrors of the Holocaust. He simply wasn't here: He was there. He walked through the exhibits like a drunk, not knowing what was going on around him. And yet he knew exactly what it was he was searching for, and not for a moment did he forget what he had come for that day.

And then — it seemed to him that he had found it …

3

J airo hurried. The funeral was set to begin in another half hour. His black Aero-Willis automobile raced through the streets of the Jardim America neighborhood where he lived. His car passed the main boulevard, the Avenida Paulista, sped down the Consolacao and, after a few hundred meters, turned left towards the high-class neighborhood, the Hygienopolis. His business partner, Francisco Machado, was already standing in front of his home, obviously impatient, waiting for him. Jairo slowed down and Francisco wordlessly entered the car.

Before he'd left his house Jairo had called and asked Francisco to accompany him to the funeral, instead of taking his own car. This was important: Jairo didn't want to go to the cemetery by himself. After the shocking conversation with the widow, a conversation that had left him angry and upset, he didn't know what to expect, what might happen to him there. Despite the deep anger that coursed through his veins, Jairo had to confess to the bitter fact that he needed the security that Francisco gave him. This as the first time in his life that he could remember needing a gentile to shield him from an anti-Semitic attack.

Jairo apologized. "I'm sorry for the delay, Francisco. You know how it is, the lights always turn red when you're in a hurry."

"No matter," came the short reply.

Francisco, a crafty and clever Brazilian, felt the tension and nervousness in his Jewish partner's voice. He'd purposely restrained himself in greeting Jairo, knowing the strong ties that bound Jairo and Alberto Hunkes. Jairo's nervousness was undoubtedly a result of the sudden loss of his close friend. Jairo's emotions were understandable, he thought. Such an event is never easy, all the more so because of the huge GAC contract, whose fate was now in doubt...

Despite their hurried ride through the streets of Sao Paulo, they were late, arriving at the gates of the cemetery ten minutes after the funeral had been called for. They saw no sign of either the Hunkes family or the pall-bearers. Only the parking lot, filled with luxury cars, gave a sign that within the walls of the cemetery a man was being laid to rest.

"Come, let's go in," said Francisco, "They're probably burying him. That's all we need, that they should notice that we're late. All the GAC people will be there, no doubt."

Jairo didn't answer, just nodded his head in silent assent. They left the car, walked through the iron gate and descended into the cemetery. Only the quiet whistling of the wind through the trees broke the deep, deathly silence of the place. They saw no one among the many varied headstones. After a walk of several minutes they finally found, a few hundred meters away, that which they sought. They turned towards the group, remaining at the edge of the small cluster of men dressed in black standing quietly and with great decorum.

"This is it, we're here," Jairo whispered. "See? That's Regina, the widow."

"Poor thing," remarked Francisco.

Jairo didn't answer. The secret of their ugly conversation lay deep within his heart. Now, surrounded by the other mourners, he could clearly feel the tension that had overwhelmed him. He felt alert, coiled like a spring. He found himself whistling quietly to himself.

Francisco gave him a hurried glance, surprised.

Jairo and Francisco carefully and quietly moved up a few steps. Now they were quite near the group surrounding the open grave. No one noticed their arrival, or else pretended not to. Jairo looked carefully at the faces of those standing near the grave. He only recognized a few of them. All stood quietly facing a tall, grey-haired man who stood erect near the top of the casket, speaking so quietly that his voice could barely be heard. Jairo stared at him; he didn't look familiar at all. But his hawklike face, his severe mien and intense expression, drew Jairo's attention. He tried to make out the words of the eulogy that the man was saying over the grave of his friend Alberto, but it was hard to hear anything clearly. From where he was standing it seemed that he was hearing German being spoken. Could he be mistaken? Jairo felt a warning bell go off in his head.

The tall man continued to whisper towards the others who listened, heads bowed, features frozen, to every word he uttered. Occasionally he would raise his voice, and Jairo would have the chance to catch a passing phrase. Frightening words, words that sent shivers down his spine. Without realizing what he was doing he grabbed at his partner, Francisco Machado. No, there was no mistake: The little Yiddish he'd heard in his home was sufficient for him to understand the gist of the words — "international Jewry," "fuehrer," "German."

When he'd finished his short eulogy the grey-haired man bowed his head, and his cold eyes swept past the people gathered there. A new wave of fear engulfed Jairo. He could clearly hear the clicking of heels of many of the participants. It had a military sound, and it sent a thrill of horror through him. But true terror engulfed him as he noticed two of the older men, standing on either side of the grave, raise their hands in the Nazi salute, holding them up through the long minutes in which the coffin was lowered into the ground and covered by earth.

Jairo felt his head aching. All he wanted to do was flee from the spot as quickly as he could. An awful thought raced through his mind. It was clear he'd been attending a Nazi funeral. Who knew how many of these people, dressed now in their dark, elegant suits, had once worn the uniform of the S.S.? What was the explanation of the awful tableau unfolding before his eyes? Had his friend Alberto, too, been a former Nazi? Even in this horrifying moment the thing seemed impossible. How could he have been such a close friend of a Jew? Alberto certainly knew that Jairo was Jewish. More than once Alberto had accompanied him to visit his parents, "graduates" of the Buchenwald concentration camp in the early years of the Nazi rule. He remembered now how patiently Alberto has listened to his father's stories of Kristalnacht, the night of broken glass when Germany's synagogues had been shattered, and of the tortures of Buchenwald. Alberto always empathized with their agony, was interested in the details, and would emotionally show how he shared the sorrow of the Jewish people. And now...now was Jairo to think that his behavior was nothing more than a cold, hypocritical mask? Impossible! It simply couldn't be. Regina was something else altogether. The morning's unfortunate conversation had revealed something ugly in her character. But Alberto? Jairo felt at that moment that he'd lost not only a good friend, but his last vestige of belief in mankind.

But Jairo, with all his burning desire to be far away from this dangerous place, remained paralyzed, rooted to the spot. He watched all that was going on without expression. Francisco stood next to him, feeling the terrible emotions that were enveloping his partner.

"*Calmo, calmo, amigo,*" Francisco whispered.

"Francisco, let's get out of here," Jairo answered quietly, but with an edge of panic in his voice. "I can't take any more. Remember, I am a Jew. What's happening here is a terrible mistake! Terrible! Apparently we've found ourselves in a crowd of Nazis! What they have to do with Alberto, I can't understand. Come, let's get out of here! I can't take any more! I've got to think!"

Francisco forcibly stopped him.

"Stop acting like a fool! Remember the contract with GAC! Get hold of yourself! Play their game.

What are you afraid of? Remember, you're in Brazil, not in Germany. I beg you."

Jairo grew silent. The crowd surrounding the grave slowly began to disperse and make its way towards the exit. Silently the participants shook each other's hands. The widow, Regina, dressed in black, stood next to her son, bowing formally to all who had come to pay their respects to her husband's memory. Jairo was afraid to approach her, afraid of her reaction when he would appear before her. Softly but firmly Francisco pushed him towards the mourners.

Jairo passed before her, Francisco behind him. He gave a polite bow, feeling his heart pounding within him. Regina proudly lifted her head, gave him a disdainful look and then ignored him, bowing towards Francisco. Eduardo, Alberto's son, also ignored his existence. It was as if Eduardo had never visited his home, as if he had never gone with Jairo to the Chacara ranch in the Eldorado, to ride horseback together within its large stables. The young man had spent many weekends with Jairo's family; had the anti-Semitic widow managed to poison his mind so against him?

Jairo noticed that the others at the funeral, too, behaved coldly towards him, with a clear though veiled enmity. Among them were several executives of GAC. Francisco, though, was accorded all the attention expected at such an event. During those difficult moments, that seemed to last a lifetime, Jairo was truly alone. *Classic Jewish loneliness*: The troubling thought slipped through his mind, a thought he immediately banished. He was a Brazilian, after all. And yet — a Brazilian Jew. He had always felt the equal to his gentile friends, never had discerned any difference. Was that why Regina had insisted on his attending the funeral? To cast him down, to make him feel alone and different and solitary, to use her husband's burial to throw into his face the deep hatred that she felt for him? But why? Why?

"Francisco," he whispered to his partner, as they slowly made their way out of the cemetery, "I can't rest until I understand what happened here! Until I know who Alberto Hunkes really was."

Francisco gave his defeated friend a pensive look.

"What do you think, what's going to happen to the GAC contract?"

To his shock, Jairo answered, "Frankly, I'm not really interested."

Francisco touched him lightly on the shoulder. "Go, *amigo*, to Santos. You know what, don't bother coming back to the office on Monday. Stay at the beach for a few days. That will help. Okay?"

Jairo didn't even have the strength to give him a grateful smile.

Three hours later, in his small apartment in the resort city of Santos, Jairo's wife handed him a letter that had been delivered just a few moments before his arrival. Impatiently, Jairo tore at it. The words added still another blow to this accursed Friday:

> *"Jairo Silverman, we know all that has passed. We have seen all — in the cemetery. We ask that you do nothing. Do not investigate anyone. Let Alberto Hunkes rest in his grave; do not disturb him or us."*

The letter was not signed.

"Who brought it?" he screamed, trembling uncontrollably.

"What are you shouting for? What's happened to you?" Paulina answered, perplexed. "It was brought by a taxi driver. He said he was asked to deliver it. Don't worry, he was paid in advance. What does it say, and who wrote it?"

Jairo didn't answer. He stared out the window at the sea. The ocean was stormy, the waves attacking the beach but never conquering it. The sky was dark, ready to shed mournful tears...

"Make me a cup of coffee. I've got to get some sleep," Jairo finally said weakly.

Jerusalem
Yad Vashem
1 Iyar 5727 (1967)

Yitzchak Austerlitz stood there, his eyes wide, almost popping out of their sockets. Slowly, so slowly, the objects surrounding him disappeared. The other visitors wandering through the exhibition evaporated. The pictures hung on the walls, the walls themselves vanished into nothingness. He stood there — alone. Yitzchak Austerlitz, alone, alone before — the picture. He felt something stab through his chest, a stabbing that took his breath away. His temples beat in a murderous rhythm. It was him! Yitzchak was certain! It was him!

From an infinite distance Yitzchak heard the horrifying sounds of that terrible morning. It had been Shabbos. He remembered it perfectly. Yitzchak Austerlitz covered his ears with his hands. No use: From within, within his heart, rose wild cries, tragic screams, as the cursed soldiers attacked the homes of his village. And then — it happened. Yes! It was him! He remembered him perfectly! Yitzchak remembered his proud bearing as he stood in the doorway. He remembered the quick, short orders he barked to the gangs of Nazis who conquered Yitzchak's home and destroyed it, as they tore his wife and three babies from him — five-year-old Devoraleh; Yosef Tzvi, two years old; and little Yaakov Yehoshua, age three months. For some unknown reason the enemy chose to allow him, the bereaved father, to remain alive. But not before grabbing him mercilessly by the beard and jerking his head up:

"What's your name, Jew?"

"Yitzchak." The answer came, unbidden.

"What else? Quickly!"

A blow to his teeth.

"Austerlitz. Yitzchak Austerlitz," he answered quickly, feeling his mouth wet with blood.

The Nazi chuckled wickedly.

"Yitzchak Austerlitz, say a nice goodbye to your young family. Tell them you'll meet them again — in hell."

He remembered how he remained dumb. Another blow ended his silence.

"Say it!"

The moment rose before him in his tortured heart. The moment when he said what he'd been commanded to say. The moment in the picture which stood before him.

Yitzchak Austerlitz began to touch the picture, pushing it back and forth, back and forth, until a strong hand grabbed his arm …

4

Paulo Chilo was the first to speak: "I'm sorry that at the last minute I couldn't make it to the funeral."

Jairo Silverman gave a bitter laugh. "And I'm sorry that I did make it!"

"In that case," Francisco Machado interjected, in order to bring the conversation back to where it belonged, "in that case, I, too, will be sorry about something. I'm sorry that there was a funeral at all! What's worrying me now is the fate of the GAC contract. That, in my opinion, is the most pressing issue now. And I think," he continued, "that, despite everything, you agree with my assessment, Jairo."

Francisco accompanied the words with a piercing look.

Jairo didn't answer. He was still drained from the events of the weekend. Now, on this Monday after that terrible Friday, the three partners sat in their Sao Paulo office conferring on what steps should be taken next. The central topic was, of course, GAC. From the look on Chilo's face, Jairo could see that his information was up to date, that Francisco had already told him what had happened at the cemetery on Friday. Still, one deep secret remained concealed within his breast. He hadn't told them about the mysterious letter that had been delivered to his Santos home. They'd been partners for nearly five years, and this was the first time he felt something tangible separating them. He was a Jew. And these two were gentiles, who would never, with all their good will, understand the Jewish spirit — particularly a Jew whose parents had reached Brazil as refugees fleeing the Holocaust. Furthermore, he remembered at that moment, Paulo Chilo was a Lebanese Arab, though a third-generation Brazilian as well.

"And so, what to do?" Francisco sent his question spinning into the air.

No one rushed to respond.

"What's clear," Jairo finally answered quietly, "I personally am out of the game. I can't help much any more. I just hope that because of me nothing gets ruined."

Francisco and Paulo exchanged a hasty glance, one which did not escape Jairo. He felt a possible crisis in their relations building up.

"Despite everything, Jairo, I think you're exaggerating," Francisco said.

"Perhaps," Jairo sighed, "and don't I wish it! Right now, though, I'm feeling pessimistic. I think you should handle the matter yourselves."

Ultimately, the decision was Jairo's: He was the senior partner in the office.

"And what does it mean?" Paulo tried to understand this new turn of events.

"Simple. From this moment you two will main-
tain all contact with the company executives.
Carefully check if it will be possible to save our joint
venture. You, Francisco, gently hint that if the contract will not be signed nothing will happen, but
somehow the public will find out that anti-Semitism
is behind it. You know that today such things are not
acceptable to the Brazilian public, and they are illegal as well. It's hard for me to believe that a concern
as respected as GAC will be ready to risk such a
public relations mess. That's it. That's all I have to
say. You'll have to take care of it."

"Jairo," Francisco said, when he'd finished speaking, "rely on us. We'll take care of everything."

They gave Jairo's shoulder a friendly pat. They understood his feelings: They shared his grief.

The conversation came to an end. Jairo returned
to his private office, and his two partners also disappeared into their rooms. From the time Jairo had
entered his office, he'd waited for the moment he'd
be alone. Without hesitation he dialed the number of
Police Officer Roberto Nunes. He knew Nunes from
way back in their university days, when they'd been
students together. They had kept strong ties between them, which had benefited both
professionally as well. A bond between a police officer conducting criminal investigations and an
attorney called upon to defend clients with doubtful
reputations was fated to be a successful one, particularly in Brazil, where one could obtain anything
by means of bribery. Jairo Silverman and Roberto
Nunes had made the most of their connection.

"Hello, Roberto; it's me, Jairo, Jairo Silverman. *Bom dia.*"

"*Bom dia,*" Roberto's cheery voice said. "How are you? What's new? How was your weekend? And what brings you calling so early this morning?"

"Everything is fine, thank G-d."

"Can I help you with something?"

"I think so. How was your vacation this week?"

"Some vacation! We had planned, my wife and I, to travel to Argentina for a week, to Buenos Aires, to her uncles there. But because of what happened they canceled all leaves in our unit. All the investigators and detectives had to stay in the city."

"Why? What happened?"

"What, didn't you hear about this weekend's murder?"

Jairo felt his breath grow short. With an effort, he mastered his trembling voice:

"And you over there in criminal investigations still get excited about murder? Roberto, how many people get murdered in Sao Paulo every day?"

There was a moment's silence.

"Jairo, don't you read the paper?"

"I read."

"Well, the facts weren't made so clear, but this was no ordinary murder. One of the bigwigs at GAC isn't murdered every day."

Jairo's heart skipped a beat. "Yes, that's right, I remember something about it. Name of Alberto Hunkes, if I'm not mistaken."

"You're not. But that was the end of my vacation. What could I do; the commissioner is giving this investigation the highest priority."

"Why?"

"Don't know. Something smells bad here. There's clear indications that this was murder. And yet the GAC company has asked us, if possible, to call off all investigation."

"Interesting."

"Does it really interest you, Jairo?"

"Not particularly. But as a lawyer you never know. Maybe the two of us will make something out of this case. Maybe the suspect will hire me to defend him and I'll have to prove that he's innocent, while you'll have to prove the opposite. This could be big business."

The two laughed. "That depends, of course, on who pays the judge more — us or you."

"So tell me more."

"Okay. It's clear it was murder."

"Clear?"

"That's right. They found poison in the abdomen of this Hunkes. Poison that he'd swallowed about an hour and a half before he collapsed at home. The chemical composition, and how it killed him, isn't important at this moment."

"Go on."

"Okay, the details that we know at this point are that Hunkes was in the company of a man who called himself Jurgen Osten of Copenhagen. The man had arrived here a day before, on a direct flight from Germany. Two hours after he'd left Hunkes in the Praca da Republica he was already on a direct Varig flight to Paris."

"And what line is the investigation taking?"

"We're still searching in the dark. We don't know what to think, what lines to follow. There are a lot of question marks. The telex that we received from the

Copenhagen police hasn't helped to clear the fog from this murder. They reported that the passport was forged. No such person exists in their population records. That's one reason my vacation was canceled. And then came this request, politely worded but urgent, of GAC's, that we stop the investigation. The official reason they gave was that it would harm the corporation's business and in any case we wouldn't be able to find the mysterious murderer. You want to know the truth? I don't like their behavior one bit."

"You're right. It certainly looks strange."

"Wait a minute. That's not all. The family too — the widow has asked us to leave it alone. She's not prepared to cooperate with us. She won't give us any details that will help us further our investigation. Actually, she hinted pretty broadly that she would be very grateful if we'd close the file. Pretty strange, huh, Jairo?"

"Very strange," Jairo replied. He felt a strong urge to tell his friend the awful things that had happened in the cemetery during the funeral. But he backed off. No. No. And not because of the note he'd gotten in Santos — though, when he thought of it, he felt a spasm of fear.

The phone line remained quiet for a few seconds. Finally, Roberto continued. "Look, Jairo, we feel that something here's not right. The family and GAC are hiding something. Their desire to close up the affair has raised our suspicions. The murderer may have come from Europe, but the murder took place here and we think it has its roots in Brazil, in Sao Paulo. You understand me?"

"I understand you perfectly. So what's next?"

"As I told you, we're still caught in a fog. We haven't a clue as to who wanted to murder Alberto Hunkes."

"If that was his real name."

"What'd you say?" The voice on the other side of the line sounded surprised.

"Nothing, nothing at all," Jairo answered hurriedly.

"But Jairo, I've completely forgotten what you wanted from me."

"Believe me, I've forgotten too."

After a short silence, he added, "What do you think, Roberto, can you join me for lunch?"

"Today?"

"Why not? Do you have something better to do?"

Roberto laughed. "If you think I know more about the affair than I've told you, you're mistaken. It'll be a waste of food."

"The food won't go to waste, Roberto." Jairo sounded confident.

"Fine. In an hour in the restaurant on the roof of the *Edificio Italia*."

"Great. *Chau.*"

"*Chau.*"

Jairo hung up the phone. For some reason he felt his spirits lift, and the misery of the past few days lighten considerably. At that moment he felt capable of taking care of office business once again. He turned towards the cabinet to pull out a file. And then he heard the phone ring.

"Hello?" he answered, in his most professional, lawyer-like tone.

"Do not dine with Police Officer Roberto Nunes. For your own good, *Senhor* Jairo Silverman."

The telephone went dead.

"Hello! Hello!" he shouted into the phone. "Who are you? Why are you listening in on my calls? What do you want from me?"

Jerusalem
Yad Vashem
1 Iyar 5727 (1967)

Yitzchak Austerlitz awoke as if from a dream. He felt the pressure of a hand grabbing his arm, pulling him from the picture whose frame he'd grasped. He felt convulsed with fear, his spirit dwelling somewhere in Hitler's Europe.

"Sir," the guard said in a stern and angry voice, "what is this crazy behavior? It is absolutely forbidden to touch the exhibits. I must ask you to leave the museum right now!"

"But…" Yitzchak Austerlitz tried to explain.

"No 'buts.' " It was the relentless voice of officialdom speaking. "You are leaving voluntarily, or else I'm calling for security and we'll throw you out of here. Understand?"

"But it's him! It's him!" Yitzchak Austerlitz shouted. His trembling finger pointed to the wall. Bored tourists wandering between the exhibits showed signs of life at the bizarre behavior unfolding before a picture, in which several Nazi officers could be seen smiling during an *aktion* somewhere in Galicia.

"There's no 'him,' sir. You must respect this place, as all visitors do. Damaging exhibits is punishable by law."

He motioned to two other guards who were in the area and together the three began to pull Yitzchak Austerlitz out, paying no attention to his objections.

"I've got to see him again. He killed my wife and children! I must have that picture! I want to know his name! I must know his name!"

Suddenly he grew silent. His body grew limp within the arms of the guards, keepers of law and order. His head lolled weakly.

"Water! Water!" the guard yelled in visible panic.

5

Yitzchak Austerlitz was laid gently down
upon the floor. The frightened security officers
called urgently for help. Deep in their hearts
they feared that the strange old religious Jew
had suffered a stroke and had died in their arms. One
of the three sped out of the exhibition hall to tell his
superiors what had happened. The few Japanese
tourists, who had been strolling peacefully between
the exhibits, were galvanized into action. Cameras
were quickly enlisted, flash equipment set up, and an
interesting shot — Jew lying on the floor of Yad
Vashem — was prepared for their souvenir photo album of their trip to the Holy Land.

The guard who'd gone for help jumped into the
hall, accompanied by a doctor and the institution's
director. They forcibly made a path through the circle of interested tourists surrounding the prostrate

figure. The doctor stooped down and began to examine Yitzchak. He carefully checked his pulse and heartbeat. After a few minutes he turned his face upwards and spoke. "He's fine. Pulse is a bit weak. He's just fainted."

The guards breathed a sigh of relief.

The doctor again turned towards his motionless patient. "Rabbi, can you hear me? Can you hear me? Wake up!"

There was no answer. The doctor gently slapped his patient's face, again and again. After a few seconds, Yitzchak Austerlitz slowly began to open his eyes. He looked at the circle of people around him without comprehension.

"Where am I?" he shouted, in sudden panic.

"Calm down, sir," the director of Yad Vashem, standing nearby watching the doctor's attempts to rouse the man, said. "First of all, rest up a little. Then, come to my office for a chat. You are in Yad Vashem."

Yitzchak didn't understand.

"Yad Vashem? What am I doing in Yad Vashem?"

"That's exactly what I'd like to know. In a little while we'll try to figure it out, together. But first — you've got to recover a little."

The director turned towards two of the guards.

"Help him up, please. Take him to one of the offices, bring him a cold drink. After he's rested a bit and is more himself, let me know."

An hour later, Yitzchak found himself sitting in the office of the director of Yad Vashem. The director had received a full report on the events in the exhibition hall, and on the wild behavior of the man sitting opposite him.

He gave a weak smile. "Well, how are you feeling?"

Yitzchak was still confused. While he had rested he heard what happened from the guards, he himself had no memory of what had occurred. When they reminded him that he'd wanted to damage one of the exhibits — a photograph of a group of Nazi officers smiling near a pile of dead Jews — he burst into bitter tears. It had taken him a great effort to stop crying, and his voice still trembled as he answered the director.

"*Baruch Hashem*, better."

"And what's your name, sir?" the director asked in a quiet and friendly tone.

"Yitzchak Austerlitz."

"Where do you live?"

"In Bnei Brak. Or perhaps in a village of Galicia. I honestly don't know where I live."

The director took his eyes off him, gave a little sigh. He forced himself to speak with a measure of confidence. "And what did you come looking for, here in Yad Vashem?"

Yitzchak Austerlitz searched for the words. Finally, he spoke. "For the murderer, who murdered me."

The director began to feel uncomfortable with this unexpected encounter. He hoped to end this conversation quickly. For a moment he considered sending for the police, having them deal with this confused old man. He pushed the thought away.

"Sir, your behavior in the exhibition hall was unacceptable. It's clear to me that you're struggling with a heavy load of strong emotions, and so I'm not going to bring the police into this. But I won't allow you to make fun of me and give me such answers. You are, thank G-d, alive. What is this, that you're looking for someone who killed you?"

Yitzchak Austerlitz gazed at the respected director with pitying eyes. Such thin skin! *How can he understand me, this pampered and spoiled young man,* he thought to himself. But his habit of judging favorably won out.

"Excuse me, sir, if I've offended you. But were you there? If, heaven forbid, you'd been there, as I was there, you would know that I am speaking the truth. My body lives in Bnei Brak, but my restless spirit and wandering soul are in the village where I was born. Where I grew up. Where I married a woman — and where I was murdered. Yes, yes, I was murdered on the day when the accursed ones took my wife and children from me, forever. Can you understand that, sir?" he asked with open fury.

"Yes, yes, I understand," the director answered, clearly uncomfortable. "But that doesn't justify what you did an hour ago. What did you want from the picture hanging on the wall?"

Yitzchak Austerlitz put his face in his hands. Then he spoke.

"You're right, sir, and I ask your pardon. But I saw him there in the picture!"

"Who?"

"The murderer! The cursed Nazi that broke into my home on that day! For many months I've been fighting myself, trying to decide whether or not to come here. I came to Yad Vashem to search for him in your pictures and documents. Again, I am sorry that I lost control. But I came here to ask for your help. Help me! Help me find him! I must know his name, if there is any news of him. Is he dead, or does he still live? If he is still alive, I must see him! I must! Do you understand?"

Yitzchak spoke heatedly. After a short, painful silence, he muttered one more sentence. "Do you understand — I must look him in the eyes."

Again, he put his face in his hands. His head trembled uncontrollably. After a moment he revealed his face and whispered: "And perhaps someone will bring him to justice."

The director attempted to calm him down. "Mr. Austerlitz," he said quietly, in almost a whisper, "you must control yourself, at all costs. You must try to forget what happened to you during the war. Many who went through that hell, like you, have built themselves new lives, new homes, here in our land. One can't live forever in the shadow of these memories. You, too, must do it!"

Yitzchak swayed in his chair. His knees trembled.

"You don't understand. I have tried to do so. I have built myself a new Jewish life after *baruch Hashem* having come to Eretz Yisrael. *Baruch Hashem!* But you, after having brought Eichmann to trial, you brought the memories back to me. From that time, I cannot rest. The wound has been reopened. I have endless nightmares. Six years ago, when I saw Eichmann sitting in his glass cage, everything was re-awakened. I saw myself once again behind the barbed wire of Auschwitz: as if it had happened yesterday. It was all so close. Close — I could almost touch it. Until that day I had felt myself so small, degraded, like a pitiful dwarf standing helplessly by the legs of the frightening German giant. The German, whose great stature blocked out even the rays of the sun. But from the day of Eichmann's judgment, all that changed. From then, I have the power and will to stand before him. To meet him. To hear from him exactly where he took my wife and children; to learn where they...they...where they died as G-d's martyrs. Can you understand?"

The last words came out as a shout. His face grew contorted. His bottom lip jutted out obstinately; his short beard seemed to stand up before him. His eyes grew small; his mouth thin and miserly. His black hat rocked upon his head like a sea-tossed ship. The director felt a moment's fear. The thought flashed through his mind: *How he resembles the wandering Jew of the Diaspora.*

The director nervously played with a pen that stood on his desk. "I understand," he said, in an attempt to placate the man sitting before him. "But you must try to overcome and ..."

Yitzchak Austerlitz didn't let him continue. He seemed to stand a little straighter.

"I'm sorry, sir. I'm asking for your help, not your advice. Can this institution help me find the name of that young officer who appears in the picture, the officer on the left? Have you any information on him? Is he dead? Or is he still alive, somewhere in the world? Every day they find Nazis who escaped and found sanctuary in far-off countries!"

"And if you knew? What then?"

Yitzchak Austerlitz turned expressive eyes upon him.

"I have told you. If I know that he's alive I will do everything to find him. Everything! I'll travel to the ends of the earth to meet him. I'll force him to speak. Or else — I don't believe my spirit will ever be able to rest."

Suddenly, Yitzchak stood up, his entire being ready for battle.

"I see, sir, that you are hesitating. It seems that you don't understand. And so I demand of you: Give me that picture. Now!"

The last word came out, a scream.

Sao Paulo, Brazil
May 15, 1967

For a long moment Jairo simply stared at the telephone in his hand. He felt waves of anger engulf him. It seemed to him that beyond the telephone receiver — whose dial tone sounded at this moment like the shriek of an alarm — he could hear the mysterious words echoing again and again:

"Do not dine with Police Officer Roberto Nunes. For your own good, *Senhor* Jairo Silverman."

Jairo racked his brain. Who could be behind this attempt to stop his meeting? Who was this terrifying eavesdropper? And what was this unknown person afraid of? How could he, a young Jewish attorney in Sao Paulo, endanger someone? He had read in the *Estado de Sao Paulo* that after Eichmann's capture by Israeli forces, Nazi organizations fought bitterly against anyone who tried to reveal the identities of war criminals who, after Hitler's downfall, had escaped to South America. These stories, that he'd read with little interest, suddenly seemed very real, and very ominous. Could it be these Nazi organizations threatening him? How could they know how he'd felt at the possibility of his friend Alberto's double identity? How could they know that he'd decided to uncover the real Alberto? He had only told his partner, Francisco. He felt stunned, struck by a bolt of lightning. Could his partner, Francisco, be working for them? Impossible; Jairo discarded the idea. But then — how could they know? And what were they afraid of? Even if he found that Alberto had been a Nazi — perhaps a highly placed Nazi — what would happen? Alberto was dead! Why protect a dead Nazi? What could they be hiding? Why did they want to stop the investigation?

Jairo set the receiver down. He could feel fear crawling through him like a worm, a deep fear of these mysterious people, who knew everything, a fear of people who could hear his telephone conversations, know his every move, reach him wherever they wished. Should he give up this desire of his, to know the true identity of Alberto Hunkes?

Jairo leaned back deeply into his chair. And suddenly he felt, with all the mystery and danger, his curiosity growing. He *must* know; it had become almost a necessity. Should he struggle with hidden, unknown obstacles and despite the warning go to the meeting with Roberto Nunes? Or should he give in and stay in his office? That was the difficult question that he had to answer in the next half hour, the amount of time left before his meeting. He felt a pain in his chest, as if a heavy stone were embedded within him, lying on his heart.

Jairo stood up and went towards the small bar in one corner of the office. He pulled out a small bottle of Chivas Regal and poured himself a drink. He needed help — and a drink would undoubtedly help.

Suddenly, his decision was made. As if pushed from within and unable to stop himself, he hastily grabbed the various papers lying on his desk and placed them in a neat pile. He straightened his tie, pulled his jacket off its hanger and jumped out of his office. He burst into Francisco's office and shouted: "Listen, Francisco, I'm going! I'm not afraid of anyone! I'll meet with him no matter what! But if I haven't come back to the office by 5 o'clock, have the police search for me, and let them find out if I've been at the *Edificio Italia*, in the rooftop restaurant."

Francisco jumped out of his chair. "What are you talking about, Jairo? What's happened to you?"

Jairo answered, "It doesn't matter. If I'm not back by 5, call the police."

Suddenly he remembered, and added, "And tell my wife, Paulina."

These last words were shouted as he hurried towards the elevator. But as the elevator doors opened before him he suddenly remembered something, and he raced back towards his office.

6

Francisco Machado was left open mouthed. "Something's happened to him," he thought. "Quiet Jairo, who never raises his voice. Jairo, always smiling, always taking things easy. These outbursts just aren't like him! What disturbed him so in the cemetery, during the funeral? Strange. So some Nazi raised his hand and yelled 'Heil Hitler.' Big deal!"

Francisco rubbed his hands together and attempted to return to the document he'd been reading before the odd interruption. But he wasn't able to concentrate. Hurriedly he left his own office and turned toward Paulo Chilo's. He'd exchange a few words with him, to see what they should do about Jairo, the boss who it seemed wasn't altogether well. But in the hallway there was an unavoidable accident as Jairo, racing back towards his office, careened directly into his astonished partner, who reflexively grabbed his wounded head with his two hands.

"Excuse me," Jairo said hurriedly, "when I return to the office I'll apologize properly. And perhaps I'll already have the answers to some of my questions, and I'll be able to explain everything."

Francisco, still clutching his head in his hands, ruefully rubbed his aching temples. With a swift motion he turned towards Jairo, staring at him as one stares at a madman. After a moment he saw Jairo again leave his office, his nervous hands attempting, unsuccessfully, to tuck a revolver into his pants pocket.

Francisco shivered.

"Jairo, what's this? Are you crazy? What are you going to do? What's that gun?" he shouted at the top of his lungs, his aching head forgotten.

"Don't worry. Nothing's going to happen."

And before Francisco could say another word, Jairo had vanished into the elevator.

"Paulo!" Francisco called, bursting into his partner's office. "He's gone crazy!"

Paulo lifted his eyes from the afternoon paper he'd been reading. He straightened in his recliner and put his startled gaze on the panic-stricken Francisco.

"Calm down. What's happened?"

"He left the office like a lunatic! If you'd seen the look in his eyes you'd also be worried. Believe me!"

"And what should I do now?"

"Nothing. I don't understand what's going on here. He's under tremendous pressure from something or someone."

Paulo Chilo pulled a cigarette out of a case and placed it between his lips, unlit. He closed his eyes. "So it would seem."

"This business," Francisco said earnestly, "what I mean is, Hunkes's death, is beginning to smell wrong to me. I can't figure out why he's so upset about it. So the widow acted strangely to him. So what? For that he's lost his mind? So two stupid Nazis danced around the grave. Is that the end of the world?"

Paulo Chilo opened his eyes slightly. His recliner swayed back and forth slowly. "Remember, Jairo is a Jew."

Francisco leaned on a corner of the desk. He bent towards Paulo Chilo in the movement of one sharing a deep secret.

"So what? He didn't know there were Nazis in the world until last Friday?"

Paulo pulled the unlit cigarette out from his mouth and slowly squeezed it between his fingers. He took the pieces and carefully placed them in the large stone ashtray that stood in the center of the desk. His right hand slid down his black, bushy hair. Francisco recognized the gesture: It was his partner's characteristic habit in times of trouble. Paulo felt himself tremble slightly, without knowing why. But at that moment, from the deep recesses of his mind, came the thought, unbidden, that he was an Arab. *Why should I think of that now?* he wondered, without finding an answer.

Francisco sat silently, shifting his weight on the corner of the desk, with one foot resting on the floor. He breathed deeply and gave Paulo a penetrating glance, as if trying to discern his every reaction. "Jairo took a gun with him."

Paulo moved nervously in his recliner. His eyes opened wide.

"A gun? What are you saying? Where did he go?"

"How should I know where he went? He went! But I don't like this one bit."

"You're absolutely right. I don't like it either. What should we do?"

Francisco spread his hands in a clear gesture of despair. "I don't know."

Paulo leaped out of his chair. "What do you mean, you don't know? We've got to do something! Before something terrible happens! Do you know what will happen to our office if Jairo does something stupid?"

After a short silence he spoke again. "And what will happen to our deal with GAC?"

The two partners were quiet. A heavy stillness lay upon the office. Only the jangling of the telephone broke the ominous silence. Neither bothered to answer it. After a few obstinate minutes the ringing ceased. Again, silence reigned. The two partners gazed at each other blankly.

Paulo was the first to rise. He pulled the telephone towards him and hastily dialed. He heard a busy signal on the other end.

"Who are you calling?" Francisco asked curiously.

Paulo didn't answer. Again he dialed. His lips murmured a quiet curse that Francisco couldn't quite make out.

"Hello!" Paulo cried into the receiver, "Is that the police? Yes. I want Roberto Nunes, yes, from Criminal Investigations. Thank you ..."

Paulo pulled the receiver away, bent towards his partner, and whispered, "Roberto Nunes is a good friend of Jairo's. I want to tell him what's happened."

He pulled the receiver close to him as a voice on the other end spoke.

"What's that? What are you saying, he's not there! When will he be available? What? You don't know. Oh, he went to a meeting."

Even as he listened to the tinny voice, Paulo's eyes grew wide, as if a thief was standing before him demanding his money.

"He went for a meeting with whom? With Jairo Silverman, the attorney? Are you certain?"

Paulo's voice grew suddenly quiet. He managed to blurt out a weak thank-you before hanging up.

He turned to Francisco. "You heard?"

"Yes."

The partners exchanged glances.

"What can we do?"

"I don't know."

They were all out of ideas.

Jairo jumped out of the elevator and raced into the street. Though he was in a hurry, he decided to walk. The traffic jams at this noon hour could cause him to be late for his meeting with Roberto. Walking would be faster. He passed the bridge, the Viaduto. Near the central post office he continued towards the Avenida Sao Juao. From there, he decided, he would go straight to the Praca da Republica, no more than a 20-minute walk. There he would turn left, to the *Edificio Italia*, whose 35th-story roof included a famed restaurant which looked down on the entire city. In half an hour he'd be sitting with Roberto.

Jairo began to cross the busy street. As a native of Sao Paulo he maneuvered between the hundreds of cars careening wildly, ignoring traffic lights and other warning signs. He'd hardly gotten into the street when a GAC Clipper screeched to a halt, almost hitting him. With a start, Jairo jumped back onto the sidewalk. But the angry driver of the GAC didn't drive on. He pulled over to the shoulder and left the car, walking swiftly towards Jairo, whose hand traveled quickly towards his pants pocket. The driver, a tall man with blond hair and a European look, began shouting at Jairo from a distance.

"Do you want to die, *senhor*?" he asked in heavily accented Portuguese. "Why aren't you careful where you're going?"

Jairo, still nervous, retorted, "I think that I, actually, was in the right. The light had just turned green. Pardon me, I had the right of way. You should have stopped!"

The driver approached Jairo with one big step. A smile covered his face.

"*Senhor*, you didn't understand me properly. You're right — you were crossing properly. I didn't ask you why you weren't careful in how you crossed — I asked why you weren't careful where you are going. And that's what I meant, Mr. Jairo Silverman! You're not being careful where you're going. Listen to me. Return to your office, and don't go to the *Edificio Italia*. We don't want you to discuss with anyone what happened in the cemetery last Friday. Is that understood?"

Before Jairo could recover the stranger had turned his back and returned with lightning speed to his car. With a roar of his engines he rejoined traffic and in a moment was part of the eddy of cars that flowed like a swift river down the busy street.

Jairo stood, dumbfounded. He cursed himself for not having noted the license number. Maybe, with that detail, he could have done something. What did these anonymous strangers want from him? Who were they? Why didn't they identify themselves and tell him exactly what he should do? Jairo was frightened, but he knew he had to continue.

He walked on. Who knew how many more warnings were awaiting him, until he reached the restaurant? He would walk, his senses alert for any strange cars.

Jairo went on his way along the sidewalk. A pity that he hadn't taken a taxi. He would have been less vulnerable in a cab than he was here, walking in the open air on a street where everyone who passed near him could be a mysterious enemy. On second thought, they would no doubt be able to reach him, even if he'd hidden in a taxi.

He was certainly no hero. Actually, he was a bit of a coward who stayed far from danger. But he was certain that nothing would happen to him. True, someone was interested in seeing that he, Jairo Silverman, return to his quiet life, and forget that he had ever had a friend by the name of Alberto Hunkes. The reason for this was a black mystery. What was clear to him, without any doubt, was that it involved hidden Nazis who were determined never to escape their anonymity. And that, Jairo thought, was the insurance that no one would harm him. Any other murders would bring the curious eyes of the police upon them. He could depend on it:

Their actions would remain mere threats.

Thus Jairo continued on his way. After half an hour he reached the restaurant. Most of the tables were full, he noticed: businessmen taking a break for lunch. His eyes traveled from table to table. Roberto wasn't there.

"How can it be?" Jairo thought. "Roberto is usually so prompt. What's happened today?"

He felt a hand fall gently on his shoulder. A chill of fear paralyzed him; it was impossible for him to turn around and see who was calling him.

"Excuse me, *senhor.* Are you Jairo Silverman, the advocate?"

"Yes," Jairo answered, tensely awaiting the next of his enemy's tactics.

The speaker turned and faced Jairo, who let out a deep breath. It was only the headwaiter, whom he'd seen many times before.

"Are you looking for Lieutenant Nunes?"

"Yes. How did you know?"

"Here, this is for you."

The waiter handed him a folded note. Impatiently, Jairo opened it. The waiter could see that the note had moved his customer. He lifted his head a bit, trying to catch a glimpse of what was written within.

> *I'm so sorry, Jairo, my friend. I had to leave the restaurant. I received an urgent summons back to the office. Another murder. I couldn't say no. The call came directly from the commissioner's office. Pardon me, and call me late tonight. Chau.*
>
> *Yours in friendship, Roberto.*

Jairo lifted his eyes and looked at the waiter with concern.

"When was he here?"

"He left 10 minutes ago. He seemed very worried."

Jairo took a deep breath. Before he left he took a long look at the other diners. Suddenly, his eyes bulged. Near one of the tables, not far from the entrance, sat a lone man, busy reading the newspaper after a satisfying meal. Jairo recognized the man. Yes, he'd seen him at Alberto's funeral. He couldn't be certain, but he thought it was one of the two who'd given the Nazi salute in Hunkes's honor.

The man noticed Jairo's close glance. Swiftly he folded his newspaper. He gave a cold and victorious smile and called the waiter for his bill ...

Jerusalem
1 Iyar 5727

Yitzchak Austerlitz repeated his request once again.

"I must have that picture now!"

He himself didn't recognize his voice — a hard, confident voice. He had never spoken to anyone like this, with absolute certainty that all must accede to his demands.

Yitzchak grew silent. His hand was outstretched before the director's face. His eyes, that held the director's eyes, were uncompromising. They made the director feel terribly uncomfortable. He searched desperately for a way out of the emotional labyrinth that he'd been placed into by this Bnei Brak Jew.

"See here, Mr. Austerlitz," he finally said, "we don't normally grant requests by individuals. This kind of work is usually handled by Simon Wiesenthal, from his headquarters in Vienna."

"So I'll go to him," Yitzchak said impatiently. "But give me that picture!"

"A little patience, sir. We cannot remove displays from our institution. But, as I have tried to tell you, as an unusual gesture, and because of personal considerations, I'll try to take care of this. On a personal basis, remember. Your pain has simply touched my heart. I'll do my best to find out the name of the Nazi officer. Okay?"

Yitzchak was impatient. "When?"

"I don't know, sir. This kind of work is difficult. There's no point in pressuring us. You have my word."

The director stood up swiftly, held his hand out in farewell. After a moment's thought, Yitzchak, too, held out his hand.

"Thank you very much, Director, for your good intentions. I'll call you in two days.

Yitzchak didn't wait for his answer. He was already on his way out. Deep in thought, deep in a different world …

7

Jairo hurriedly left the restaurant and hastened towards the street. The ear-splitting noise of hundreds of automobiles roaring through the large and busy *praca* hit him like a fierce wave. His heart beat wildly. A combination of unutterable rage and the fear of a beast stalked by a hunter propelled him forward through the teeming mass on the sidewalk that overflowed into the busy street itself. Passersby gazed with angry eyes at the young, well-dressed man who pushed them heedlessly in his swift progress. His hand moved frantically back and forth, trying to hail a cruising taxi. But it was lunchtime; impossible to find a free cab. Tens of thousands of people had all left their offices in the skyscrapers of the Praca da Republica, each hailing a taxi as they hurried home for their afternoon rest.

At first Jairo didn't notice the taxi that suddenly swerved out of the center lane in which it had been cruising. It succeeded, by weaving and turning and dangerously cutting off several cars, to reach the right lane of traffic snaking past. With a screech it pulled up right next to Jairo. The driver hurriedly opened the door to invite him in. Jairo refused. A terrible fear overcame him: Could it be coincidence that the cab, a GAC, product of the firm that Alberto had worked for, had stopped right next to him? His suspicions, like his fears, were aroused. Could "they" be trying to kidnap him?

Jairo waved him on. The driver favored him with a look of astonishment.

"Why are you hailing cabs, if you don't plan on driving in them?" he hissed angrily. "Didn't you see what I did to get here next to you? What kind of people are there in Brazil?"

Jairo looked at him in consternation and embarrassment.

"I'm sorry," he apologized. "I didn't notice that you were a cab."

And after a moment's hesitation, he entered into the taxi. *What is happening to me?* he thought. *What are these mad suspicions? What am I so afraid of?* But he could find no answers.

"Where to?" asked the driver, restored to his normal cheerfulness.

After a moment's hesitation he answered, "Jardim America, Franca Boulevard, please."

A 15-minute ride and Jairo was home. Though normally he'd still be in his office at this hour, he felt too exhausted to return to work. Still, he hurried to phone the office to reassure his partners. He was certain that he'd given them a good fright, with his strange behavior an hour before. Now, in his house, after downing a small glass of whiskey and slowly smoking a fine cigarette, he wasn't certain if he understood himself what he'd done. He certainly felt uncomfortable about what had happened. He must apologize to Francisco for having lunged into him and hurt his head, unintentionally of course.

He slowly dialed the familiar number. He could feel a steady pressure in his temples.

"Hello, Francisco, it's me, Jairo."

Francisco, at the other end of the line, grasped the receiver with a steely grip.

"Jairo," he yelled wildly, "where are you?"

"Don't worry, everything's all right. I'm at home, and everything is okay. Don't worry. First of all, let me apologize for having bumped into you. You must have seen how upset I was. I'm ashamed of myself, but I simply lost control."

"No matter. I understand, it happens to me, too, sometimes. Forget about it. Did you meet with Lieutenant Nunes?"

Jairo stopped, astonished. The words froze in his mouth. How did he know? He hadn't told a soul that he was meeting Roberto. For an endless moment he was silent. He felt his hands trembling.

Finally, he shouted into the receiver with a terrible fury.

"What's going on here? Are you also after me? What does everyone want from me?"

Francisco couldn't understand this new outburst.

"Who's after you, Jairo? Calm down, okay. What kind of talk is this? What's happened to you? All because of that cursed funeral on Friday. Forget about it already! What do you mean, we're after you? We were simply worried about you. I saw that you took a gun with you when you left the office. How should I know what you were planning to do? We called the lieutenant's office, to help us deal with you! Isn't he your friend? His secretary told us that he'd gone out to meet you. I think she mentioned the *Edificio Italia*. Why are you carrying on? What's all this?"

Jairo quickly calmed down. He realized that he was behaving outrageously.

"It seems," he said, in a quiet and patient voice, "it seems that I'll be spending the entire day in apologies. Once again, I'm sorry."

Francisco took a deep breath.

"It's not a question of sorry, Jairo. Something is bothering you, and I don't know what. Maybe I can help you. Tell me, who is after you?"

"Forget it, Francisco. It's not for the phone. Just forget it."

After a moment Francisco's voice came on again. He was suddenly soft and fatherly.

"Jairo?"

"Yes?"

"Jairo, don't get angry with me, but maybe you should see a doctor?"

Jairo began to laugh.

"I understand. You think I've gone crazy, out of my mind. My nerves, it's true, are rather frayed these past few days, but I've still got my sanity. Don't worry, Francisco."

"Tell the truth. It's all because of Hunkes's funeral?"

"Yes."

"You don't think you're ... exaggerating?"

"I don't know. I guess I'm more Jewish than I ever thought I was."

Francisco didn't understand. "What does that have to do with it?"

Jairo decided not to answer. Instead, he said, "*Chau*, Francisco."

Francisco sensed Jairo's evasiveness. This time, he let it go.

"*Chau*, Jairo. And watch over yourself."

The conversation was over. And yet Jairo didn't rush to hang up the phone. His last sentence had shocked him. He — a Brazilian-born man whose parents had done their all to have him grow up a part of his Brazilian society, free of all the fears that had been their lot as Jews in the old country of Europe — he suddenly felt the burden of the Jewish destiny, and particularly the Holocaust, settle upon his shoulders. He, whose father had intentionally sent him to Sao Paulo's non-Jewish schools, so that his friends would not be Jewish. And truly, his being Jewish had never been an issue, had hardly been mentioned, in his relationships with his fellow students, both in high school and university. And yet, he suddenly knew that the words he'd uttered to Francisco had created a wall between them. From this day on, he felt, the wall, no less real for it being invisible, would exist between them. Who knew if this new fact of life wouldn't have an effect on their joint work in the office? And what about his relationship with Paulo, who was an Arab as well as a non-Jew? The Jews and the Arabs, after all, were not living peacefully together in the Middle East.

But Jairo had little time for painful thoughts. Any minute now his wife would arrive home from school with the children. He must speak to Roberto urgently. He must know what had happened.

"Roberto?"

"Who is this? Jairo! I'm so glad you called. Truly, I'm sorry. You know, in the life of a police officer we have unexpected surprises happening all the time."

"It's okay, I understand. What's the story on this new murder? I see that Sao Paulo can't get along without you anymore! Don't give me all the details — I'm just curious."

"You'll never believe it, Jairo. There was no murder!"

"I don't understand. Why did they call you?"

"They didn't. The commissioner never sent for me."

Jairo could feel the blood rush to his head. "Roberto, can you explain what you've just said? Didn't you write me that note in the restaurant?"

"Yes I did, but I was wrong. Someone tricked me, pretended to be the commissioner. He fooled me completely."

Jairo trembled.

"You're telling me that everything was made up. It never happened?"

"Exactly, Jairo."

Jairo could hear his friend's rueful laugh. "I guess someone didn't want us to have a chat."

"You don't know how right you are."

"I was just joking, Jairo. Don't be so serious."

"But I'm not joking, Roberto. I am serious."

A moment's silence.

"Jairo?"

"Yes."

"You're serious?"

"Very serious. Unfortunately, very, very serious."

"My friend, you're beginning to interest me. When can we meet?"

"I don't know. I'll be very busy the next few days. Maybe next week? I owe you a lunch."

"Can we meet today? You've made me curious. Why don't you drop by my house tonight?"

"Sorry, Roberto, I've got other obligations. Don't worry, I'll call you."

Jairo, concerned that someone was listening, carefully watched his every word. His mysterious enemies had succeeded in keeping him away from his meeting. Who knew what else they were planning? For him, for now, caution was the watchword.

Quickly, he added, "*Chau*, Roberto."

"*Chau*. But I'm not giving up on your story."

"I'll remember that. *Chau*."

Jairo held his face in his hands. *What now?* A despairing voice called from deep within him. *What trouble have I gotten myself into? Should I give in? Should I forget it? But then I'll never know who Alberto Hunkes really was. So what? So he was a Nazi war criminal playing an ugly game with me. Why should I care? Why should that change my life? Should I destroy my life for a little information? Francisco is right: Forget about it and that's all!*

Jairo lit another cigarette and paced back and forth in his spacious living room.

That's right, the thoughts passed swiftly through his brain, *that's right. Logic says forget about it, return to reality, to your normal life. You have a house, you have a wife, you have children.* But was it mere curiosity propelling him to find out what mystery lurked behind the amiable face of his friend? It seemed it was more than that. The deep hatred of the widow; her accusing the Jews of her husband's death; the obvious efforts that she and others — he still didn't know who they were — had made to stop the investigation; all whispered to him that Alberto Hunkes was not dead! His body, yes; but his spirit lived! Something mysterious, and possibly dangerous, continued to exist even after his funeral.

Jairo lit another cigarette from the embers of the previous one.

And so what? his thoughts continued relentlessly, one contending with the other. *So what? Am I a police officer? Am I in charge of public order? Do I have to expose Alberto? To find out if he was a member of some Nazi underground that exists in Brazil? And that his friendship with the Jew Jairo was nothing more than a blind, or who knows what else? For what?*

Suddenly, standing in the middle of his living room, a thought came, a blinding thought that conquered all others with its strength.

It seems that what I told Francisco is true. I am much more of a Jew than I had believed! The affair of Hunkes's death and funeral has unearthed this part of my soul. Pa wanted to suffocate the fact of my Jewishness. But it seems that the inner reality is too strong for that!

Jairo felt a strange emotion slowly overcome him. And with that unfamiliar feeling came fear, as he realized what it was that was forcing him onto a dangerous path, a path whose end was still hidden.

And with that, he knew deep in his heart that he had no choice. There was no turning back.

His head ached. The best thing he could do now was sleep — sleep, until the morning. It was 4 in the afternoon. Fourteen hours of sleep might help calm his shaken nerves.

Jairo turned to his bed. But five minutes after he'd put his head on his pillow, with thoughts still racing through his fevered brain, he jumped out of bed. He grabbed his alarm clock and set it for 2 — 2 in the morning. Suddenly he felt better. The plan he'd just come up with suited him just fine ...

Jerusalem
2 Iyar 5727

The phone rang. The director of Yad Vashem picked up the receiver.

"Yes?"

He was silent for a moment. Then his face grew angry.

"Excuse me, Mr. Austerlitz, I don't understand. You were here yesterday, and you already want an answer?"

He listened once again.

"After you left, we sent a number of telexes to information bureaus throughout the world in order to find information on the man you seek. Did you really think we'd already have an answer?"

Another moment of silence.

"You don't have confidence in me! Really, sir, this isn't fair! You'll have to be patient. I gave you my personal promise. And I'll do my best to keep it. Believe me, Mr. Austerlitz, I deserve better from you!"

The director once again heard the speaker on the

other side of the wire.

"Okay, I forgive you. I understand your concern. But be patient. I'll call you the minute I have an answer. Good-bye."

He slammed the phone down and returned to work.

8

P aulo Chilo's eyes were riveted to Francisco, sitting quietly after his conversation with Jairo.

"What happened?" Chilo finally asked, after Francisco had slowly hung up the phone.

"Didn't you understand?"

"With all due respect to my startling brilliance — no!"

Francisco took a deep breath. "It seems to me that Jairo isn't quite all right."

"Did something happen?"

"Thank heavens, nothing happened. That is — so far, nothing's happened. He didn't meet Nunes. And instead of returning to the office, he decided to go home."

Paulo stood up, took a few steps towards Francisco.

"And with all that, something about his behavior is worrying you."

Francisco, too, stood up.

"Absolutely. He's full of delusions of persecution. He's acting paranoid. He thinks someone is after him."

Paulo looked at him incredulously. "You're joking."

"It's no joke."

Paulo pulled a pack of cigarettes from his jacket, took one for himself and offered another to his partner. The match gave off a tiny spark of light; a thick cloud of smoke floated above them in the office.

"What do you think, why did it happen to him?"

Francisco didn't hurry with a reply. He searched for the correct words to describe what he felt was the problem.

"I think it began at the funeral. Yes, for certain, that's when it started. You weren't there, Paulo, so I'm not sure you can understand. And it wasn't only his imagination. Jairo was in a bad position — you should have seen with what hatred they looked at him. That widow, particularly … "

"Yes, and then what?"

"Don't forget, Paulo, that Jairo is a Jew. Jews always feel persecuted, even though here in Brazil there's no reason to feel that way. It seems that fear of persecution is deep in the Jew's genetic heritage: a sad inheritance from their ancestors."

After a silence, he added:

"And don't forget that his father spent some time in a concentration camp at the time of the Second World War and fled to Brazil just before the gates slammed shut. It was no party, by all accounts. So any connection with Nazis or neo-Nazis can knock him off balance."

Paulo didn't respond. The fact of their senior partner's Jewishness was not news to him. But this was the first time, in all their years of partnership, that the issue had ever come up. With all their might the two of them — Paulo Chilo, the Arab, and Jairo Silverman, the Jew — had avoided bringing up the burning issue of the war between Jew and Arab in the Middle East. The two had made fanatical efforts to bridge any gap between them by their common identity as Brazilians. Paulo felt no special bond with Lebanon, his grandparents' birthplace. As far as Paulo was concerned, Jairo had no problem with the issue either. His country, after all, was Brazil! What connection did he have with Palestine?

Francisco was the first to break the silence.

"What are you thinking about?"

Paulo awoke from his reverie.

"Oh, nothing," he said quietly. "Nothing at all."

He gave his hand a dismissive shake and, to get Francisco's mind off his question, continued.

"We've completely forgotten about GAC."

"You're right. Okay, let's get on with it. Call them and try to get the meeting rescheduled for today. By tomorrow I don't know what will have happened with Jairo. Best that we try to close the deal with them right now."

"Got it."

Paulo pulled the telephone receiver towards him. "Hello. Can you please connect me with *Senhor* Orlando Toncardo? Thank you very much."

And after a moment:

"Good afternoon, *Senhor*. Is everything all right? Good. This is Paulo Chilo from the law firm 'Silverman, Machado and Chilo.' Yes, exactly... Because of various circumstances beyond our control we will be unable to meet with you tomorrow morning as planned. We've got to leave urgently to Brasilia. Yes, yes, it can't be postponed. What? What are you saying? You want to cancel the meeting? No, no, Jairo Silverman will not be coming. Just the two of us, Francisco Machado and myself. No, no, *Senhor* Silverman has not left the firm, but he will not be in the office for several weeks. Why? Family reasons, I'm not certain exactly. What? What are you saying? No, *Senhor*, we can't put the matter off for another time. According to our plans, Francisco will be leaving to Europe in two days for a full month."

Francisco saw Paulo's face grow ashen with anger. After a few minutes of listening, Paulo began to speak once again.

"*Senhor*, this is very irregular. We are a law firm, and please don't forget that! We are a well-known and respected firm and will not accept such behavior. I suggest, in view of proper business relationships, that we meet today. That's right, today! Right now! To meet and clarify the issues that need clarification. We are willing to forego signing the contract with you, but we will not forego the basic common courtesy that is due us, is that understood?"

Paulo balled his fist, as if preparing to assault an unseen opponent. Francisco could understand, from what he heard, that the resistance from the other side was somehow connected to Jairo Silverman.

"Okay, *Senhor*" — Francisco once again heard Paulo's voice —"Okay, I agree. An unofficial talk, an informal meeting. In half an hour? Yes ... yes. Where did you say? In the Cafe Fazano on Avenida Paulista? Fine ... we'll be there!"

With a swift gesture Paulo hung up the phone.

"Come," he yelled towards Francisco, "quickly, and maybe we'll be able to salvage something of the contract. The fools regret the entire deal. Suddenly they don't like Jairo. Have you seen such a thing! I had to convince him that only the two of us would come to a meeting. We may actually have to place Jairo on the side lines for a while. Suddenly his Jewishness is a business problem!"

Francisco grabbed his attache case, straightened his tie, and hurried behind Paulo, who was already standing by the elevator, pressing the button with all his strength.

"What did they say?" Francisco asked, his breath heavy.

"They're trying to get out of it. The director stuttered something or other, and really had no idea of how to get rid of me. He couldn't give me any reasonable excuse for withdrawing from the deal. I'm beginning to get a little curious myself. Who was Alberto Hunkes, and what were his dealings with Jairo? Because they've buried him, is it impossible to continue with our contract? Come, let's be quick. We've got to be in the cafe on time. That's all that we need, that they be able to slip away from us!"

The meeting at the Fazano was frigid and formal. The director of GAC appeared with three men, unknown to them. But after a moment a frightening memory came to Francisco. It seemed to him that one of them was familiar — the one sitting at the corner of the table, the eldest of the three. Francisco couldn't be certain, but it seemed to him that they had met before. He'd seen him at Hunkes's funeral. He was one of the men who'd marched towards the grave, giving the Nazi salute …

Jairo didn't hear the alarm clock. It rang, as set, at 2 in the morning. His wife, Paulina, awoke in a panic.

"Jairo!" she nudged her husband, "Who set the clock for this hour? It's the middle of the night!"

Jairo jumped out of bed, wiping the sleep from his eyes.

"What do I know? Maybe the children played with it. I've told you more than once that they shouldn't be allowed in this room! Go back to bed, I'm just going to get a drink."

His wife murmured something and turned back into a deep sleep.

Jairo was satisfied. His wife knew that he'd left the room and wouldn't worry if she woke up in a few hours and didn't find him sleeping there. He got out of bed, dressed, and quietly left the bedroom. He didn't turn the lights on in the living room or kitchen. He looked out of the large window in the living room that overlooked the street, and carefully pulled the curtain open. Nothing. No suspicious traffic in the street, nothing to indicate anyone lying in wait for him. With exaggerated caution he looked through the kitchen window at the back yard. The outline of the cars parked there, in the house's parking lot, were all those of his neighbors. He couldn't be 100 percent certain; still he hoped that at least at this hour of the night his footsteps wouldn't be dogged by the enemy.

He left the apartment through the kitchen exit and decided to use the service elevator. That way he'd avoid the *zelador,* the apartment house security guard who always sat in the house's spacious lobby. When he reached the ground floor he snuck quietly from the elevator to the yard. A deep blackness greeted him outside. The windows of the multistoried homes around him were darkened; not a light could be seen. Sao Paulo slept. Carefully, ever so slowly, he began to walk on the asphalt where cars entered the parking lot. He did all he could to stifle the sound of his footsteps. He knew that the guard ("if he's awake at all," a wicked voice said within him) would not hear him as he left this way. A nocturnal walk such as this, after all, was liable to raise suspicions that Jairo wanted at all costs to avoid.

Suddenly he heard a noise. On the silent street a shadowy figure approached. Jairo clung to the wall, paralyzed with fright. But it was too late. His neighbor's Doberman gave a loud howl and jumped upon him in fond joy. Jairo gave a sigh of relief. The dog, an old friend, had recognized him even in the pitch blackness. Tonight, though, Jairo could have done without the friendly greeting.

"Sshhh, sshhh…" Jairo patted his head and finally succeeded in quieting him down. But what was he doing here? Why had his owners let him loose? Maybe he was following him. "Jairo, you've gone stark raving mad," he heard himself murmur quietly. The dog gave another shake of the tail, sniffed a bit, and disappeared. Jairo reached the street.

He walked quickly down Bela Cintra Street, passed through several deserted blocks. After twenty minutes he came to a wide avenue, Estados Unidos. He looked back and forth and walked towards one of the one-story villas that graced the area. Without pausing for more than a moment he rang the bell. No answer. He rang again, a longer ring. His tension eased somewhat; someone in the house lit a light in the living room and carefully peeked through the curtain. Jairo raised his hand and waved wildly, trying to get his attention. It seemed, from the silhouette on the curtain, that it was he.

The man behind the curtain saw his wild gestures. Apparently he recognized him, despite the darkness. He swiftly put on a robe, opened the door, and jumped towards the gate.

"What's happened to you?" he asked. "Why have you come at such a crazy hour?"

"Let me in, I must speak to you urgently. Open the gate! Quickly! Before someone recognizes me!"

"Jairo, have you gone mad?" he answered, even as he opened the gates.

Bnei Brak, Israel
2 Iyar 5727 (1967)

Rivka, wife of Yitzchak Austerlitz, was beginning to get worried. Since he'd returned yesterday from Yerushalayim her husband had undergone a drastic change. He had withdrawn into himself. Silent, never speaking. Even before this, he hadn't been a big talker. And yet …

She'd seen it as soon as he'd come home that night. He had gone out to daven *Ma'ariv*, asked for something to eat, and immediately gone to bed.

He'd skipped even his daily *shiur* in *Mishnayos*. Normally when he returned from a visit to the yeshiva he'd give a full report on how he'd found their son. These were always hours of *nachas*, hours that made up just a little for the loss of his first family, there in Poland. But this time he told her nothing. Perhaps, the suspicion entered her heart, perhaps something had befallen her Yaakov Yehoshua — may Hashem guard him! Had he fallen onto an evil pathway?

Rivka didn't know what she should do. How to make him speak? This morning, after an entire day of deep and heavy silence, she heard him yelling at someone on the phone. He was speaking about some picture or other. What picture could he be referring to? Rivka had no idea.

And then, an hour before Shabbos, before nightfall, she finally made the attempt — "Yitzchak, you returned from Yerushalayim yesterday without a word about Yaakov Yehoshua. Aren't I entitled to know?"

Yitzchak saw the justice of her words.

"Everything's fine with him, thank G-d."

Rivka sent a searching glance upon him.

"And with you?"

"With me — less."

"What happened?"

Her voice was worried.

Yitzchak turned to leave the room. "It's not for now. Shabbos is almost here."

"For when, then?"

Yitzchak was already on the threshold, dressed in his white Shabbos shirt and black *kapote*. He paused for a moment. Suddenly, he turned and gave her a strange and fearful look, a look she'd never seen.

"The day will come and you'll know!" he shouted. "A few more days and you'll understand! I won't give up! Leave me alone and don't ask me anything, please!"

A small tear formed in her eye as he slammed the door in fury — for the first time in his life. And with that, Shabbos entered.

9

I n the Cafe Fazano, Francisco stared at the representatives of GAC and made a decision: He would take the initiative. Outwardly patient and inwardly seething, he waited for the moment when the waiter would finally be done pouring out the steins of beer that he'd ordered — on his tab — for each one. But when he tried to speak he felt Paulo's foot give him a gentle kick. He turned involuntarily to face him, his eyes asking a question.

"Wait a minute. Don't begin," Paulo whispered. "Let them take a few drinks. Maybe the atmosphere around the table will lighten up a bit."

The GAC representatives didn't catch Paulo's words. Certainly they noticed the quiet conference going on between the two attorneys sitting across from them, but they said nothing. Their looks continued to be frigid. They began to slowly sip the beer, working hard to avoid meeting the lawyers' eyes.

"I am glad," Francisco finally began in a quiet, halting voice, in which perplexity and lack of confidence was apparent, "I am glad that we've finally been able to work out a detailed contract between us — our firm — and yours — GAC."

The GAC executives remained silent.

"As you know," he continued, "the contract has gone through many versions. The final wording, now in your possession, clearly serves your interests as the largest automobile manufacturer in South America. I believe," Francisco added a compliment, "I believe that you are the most profitable of all GAC divisions, are you not?"

It didn't work. The men continued to slowly sip their cold beer, sitting motionless, in stony silence.

Francisco gave a confused smile. Though inside he was furious, he still spoke in a pleasant and friendly tone.

"So let's give the contract one last read-through and sign on it, shall we?"

Francisco gestured towards Paulo, who handed him a black leather case. Without waiting for their answer he began to pull out thin cardboard files containing copies of the contract. At first the GAC executives didn't react. Slowly they turned towards one of their group, as if waiting for him to speak. Paulo and Francisco, too, turned their gazes to the man. It seemed that the decision rested with him alone.

The man was not Brazilian; he was clearly a European, probably German. Francisco had seen that almost as soon as he'd entered the cafe. He was a handsome man of about 50. His face was smooth and unlined, young for his age; it possessed the strength and determination of one who knows what to expect of the future. His sharp nose, like an eagle's beak, was held aloft and his eyes seemed locked at a point somewhere above the others' heads. The thought flitted through Francisco's mind: *I didn't see him at Hunkes's funeral.*

Suddenly he bent his gaze towards the young lawyers.

"My name," he said, "is Otto Von Dorfman. I am a representative of the company, and I arrived yesterday from Germany. One of the points that I've been asked to take care of by the company is the question of the signing of this contract. A signing that has become very complicated since last weekend."

The words were spoken heavily in German. One of the executives of the local company, who spoke the language fluently, translated them into Portuguese.

"What complications?" Francisco asked hurriedly.

The German turned a contemptuous face upon him. "Don't you know? The murder of our company executive, Alberto Hunkes!"

Francisco didn't understand.

"What has that to do with the contract?" He spoke slowly, enunciating every word. "We recognize the victim's great contribution to the project. But why should his tragic death force you to change the mutual decision to sign the contract?"

The German gave Francisco a chilly smile.

"Your partner, the Jew," he finally said.

Francisco jumped up. "My partner, the Jew, my dear *Senhor* Von Dorfman, my partner the Jew, Jairo Silverman, was a close friend of Alberto Hunkes!

He was in shock when he heard of the man's sudden death! What does he have to do with this?"

The GAC representatives took another long, slow drink of their beer, wicked smiles still on their faces. They knew a secret, one hidden from Jairo's partners, Francisco and Paulo.

Jairo quickly entered the open gate, terrified. The owner of the house, Police Lieutenant Roberto Nunes, tried to calm him.

"What's happened, Jairo? Couldn't it wait until morning? Speak to me!"

Jairo felt uncomfortable in his friend's brightly lit living room.

"Put out the lights! Let's speak in the darkness. I can't be sure that they're not coming after me, even now."

Roberto began to wonder if something hadn't happened to his friend. Still, he shut the light.

"Who's after you? What's going on?"

Jairo didn't answer. "Why didn't you come to the restaurant today?" he demanded.

Roberto spoke quietly, putting his finger on his lips to show his friend that he, too, should not raise his voice.

"I told you, Jairo, they called me urgently to return to the office."

"Did they really call you?"

"No. It was a practical joke."

"A practical joke, you say! That's your mistake! They've been trying to prevent us from meeting since Friday."

"Who is 'they'?"

"I wish I knew!"

"And what happened on Friday?"

"The funeral of Alberto Hunkes, whom you say was murdered."

Roberto straightened in the chair in which he was sitting. In the darkness, he bumped his knee in the living room's coffee table. Despite the shooting pain, he quickly sprang up towards Jairo's armchair.

"What do you have to do with that, Jairo?" Roberto said, suddenly alert, his policeman's sixth-sense awakening.

"I was his good friend. Maybe his best friend. But during the funeral his widow insulted me."

Roberto said nothing, waiting for Jairo to continue.

"She said the Jews had murdered her husband. Why? Why should she think that? That she would-n't tell me. But you should know, it was a Nazi funeral. I still haven't calmed down from what I experienced. I'm Jewish, you know."

Jairo had surprised himself. Those last words — I'm Jewish — had nothing to do with the matter. So why had he said them? He had no idea.

Roberto remained silent. He stood up, headed towards the kitchen. His hands groped through the darkness to the refrigerator. He pulled out a bottle of Coca Cola, a family-size bottle. He took a cup off a shelf and returned to Jairo, comfortably ensconced in an armchair.

Roberto poured his friend a drink, and asked, "And what happened then?"

"They've warned me not to get involved in the affair. That I should stop trying to find out who Alberto Hunkes actually was. They're after me all the time to stop investigating and leave the whole thing alone. They heard our phone conversation and warned me not to meet you. When they saw me leave, despite them, towards the *Edificio Italia* , they managed to sidetrack you."

Roberto didn't answer. True, he'd seen the lack of cooperation by the family in the murder investigation. The widow didn't want to give a single detail that would advance the investigation and help the police make some logical deductions as to the murderers' identities. GAC, too, would be pleased if the police closed this particular file without ever completing their investigation. What was everyone hiding? Of even more interest, the police commissioner himself had suddenly played down the importance of the case. Who knows how much they'd paid him, those men in GAC?

These strange details that Jairo was offering him now certainly aroused the curiosity and inflamed the imagination. Murder …Nazis …Jews …The tale seemed to Roberto like a good detective story! But what did they want of Jairo? And who was it that wanted something of him?

Jairo drank up the Coke. It calmed him down somewhat.

"Thanks a lot, *amigo,*" he whispered. "What do you plan on doing?" he added.

"What can I do? Suddenly the commissioner isn't very interested in investigating the affair. You can figure out why."

Jairo certainly could. In all probability, there were large sums of money involved. Instead of answering, Jairo began to rummage through his jacket, finally pulling out a thin packet and handing it to Roberto.

"Count," he said to Roberto, "count it. There's a thousand dollars there! That's just an advance for you; I promise there's more coming. All I ask is that you continue to investigate; help me to find out who Alberto Hunkes really was! It's vital to me!"

Roberto held the package without opening it.

"Jairo," he said, after a moment of profound silence, "what do you need this for? If what you've told me is true, mighty forces are ranged against you. I don't know exactly who or what. We've got a lot of information on Nazi organizations working in the country. Why get involved with them? Do you want to die young? Think of your wife and children!"

Jairo rose from his chair and stood close to Roberto. In the dimness he cast a piercing glance at his friend. The police officer was clearly aware of it. Then Jairo began to pace nervously back and forth in the living room.

Finally he said, "You're lucky, Roberto. You're not a Jew. You're a Brazilian. You didn't suffer during the Holocaust at the filthy hands of the Germans, as my family suffered."

"But you live in Brazil, Jairo," Roberto cried out hotly, "and there's no anti-Semitism here! You can live here in peace and quiet. Give it up, forget the past for the sake of a better future!"

"You're right, and thank G-d for it. That was true for me until the moment of the funeral, when I stood, for the first time in my life, right next to Nazis. And I — I can't! I simply can't! Can you understand? I can't! The fact that I am a Jew was aroused in me in a way that I can never understand. And that's why it's so important for me to know if my friend, Hunkes, belonged to that murderous gang of criminals. By all the evidence I saw at the funeral I suspect that it's so. I will wipe him out of my memory, take revenge, at the very least, in my thoughts. Revenge because he took advantage, coldly and hypocritically, of my innocence, my friendship, to live peacefully in this blessed land. Do you know how many times I — a Jew — helped him? So that his widow should behave so at his funeral? No! To think of it, that he would come to my parents' house, hear what my father had suffered in Buchenwald, and nod his head in sympathy! And to think that all this was nothing more than a miserable act to soothe my feelings! No! I can't give it up! And I'm asking that you help me. You'll make a lot from me, Roberto; this is a wonderful opportunity for you. Count the money, I beg you!" he beseeched.

The police officer hesitantly tore open the package, never taking an eye off his friend. His fingers, accustomed to accepting illegal payments, counted, as if of their own accord, the bills that rustled through his deft hands, like the rustling of a brook wending its way down a hill. When he'd finished he pressed the envelope into the pocket of his robe. He shook Jairo's hand and said, "Okay, I'll continue. But you should know that I'm not doing it for the money, but for the friendship that I feel for you. Besides, I don't like Nazis, just as you don't."

"Don't be angry at me. I believe you, that you hate them too. But my hatred is different from yours."

"For the work ahead of us, that's not important."

"That's true. And now, what I'm asking of you, try to find out every detail of Alberto's life. Since he wasn't born in Brazil, try to determine where he came from, and when. He told me he was Danish. I'm interested to know if that's the whole truth."

"Okay."

"But remember, no details over the phone. I'll take care of being in touch with you."

"Fine, but not this time of night."

Even in the darkness, the two could sense each others' smiles.

Half an hour later, Jairo sneaked into his apartment. He hoped, with all his heart, that no one had followed him. But as he left the elevator he saw the light in his living room. His heart began to pound. Were they there, waiting for him?

He slowly opened the door, making a monumental effort not to make a sound. To his surprise, he found his wife sitting in the living room, furious.

"Where have you been?" she hissed between tight lips. "And what was the meaning of the phone call I received half an hour ago?"

10

Rivka put down the *siddur*. She had barely managed to say *Kabbolas Shabbos*, and she simply couldn't *daven* any more. She closed the *siddur* with a nervous motion, straightened the scarf on her head, and left the house. It was a lightning decision, taken as she'd recited the verses of *Lechu Niranenah* while the tears, uncontrollable, had poured down her face and obscured the words dancing before her eyes. The slamming door, her husband's shouts, coming from a tortured soul, had buzzed in her ears with a frightening sound, leaving her no peace to concentrate on her prayers. And then came the decision, to share her pain and fears with the wife of her husband's *chavrusah*, Rabbi Yitzchak Mandelkorn, a learned man who, despite his youth, had an excellent and important influence on her husband.

Rivka walked through the streets of Bnei Brak, still wrapped in a twilight softness. The deepening night brought with it the wonderful fragrance of a Sabbath stillness. Latecomers to prayers hurried through the streets to their *shuls*, and here and there one could spot young women pushing baby carriages, two or three little ones hanging on to their hands or their skirts. How Rivka loved this scene! It was a sign to her of Hashem's goodness, after the horrors of the Holocaust, which had uprooted her, a young girl, from her warm, loving home in Galicia. It was the incredible kindness of the rebirth of *Am Yisrael*. Each time she walked through the streets she felt joy as she looked upon the children, though she, a survivor, had merited only one son— her Yaakov Yehoshua. Yaakov Yehoshua, who, it seemed, was the cause of the frightening change in her husband's behavior, one day after his weekly visit to the yeshiva. She didn't understand what had happened, but she trembled before it, from the horrifying danger approaching like a thunderstorm.

She knocked gently on the Mandelkorn door. The rebbetzin herself answered.

"*Shabbat shalom,* Rivka," she said, with the happiness of a true hostess. But her joy immediately evaporated; she could sense that all was not well.

"*Shabbat shalom,*" Rivka answered quietly, forcing herself to return a pleasant smile.

Her hostess was a practical woman. She led Rivka into the living room, a beautifully set table glowing in its center, and before even offering her a seat asked, "Has something happened?"

Rivka sat down on the sofa and indicated with a glance the children surrounding them in the living room, staring with interest at the unexpected guest. Her hostess took the hint.

"Children," she said, turning to them, "go play in your room, please."

The rebbetzin sat down next to Rivka, her eyes trying to delve deep into Rivka's heart.

Rivka spoke quietly, tapping her fingers nervously. "No. Nothing's happened."

Again she tried to muster the ghost of a smile, without success.

Her hostess prodded her. "And yet …?"

"I am afraid," Rivka said, in a voice not her own, "that something will happen. I hope, with all my heart, that it hasn't happened yet."

The rebbetzin, her hostess, felt her discomfort. She knew that at moments such as these, one had to do a little probing.

"If you've come to me, that's a sign that you want to tell me. Please, don't speak in riddles."

"Yes. It's true. You're right. But it's hard. Give me a minute to recover. To collect my thoughts. I don't know exactly where to begin."

A few moments of deep silence passed. From the Shabbos table came the gentle hiss of the flames as the wicks burned. Finally, Rivka's hushed words broke through the peace.

"You know that my husband is a survivor of the war."

"Yes, I do."

"He lost a wife and children."

"I didn't know that."

"A wife and three small children."

The rebbetzin gave a deep sigh. "Hashem should have mercy."

"Our only son is named for the baby the Germans killed — Yaakov Yehoshua."

The rebbetzin gave no answer. She waited for Rivka to continue.

"Today I regret that I agreed to name him for the poor, martyred little boy."

The rebbetzin felt Rivka's tension. Yet she still didn't understand what Rivka wanted of her. She remained silent. Rivka continued.

"It's not good. I wish I could change his name now. Would that be allowed?"

The rebbetzin was taken aback by the strange idea. "I don't know if it's permitted or not. But why isn't his name a good one? What's happened?"

Rivka was silent. The rebbetzin could see her guest's breath coming in quick, short gasps; she felt she could even hear the uneven beating of her troubled heart. Clearly, Rivka was searching for the correct words.

"My husband. My husband," Rivka said in a choked voice. "He can't forget what happened to him during the war. Yaakov Yehoshua reminds him, endlessly reminds him, of his previous child. He looks at him and sighs. All day he imagines how his son would have looked, had he lived. It's the name that causes him these tortures. One simply feels that he is constantly reliving that awful moment when the Nazis, *yimach shemam*, took his son from him."

She lapsed into silence, put her face into her hands as if to hold off the flood of tears. After a moment she continued.

"Every week Yitzchak travels to our son's yeshiva in Yerushalayim, in Bayit Vegan. I know that the boy doesn't really enjoy these visits. It's a big pressure on him. But thank G-d he's a perceptive boy, and he knows and senses what his father has gone through. So he's patient with him. Truly, he's a good boy."

The rebbetzin was silent, listening intently to each word, trying to uncover what lay behind them. Did Rivka want something specific, or had she come simply to find a little relief from her constant anxiety? For now, she would be quiet, waiting for more.

"Every week," Rivka continued, "he returns from his visit, crushed. He tells me how Yaakov Yehoshua is succeeding in his learning, how sensitive and dedicated he is, and how the *mashgiach* is full of his praises. Yes, we certainly have our share of *nachas* from him. But each time he says the name 'Yaakov Yehoshua' it ends in deep, anguished sighs and often in heartbreaking tears. I can't stand seeing it. I can't take it any more."

Finally, Rivka let her tears flow. For a few long minutes she sat upon the sofa in her friend's house, sobbing into the hands that enveloped her miserable face. The rebbetzin carefully placed one soft hand on her friend's shoulder, gently patting her, while using the other hand to forcefully signal to the curious youngsters peeking into the living room door.

"Calm down, Rivka. It's Shabbos," she said quietly, in a soothing tone. "Shabbos, *Shabbos kodesh*. Be strong, Rivka."

Rivka wouldn't calm down. From behind her hands, she continued sobbing, even as she spoke.

"But this week was the worst. He returned to our house completely broken. I felt that something unusual had happened. I asked him, but he wouldn't speak to me at all. He was evasive, he was silent, he was completely turned inward. He hardly ate dinner, and most of the night he couldn't sleep. He paced back and forth in the living room. I saw him take a *Sefer Tehillim* in his hand, and try to say a few chapters, but he couldn't. He opened his *Gemara* and a few minutes later it was shut. I thought my heart would burst. I was afraid to speak with him. I knew that something was oppressing him terribly, but I didn't know what it was. I don't know what it is. And I am afraid. I am so afraid."

The rebbetzin found the chance to interject a few words.

"What are you afraid of? You know very well that, unfortunately, your husband is not the only one who couldn't recover from what happened in Poland during the Holocaust. Our generation must live with that. What can we do? It's the will of Hashem! We've got to strengthen our faith in G-d, and endlessly repeat: All that G-d does is done for the good. And most importantly: We must *daven. Daven* a lot."

"No, you don't understand. I've gotten used to that situation and I can live with it. To my sorrow, I know that this is what it's going to be like, perhaps for all our lives. I am so thankful to Hashem for having allowed me to escape the ghetto, reach Eretz Yisrael, rebuild a home, and have a son who learns Torah. Thank G-d for all His favors. And deep in my heart I hope that my husband will, with the passing of years, calm down."

"So what are you afraid of?"

"Of what happened this morning."

"What does that mean?"

"I don't know exactly what happened. There was something oppressive in the air. Yitzchak called someone, shouted at him, spoke about a picture that he wanted. I don't know what he meant. But I know that it was terrible."

The rebbetzin was silent. She didn't know exactly what she should do. She could see the worry in her friend's eyes. She understood her feelings and searched for words of comfort, words to strengthen her. After a brief wait, she tried to speak.

"Listen, Rivka ..."

She couldn't continue. At the same moment, Rivka finally formed the difficult words that had sent her to this woman, wife of her husband's *chavrusah*:

"And what disturbs me the most is the way he shouted at me. This was the first time in all our married life that he behaved like that. His eyes were like a madman's. I think something horrible happened to him, and I don't know what. I just don't know."

After a moment she added, "And he ...he spoke ...like a madman."

Again, silence.

"He screamed, 'The day will come and you'll know. A few more days and you'll understand. I won't give in!' "

"Won't give in to whom?" the rebbetzin wanted to know.

Rivka again dissolved in tears.

"I wish I knew! I'm certain that it's something connected with the Holocaust. Something connected with what happened to his previous family. And I'm worried. I'm afraid the images he lives with are taking away his sanity, that he can't control them, that they are leading him to complete disaster!"

Rivka stood up. She dried her tears with a small handkerchief clutched in her hand. She gave a sad, endearing smile.

"I didn't come to you only to pour my heart out. I've come, for I want your husband to speak with him. Tomorrow. They *daven* in the same *shul*. Let him speak to him. I don't have to tell you that Yitzchak must not find out that I've been here and spoken with you. *Shabbat shalom* — and thanks."

"*Shabbat shalom*, Rivka, and remember — Hashem's salvation can come in the wink of an eye."

On her way out, standing next to the doorway, Rivka turned to the rebbetzin:

"Remember to ask your husband if it is permissible to change a name for this reason. Let him ask the *gedolim* on my behalf."

The rebbetzin gave her a warm smile. "Okay, I'll ask him."

Rivka left the house. The street lights shot their golden glow onto the sidewalks. One could see the congregants making their way home. She must hurry. She must reach her home before Yitzchak did ...

Sao Paulo, Brazil
May 15, 1967

Jairo stood, confused, before his wife. It was 4:30 in the morning. Clearly, she had been waiting for him in the living room this entire time. Quickly, he recovered. Her words, her mention of a phone call, had terrified him.

"What phone call are you talking about? Who called you at this hour?"

She didn't reply. She was trembling with rage. From her mouth emerged the same four words: "Where have you been?"

Jairo's hand nervously pushed back a lock of hair. He had no patience for this.

"Okay, I'll tell you, Paulina. But first, you must tell me about the phone call! What did he want? I very much suspect that it's connected with the reason I left the house. Tell me!"

The angry Paulina didn't rush to do his bidding. She could sense his impatience and anxiety to hear what the anonymous caller had said. She made a terrific attempt to understand what was happening here at the time when honest people slept.

"Tell me already!" The words came out a shriek. "What did he say? What did he want?"

She remained silent and would not answer. Her gaze was riveted to a certain spot on the curtain that covered the large living room window; her knees knocked together nervously.

Jairo approached her threateningly, his voice tight and frightening: "What did the man on the phone want?"

"It was an unknown voice, and it asked me ..."

"What?" Jairo shouted, not letting her finish the sentence.

Paulina's anger subsided before a deep fear. Jairo's hysterical behavior worried her.

"What's happened to you, Jairo? Why are you so nervous?"

But Jairo wouldn't be deterred. "What did you hear on the phone?"

"That's all, Jairo! I give in, and start to tell you, and you won't let me finish my sentence! What's happened to you?"

Another minute of this, Jairo felt, and he would burst into tears.

"*Por favor,*" he pleaded, "don't give me lectures now! Later! Now, just tell me what he wanted."

"He asked if you were home."

"Yes, and what did you say?"

"Yes, of course."

"And?"

"He suggested that I check to see if you really were home."

"And?"

"Well, I checked, and discovered that you'd disappeared!"

"And then?"

"And then, when I'd returned to the telephone he'd hung up! The anonymous caller was gone! What's this about, Jairo?"

Jairo searched for the closest chair and collapsed weakly into it. After a long minute, he told his wife all that had happened.

Paulina stood, shocked. Suddenly, as she began to understand the implications of the frightening story, she began to tremble.

"Jairo," she whispered in obvious terror.

"What?"

"Jairo, I'm frightened! Leave it alone! Think of me and the children! Leave it!"

"I can't!"

"What's happened to you?"

"I'm a Jew!"

"And I'm a Jew too! What does that have to do with it?"

"I don't know! Suddenly, I've begun to acknowledge this fact. And I don't know why."

11

In the cafe, Francisco and Paulo sat, paralyzed. They stared at the representatives of GAC. Events had taken a surprising, unexpected turn, they realized. *These men are hiding something,* a doleful voice whispered in Francisco's heart. But what could it be? He thought of Hunkes's funeral, with its obvious Nazi overtones. Was there a connection? If so, what was it? He cast a quick glance at Paulo, whose nervousness and anger were becoming more apparent. Suddenly, Paulo decided to take matters into his own hands.

"*Senhores,*" he said, "my name is Paulo Chilo, and I am an Arab. An Arab of Lebanon. My friend, *Senhor* Francisco Machado, is a Brazilian for many generations. I don't understand why all the emphasis on our third partner who is, after all, a Jew."

Paulo grew silent. His eyes examined the faces of the three GAC men, trying to gauge their reactions.

But their countenances remained sealed: There was no emotion revealed. If they found anything interesting in this partnership between Arab and Jew, they showed no sign, no hint of it.

"I think," Francisco quickly interrupted, "that you should be wary of any position that might be construed as racist. Brazil has no love for this. I think that respected men such as yourselves understand this well. It would not be desirable that a concern as well respected as yours would fall prey to something so unpleasant. At the very least, I assume public opinion means something to the company."

Finally, signs of life could be read upon the faces of the Germans sitting across from them at the table. The GAC executives shifted uncomfortably in their hard plastic chairs. They turned their gazes towards the Avenida Paulista, the busy and attractive boulevard that bisected Sao Paulo. This last point that Francisco had brought up was disturbing: Clearly, they had no desire to be viewed by the Brazilian public as anti-Semitic. As a German company they were well aware of public sensitivity to the Nazi crimes. The Jews might make a fuss, cause a furor in the media. No. It wasn't worth it. Company sales might be damaged.

One of the men sitting near Von Dorfman whispered a German translation of Francisco's words. The German cleared his throat slightly; his face softened, and the ghost of a smile appeared in his eyes, trying to give his eagle-like features a more pleasant cast. He turned slightly towards Paulo and Francisco.

"*Meine herren*," he said calmly, "you have clearly not understood the real reason for my mentioning your Jewish partner."

He was silent for a moment, then continued.

"Let me make this clear. We have no objections to the Jew because he is Jewish. That is self-evident!"

His authoritative glance swept over the GAC executives. They nodded their heads gently in agreement.

"The days of the Nazis are gone, never to return. Thank G-d. And we know this! Obviously a respected concern such as ours will not be embroiled in such things. But in this unusual instance specific problems exist, and we do not know how to overcome them. I refer, as you must know, to the widow, Hunkes's wife. She is persuaded that her husband was killed by the Jews, and as a result she loathes them. One can understand her. We believe that with time the wounds will heal, and she will calm down. But in the meantime — that is the situation. And we, in respect to her husband's memory, do not wish to hurt or offend her further."

Francisco was confused. "I don't understand. Why should she say the Jews killed him? What did he do to them?" The surprise in his voice was apparent.

Von Dorfman shrugged his shoulders. The others looked perplexed; they had no knowledge of the matter. It was clear, though, that they wished to end this meeting, forced upon them, as quickly as they could.

Francisco drummed his fingers quietly on the table. His mind worked feverishly. He, too, searched for ways to escape this unpleasant encounter. Suspicion of the true motives of the men sitting across from him mounted — at the very least, those who were not Brazilian, who looked foreign, European. Who knew who they were? And what they'd done when they were young, 25 years ago, when war raged throughout Europe. In the light of his dark suspicions he looked at

Jairo's escapades of the past few days with a different perspective. A sixth sense whispered to him that he was dealing with a mystery. When he'd return to the office he'd try to speak with Jairo. In the meantime, he continued attacking Von Dorfman's position.

"Excuse me, sir, would you have us believe that the caprices of a widow and her baseless feelings of enmity is what makes the policy at GAC? I wonder how the business world will react when they read this strange story tomorrow in the *Estado de Sao Paulo*!"

Von Dorfman's face grew scarlet with rage. He stood up, straightened himself to his full height, his eyes shooting barbs of intense hate towards Francisco.

"Is that a threat, *Senhor* Francisco?"

Francisco, too, stood up.

"I don't know! You see, I have a minor problem. The editor of the business page of the *Estado* is a close friend. He knows that we are currently meeting to sign on a contract of mutual, multinational cooperation. This is precisely the sort of topic he'd like to report on. A small scoop, you know. He's waiting for me. He wants to know the results of our talk. What should I tell him, when he asks for the reasons behind canceling the contract?"

Now it was Von Dorfman's turn to be perplexed. Francisco felt a twinge of triumph within him. The idea of the reporter had just flashed through his head. He'd see how the German would respond to the challenge he'd leveled at him.

Von Dorfman returned to his seat, a little bewildered. After a moment, he burst out laughing. But Francisco's ears caught the false note behind the laughter.

"And so, *Senhor* ..." For a moment Von Dorfman couldn't recall his name.

"Francisco. Francisco Machado de Oliveira," Francisco volunteered.

"And so, *Senhor* Francisco, I think that our conversation has become more complicated than necessary. You have not heard from me that we are canceling all agreements between us. Our management in Germany has asked that I clarify all the ramifications of the contract on the company and its future. It's obvious that the whims of a widow cannot set our company policy. We don't need a respected attorney to tell us that. But sometimes economic considerations are intertwined with sensitive psychological assessments regarding company morale and business success. Our business sense tells us that there is a problem here, despite the fact that we cannot point an exact finger to what it is that disturbs us."

Francisco took a deep breath. The long speech in which the German attempted to camouflage his inability to explain himself upset him, without in the least convincing him. He didn't believe the German. But he understood that there was no reason to continue this fruitless meeting. Still, out of politeness, he asked:

"And so, what do you propose to do at this time?"

"I want you to understand," Von Dorfman hastened to say, "we stand before a difficult decision, with a dilemma whose solution is not clear at this time. On the one hand, we admit that we have obligated ourselves to sign the contract with you; on the other, *Senhor* Jairo Silverman's role in the deal is a serious obstacle. We have therefore decided to delay, for the meantime, the signing, to put a freeze on it for a short time, and to bring it to a decision by the head directorate in Germany. After a careful scrutiny, no doubt we will sign! Let it be clear — we are not anti-Semitic!"

"But what is happening in this matter is clearly an anti-Semitic attitude!" Francisco said emotionally.

"I don't believe so and in my opinion it is not fair for you to accuse our respected firm of such a terrible thing," Von Dorfman replied in icy tones.

The men grew silent. The waiters, in their white uniforms, glided silently through the restaurant. One of them noticed, out of the corner of his eye, that the steins of beer of the respected businessmen were empty, and he approached with a new supply. Without a word, he filled the glasses once again. No one drank.

"And if," Paulo Chilo's quiet voice broke the silence, "and if *Senhor* Jairo Silverman will be terminated from the office, would that make a difference regarding the conditions of signing the contract?"

Francisco favored him with an angry glance. He understood quite well where his colleague was headed, and the matter infuriated him. Paulo's clear attempt to sacrifice Jairo, and reach a business understanding without him, seemed to him treachery of the lowest order. *Why is he acting this way*, Francisco thought to himself. Paulo, from his side, ignored Francisco utterly. The thought that they might lose the contract had shocked him to the core.

On the other side of the table everyone perked up. Von Dorfman's eyes lit up. Perhaps he'd been meaning to reach this goal all along.

"Certainly, my young friend," he responded quickly to the new challenge, "certainly these would be new conditions, which would ensure a new response. And I can promise that it would be a warm and positive response."

Von Dorfman was the first to rise. The GAC executives followed him, as if bewitched. Their vast respect for the German representative was obvious.

"*Meine herren*," he said, as he held his hand out to Francisco, "I think we've made our position clear. We'll be glad to hear from you if you have news for us."

He gave Paulo a special smile as he gave him a farewell handshake. "Your idea can truly bring a speedy resolution to this complicated situation. I am certain that the two of us can work something out to our mutual benefit."

He ruffled through his wallet, pulled out a small business card, and handed it to Paulo.

"Here, this has my phone number in the Ipiranga Hotel, where I'm staying these days. The GAC office will know where I can be reached during the day. After business hours I'll be in my hotel room. You can call me in the evening, whenever you wish. I'm certain we'll have something to talk about."

The GAC executives were the first to leave. Francisco and Paulo stayed behind to pay the bill. When their eyes glanced at the restaurant door they saw the figure of an older man, with grey hair combed back. It was the man Francisco had seen giving the Nazi salute over Hunkes's grave and here he was, returning, walking towards them ...

Bnei Brak
3 Iyar 5727 (1967)

It was 7:30 in the morning. Shabbos morning. Yitzchak Austerlitz didn't get out of bed. Rivka had awoken early, in order to say some chapters of *Tehillim* for the success of her husband's talk with Rabbi

Mandelkorn, his *chavrusah*. And now it was late, and her husband wasn't up yet. Prayers began in half an hour and he was still lying in bed. This didn't happen. Never. He was scrupulous in *davening* with a *minyan*. What had happened today?

She was apprehensive about returning to the bedroom to awaken him. Last night's events were still fresh in her mind, burned like a torch in her heart, and now she was afraid of his reactions. Slowly, carefully she opened the door. Yitzchak didn't move. Had something happened to him?

Yitzchak lay in bed, pretending to sleep. His outburst towards his wife yesterday before *davening* distressed him enormously: another wound on his already scarred heart. He felt a deep misery that sapped him of his strength. He had no desire to rise. His headache felt like a balled fist in his brain.

He knew his wife was standing in the doorway, watching him. Still, he didn't move, hoping she'd think him asleep.

Finally, after long moments, he heard her quiet voice.

"Yitzchak, 15 minutes till *davening*."

No answer.

"Yitzchak, you'll be late!"

He felt horribly guilty. At that moment he wanted more than anything to show her he wasn't angry with her. He turned around and said, "I'm not feeling well. I'm not going today. I'll *daven* at home."

Rivka felt her world darken. She had counted so much on his *chavrusah's* talk with him! After she'd revealed herself to her friend, she didn't want this opportunity to disappear.

Her voice turned stern. "I want you to go."

She was frightened by her tone of command. Yitzchak looked at her with puzzled eyes; he didn't understand her harshness. Still, he arose, without a word, and did as she had bid him.

12

Tensely, Francisco looked towards the GAC employee who'd returned to the restaurant. What did this grey-haired man want from them? Francisco took his change from the cashier and grabbed Paulo's arm to get his attention. Paulo gave him a questioning glance.

"Pay attention. There, near the entrance," Francisco whispered. "One of them has returned to us."

The two partners didn't stir. They stared at the man who was approaching them.

"*Senhores,*" he said with a wide smile, once he was next to them, "my name is Hermann Schmidt. I wanted to ask something of you, but not in the presence of the others."

Francisco and Paulo nodded. In Francisco's mind came the infuriating image, once again, of what he'd seen at the cemetery. He couldn't escape the memory of how this man had stood next to the grave, his hand held out aloft in the classic "Heil Hitler" salute that the Nazis had given their mad leader.

"Can we sit for a few more minutes?" he asked politely.

"See here, gentlemen," he began immediately in German-accented Portuguese, "your Jewish partner is making trouble for us!"

"Who is 'us'?" Francisco interrupted. Perhaps, he thought, he'd be able to get some answers that would explain Jairo's recent strange behavior.

Hermann Schmidt evaded the question. "Us!" he said with strict politeness, his meaning clear: Accept the fact and don't inquire too deeply.

Francisco felt his anger mounting. With this, he asked frigidly, "And what are the troubles that he's making for you? If that is permitted for us to know?"

Mr. Schmidt ignored the insulting tone. "Your partner is interfering with a police investigation."

Francisco laughed. "The police asked you to report to us? Interesting!"

Schmidt began to laugh, laughter that Francisco felt hid his bafflement.

"Oh, heavens, no! But we know that he is trying to uncover the murderers of our Alberto Hunkes!"

"And what's so detrimental about that? Wasn't he your friend?" Francisco continued.

"You're right. But we are interested in seeing him forget the entire affair."

"Again, 'we,' " Francisco said ironically.

"Yes, again, 'we,' " the GAC employee said in sterner tones. "These investigations may ultimately cause damage to the company and we are not interested in them."

"The company has something to hide?"

Hermann Schmidt began to show clear signs of impatience. He breathed deeply and, hardly aware of it, pulled a cigarette case out of his pocket. He answered harshly. "Our company has nothing to hide, sir! But investigations such as these, by their very nature, lead to rumors, rumors which can damage an important and respected company. After all, though we've nothing to do with the matter, GAC is a German company. We remember this fact well and try, with all our might, to keep our good name in the public eye. I assume you understand what I'm talking about."

"I understand," Paulo responded quickly. He saw no point to the entire conversation. All his attention was centered on how to restore, by any means, the contract. With Jairo — or without him.

Francisco, though, continued. "No. Pardon me, but I don't understand. Does your firm have some sort of connection with the Nazis who fled to Brazil?"

Francisco sent out the sentence as a trial balloon. He was very much interested in seeing the reaction of Mr. Schmidt. *If that's his real name*, the strange thought flew through his mind.

Hermann Schmidt looked nervously around him. "Why, *senhor*, should you bring up such a possibility? We're a clean company! We're simply looking for quiet to enable us to carry out our business. To our sorrow our Alberto, Alberto Hunkes, will not return to life. Continuing to dwell on the affair will damage our good name. Considerably!"

Francisco gave him an unbelieving look. "And that's all?"

"Yes. That's all," Schmidt answered vehemently.

"If so, what are you asking of us?"

Hermann Schmidt examined Francisco suspiciously. He couldn't understand where the Jew's partner stood. He didn't know how much he could trust him.

"In order to renew the atmosphere of goodwill between us," he finally said, "we would be very happy if you would stop your partner from the ruinous activities he's been pursuing since Hunkes's death. He must end his investigations! If he does so, it will assist in enabling us to ultimately sign the contract. Do you understand what I'm saying?"

Francisco formulated his response for a long moment.

"We will try," he finally said. Then, after a minute's thought, he added, "I don't understand one thing. Why couldn't Von Dorfman tell us this? Why only you, and only in private?"

Schmidt's surprise was obvious. At least, that's the way it seemed to Francisco. With that, a voice within whispered: *This man is playing a part!*

"Please understand, Mr. ..."

"Machado. Francisco Machado."

"See here, Mr. Machado," Schmidt said quietly, in a soft voice, a voice that tried, at any cost, to be believed. "This topic, German or Nazi, is a very sensitive one. Since Israel uncovered Adolf Eichmann a few years ago, and sentenced him to death, we are doing all we can to distance ourselves from any possible suspicion. In the countries of South America today every German is suspect as a fleeing Nazi. We simply don't want to draw attention to ourselves. The others at the meeting that ended a few minutes ago didn't want to publicly discuss this issue, particularly since local representatives of the company were there. Do you understand me?"

"Not really," Francisco admitted openly. He had an overpowering urge to reveal to the man sitting across from him what he knew of him. How he'd seen him behave as a loyal Nazi there in the cemetery. But he held himself back. He didn't need to hear more of his fairy tales. The man had succeeded in arousing his curiosity: He hoped that Jairo would fill in the blanks.

Hermann Schmidt, the man with the steely grey hair, wanted to end the conversation. He stood up, said goodbye to the two attorneys, and turned towards the big glass door that stood open. Suddenly he whirled around and, with a false smile, spoke to Francisco and Paulo: "You'd better take care of this business quickly! Otherwise the responsibility — and the consequences — will fall upon you as well!"

Francisco's anger got the better of him. He stood up, ready to run after the impudent German. But Paulo grabbed his sleeve and held on to him.

"Calm down, Francisco. Calm down!"

But Francisco could still throw his barbed question towards the German.

"Is that a threat?"

Schmidt gave a frosty smile. "You may interpret it any way you wish."

The grey-haired man hurriedly left the restaurant. In another minute, he'd been swept into the tide of pedestrians swarming down the Avenida Paulista, and Francisco could see him no longer.

Police officer Roberto Nunes woke up at 7 in the morning. This, despite the strange nocturnal conversation he'd had with his Jewish friend, Jairo Silverman. He decided to appear at work in civilian garb, rather than in his uniform. His uniform might interfere with the job he was planning on doing today. From the moment he'd awakened, he hadn't stopped thinking about Jairo's surprising words. Here, certainly, was a thought-provoking development in the Hunkes murder case. The details of Nazi involvement that Jairo had brought up — and he had no reason not to believe him — added an interesting twist to the entire story. The affair had turned into one that was worth his putting effort into. Who knew? Perhaps he held in his hand one end of a long and involved string. If he could uncover it, he, *Delegado* Roberto Nunes, would surely capture the headlines! He certainly would be up for promotion! And besides, he couldn't forget Jairo's personal promise to pay well, if he could identify the true Alberto Hunkes. The murderer was already less interesting than the victim. Who was it who was trying to stop the investigation — and why? What did they have to hide? These were all questions he'd have to deal with. The generous advance of one thousand dollars that Jairo had given him on account gave him a strong push forward. A good friend, Jairo, a true friend!

Roberto didn't hurry. He drank his morning coffee calmly, listened with half an ear to the news on the radio, the entire time his mind on the Hunkes file. He was pleased that the commissioner had, last weekend, placed the investigation in his hands, though at the time he'd merely grumbled aloud at the responsibility.

At 8:30 he left his home in Jardim Europa, one of Sao Paulo's luxury neighborhoods. Half an hour of driving in the busy and crowded city streets brought him to police headquarters next to the train station, which hugged the Bom Retiro neighborhood. This was where most of the city's Jewish population lived, among them many survivors of the Holocaust. If he would manage to uncover Nazis beneath this ordinary murder, he would be a hero in this neighborhood. A warm feeling coursed through his body at the thought.

He parked in the police lot and with light steps made his way to his office. As he walked through the long corridors he graciously flung "Good Mornings" to whomever he passed. When he reached the third floor, where his office was located, he thought that it seemed rather quiet. The closer he got to his office the more he felt a dim sense of foreboding. He couldn't explain what he was nervous about, but, relying on the well-developed reflexes of an experienced police officer, he knew he had to be careful. A few steps before his office, he saw, to his astonishment, that the door was wide open. His suspicions grew. There was enough in Jairo's stories to make him alert and on his guard. Maybe "they," the mysterious "they," knew of his connection with Jairo?

His right hand instinctively grabbed the butt of the revolver hanging around his hips. He approached the door with slow, silent steps. He knew he must be careful of whatever surprise awaited him on the other side of the door. When he was right next to the door he pulled the revolver quickly out of its holster and, in one motion, bounded into the room, the revolver squarely pointed at his desk.

But the office was empty; no one was waiting for him. Roberto slowly returned the revolver to its place, oddly disappointed and rather embarrassed. How could he have allowed his feelings and fantasies to overcome him? But with all that — how had the door come to be open? Who had opened it? Roberto had no idea. But when he sat down at his desk he saw that he'd had a visitor: His papers had been searched. Someone had gone through his documents, pulled files out of the cabinet. And he had done it in a way that ensured that Roberto knew he'd been there — and that he would draw the conclusions that "they" wanted him to draw.

13

Though his gun was safely back in its holster, Roberto felt his tension grow stronger. This unexpected visit to his office, and particularly the insolence that it showed, unnerved him, or, more precisely, aroused his suspicions of the forces arrayed against him. Roberto was no coward: Conversely, from his youth he was known for his bravery, and in his chosen profession in the police he had often proven himself. More than once he'd come face to face with death. In his career as a detective he had several times been in gunfights with criminal gangs, particularly drug dealers. He was particularly remembered for a shootout he'd had with leftist terrorists on one of the city's main streets. He had often been commended for bravery. He had never turned away from trouble, despite the danger to his life.

This time, for some reason, he felt something new. He couldn't recognize the mysterious enemy standing before him. This enemy was of a high caliber, clever and unexpected. The impudence of it, to sneak into police headquarters, into his locked office, and do whatever he wished: It showed massive self-confidence. And how, indeed, had he gotten into such a well-guarded building?

Roberto suddenly broke into a cold sweat. The thought was inescapable: *Maybe the unknown who'd broken in on "their" command is someone on the inside, someone in this building? Otherwise, why did no one notice the intruder in the corridors, where everyone recognizes everyone else?* Roberto became aware of the tremendous challenge that lay before him, the mystery whose solution — the correct solution — he must find. What was clear to him was that if he combined the stories Jairo had told him last night with the evidence before his eyes this morning, he must be doubly careful with every step he'd take.

Roberto crouched down and collected the papers spread around the floor. He piled them up on the desk and began to file them. He examined page after page, file after file, to try and uncover what they had searched for in his office. No surprises: His guess had been correct. "They" had interested themselves in only one file — the murder of Alberto Hunkes. On the file folder he found one word that "he" — whoever he was — had written in blood-red ink: Caution! He noticed that several pages were missing — the testimony of the restaurant owner who'd described the man who'd sat with Hunkes during his fateful last lunch. Luckily, he had another copy in his house safe. In addition, all the documents that Varig Airlines had supplied, and those of the border patrol concerning the suspect's passport, dates of entry and exit, and travel plans after the murder were also gone. Interesting that all of the details on Hunkes himself that he'd begun to collect had remained in the file, and the mysterious hand hadn't touched them at all.

Roberto ensconced himself in his executive's chair. This last fact was baffling. His senses, as a police investigator, were sharp. Something very strange here, impossible to explain. Something didn't fit with the theory he'd been developing, a theory based, in large part, on Jairo's narrative. Up until this moment he'd been sure that the hand of the Nazis was involved, in an effort to undermine the investigation. An investigation such as this could very well reveal their true identities and disturb the lives they were living, under assumed names, here in Brazil. The precedent of Adolf Eichmann, who'd been kidnapped from Argentina and brought to judgment in Israel, was enough to frighten the entire underground network of Nazis living in South America. To make them very, very cautious — up to the point of murder! But if so, the entire file should have disappeared, particularly, those documents relating to the identity of Alberto Hunkes himself. And yet the mysterious thief had taken only those papers connected to the murder investigation and the possible identity of the murderer. For some reason, he was anxious to conceal the murderer's identity, not that of the victim. But it was the victim's true identity that interested his Jewish friend, Jairo. So who was it who was meddling in the matter — and what did they want?

There was no one in the entire police headquarters who could give him a straight and clear answer. He must collect every detail in order to reach a satisfactory conclusion. Piece by piece he would try to form a complete picture. Perhaps this simple murder concealed something earth shattering? Perhaps the murder had come to cover up even greater crimes?

Roberto gently scratched his forehead, and his lips mouthed the question: "What can it all mean?"

But the fog and secrecy that seemed to envelop everything that had happened only served to push Roberto further into the investigation.

He turned to the telex department of the police.

"Good morning," he greeted the bored clerk who sat behind the counter, reading a novel concealed on her lap.

"Listen," Roberto asked, "send telexes to the following places. First, to the Brazilian Interior Ministry. Second, to the political branch of the police department here in Sao Paulo. Also, I need a telex sent to the Justice Department in Copenhagen, Denmark, and another to Interpol."

Roberto gave her the text of each telex. She followed his instructions closely. Finally, he thanked her warmly. "When there are answers telephone me, *Delegado* Roberto Nunes, third floor, room 312. The switchboard will give you my extension. Okay?"

"*Si, senhor.*"

After two hours the replies lay on his desk, and a satisfied smile was spread upon his face. His hand reached for his telephone; he wanted to share his findings with Jairo. But, at the last minute, he stopped. He must take care. It was possible that they would not be alone on the phone line.

Instead, he telephoned the home of Alberto Hunkes's widow — *Senhora* Regina.

Regina Hunkes was sitting on the couch in her living room, her eyes skimming the afternoon paper, when she heard the doorbell. She realized immediately that it wasn't the main entrance; rather, the bell ringing was near the exit from the kitchen, which faced the service elevator. She slowly made her way to the door, and opened it with a weary motion. A young woman stood before her, almost filling the entranceway.

"Good afternoon, ma'am," the woman began in a subdued voice.

"Good afternoon," came the polite reply, with just a trace of impatience. *Senhora* Hunkes stared suspiciously at the unlooked-for guest, and asked, "Can I help you?"

"*Senhora*, downstairs the *zelador* told me you are looking for household help. The *zelador* said good things about you. He also added that you need a maid who is cultured and I," the young woman began to laugh quietly, "I certainly am!"

Regina didn't know, at first, how to react. The maid's self-confidence amused her. Despite the bitterness frozen on her face from the time of her husband's murder, Regina gave a faint smile. The maid sensed it, and decided to continue. "Yes, yes," she said, with the enthusiasm of a small child, "I am more cultured than any other maid around here. I have gone to school. I know German as well as Portuguese."

Again, she burst out laughing. Mrs. Hunkes suddenly looked interested.

"German? What do you mean, you know German? Did you work with a German-speaking family?"

The young maid, heartened by her interest, quickly replied, "No. I myself am German."

Senhora Hunkes looked at her with clear disbelief. The young woman was dressed like a typical Brazilian. Her poverty was obvious. Her Portuguese was perfect. Obviously, she'd been born in Brazil.

"German? And you want to be a maid?"

The young woman laughed again.

"I'm not a German born in Germany. I've come to Sao Paulo from Santa Catarina, from the city of Blumenau. Has the *senhora* heard of Santa Catarina?"

Certainly, Regina had heard of it. She'd visited the southern region with her husband more than once. It was a state, part of the United States of Brazil, whose residents had almost all emigrated, generations earlier, from Germany. The German language was spoken there, in addition to Portuguese.

"But why is the *senhora* so interested in my German?" The voice broke into Mrs. Hunkes's thought and memories of the Santa Catarina cities of Blumenau and Joinville.

Regina softened somewhat. "I, too, speak that language. I myself came to Brazil from Denmark. But my parents also spoke German in the house. My father was a Danish diplomat, and he spent several good years in Berlin. So I understand the language. Interesting."

The young woman gave her a searching look. "So, may I come in?"

Something in the woman's personality attracted Mrs. Hunkes. She had a spark of friendliness, the talent of getting along with others.

"All right, come in," she said, after a moment's hesitation. "But you understand that my house is not a language school. I need good service, with or without German. Let's see what you can do. What's your name?"

The young woman had already stepped into the kitchen. "They call me Celia, Celia Baumgarten."

"A real German name. Nice."

It seemed that the young maid was enjoying the interest of the mistress of the house. But she remained silent. The main thing was, she was now in the apartment.

Regina got down to practical matters. "See here, Celia. Today, to my regret, there isn't much to be done in my house. My son doesn't live here anymore and I ... I ..." Regina sighed deeply, "I live by myself."

It was obvious that the last sentence was difficult for her to say.

Celia dared asked the question. "Alone?"

Mrs. Hunkes looked at her with miserable eyes, sighed, and said, "My husband died. Last week."

The young woman's face took on an aspect of sympathetic sorrow. "You poor thing! But you are so young. Was your husband also young?"

Regina gave her a sad look. "To be sure, he wasn't old."

Celia was quiet for a moment, thinking. Finally, she asked, "And he died? Suddenly?"

"To my great sorrow, he didn't take care of himself as he should have. Heart attack, you know ..."

"A pity," the young woman again demonstrated her empathy in her new mistress's sorrow.

The telephone shrilled loudly. Listlessly, Regina lifted the receiver. The sharp ring had torn through the memories of her husband that she was sharing with this unfamiliar new maid.

She listened with fashionable Brazilian patience to the voice on the other end of the line. Slowly her face grew cold and angry. Other than repeating one word — *si, si* — she said nothing. The conversation ended in a minute or two. She replaced the receiver on the hook and leaned weakly against the wall. Her left hand rubbed her forehead in a nervous gesture, and it seemed to Celia from Santa Catarina that she could hear a sigh escape.

"Has something happened, *senhora*?" she asked worriedly.

Regaining her composure, Regina answered, "No. Nothing special. Nothing of consequence ..."

Words, followed by a long moment of thought. Suddenly, she said, "Celia, wait for me here in the kitchen. I'll be right back."

The mistress of the house left the kitchen, closing the door. Celia heard her dialing the living room phone and quickly pulled a small piece of equipment out of her bag, attached it to the phone connection in the kitchen, and listened ...

"Eduardo?"

"Yes, who is this?"

"Your mother, Eduardo. Good afternoon."

"Yes, Mother, what's happened?"

"A police officer called me."

"Which one?"

"The one investigating the murder. Father's murder."

"Ah, yes. What did he want?"

"I don't know exactly. But I'm worried."

"What did he say?"

"It wasn't clear. He wants to meet with me."

"Okay. But what exactly did he say?"

"He wants to show me several documents that he's gotten concerning Father. He wants me to verify them. I'm worried, Eduardo."

Silence. Finally, Eduardo's voice came on the line. "So what do you want me to do?"

"I don't know. In any case, I want you to come. Be with me in the house when he comes."

"Okay. When is the meeting set for?"

"Another hour."

"What time is it now?"

"Three. Three in the afternoon."

Again, a short silence.

"Look, Mother, I must finish my column for tomorrow morning's *Estado*. I hope to come, but if I'm a little late, don't worry."

"No, Eduardo. Be on time!" Her voice was cold and commanding.

"I see you're really nervous."

"Yes. You're right. And I hope you'll do as I say. In three quarters of an hour you'll be here. Okay?"

Again, silence. "Yes, Mother, I'll try. *Chau*."

"*Chau*."

Celia quickly disconnected the telephone equipment and hid it within her plastic pocketbook. When Regina Hunkes returned to the kitchen, feeling calmer, Celia was busy reading one of the illustrated magazines that she'd taken from a stack that lay piled neatly beside the kitchen table.

14

"Maybe we shouldn't learn today?"
Yitzchak Austerlitz was still wrapped in his *tallis*. Most of the others had already left the *shul* after the Shabbos prayers and were on their way home for their Shabbos meal. Here and there, within the *shul*, a few *chavrusahs* remained to learn. And on this Shabbos he, Yitzchak Austerlitz, wanted to ignore his weekly custom and rush home.

His *chavrusah*, Rabbi Yitzchak Mandelkorn, gave him an understanding look. His wife had told him last night about her painful discussion with Austerlitz's wife. As a result, he was particularly interested in learning with him this morning. Perhaps he could lead the conversation towards the personal. Yitzchak's request was thus an unpleasant surprise.

"What happened today?" he asked, openly shocked.

Yitzchak Austerlitz didn't meet his eyes. "I've got a headache. It's hard for me to concentrate."

But Rabbi Mandelkorn wouldn't give up. "You know what? Let's learn just a little. It's not good to completely skip something so regular."

Yitzchak was impatient. "I know. But my head is really hurting. I want to go take a nap. I'll try to come before *Minchah* and we can learn then."

The *Gemara* already lay open in front of Rabbi Mandelkorn. He closed it slowly, perplexed. He felt Austerlitz's obstinacy, and saw no benefit in pushing him further. But he, too, could be obstinate, and he wanted to speak with him at all costs. He couldn't put this conversation off: From what his wife had told him, the situation at Austerlitz's home wasn't good and things could get worse. He had no choice. Now was the time.

"Can I walk home with you?"

Yitzchak Austerlitz didn't want the escort. More than anything, he wanted to be alone ... Alone. Let them leave him alone. But he also didn't want to insult his respected *chavrusah*. With no choice, he agreed.

They left, each wrapped in his *tallis*. From Rabbi Tarfon Street they turned towards Rabbi Akiva Street, walking slowly and heavily. Bnei Brak was flooded by sunlight; the weather was pleasant. But Yitzchak, sunk deep into thought, took no enjoyment from his surroundings. Rabbi Mandelkorn, walking alongside him, also was silent. As they approached Austerlitz's home, Rabbi Mandelkorn could feel his tension grow. *Another few minutes and he'll dive into his house and I — I haven't yet spoken with him. Go on, Yitzchak, this is your chance. Don't miss it!*

His breath came heavily. He searched for the right words to open the conversation, a conversation that would be a difficult one. From the corner of his eye he looked at the quiet man walking next to him. Austerlitz didn't even notice Rabbi Mandelkorn's gaze. His head was bent, his eyes locked onto the ground beneath him. A man enveloped in blackness.

"Reb Yitzchak!"

Rabbi Mandelkorn's voice was clear and sharp. Yitzchak Austerlitz raised his head, surprised.

"Reb Yitzchak, I beg of you, tell me the truth."

Yitzchak Austerlitz stopped short. His eyes showed a deep wonderment, and he stared at his *chavrusah*, who'd stopped short next to him.

"I don't understand. What 'truth?' "

"Reb Yitzchak, let's sit down on this bench for a little while."

Yitzchak Austerlitz looked around at the people passing by. "Here, in middle of Rechov Rabbi Akiva? In front of all the people coming home from *shul*?"

Rabbi Mandelkorn, who'd finally found his courage, refused to give way.

"Yes, now, in middle of Rabbi Akiva. The bench was put there for people to sit on, right?"

They sat. Yitzchak Austerlitz felt himself surrendering; from the moment he'd stopped he knew that he would do his *chavrusah*'s bidding. He stared at Rabbi Mandelkorn, saw clearly the tension on his face. He noticed that his friend's eyes were darting back and forth in obvious restlessness. Yitzchak Austerlitz didn't understand what had happened to him. Suddenly, he heard his voice:

"See here, Reb Yitzchak. We've been learning together for almost five years now. Thank G-d we've gone through several *masechtos*, and we've mastered them. *Baruch Hashem*. There has been enough time for us to get to know each other. I know you, you know me, at least I hope so. And I am worried about you. That's the truth. And I want to know if I can help."

Yitzchak Austerlitz made no reply. He stared into the street, full of people who'd just finished *davening* with the Great Synagogue's second *minyan*.

"*Gut Shabbos*, Reb Yitzchak!" came a voice from among the walkers. Yitzchak Austerlitz didn't answer, though Rabbi Mandelkorn gave a warm reply and a nod.

After a few moments of silence, Yitzchak Austerlitz quietly spoke. "I don't think you can help me."

Yitzchak Austerlitz shocked himself with his words. This was the first time he'd confessed to another that something was disturbing him. He trembled for having revealed, for no reason, his deep secret.

Rabbi Mandelkorn moved nearer to Austerlitz. "How do you know? Maybe I can help! Doesn't it say in *Mishlei*: 'A man who has a worry within his heart, let him speak of it'? A man may not keep his problems buried within him. Just speaking of them often lightens the burden."

Another long, cold, grey silence.

"No! I'm not interested in talking about it! It's too hard. I must carry my sorrow in silence, and hope that Hashem will save me from my anguish."

Rabbi Mandelkorn wouldn't give in. "And yet — "

Yitzchak Austerlitz gave a melancholy smile. "I'm sorry, my friend. We belong to two separate worlds."

Rabbi Yitzchak Mandelkorn gently put his arm on his *chavrusah's* shoulder.

"Is it … is it connected with what happened…there, in the Holocaust?"

Yitzchak Austerlitz didn't answer. He merely nodded his head.

Silence descended once again. Neither knew how to continue the conversation that, in Rabbi Mandelkorn's eyes at least, had not really begun.

Yitzchak Austerlitz was the first to break the silence. "May I please go home now? I've already said too much!"

He stood up, a clear indication that in his opinion the dialogue had ended. Rabbi Mandelkorn, too, rose, shook his friend's hand, and said, "It's a shame, Reb Yitzchak, that you show such a lack of faith, one that almost borders on apostasy."

Yitzchak Austerlitz, one foot already stepping forward, trembled. Trembled — to the depths of his soul. Now he wanted to continue to speak.

"Are you saying that I am a non-believer?"

Rabbi Mandelkorn sat down once again and waited for his friend to do the same. Austerlitz followed, shaken by the accusation that his *chavrusah* had leveled against him.

Rabbi Mandelkorn began to sway, as he would during a *shiur* in *Gemara*:

"You want to know why I say this? I haven't said it — the *Gemara* has! The *Gemara* in *Moed Kattan* says: 'Three days for crying, seven for eulogy, thirty for mourning. More than that, says G-d, don't be more merciful than I.' We understand from this that to mourn beyond these limits for loved ones who have died implies that G-d, so to speak, is not sufficiently merciful and we flesh and blood humans show greater mercy than He. The *Gemara* makes this demand upon us."

He was quiet for a minute and then continued, with increasing force.

"My poor, suffering friend, Reb Yitzchak! Of course, no one can ever forget his family, taken from him during the Holocaust. G-d does not demand this of a man. You are right, too, that we belong to two different worlds. Thank G-d I was born in Eretz Yisrael. Never, never will I be able to descend into the depths of your frightful world, may G-d have mercy. But with that, Reb Yitzchak, we must remember that there is one kind of mourning and another type of mourning. There is the mourning of the first week, the first month, the first year. And the mourning of 'after the year.' And each mourning has its own boundaries. The *Gemara* teaches us that we may not mourn with the fervor of the first month during the first year. And certainly we may not mourn as we do during the first year — for all of our lives! Forgive me, even though I am younger than you, for saying this. It seems to me that you are mourning as during the week of *shivah* up until this day, 25 years later! True, we cannot delve into the judgment of the Creator and understand why He allowed this to happen. But it was the Chazon Ish *zt"l* who said that when we see a tailor tearing material from a roll, we know he is preparing to sew a suit. This was the way the Chazon Ish viewed the horrors of Hitler. Can't you see G-d's mercy — you survived! You survived, you reached this land. You created a family. You have a son who learns Torah. Reb Yitzchak, with all the pain, you may not destroy your entire life, your home and your future. It was G-d's will. If you don't accept this, you've repaid G-d's good with evil."

Rabbi Mandelkorn was torn with emotion as he said the words. It was hard for him, terribly hard, but he knew his obligation at this moment. He had spoken with his eyes firmly cast downwards, trying not to look at the one he was addressing. Now he shifted his gaze. Yitzchak Austerlitz was sitting silently on the bench, staring at him with melancholy eyes, tears dripping down his face onto his beard, undisturbed.

Rabbi Mandelkorn felt a wave of discomfort. Had he hurt him more than necessary, more than was permitted? He had meant well. He wanted to strengthen his *chavrusah*'s heart, his faith that all that Heaven had done had been done for good. But who knew? Perhaps he'd overstepped his bounds. Who could probe the depths of a soul that had survived Hitler's hell?

"I hope I haven't insulted you. If I have, forgive me."

From amidst his tears, Austerlitz sent a warm smile to his friend, younger than he in years, yet greater in Torah knowledge. He understood that he intended only to help.

"No, no, heaven forbid, you haven't insulted me. You're right. I still mourn my murdered family, particularly my son, Yaakov Yehoshua, may Hashem avenge his blood."

And after a moment of silence he added, "As Yaakov Avinu mourned his son Yosef for 22 years."

Rabbi Mandelkorn well understood Austerlitz's hinted defense: If Yaakov Avinu was permitted to mourn for 22 years, he, too, could mourn his lost family. Rabbi Mandelkorn felt the need to make his point more clearly:

"That is something else. We know that the pain of death is ultimately lessened. In the case of Yaakov Avinu, Yosef was still alive, and thus Yaakov couldn't forget him, and so he mourned as he did. What does that have to do with this?"

Yitzchak Austerlitz's eyes suddenly opened wide. Rabbi Mandelkorn could feel a sudden change come over him. He saw Austerlitz's breath begin to come unevenly. He saw him grab a corner of the *tallis* which he was wearing, pulling so hard he almost tore one of the *tzitzis* off it. A feeling of dread overwhelmed Mandelkorn. He tried to remember what it was that he'd said that could so excite Austerlitz, but there was nothing.

"Don't you feel well?" he asked worriedly.

But Yitzchak Austerlitz didn't respond. He didn't even hear Mandelkorn speak to him. His soul had suddenly passed to another world, far, far away. A wild idea seized him when he'd heard his *chavrusah*'s words. The words echoed in his brain like the tomtom of a drum: The pain of death is ultimately lessened ...Yosef was still alive ...Yaakov couldn't forget him ...Those were Mandelkorn's words. He'd heard them clearly. He knew. It was there in the *Gemara*. In the *Midrash*. Perhaps ... perhaps that was why he couldn't forget his Yaakov Yehoshua! Because ... because ... he was alive ... alive somewhere on this earth!

Yitzchak Austerlitz cradled his head in his hands. Another minute and he would burst. He knew this was foolishness. It could not be. His Yaakov Yehoshua had been murdered along with his wife and two other children. If he were alive, Austerlitz would know of it. But this mad fantasy had settled in his brain and now dominated it. He shook his head back and forth, trying to banish the wild thought from his brain. *After all, it simply can't be. It can't be! Can't be! Why do I think such things? Please, G-d, have mercy upon me. Save me! Enough of my troubles! Take these foolish and terrible thoughts from me. I can't stand more!* "Enough! Enough!"

The two last words burst from his mouth in a scream. Rabbi Yitzchak Mandelkorn stared worriedly at his friend. He couldn't understand what had suddenly happened to him. He felt terrible. He had wanted to help; who knew what harm he'd caused instead. And what should he do now?

Yitzchak Austerlitz stood up and, without a goodbye, turned homeward. He walked slowly, like an old man whose illness has sapped him of strength. Rabbi Mandelkorn remained seated on the bench, unmoving, his anxious eyes following Austerlitz as he disappeared down Rechov Rabbi Akiva.

15

The small room was hazy with cigarette smoke. Four men were crowded in it during this noon hour. They had arrived at the high-rise building at 15 minute intervals, had each taken the elevator to the 10th floor and, after making certain no one had been watching them, had entered the small apartment. Their host, the tall grey-haired GAC executive, Hermann Schmidt, was scrupulously dressed, his hair combed back. He sat on the sofa, one leg carelessly slung over the other, and stared at his colleagues sitting near him. It was only an hour ago that he'd called them for this emergency meeting.

He could see the tension outlined on the short man who sat, almost lost, in a deep recliner, smoking cigarette after cigarette. The man had come to Brazil just yesterday in order to be close to developments.

The grey-haired man's gaze then fell upon a thin man, whose mustache adorned a sharp face, who leaned nervously on the door. The thin man was an active partner in certain activities that took place in Sao Paulo, a native who was of great help to them. He had been partly taken into their confidence and they had spent many hours together in dangerous and nerve-wracking work.

The fourth man was heavy set, of average height, with a Middle East look. His figure radiated power and, despite his advanced years, his bodily strength was apparent.

From outside came the sounds of the teeming street, the Nuevo de Julio, that gigantic boulevard that bisected Sao Paulo. As always at this time, tens of thousand of cars traveling back and forth made a noise like that of a storm at sea.

All were silent, awaiting the words of the grey-haired man.

"That's it," he finally said. "So far, we haven't been able to stop the mischief of the young attorney, Jairo Silverman. It seems that he's managed to meet with the police officer, Roberto Nunes. By all the signs that we have, it seems the policeman will be involved in the investigation."

"When and where did they meet?" the short man asked in a quiet tone, almost a whisper.

"That's the problem. We managed to prevent several rendezvous between them but still, somehow, they got together. Probably last night. We haven't been able to find out where they met. But we know for certain that Jairo was not in his house in the late hours of night."

"And now?" the short man spoke again. The others waited in perfect silence.

"Now, this is the problem. I am afraid that all the furor that this stupid policeman will raise will frighten the bereaved widow out of her cage before we've succeeded."

The thin man left the doorway and stood, legs apart, across from the grey-haired man.

"I want to know what new developments there have been? We already know all that you've told us."

At that the short man in the recliner rose and stood angrily before him. "You know all this?" he said, surprised.

The man with the iron-grey hair gave a frosty smile. "You want something new? Well, then, Roberto Nunes, police officer, is at this moment sitting in the home of the Hunkes widow."

The short man sat down again.

He glanced at his watch and added, "Excuse me, I am in error. They made up to meet at 4 and it's only 3 now."

Schmidt's eyes flitted from one to the other to see their reactions to his precise information. But no one showed any emotion.

Schmidt continued. "She called her son, Eduardo, that young genius who works at the *Estado*, to join her at the meeting. She's worried about the investigation. And I am afraid, terribly afraid, that she will make a hasty decision to disappear and return to Europe, before we can implement our plan. That's all."

The short man shifted in his seat. His deep voice whispered, "How do you know that this Roberto is already on his way?"

Schmidt had waited for this question.

"Well," he said, "we've managed to plant Helena in the Hunkes house. She overheard the conversation."

"Good, that's progress," the elder of the group volunteered.

The thin man asked, "When did she get there?"

Schmidt gave a slight sigh. "That's the problem. Only this morning. It's hard to believe she can put the plan into effect so quickly. The meeting with Roberto Nunes is damaging, very damaging! It is necessary that everybody be kept quiet right now!"

From downstairs came the frightening sound of hundreds of car horns being honked. Another traffic jam, no doubt, to enrage Sao Paulo drivers. In the room, cigarettes were lit endlessly.

"What do we do now?" asked the short man, demanding action.

"That's the problem! What do we do?"

The thin man rubbed his forehead, threw his cigar stub to the ground, and said, "I'm going to make myself a *cafejinho* (cappucino). Anyone interested?"

The others shook their heads, no. When he was standing next to the kitchen door, the thin man turned around and said, "Perhaps we can use the telephone trick once again?"

Schmidt lifted his hand in a gesture of rejection. "No. Roberto Nunes won't fall for it. That tactic, that prevented them from meeting in the restaurant, is too transparent. We're not talking about a naive college student."

The thin man returned from the kitchen, without the *cafejinho*, and spoke earnestly. "You didn't understand what I meant. This time, we'll use it against her. We'll find a way to get the respected Mrs. Hunkes out of the house, so she won't meet the curious Nunes. We have half an hour, you say? And if Helena is in the apartment by herself, perhaps we can finish the job today!"

Schmidt nodded his head in satisfaction. The others kept their feelings safely hidden. The grey-haired man stood up and approached the telephone.

"We can try. It's hard to believe. She's extremely suspicious, this woman."

With all that, Schmidt began to dial …

Paulo Chilo was upset. He arrived at the office that morning, his mind made up. He went directly to Francisco's office.

"Francisco," he said, without a word of welcome, "we've got to get things settled! We can't leave them hanging like this!"

Francisco was surprised by the junior partner's aggressive tone. He lifted his legs from the desk, where they'd been resting comfortably, removed his reading glasses and placed the document that he'd been perusing, slowly and carefully, before this unexpected intrusion.

"Calm down, Paulo." Francisco tried to restore some serenity into the stormy atmosphere. "I agree with you, generally, that affairs should be settled. But what's all the eagerness this morning?"

"Francisco, you're not as naive as all that. You know very well that I'm talking about the GAC contract. I don't know why, but you've been blinded by something, and you don't seem to realize what an opportunity it presents to the two of us."

Francisco's face grew serious. "Sit down," he commanded Paulo.

Paulo dropped down into an armchair that stood near the wall, far from Francisco's desk. He was uneasy.

"I don't understand, Paulo. What did you say? The

contract is an opportunity for the two of us. What's this — the two of us?"

Paulo rubbed his hands together in a nervous gesture.

"Francisco, didn't you realize that the firm won't sign with us as long as Jairo is involved? Believe me, I've nothing against Jairo. He's a good attorney, personally helped me a lot. I admit it! But I don't have to give up my life for him. And I don't have to give up the contract! Don't you think so?"

"No. I don't think so."

"Why not?"

"Loyalty, my friend, is also worth something. At least, to me it is. You don't do everything for money!"

Paulo coughed, trying to hide his bafflement. This reprimand came as a surprise to him.

"Francisco, I also know the meaning of loyalty. I wasn't born yesterday! But what does that have to do with this?" The protest in his voice was apparent.

"And why not?"

"You know very well that from the company's point of view this also has nothing special to do with Jairo. There's some kind of complication with the wife of this Hunkes. And they simply don't want to offend her. So because of that we won't sign? Believe me, Jairo will understand. Is there something so vital here that we have to show our loyalty? I'm convinced that with time the whole affair will be forgotten, and Jairo will join us. What's the big deal?"

Francisco placed his hands behind his head and tensed up. His eyes were firmly fixed upon Paulo's restless ones.

"With all that, I'm not satisfied, Paulo. There's something that really smells here; like anti-Semitism.

What's going on here? That conversation we had with the grey-haired man before we left the restaurant. The whole thing is suspicious."

"You're becoming just like the Jews. Whatever happens, they see anti-Semitism!"

Francisco straightened up, placed his hands on the desk. He lit a cigarette, playing for time, trying to calm himself from the insult that Paulo had flung at him, no doubt unintentionally.

"Paulo," he finally said, carefully and quietly, "I'm asking you. And …"

Suddenly, he grew silent, remembering Paulo's Arab heritage. A deep feeling within him told him that he should not, at this time, sharpen the conflict between Jairo the Jew and Paulo the Arab. The two nations were now in the midst of a state of war in the Middle East. It wouldn't be very smart to import that war to Brazil, to their own office.

Paulo shifted his seat. "Why'd you grow quiet? What did you want to say?"

"Nothing. It's not important."

Paulo didn't believe him. With that, he returned to his first argument.

"What's important is to close the deal with GAC today! They'll run away from us, my friend. Don't you understand? Why can't you decide? Do you want me to speak with Jairo? I'm prepared to do that! I'll be firm with him."

"You're going too fast, *amigo*. Wait a bit, the day has just begun. Jairo will arrive and we'll discuss everything. Why do we have to argue?"

Paulo laughed. "Did you see how hysterical your Jew-boy was yesterday? Mention Germans and he breaks out in a rash! The whole GAC affair is no longer for him! And I won't agree to have him mess it up for us, just because he's a Jew! A Jew who hates the Germans, who did or didn't do what the Jews accuse them of."

"Paulo, I'm really not happy with you now. You're mentioning Jairo's Jewishness far too often! I don't like it!"

"What can I do? There'll be things you like, and there'll be things you don't like. Learn to live with it, Francisco."

Francisco felt uncomfortable during the entire discussion. In his eyes he could see their partnership destroyed because of nationalistic infighting. The whole thing was foolish. A shame. They had created a successful, profitable establishment. They'd worked together harmoniously. There'd never been any grievance that he was a Brazilian, Jairo a Jew, Paulo an Arab. So what? He wouldn't let Paulo poison the atmosphere because of some unsigned contract.

"Look," Francisco finally said, "I repeat: Let's first see what Jairo has to say. I'll push him this morning, force him to tell me all that's going on. I can't understand all this talk about being followed. It's got something to do with that grey-haired Nazi who told us to get Jairo out of investigating Hunkes's death. The mystery is beginning to interest even me."

"It will only interest me after that cursed contract is signed!" Paulo answered quickly. "Help me, Francisco! Even at the price of a confrontation with Jairo."

Paulo stood up, ready to return to his office. He opened the door and almost collided with Jairo, who had just arrived and had been heading to Francisco. Jairo smiled at his partner's startled and puzzled face. He could see Francisco's slightly embarrassed expression. He himself was feeling good.

"Has something happened?" he asked, breaking the other's deep silence.

Bnei Brak
4 Iyar 5727

The telephone rang Sunday morning in the home of Yitzchak Austerlitz. Luckily, he hadn't yet left to work. On the other end of the line, he could hear the clear voice of the director of Yad Vashem, with whom he'd fought the other day.

"Mr. Austerlitz?"

"Yes."

"Good morning, I'm speaking from Yad Vashem. Do you remember me?"

"Of course." Austerlitz's heart began to pound.

"I have good news for you …"

The voice on the other end grew faint; Austerlitz felt a sharp pain in his head.

"Actually," the voice continued at last, "it's strange to call it 'good news.' I meant to say that we've had some serious progress on your request. From the Simon Wiesenthal Center in Vienna I have received the information that they recognize the man. They know his identity by the number of the picture, which I sent them in my telegram."

With difficulty, Austerlitz controlled himself.

"What's his name? Is he still alive? Where? I must find him! At all costs!"

The last words came out as a shriek.

"I apologize," the director of Yad Vashem said. "For obvious reasons, we cannot give you that information over the phone. If you come to our office, we'll give you all the details that we've collected. *Shalom.*"

"But …" Yitzchak Austerlitz tried, but he was too late. Only the sound of the dial tone issued from the receiver.

16

The grey-haired man didn't give up. He dialed the number once again. In the room, the tension grew thicker. All the men stared at him. No one spoke, no one commented on his lack of success in getting through to Regina Hunkes. They noticed that Schmidt was beginning to seem impatient. The thin man couldn't be certain but it seemed that Schmidt's finger was dialing just a little too hastily, a little too firmly, as if that would persuade the one on the other side to pick up the receiver.

But there was no answer …

The grey-haired man looked at his comrades and raised his arms in a gesture of despair.

"No one answers," he said.

"Perhaps she's not at home," one of the others volunteered.

"Impossible! Helena would have reported it. She *must* be home! Her meeting with the police officer is set for 4 o'clock. That is, if everything is all right — I repeat, if everything is all right — it will begin in half an hour."

"And what will happen?"

Schmidt gave the thin man an angry look.

"What's your solution to the problem?"

The thin man looked confused. Schmidt was his direct superior, and he knew that he didn't like surrender, doubts, and lack of confidence. The thin man realized he'd made a mistake.

"Sorry," he hurriedly said.

Schmidt, angry, didn't deign to show he'd even heard him. With characteristic stubbornness he began to dial again.

The short man, who'd come from abroad, also began to lose his patience.

"Time is running out. Twenty minutes and the meeting will begin in the widow's house. We've got to stop it at any cost. Do you understand — at any cost!"

That was the sign for the grey-haired man to leave the telephone. He turned to the thin man and commanded, "Go and find him."

The thin man tensed up. "Who?"

The grey-haired man's face took on a yellow tinge, looking a bit like a rotten fruit. "*Delegado* Roberto Nunes, that's who!" he barked angrily. "Haven't you been with us for the past hour? Don't you know what we're talking about?"

The thin man was insulted. "Okay … okay …" he said, resigned to his fate, "but you don't have to yell at me!"

"Quickly! There's no time! You've got to stop him, come what may! You can even cause a minor traffic accident; I'm not interested in how you do it. The main thing is that Roberto Nunes must not meet with the widow and her unpleasant son. Understand?"

The thin man was already next to the door. He was prepared to carry out his mission, though he wasn't certain what he was to do. But Schmidt stopped him, grabbed his arm roughly, and said,"Wait a minute. Do you have any idea where to find him?"

The thin man answered, embarrassed, "No."

Schmidt didn't reply. Instead, he pulled the receiver up from the phone and dialed once again.

"Good afternoon," he said, in a pleasant voice, "is this Police Headquarters? ... Good. May I speak with *Delegado* Roberto Nunes? ... I understand. When did he go out? Ten minutes ago? Interesting, he was supposed to wait for my call ... Who am I? Oh, it's not important. I'll call him tomorrow. But perhaps you know where he went? ... To an important meeting? I understand. Thank you very much. *Chau.*"

The grey-haired man replaced the telephone on the hook. "Did you hear that?" he turned to the thin man. "He left 10 minutes ago. From Police Headquarters, that's next to Bom Retiro. Let's study the situation for a moment. To get to the parking lot, he'll need 4 to 5 minutes. By my reckoning, he could be at the Avenida Sao Luis by now. If we take the next 10 minutes into account, with you leaving now and moving quickly, you can reach the Paulista in 3 minutes. You can get to the Avenida Angelica in the Hygienopolis in a quarter of an hour. That gives you 5 minutes to search the roads for Nunes. Drive around the streets that lead to Piaui. I hope you'll use all of your varied talents to stop this meeting with Mrs. Hunkes, our revered widow. Understood?"

The thin man straightened, his confidence returning. This plan restored, in his eyes at least, his lost honor. Even though he still didn't quite understand what he was to do.

"Yes," he answered shortly.

He rushed out the door, but Schmidt's peremptory voice stopped him short. "Wait!"

The thin man swirled around and angrily stopped. His superior's abusive attitude was beginning to make him nervous.

"Yes?"

"You know him, Nunes?"

"Yes."

"Good. But do you know what car he drives?"

The question was not a pleasant one. Again, the thin man was forced to admit his professional ineptitude. In the critical moment, he'd forgotten to ask the most basic questions. He felt foolish, although deep inside he justified himself. After all, he was Brazilian, not European, and he was simply helping them with various schemes for which he'd never been adequately trained. They shouldn't make such demands on him. Still, he felt he'd not proven himself before Schmidt and the others.

"No," he answered weakly.

"It doesn't matter. There's no way you could know." Schmidt's voice was conciliating; he felt he'd gone too far in insulting this hired hand. He put his arm on the other's shoulder in a gesture of friendship and explained. "Lately, he's been driving a new, blue Gordini. His father-in-law bought it for him as a birthday present. On the left, on the bottom of the door, there's a noticeable dent, and the paint is chipped. If there's no choice — do you hear me, no choice — you might want to deepen the dent. Do you understand what I'm saying? But obviously, I'll be very happy if you can find a more sophisticated way of stopping him. A way that won't involve the law."

As the thin man finally left the room, Schmidt added, with the ghost of a smile. "I'm counting on you."

Like a car engine newly revved up, the thin man raced through the door.

Jairo looked at his partners and repeated his question. "Has anything happened?"

"Why do you think so?" Francisco quickly replied.

Before Jairo could answer, Paulo left the office, without a word. Jairo stared after him in open amazement. He had seen Francisco trying to calm Paulo down with a swift look.

"What's going on, Francisco?"

Francisco hesitated. Finally, he spoke. "He is angry."

"Angry over what?"

"He's angry that the GAC contract hasn't been signed yet."

"Very good of him! One would think that he would put in all his efforts into finalizing it!"

Jairo put his leather attache down on the desk, chose the nearest chair and sat down. His eyes sought to discover if Francisco was hiding something from him. But his look was honest and clear. Jairo could even see a twinkle in his eyes.

Jairo realized that though he was senior partner in the office, he must now explain what had happened these past few days. Not that Paulo had the right to be angry. Still, his behavior had been eccentric, to say the least. He sensed that he owed his colleagues an explanation.

"Look," he said, an embarrassed smile on his face, "I was a little wild these past few days, I admit, but that's it! I'm back to normal."

Jairo gave a boisterous laugh. Francisco didn't join him; he realized that it merely masked Jairo's confusion. It seemed that Jairo was ashamed of his strange behavior before his partners.

Francisco, curious, decided to gently do a bit of probing.

"I understand. The scene at the cemetery made a big impression on you. I understand: the Holocaust, Nazis, things like that. It's hard for a Jew to take part in that. I understand."

"No," Jairo said, carefully selecting each word, "it's not exactly that. I admit that my father's stories about the Holocaust seemed to come alive before my eyes. Something stirred in me, when I saw that grey-haired man lift his hand in a Nazi salute. I still haven't forgotten that awful sight."

Jairo lapsed into silence. Beads of sweat suddenly appeared on his brow.

"Yesterday I met him again! But where?" Jairo tried to prod his memory. Suddenly, he remembered: in the restaurant, where he'd gone to meet Roberto, who hadn't turned up. But he kept this fact to himself and didn't share it with his partner.

"His name is Hermann Schmidt," Francisco offered the information.

Jairo's surprise was great. "You know him?"

"Yes," Francisco said in an offhand manner, adding, "what's so important about that?"

"From where? From where do you know him?" Jairo shot another question.

Francisco laughed. "You said you've gone back to normal, Jairo! I see that's not exactly so."

Jairo felt he'd gone too far. "I'm sorry."

Francisco ignored him. "Hermann Schmidt is a GAC executive."

"And ..."

"You weren't here, Jairo. We couldn't tell you that we met with the GAC people."

Jairo's face froze. He looked worriedly at Francisco. He remembered that he'd told them to work it out without him. Still, the knowledge that his partners had met with the company's men behind his back angered him. In normal times, he would know how to react, but now he couldn't fault them. He knew that he was to blame for these developments, and that they might very well damage his standing in the office. Now he had to control himself, slowly reinstate his position of power. His voice suddenly grew quiet and businesslike as he tried, without success, to radiate authority with his words. "When was the meeting?"

Francisco was no fool. He could feel his senior partner's surging emotions, beneath the quiet and cool exterior. He decided to continue the conversation, curious to see where it would lead. He lit up a cigarette.

"Yesterday," he answered shortly.

Jairo thought for a moment. Finally he asked, again in an even and controlled voice, "Why didn't you tell me?"

"But Jairo, you yourself told us to do what we thought best. What do you want now?"

"You could have told me, at the very least!"

Francisco sensed the accusation.

"What do you want from us? Did you leave us an address where we could speak with you? You left the office like a whirlwind, and no one knew where you'd disappeared to! It seems you don't remember what you looked like, what came over you yesterday!"

"I understand. And yet, to go to a meeting without notifying the main one concerned?"

Francisco took a deep breath. "We didn't want to break our connection with them. You understand that we wouldn't have signed anything without you."

"And what happened at the conference?" Jairo continued.

Francisco understood: The moment of truth had arrived.

"They don't want you, Jairo. I don't know why. They'll accept the contract only if you're not involved, that you don't sign it, and have no part in it!"

Jairo's eyes opened wide. "The Jew."

Francisco felt distinctly uncomfortable. "They didn't say that openly; they didn't even hint at it. By the way, what did Hunkes's wife do to you?"

"She hasn't done anything! They told you they're against me because of that woman?"

"Yes. They said it specifically! Coincidentally, Jairo, tell me the truth — are you working on a private inquiry into Hunkes's death?"

"Why do you say that? What foolishness!"

Francisco looked at him unbelievingly. He spoke slowly, watching for Jairo's reaction. "Hermann Schmidt, the grey-haired man that we saw in the cemetery, took part in the meeting. He asked me to see to it that you stop interfering. That you shouldn't ask too many questions into Hunkes's death. That you stop it immediately! What's going on with you, Jairo? What are you doing, getting involved in this?"

Jairo was stunned. Suddenly he realized who was after him. It was none other than GAC! At that moment his suspicions of Hunkes's identity as a Nazi grew even greater. The picture was becoming clearer, though he still couldn't tell what they had to fear from him, Jairo, if he uncovered the true identity of his murdered friend.

Jairo didn't answer. He stood up, grabbed his attache, and turned to the door.

"Listen to me, Francisco. Without me there is not, and will not be, a contract with GAC! Is that understood?"

"Not really, Jairo. Paulo wants to strike out on his own. And GAC is pressuring him, and making him all sorts of promises. Can you stop him?"

Jairo returned to Francisco's office, sat down once again. He opened his mouth as if to speak, suddenly shut it again. He sat for a few moments in absolute silence, thunderstruck. He hadn't expected such a betrayal, such treachery in the office. Francisco had placed the blame entirely on Paulo. But what about him? Was he, too, prepared to throw away a profitable partnership for the contract? Was he, too, uninterested in the anti-Semitic leanings of the giant firm? Jairo felt, again, the aloneness of the Jew. So alone, without friends to stand by him in his time of trouble. An unseen wall had suddenly sprung up between him and Francisco, his colleague for so many years!

After a few seconds of silence, Jairo stood up. Before leaving, he said, "Without me the contract will not be signed, my friend. Watch for unexpected developments! And I say to you personally — stay away, and beware! It's dangerous! Very dangerous!"

Jairo didn't explain his warning. He just sped out of the room.

17

Sao Paulo, Brazil
May 16, 1967

Roberto carefully drove through the busy streets of Sao Paulo. Getting through the hub-bub of Sao Luis was almost impossible. Anxiously he glanced at his wristwatch: Already 3:45. Would he manage to get to Mrs. Hunkes's house in 15 minutes? Would he find a parking space immediately? He had realized, during his telephone conversation with her, that she was anxious to avoid this meeting and at the very least hoped to put it off. All the more reason for him to want to speak with her — particularly in light of the curious replies he'd received to the telexes he'd sent. Interesting to see her face when he shared some of his discoveries.

Roberto turned left on the Rua Consolacao. He passed the Praca Roosevelt and sped up to the first right turn, that would bring him to the Angelica. At this hour, it seemed to him the easiest and fastest route. He knew he must arrive on time. The honorable widow must surely hear the truth, the truth that had begun to be clear to him from the reports he'd just received. She might use his tardiness as an excuse to leave the house. Afterwards, she'd undoubtedly apologize, with every indication of regret, pointing out that it had been *Delegado* Roberto Nunes who had missed the meeting, and she had had to go shopping or whatever other excuse she could think of.

Roberto was disturbed by his friend Jairo's complicated connection to the affair. The document that Roberto had obtained from Brasilia had aroused dim suspicions that made him distinctly uncomfortable. Why had Jairo insisted that he investigate the matter for him? Wasn't Jairo aware of what he himself had done? Roberto had no answer.

Suddenly he hit his forehead with a finger. "What a fool I am!" he said aloud to himself, his voice mixing with the smooth tones of the announcer on Channel 7 of his car radio. "How could I have forgotten to have a telex sent to the Buenos Aires police?" That was the most important thing for him to have done, even more vital than setting up this meeting. The answers he would receive might be the turning point of the entire investigation. Should he go back, skip the meeting, in order to see what the Argentinians had to say? No! He'd go on!

Roberto had made the right onto the Angelica. He slowed down somewhat; he didn't want to miss the turn onto Piaui Street. He bit his lips. *Buenos Aires! Buenos Aires! It was there that part of the picture would be revealed!* How could he have forgotten to take care of it before rushing off to meet the widow?

He stopped at a corner. The light had begun to change as he reached the intersection, but the traffic coming from his right continued, despite the red signal. Five minutes to 4. Traffic was blocking his way completely. Roberto felt himself losing control; the long, snaking line of cars was infuriating. He was tense: Who knew what the coming meeting would bring? More than that, he was anxious about Jairo. His wonder was growing by the minute: He couldn't understand the reasons for Jairo's involvement in the Hunkes affair — an involvement that had been noted in the telexes that were safely placed in the black leather attache next to him. After all, Jairo was a Jew ...

And then it happened.

The station wagon, loaded with merchandise, swerved out of its lane and rammed the lieutenant's Gordini. Roberto could feel his body fling towards his car's front window, his head sustaining a stunning blow. Within seconds he was lolling back in his seat, momentarily unconscious, his head dropping down on his chest. Passersby rushed to the stricken automobile, whose front fender had been badly dented. In another moment drivers of cars that had come to a shrieking halt joined the crowd, trying to assist the stricken man in the small automobile. The driver of the station wagon, a thin young man, came out, almost in tears, his body trembling.

"When did you get your license?" an older man yelled at him.

"He learned driving in a correspondence course!" a younger man said sarcastically, not bothering to join the crowd who'd gathered to give the wounded man first aid.

The guilty driver didn't answer. He hurried towards Nunes's car. He pushed through the crowd to reach the wounded man. Just as he'd managed to make his way through, he saw the driver open his eyes and look around in obvious confusion.

"I'm sorry," the thin man said in a beseeching tone, even as he glanced at his watch. The time, he noticed with satisfaction, was 4 o'clock.

"I'm so sorry," he repeated. The others threw hostile glances at him, that would, under other circumstances, have sent him fleeing the spot.

"*Senhor*," the thin man said, "how are you feeling? I'll pay for all the damages! Money is no object for me. *Senhor*, shall I take you to the hospital?"

Roberto was still confused. His head ached terribly. And yet, even in his fog, he heard the young driver's words. It seemed that he hadn't been badly hurt, despite the loss of consciousness that had lasted a few seconds. The others surrounding him began to speak more kindly to the careless driver.

The driver again asked, "Shall I take you to the hospital?"

Roberto had begun to recover. "No, thank you. I'm rushing to an appointment. I'll be all right. But why aren't you more careful? Let me see your papers. I'm a policeman. Lieutenant Roberto Nunes. I have the authority."

The thin man felt his heart skip a beat. He hadn't been mistaken. The accident had succeeded.

"*Senhor* Lieutenant," the thin man hastily answered, "I ask your pardon once again. I don't know what happened to me. And as I said before, I'll pay for all damages. Why get the police involved?"

"We'll speak about that later. In the meantime, let me see your license and papers."

The thin man hesitated. He stared thoughtfully at Roberto, trying to assess the situation. It seemed that the police officer hadn't been seriously injured. He'd received a blow to the forehead. It was a 2-minute drive, a 10-minute walk, from here to the Hunkes home. His assignment was not yet complete. Nunes could still reach his destination.

The thin man returned to his station wagon. He slowly pulled out his documents. He returned to Roberto, who was sitting in his car, his hands supporting his throbbing head. The thin man handed him the papers. The circle of bystanders had dwindled considerably.

The mission continued: The thin man must delay as long as possible. As Roberto skimmed through his papers, he said, "*Senhor*, are you feeling all right? I feel terrible! Are you certain I shouldn't take you to a hospital? Samaritan Hospital is not far from here."

Suddenly Roberto lifted his head and stared at the thin man. A quiet voice within him said that all was not right here. He remembered Jairo's tales of people following him, trying at all costs to impede the investigation and hide Alberto Hunkes's mysterious identity. Despite his weakness Roberto stepped out of his car and stood up. With a swift motion he grabbed at the thin man's shirt, put his face next to the frightened driver, stared directly into his eyes and hissed, "Tell me the truth: Who sent you?"

The thin man began to tremble.

"What are you talking about? I work for Caribe, and he sent me with merchandise to deliver to the Vila Mariana. Through my carelessness I caused an accident, and I've destroyed my life! Have pity! My parents will pay for everything! They have money, Officer."

The thin man was content. Nunes's suspicions had caused him to forget the appointment. He glanced surreptitiously at his watch. Already 4:15. Excellent. Schmidt would certainly appreciate the efforts he'd made to keep this police lieutenant away from the widow.

The driver's pleas left Roberto Nunes unmoved.

"Tell me, who are you? Who sent you to crash into me? Talk! Quickly!"

Roberto gave him a strong shake; his strength had returned. The thin man began to cry.

"I haven't the slightest idea, Officer, what you're talking about! Who should have sent me, and for what? No one sent me, in the name of all that's holy!"

Roberto remained unpersuaded. As an experienced police officer, he knew how much credence to give to the pleas and cries of suspects. His hand grasped the thin man's shirt firmly. Nunes pulled the driver towards him.

"Come with me!"

Jerusalem
4 Iyar 5727

Yitzchak Austerlitz didn't wait. He left for Jerusalem immediately. It was noontime when he reached Yad Vashem. Without hesitation, he approached the director's office.

"Hello, I've arrived," he announced abruptly.

The director raised his eyes in surprise. Then he smiled.

"Hello. I'll be with you in a minute."

Yitzchak waited impatiently. In his heart he prayed that G-d grant him the strength to bear it, now that it seemed that all would be revealed. He asked that He give him the ability to survive these next few minutes as he awaited the director sitting before him, hardly aware of the torment he was causing by delaying his answer. Yitzchak's heart, the heart of a Jew destroyed in the Holocaust, was about to burst!

The director finished the letter he was writing, raised his eyes towards Yitzchak, and said, "So, Mr. Austerlitz, it wasn't a monumental task, thank G-d. We actually had received the picture you saw from the Institute to Investigate Nazi War Crimes in Vienna. Each picture is assigned a number that appears on every copy handed out to various Nazi-hunting organizations throughout the world."

"And so, what's his name?" None of these details interested Yitzchak Austerlitz.

"As told to us by Simon Wiesenthal, his name is Heinz Krantz. Born in the city of Dresden, on the seventeenth of September, 1918. And ..."

Yitzchak's eyes narrowed. "Heinz Krantz ...Heinz Krantz ..." Austerlitz repeated the despised name again and again. Finally, the pain evident in his broken voice, he asked, "And where is he today? Is there information on him?"

The director bent towards him, as if wishing to tell him a secret. In a quiet, confident tone he said, "Up until recently there was no knowledge of his whereabouts. But lately information has come to light which may enable us to locate where he is hiding, if he is alive. Mr. Wiesenthal told me, confidentially of course, that he is checking all his sources of information. The investigation is proceeding in a satisfactory manner. This murderer, Heinz Krantz, killed tens of thousands of innocent Jews."

Yitzchak Austerlitz sat across from the director, his face a frozen mask.

"Heinz Krantz! Heinz Krantz!" Through a fog, he could hear himself repeating that accursed name, over and over. He would give anything to meet that man-beast. To look deeply into his eyes and try to understand how he could murder babies, his babies, the next generation of the Austerlitz family. But he knew that he must now conduct himself with tight self-control, if he wanted to get the information he needed …

"Do they have any identifying characteristics about this man?"

"Very little, I'm afraid. I don't know much about him. We know he went underground immediately after the war. He escaped to a village in Upper Silesia and disguised himself as a farmer. We also know that some Church figures helped him obtain forged papers. With their help, he escaped."

Austerlitz felt his whole body tremble.

"Escaped where? Do you know where?"

"Yes."

Yitzchak's heart skipped a beat. "Where?" he finally croaked.

"As far as we know, he fled to Syria. He lived there, in the same neighborhood as another war criminal called Bruner, who also found haven in Damascus."

Yitzchak Austerlitz's face paled. His eyes showed their deep disappointment. How he'd hoped, with all his heart, to one day face the man who'd killed his family, to tell him what he thought of him, this murdering beast. Now he could forget this dream. Syria? How could he ever dream of getting there, to the State of Israel's bitterest foe? And yet he asked, "Is it known exactly where he lives? Is the investigation continuing?"

"Yes, it's ongoing. But it's difficult. The Nazis fled to all corners of the earth, and did everything to cover their tracks. We can clearly see the long and skillful arm of the Spider."

"Spider? What? What's the 'Spider'?"

"Oh, that's a long story. It's the name of a dangerous and mysterious organization. But Mr. Austerlitz, I'm afraid I've got to rush to a meeting in Tel Aviv. You came at a somewhat inconvenient hour. I'm glad to have passed the information on to you."

He shook Austerlitz's arm and was out of the office, leaving Yitzchak gazing after him, open mouthed.

18

The grey-haired man chain smoked. Every few minutes the men in the room looked surreptitiously at their watches and then looked vacantly around them. No one spoke. It was almost 5 o'clock and they still had no idea if the thin man had successfully completed his assignment to prevent the widow's interrogation.

Ten minutes later an operative sent to follow the thin man and report on his activities made his breathless appearance.

"He got him!" he said, puffing hard.

The others jumped from their places. "Who?"

The man searched for the right words. "Don't you understand? The police officer has arrested him!"

One of the men brought the near-hysterical man a cup of *guarana*. He downed it in a gulp. Schmidt remained in control of himself.

"So the meeting with the widow did not take place?"

The man's breath still came rapidly and unevenly, but slowly he calmed down. "As far as I saw — no. Our man collided with Nunes at exactly 10 to 4. The police officer left his car. They exchanged stormy words. I couldn't hear what they were saying, because of all the passersby surrounding them. Suddenly, after more than 10 minutes, the police officer forced him into his car, which was damaged but still working. He started the car and disappeared with his prisoner."

Schmidt blinked. It was characteristic of him, whenever he had some deep thinking to do. After a minute, he said, "Okay, we can't find out where he's been taken. There's the possibility that the kid will begin to 'talk.' The police may arrive here. We've got to be very careful. We must get out of here immediately. We'll leave one by one, at 5 minute intervals. Quietly go down to the street, and each one take a separate cab. The main thing is not to arouse any attention. In two hours, we'll meet at the apartment we rented yesterday on Gabriel Monteiro da Silva Street, on the corner of Estados Unidos Avenue. Understood?"

The men nodded their heads in assent, and one by one abandoned the room. Schmidt left last. Before he went, he made a careful search of the two small rooms and kitchenette, ensuring that nothing suspicious had been forgotten. As he locked the door, he left an innocuous note behind: "To Daisy and the kids — We've gone to Uncle Julio in the Eldorado. Be well and see you soon."

The thin man knew what he was to do, in the event that he could escape and reach the closed door. He didn't know the new address on Gabriel Monteiro da Silva. Schmidt was glad he hadn't passed on any information regarding their newest location.

Tel Aviv
6 Iyar 5727

Yitzchak Austerlitz entered the Tel Aviv municipal library with hesitating steps.

"Where can I find material on the Spider?"

The elderly librarian gave the religious Jew a cool stare. She didn't like patrons such as this one, who came to wander through the library not really knowing what they were looking for. Why should this religious Jew need material on spiders? To fulfill one of his commandments? Who knew?

With a shrug of the shoulders, she answered, "There, on the bottom shelf, in the long cabinet on the left, there's a series of books on nature. You'll find something about spiders there."

Yitzchak felt tears rise up in his throat, choking him, ready to cascade down his face. Luckily, the librarian didn't notice his reaction to her reply. She had already turned her attention to the stack of newspapers that had gathered on the shelf and that waited, with the patience of day-old news, to be catalogued and filed away.

"I'm not looking for insects, Miss. I'm looking for a Spider that is much worse than that!"

He spoke loudly and angrily. The librarian turned to him with evident surprise. She didn't know how to react.

"I don't understand, sir. What are you talking about? You asked for spiders. I told you where you could find them."

"No!" He had no patience for this. "I mean Nazis! The Spider organization!"

The librarian spread her hands, gesturing that she'd never heard of it.

One of the library's regulars, sitting nearby, took off his glasses, put down the newspaper he'd been reading, and said loudly, "Ask her to give you the file of *Chadashot* from last year. I remember reading a long piece on the Spider there."

With hands trembling, Yitzchak took the file that contained copies of last year's newspapers. After a swift search, he found it. He placed it on one of the empty desks in the library. He sat down, casting careful looks at the surrounding tables to see if anyone had noticed his emotion at seeing the headline of the piece, a headline that read: *The church the "Spider."*

With a sigh of relief Yitzchak realized that in a library each person keeps to himself and his business, and no one pays attention to anyone else. He could read on, undisturbed.

> *The discovery and kidnapping of Adolph Eichmann in Buenos Aires five years ago focused attention again on one of the most mysterious aspects of the World War's end. On the day of Germany's defeat, tens of thousands of Nazi war criminals vanished, as if the earth had swallowed them up. The Allied forces were not successful in laying their hands on most of these fugitives, who disappeared without a trace. With the passing of the years interest in the missing Nazis waned, and, with the exception of certain Jewish institutions such as that of Simon Wiesenthal in Vienna and Tuvia Friedman in Israel, no one seemed to care. Eichmann's trial in Israel, and revelations of his evil deeds, brought the matter to life once again.*

Searches through confidential records and the ceaseless collection of such crumbs of information as can be discovered from all corners of the earth enable one to draw a partial picture of the horrendous way in which many Nazis escaped prison. Even before the fall of Nazi Germany it was known that the leaders had prepared escape routes for themselves, in the event that Germany would surrender to the Allies. But the exposure of the means of escape and, specifically, the international organizations that aided the felons in avoiding judgment and the specter of the gallows, casts a terrible stain on the face of humanity. This, when the details of the terrible genocide of the Jews in concentration camps had begun to be heard throughout the world.

It is clear that some of the world's most important institutions were partners in bringing the Nazis to freedom instead of having them answer for their crimes against humanity. The difficulties of finding out the truth comes, in part, from the fact that the governments of America and the Soviet Union, too, took part in the concealment of Nazis. But the worst chapter in the story is the compliance of the Catholic Church. The merciful Church that, throughout the course of the war, in the name of strict neutrality never raised its voice against the massacres and destruction of the Jews, was complicit in helping Nazi criminals escape punishment.

Yitzchak Austerlitz gave an audible sigh. He remembered the apathy, and occasionally the joy, of his Polish neighbors, when the grip of the Gestapo began to tighten around the Jews. He remembered, as if it were yesterday, how the village priest had personally led the young S.S. officer through the town, pointing out the homes of wealthy Jews.

He continued to read:

> One of these escape plans was called "Spider."
> With the war's end, many Nazis hid under the
> wings of the Church. Felons found their first
> refuge in monasteries throughout Europe. An en-
> tire system, under the supervision of certain
> priests, forging papers and passports that gave its
> bearers new identities. With these they could
> travel in relative safety throughout Europe and, fi-
> nally, find new homes elsewhere. From documents
> now found, it appears that this "spider's web"
> spread all over the world.
>
> The preferred destination of the fugitives were
> countries in the Middle East, South America, and
> even the United States. The Arab states, in their
> attempts to stop the resettlement of Jews in Israel
> even before the war, found sympathetic friends in
> the Nazis. Now a remnant of these Nazis needed a
> home in Egypt, Syria, and Iraq. And they were
> ready to offer their professional services to their
> new masters, who were preparing for war with the
> fledgling Jewish state. Many of these Nazis found
> a haven in Damascus, Syria's capital city.
> (Austerlitz felt his breath come and go rap-
> idly and unevenly.) They became the trusted
> advisers of the dictators that appeared and disap-
> peared with great frequency. One of the advisers to
> the Syrian government is the Nazi war criminal
> Bruner, who is fully protected in Damascus by the

Syrian security forces. (And what of Heinz Krantz? What of Heinz Krantz?)

Latin America, too, is a safe haven. It is conjectured that many found refuge in its barren land. Unofficial information has Martin Bormann, Hitler's deputy, living in Argentina. There have been frequent sightings of Josef Mengele, the bloodthirsty doctor of Auschwitz, in Brazil. An attorney in Sao Paulo, Brazil, told an American journalist that a police officer in Sao Paulo had confessed to him that he had found Mengele in a routine investigation of aliens living in the city. The murderer's friends counted out $50,000 in bribe money; after his release, Mengele disappeared. Rumor has it that he lives in the state of Parana in southern Brazil or in the jungle near the borders of Paraguay, Brazil, and Argentina.

These Nazis are connected; each helps the other as needed, and support an underground for the security of the war criminals. Not long ago, two bodies were found floating in the Parana River. They were identified as being members of Israel's Mossad, dressed up as priests, who had apparently been on Mengele's trail and met their deaths during their mission. The "spider" continues, it appears, to live on ...

Yitzchak Austerlitz was completely absorbed in reading. His heart thudded wildly. Beads of sweat gathered on his forehead and fell down his face like teardrops. The horrifying, dark days returned and stood before him in all their hellishness. He was in Auschwitz. And a dybbuk had entered him, forcing him to travel to the four corners of the earth, until he'd found Heinz Krantz. Found him, and stared down into the evil murderer's eyes ...

When he felt the heavy arm suddenly fall on his shoulder, he began to tremble uncontrollably. Fear hit him squarely, and he dared not lift his head.

19

Sao Paulo, Brazil
May 16, 1967

"Celia," Regina Hunkes called to her new maid.

The kitchen door opened and Celia's head popped out into the living room.

"*Si, senhora,*" she answered, as if ready to fulfill any command.

"I'm expecting a visitor in about a quarter of an hour. Please prepare some drinks and glasses. Whatever you find in the refrigerator. Okay?"

The maid disappeared behind the kitchen door. Regina nervously tapped the face of her watch. It was 10 minutes to 4. Where was Eduardo? She didn't want to meet the police officer by herself. She'd feel more sure of herself if Eduardo was there. Who knew what the industrious officer had managed to find out about her husband's identity? She didn't believe she could keep a cool demeanor; her emotions would betray her.

Where would it all lead? Police officers were always dangerous, even when they spoke quietly and pleasantly. Dangerous!

She rose from her chair and sat down on the couch, arms outstretched. Her taut nerves could use a rest; she knew, however, that she couldn't afford such a small pleasure. Worry about future developments robbed her of all serenity.

The ringing of the doorbell pulled her out of her seat. She opened the door and breathed a sigh of relief.

"Good afternoon, Mother."

She shook her head sternly. "I didn't know what to do and what to think! It's almost 4, and the lieutenant can come in any minute now!"

Eduardo smiled, like a student caught in a mischievous prank.

"But you see, here I am! I've arrived! I hope you'll forgive me, but I was delayed. There were problems with the military edition that I've been editing. By the way, we had good news just as I left the office. There's high tension on the border between Israel and Egypt. There's a strong possibility of a war between the Arabs and the Jewish State."

Regina waved this away. "For my part, let the whole world end there. I've got my own problems. I wanted to talk to you before the questioning began. I'm afraid."

Eduardo stopped. "You're worrying me, Mother. We've got nothing to hide."

Regina laughed softly. "Come, sit down. Maybe we'll have a few minutes to talk before this unwelcome 'royal visit.' "

Celia, the maid, came in, bearing a tray full of drinks. She put it on the small coffee table that stood between the sofa and the leather armchairs where Regina and her son were sitting.

"This is your guest?" she asked innocently.

Regina gave her a look, to remind her of her place.

"No," she said firmly, "this is my son, Eduardo. And remember, please, that you haven't been working here even one day!"

Celia turned away, shyly apologizing. "I'm sorry, *Senhora*."

Regina waited for the kitchen door to be firmly shut, and then she turned to her son.

"Will you have a drink?"

"Yes, but what's going on? You're worrying me."

"Don't worry so much. What are you drinking?"

"Coca Cola. Mother, I feel you're hiding something from me."

Regina poured herself a cup of *agua tonica* and a cup of Coke for her son.

"Why do you think so?"

Eduardo took a sip.

"Thanks. You want to know why I think so? Because you're so afraid of the investigation! You told me yourself! Someone killed Father. That's a proven fact. Do you think the lieutenant suspects you of the murder? And if so, why? What do you have to hide? I don't understand."

Regina shook her head in a negative gesture. She took another sip from her cup, held in her right hand, as her left hand played with a small set of keys. Until that moment Eduardo hadn't noticed the key chain; it seemed he was seeing it for the first time. Some sixth sense told him that his mother was calling his attention to it.

Regina remained silent, searching for the right words.

"Your imagination, Eduardo, is getting the better of you! How can you discuss my involvement in a murder that's destroyed my life? But you know, when they begin to search around in a family's life, they sometimes find other things that the police should not know of."

Eduardo placed his empty cup down next to him. His tongue played over his bottom lip, licking up the last of the beverage.

"Our family too?" he asked, surprised.

"Not exactly. It depends on your perspective."

She stared at her watch. "It's already 4:15! Why hasn't he come yet? I'm so nervous!"

Eduardo was still shocked by her statement. "What do you mean, 'It depends on your perspective'? What things, and what perspective?"

Regina took a deep breath. She sipped a little more of her drink. It seemed to Eduardo that her hand trembled slightly. She gazed into his eyes with a look that he couldn't understand.

"Eduardo, my hands are full. Light me a cigarette."

Eduardo felt her growing nervousness. He hurried to fill her request. He didn't understand why she wouldn't let go of the mysterious keys for even a moment. He waited impatiently for her to continue.

"Eduardo, you know that we are not native Brazilians. We came from Europe when you were a baby."

"Yes, I know. So what of it?"

"Inquisitive investigators can try to find out why the move from Europe to South America."

Eduardo shifted in his chair. To conceal his growing anxiety, he crossed his hands behind his head. After a few seconds of quiet, he said, "So what? I know what you're talking about. Father was a Dane who collaborated with the Nazi regime at the time of the Occupation. After the war, he and his family fled to Brazil, because he was afraid of the Danish justice system. These stories are of no interest to Brazilians. I grew up here, and I know them well. Even if they knew everything, they would do nothing. I think, Mother, that you're overreacting."

Regina put down her cup and pulled the cigarette out from her mouth. She inhaled deeply, gave a slight cough. The cough was good for her: It hid the feelings that threatened to overwhelm her. She didn't know how to continue the conversation. She was not prepared for it …

"Look here, Eduardo. Father is dead. You know who I suspect is behind it?"

"Yes, the Jews."

"That's right! Now, right after this cold-blooded murder, when I was still in shock, I passed my suspicions on to the police. It was even before the autopsy, before anyone had even mentioned the possibility of homicide. Those irresponsible words of mine undoubtedly raised some questions in their minds: Who was this Alberto Hunkes, whose widow knows that he was murdered by the Jews — of all people? At a time when all the outward signs indicated death by heart attack. Do you understand, Eduardo, that I've gotten myself into trouble?"

Eduardo poured himself another cup. This time, he chose *guarana*.

"Not really. Father is dead. You can reveal the truth of his past quietly. Denmark can't arrest him. And you? You're not guilty of what your husband did. I just don't see the problem and the reason you're so nervous!"

But her tension increased still more.

"I see that you really don't understand. A professional police officer will no doubt ask himself: Why should the Jews want to kill some small-time collaborator from Denmark? The Israelis kidnapped Adolph Eichmann and charged him with the deaths of millions of Jews. From time to time South American citizens are killed and after investigations are held, it comes out that they were on the staff in the concentration camps, in the Gestapo and S.S., and they lived in South America with false identities. Do you understand? Logic will mandate that they ask me hard questions."

Eduardo jumped up. Now, finally — he understood. A strange sensation lurched through him. He realized that his mother was hiding important information from him. She was keeping a secret, a mysterious secret. And now, he could, perhaps, see the reason behind his father's death.

His curiosity was aroused. He wanted very much to know what she was referring to. He felt that at this moment he had to know the answer to the question she expected from the police: Why had she decided that the Jews had killed Father? He remembered his mother's insulting behavior to his father's Jewish friend, Jairo Silverman, at the time of the funeral.

At the same time, a second inner voice commanded him not to surrender to curiosity. If he should find the answers, he was afraid that his life would never be the same. Europe was nothing to him, a pleasant place for a tour, that was all. He had no connection with it. He was Brazilian, and he was happy with his identity. Why should he have anything to do with the Second World War? He realized that his mother's hints were connected with the slaughter of the nations of Europe 25 years ago. He himself didn't love the Jews. Perhaps he even hated them. Who, after all, did like them? But he didn't care about them. He had several Jewish colleagues in his office, that was it. So what? Today, the world was a different place.

Finally, he said, "What are you trying to tell me?"

"Nothing. Just that I have no strength for an investigation, and I want you near me."

Eduardo didn't believe her. He sat silently, lost in thought. Suddenly, he raised his head.

"Mother, perhaps you're ready to tell me the truth. I'm a big boy now. I can know. Are we from Denmark? Is our name Hunkes?"

Regina was taken aback. It seemed to her that the conversation was moving much too fast. Faster than she'd expected.

"Certainly," she answered quickly. "Why do you think I'm hiding something from you?"

"So why would the Jews kill Father, though they know that there are thousands of Nazis living in South America? Do you have an answer to the question that the police officer we're waiting for might very well put to you? Give me an answer, one that will satisfy me."

Mrs. Hunkes looked at her watch and said, startled, "It's already a quarter to 5! What could have happened to him?"

"Don't worry, Mother, he'll be here. These men never give up on their sacrificial lambs. But what will you say to him? What do you want me to say?"

Regina understood quite well that the moment of truth had arrived.

"Eduardo," she said quietly, her confidence returning, "Eduardo, I think I've got to lay my cards out in front of you. I hope it will work out and won't damage our relationship."

She stood up. In her left hand she feverishly grasped the small set of keys.

"I'll be right back. I'm just going to the safe."

Eduardo stared after her, surprised. "What safe?" he called out.

Regina smiled. "I know, you knew nothing of it. It's our secret vault. Top secret. Hidden within is explosive political and social material. No one but Father and I knew of it. We built it in our bedroom and opened it only rarely. I need it now, so that you, too, will know what's inside. I don't know what will happen to me tomorrow. Do you understand? Or do I have to explain it to you? I want to show you something. Perhaps you'll understand me better. I'll be right back."

Regina extinguished her cigarette in the stone ashtray and went into her bedroom.

Celia the maid, standing in the kitchen, swiftly moved away from the door. She rushed to the sink, opened the tap, and began washing pots. What she'd heard just now on the other side had certainly helped in her assignment.

After a few minutes Regina returned from the bedroom, her face blank.

"No. I've changed my mind," she said in a dry, withered tone.

Eduardo stood up. "Why? What's happened?"

"I've decided that at this point I'm not ready to show you anything or to continue to discuss the affair."

Eduardo, astounded, remained quiet. He knew his mother's obstinacy, her tough personality. Nothing he would say would help. But deep inside his heart he felt something had happened to him. Something he couldn't exactly describe ...

20

Jairo slammed his office door shut. The harsh conversation he'd had just now with Francisco had upset him. Helplessly, he dropped down into his recliner, beset by anxious thoughts. Was this the first crack in the fine partnership that he'd built with Francisco and Paulo? Was the end approaching? Was the law firm that he'd created about to fall apart? Jairo stared at the files lying on his desk in a disorderly pile. Right now he had no patience to deal with any of them, or even to see which ones needed his immediate attention. Among the files was a red folder containing the GAC papers, including the draft of the contract that had remained unsigned until now. Until now? Would it ever be signed? With an instinctive gesture his left hand pulled at a corner of the file and, in a surge of fury, flung it across the room. This file, that was to have been the crowning jewel in his career, that would have made him a success story for every financial newspaper to report had turned into an obstacle, the reason for the possible breakup of his firm. Who could tell what destiny lay before a man? A man who until now thought he could do anything?

Jairo turned his chair towards the large window that faced the city center. The sharp, tall building of Banco do Brasil stood out among the skyscrapers that surrounded it on Sao Juao Street — the throbbing heart of the business district. Downstairs, on the wide bridges that overhung the Valey de Anhangabahu, tens of thousands of people scurried back and forth. Jairo usually loved the sight. He loved the dynamic flow of the city center, the enormous power of Sao Paulo. This time, though, the scene infuriated him.

Jairo thought endlessly about the argument that had broken out between him and Francisco. Deep in his heart he felt the breach between them widening. His father, a refugee of the Holocaust, had believed, in his naiveté, that by fleeing to Brazil he could escape his destiny as a Jew. He had done all he could so that he, Jairo, would not feel Jewish. Jairo never attended Jewish schools. His father saw to it that he kept company with Brazilians. Jairo had never felt any differences between him and his gentile friends, even though he'd traveled to synagogue with his father on Yom Kippur morning. No, he hadn't fasted, as he understood other Jews did. He was a Brazilian from birth.

But this past Friday, there in the cemetery, something had happened. He had reacted differently than Francisco at the sight of the Nazi salute over Hunkes's grave. Why? Disquiet and fear hadn't left him, from that moment on. Why? Hadn't both he and Francisco been born and raised in this free, wonderful city? He had never felt any discrimination. He couldn't remember any insult leveled at him for his Jewishness, a Jewishness that meant nothing to him. If so — why? Why such different feelings in the cemetery? It seemed that the Jewish fate was inscribed deep in his heart, deeper than he'd ever imagined. Some mysterious Jewish gene must be passed down, it seemed, an inheritance from father to son, and one couldn't escape it. And now GAC wouldn't sign on their business contract because he was a … Jew. Absurd! Why did fate insist on reminding him that he was a Jew? This fresh remembrance angered him. His father's dream of a pleasant existence for his children, free of any anti-Semitism, had exploded and disappeared. From moment to moment it became clearer to him that his father had made a terrible miscalculation. He, Jairo, could never become a Brazilian in the full sense of the word. On the day this nightmare would come to an end (would it ever end?) — on that day he would tell his old, sick father, still fleeing the horrors of the Holocaust, about the Hunkes affair — he would take up this issue as well. But now, he must…

The telephone rang shrilly, interrupting his thoughts. Jairo's hand reached for the receiver. But, in the last second, he reconsidered and didn't pick it up. The sharp ring continued to fill the room. He felt, for the first time in many years, oddly disconnected. How could he get away from this? Perhaps, by dropping his quest for Alberto Hunkes's true identity. Nazi or not —what was the difference? Perhaps he should try to forget all that he'd seen in the cemetery, and all that had followed. To remember them as unpleasant incidents, worthy only of being banished from his consciousness. Should he torment himself so?

Damage his professional life? His career? His partners? His family? His wife and children? The entire pleasant life he'd built so laboriously for himself?

Jairo felt his face harden. He balled up the fingers of his left hand into a hard fist and smacked it roughly into his right palm: a sign of his unyielding decision to continue to the end. The end! Not to rest and not to stay quiet, until he knew the secret. He felt that, despite the danger, he could not go on without knowing the mystery's solution. He tried to understand why he had decided to wage this personal battle — but failed.

Resolutely he swiveled his chair around, towards the window once again. With a determined motion he grabbed for the phone. And, after a moment's hesitation, he dialed police headquarters.

"Hello? Good afternoon, could I please speak to Lieutenant Nunes?"

Jairo listened in silence to the reply on the other end.

"I understand," he said. "Did he say when he expected to return to the office?"

Jairo's face reflected disappointment.

"Thank you. What? No, no message. I'll call back tomorrow. *Chau*."

Jairo replaced the receiver and tried to collect his thoughts and put them in some sort of order, so that he could decide, in a logical fashion, what he should do next. But he didn't get the chance to finish: His office door suddenly burst open. Before him Lieutenant Roberto Nunes blew in like a gust of wind. Jairo, shocked, saw that he was grasping a young man, thin and obviously frightened. The police officer was clearly agitated.

"Jairo," he said, breathing deeply, "do you recognize him?"

Tel Aviv, Israel
6 Iyar 5727

"Why are you trembling, sir?"

Yitzchak Austerlitz waited, petrified. It seemed that he recognized the voice speaking to him. The anonymous speaker was correct: He was shaking uncontrollably. The fears that had burst forth from his heart as he read the report on the Spider organization had overpowered him. He felt unable to pick up his head and face the person speaking to him: a habit left from the fearful days of the forests and the camps. The man's arm still clasped his shoulder. Austerlitz did not answer. Where had he heard that voice before?

The man took his arm off him, pulled up one of the library chairs and sat down next to him. Yitzchak forced his eyes up from the newspaper and looked at the man. Yes, it was the one who'd heard his request from the librarian for material on Spider. The one who knew exactly where the column could be found.

The man smiled. "Are you from there?"

Yitzchak nodded his head slowly. His tension abated somewhat. But he felt increasingly nervous.

The two were silent. After a moment, the man said, "Me, too."

Again, heavy silence. A silence that screamed within the quiet serenity of the library. The man asked, "Auschwitz? Majdanek? Treblinka? Or ... what?"

"Auschwitz."

The man nodded. He understood. Understood well.

"And I — Treblinka," he said wearily.

They didn't have to explain what they were talking about.

The man continued. "What's your interest in the story of the Spider?"

Yitzchak slowly closed the newspaper file. He stared for a few long minutes into the man's face. In his years in Israel, he'd learned to be suspicious of strangers. Learned to conceal what had happened and was happening to him. For never, never would he be able to tell his story. Deep in their hearts, they were simply not interested. They had no time, they had no desire. And so he grew silent, not showing to anyone the depths of his heart. He hadn't been like that, not before the deluge of fire and blood that had descended on all Poland and on his family.

But here, in the library, he felt different. In the silence that enveloped them, like the silence in the village after the *aktion*, sitting near this unknown man, he knew that his heart could open. They had a bond of horror and memories that tied them in a covenant of blood. The unknown man in the library liberated something long trapped in Austerlitz's broken heart.

Yitzchak Austerlitz felt that the man awaited his response.

"Excuse me, did you ask me something?"

The man calmly crossed his legs and patiently repeated, "I asked, what interests you in the story of the Spider?"

"I am searching for the one who murdered my family."

The man gave a laugh. "And you think you'll find him in the newspaper?"

"No. But I saw his picture in Yad Vashem. They managed to find out his name for me. They mentioned this organization, the Spider. I wanted to know what they were talking about."

"And if you know his name, what will be?"

"I'll search for where he's living!"

The man made a face. "And if you know where he lives, what then?"

Austerlitz gave him a hard look. His eyes narrowed, and he hissed in a determined and quiet voice, "I will travel there!"

The man nodded his head, his hand scratching his forehead, hidden under a cap.

"Don't you have enough troubles?"

"No! That is, I don't know! But I can't calm down. I am there every day. What can I do? That awful minute when he took my wife and children away still lives before me, even at this very moment."

The man closed his eyes and made no reply. Yitzchak, moved and excited, wanted him to speak. To say something. He wanted to hear what he had to say. He, too, had been there. But the man said nothing.

"And perhaps I cannot forget, for only the dead are forgotten. One who lives is not forgotten ..."

Yitzchak cut short the strange words that had thoughtlessly fallen from his lips. He was frightened: What had happened to him? Why was he letting the mighty emotions that had gripped him on Shabbos, as he spoke to his *chavrusah* on Rabbi Akiva Street, get the best of him? Foolishness! Nonsense! In that hell, no one stayed alive. Why had this insanity gripped him? Why?

The man sat next to him, not saying a word. He pretended not to notice Austerlitz's deeply felt emotions. But he saw all. He understood all. He, too, had been there.

Finally, he asked, "You said you know the murderer's name?"

"Yes."

"So…"

"Heinz Krantz."

The man's eyes widened. "Heinz Krantz?!"

Austerlitz felt a tremor run through his spine. "You've heard of him? You know him?"

"No, I don't know him. But I've read of him. He was in Galicia, right? From Austria?"

"Yes! Where did you read about him?" Yitzchak asked excitedly.

The man furrowed his brow in an effort of memory. He spent entire days in the library, reading all that was available on the Holocaust. He nodded his head back and forth in a sign of failure.

"No. I can't remember where. Give me a minute to think … No. I'm sorry. I don't remember. But it seems that it said he'd fled to Argentina or someplace like that."

"What? In Yad Vashem they told me he was hiding in Syria."

"I don't know. I read that he'd reached South America. It's not important."

"It *is* important! Very important to me! I must know!"

The last words came out as a scream. From the tables spread around the room, heads bobbed up in astonishment. The librarian hissed something at him, but he couldn't make out the words. Certainly, they were less than flattering. Even the man who'd begun talking with Austerlitz was startled. Still, he said, "You know what, I'm prepared to help you. My brother lives in Brazil. He, like you, was in Auschwitz. His name is …"

The librarian turned up the radio so that everyone could hear the news.

> *The IDF spokesman has announced that the Egyptian army has advanced military units in the Sinai Desert. The IDF has declared heightened preparedness and has announced a limited reserve call-up. In Cairo, voices are calling for a jihad. Our military commentator, Moshe ...*

Yitzchak and the man sitting next to them listened no further. They simply exchanged a glance, one that could only be understood by someone who'd gone through Auschwitz or Treblinka.

21

Jairo was astounded. "What's going on?" he asked, confused, his eyes darting back and forth between the police officer and the frightened young man held in Nunes's firm grasp.

Roberto Nunes was furious. "I asked you if you recognize him! First, answer me!"

Jairo did not like his tone of voice. In his heart, suspicion began to grow — but he didn't know what to suspect.

"No. I don't recognize him. Now, will you answer me?"

Roberto slowly relaxed. His fingers released the thin man's arm. He stuttered slightly. "I ... I don't know. I thought you might know him."

Jairo shifted uncomfortably in his chair. He spoke quickly. "Roberto, enough! Why should I recognize him? Tell me what's happening here."

Roberto ran his hand through his unkempt hair, a reflex when he was confused.

"It looks like I've caught it from you, Jairo. All your stories about people following you, tapping your phone, who knows what else!"

"I don't understand a word of what you're saying. What does this have to do with your bursting into my office, with this man in tow?"

Roberto gave a short, bitter laugh.

"Of course it's got something to do with it! This young man collided with my car, just as I was trying to do what you'd asked me, and interrogate Hunkes's widow. Have you forgotten the stories you told me last night, when you came to my house trembling? Maybe your Nazis are after me too! I wanted to know if you recognized him, this man who knocked into my Gordini. And you know what …"

Roberto *f* finish his heated words when Jairo gave a shocked cry: "Hey, you there …"

Roberto jumped towards the spot where Jairo had turned his surprised gaze. Roberto managed to get a glimpse of him, the young, thin man, as he escaped through the open door of the office. Without losing a second, he sprang towards the door. Too late. The thin man had slammed it shut right into Roberto's head. He vented a cry of pain and nestled his aching forehead between his two hands, as Jairo flew up to support him.

"Are you hurt?"

"Yes, but it's not too bad."

Roberto tried to open the door, hoping to run after the escaping man. But Jairo stopped him.

"Leave it! Don't go after him. You'll never catch him now. Besides, perhaps he does belong to the gang.

In that case, you don't know who is waiting for you downstairs."

After a minute he added, "Should I make you a cappucino?"

"No thanks."

Roberto was still rubbing his forehead. "Something cold?"

"That sounds better."

Jairo hurried to the small refrigerator in the corner of the office, pulled out a bottle of *guarana*. While he was still drinking, Roberto asked, "Where's the phone?"

"Here," Jairo pointed to the other side of his large desk. "Whom are you calling?"

"The widow! I'll go now. I'm not giving up on this investigation!"

"That's good!"

He dialed. "Hello, *Senhora* Hunkes? Good afternoon. This is Lieutenant Nunes. I am sorry I didn't arrive on time. I was close to your home, but some silly young man crashed into my car. What? What are you saying? Yes. That's right. No, no, not exactly. But this accident seems very strange to me, I might even say, suspicious. You don't think so. I know. Perhaps someone is interested in ending this investigation. You have no idea of what I'm talking about. Interesting. Mrs. Hunkes, I'm on my way to you. Oh, I understand. You've got to leave the house now. It would be worth your while to put off that appointment and wait for me. You wouldn't want the police to suspect that you've got something to hide. I'll see you soon."

As he hung up the phone, Roberto was amused. "Your friend is panicking. This business is getting interesting."

"How can you tell?"

"You should have heard her voice when she realized who was speaking."

Jairo was satisfied. "So, Roberto, go to her quickly, before the bird leaves the cage. I think that you, too, are convinced that this murder is hiding something interesting. It's worth rushing."

Roberto took a last drink from his cup, put it on the desk, and turned towards the door.

"Okay, I'm going. *Chau*."

"*Chau*, and good luck."

Suddenly, next to the door, Roberto came to a halt. After a moment's hesitation, he returned and stood across from Jairo, who had sat down again in his chair.

"Jairo," he said in an official-sounding voice.

"Yes, what now?"

"See here, you asked me to investigate this matter."

"Absolutely."

"You know, an investigation is an investigation. You understand?"

"Of course I do."

Roberto rubbed his temples before continuing.

"And when we begin to search, we find things. You agree?"

Jairo tensed up. He put his arms near his chest, trying to make out where this was leading.

Roberto didn't take his eyes off Jairo's face. After a moment's silence, he continued.

"I want to show you something."

Jairo leaned forward. He watched every move of the police officer, who pulled a sheaf of papers out of his jacket pocket and read through them.

"Here it is," Roberto handed Jairo a document. Jairo, with the professional eyes of an attorney, recognized the paper immediately. It was an official telegram from the Brazilian Ministry of the Interior in the country's capital city, Brasilia.

Jairo looked at the paper for a long minute. His face paled. He looked past the police officer, who hadn't moved his gaze from Jairo. Jairo handed the telegram back to Roberto and said quietly, ever so quietly, "Exactly what are you accusing me of?"

Paulo Chilo, upset and disgruntled, sat in the office shared by him, Jairo, and Francisco. Radio Tupi, one of the new Sao Paulo stations, was broadcasting a mixture of news, music, and announcements. The affair of the unsigned GAC contract had robbed him of all serenity. He saw their incredible success, just within reach, now slipping away. And all because of Jairo. Jairo, the Jew. No, he didn't hate Jews. Absolutely not. But, to be perfectly honest, he didn't particularly like them either. Yes, he was Brazilian. But his family was in Beirut. He heard much in the house of the *Yahud*, who made all sorts of problems in the Middle East, among his people, the Arabs. Yes, he had to admit that Jairo Silverman had welcomed him warmly into the office and helped him advance considerably as an attorney. He felt indebted to Jairo for that. But was he obligated to lose such an incredible business deal for it? A deal that came, perhaps, only once in a lifetime? That was too much!

Paulo lit up a cigarette. His blood pulsed through his temples; his thoughts galloped like horses at the beginning of a race.

Francisco spoke constantly of being faithful, of not abandoning a friend in a difficult time, of not betraying him in his need. Naive, that one! If the position was reversed, if some firm didn't want an Arab attorney, would Jairo the Jew not have abandoned him? Weren't the Jews traitors by their very nature?

Paulo realized that this was the first time such thoughts had flitted through his brain. For a minute he felt uncomfortable with the idea; he soon recovered. It was true: Treachery was second nature to the Jews. He had nothing against Jairo personally. But he was more interested in signing the contract with GAC.

Paulo stood up and began to pace up and down his small office. The wall-to-wall carpet swallowed up the sound of his nervous footsteps.

What to do? Von Dorfman, the GAC representative from Germany, was waiting for his call. That's what he'd said in the restaurant. One phone call, and he was directed on a new course in his career! One call! Good heavens! One call and he was set up for life. Money, a lot of money. Position, luxury — everything! So why was he hesitating? What was he afraid of?

From the radio came the sound of the announcer giving the country's soccer scores. Paulo paid no attention. He returned to the depths of his recliner, feeling uneasy. His long legs were thrust forward, beneath his desk.

If only Francisco would cooperate! If they worked together, they could confront Jairo with a *fait accompli*. They would give him the percentage coming to him and let him stew in his own Jewish juice, with his thoughts about Nazis. What did he care? But Francisco didn't want to do it. Suddenly he'd become a man of integrity! And he, Paulo, lacked the courage to go out on his own.

He took a deep pull on his cigarette, as if wanting to swallow the smoke. What to do with this fear, this lack of self-confidence of his?

The radio announcer stopped listing the scores. "Attention. It appears that a war will shortly be breaking out in the Middle East, between Israel and Egypt. Will tiny David once again defeat the great Egyptian Goliath? Bulletins arriving from the region speak of vast military movements on the part of the Egyptians towards the international border in Sinai. The Egyptian forces are in full battle-readiness. The president of Egypt, Gamel Abdul Nasser, has announced that the time to liberate the occupied lands of Palestine has arrived. Many are dancing in the streets of Cairo. The government in Tel Aviv is in confusion, and has announced a call-up of reserves. And now, here's more from Radio Tupi …"

Paulo froze in his chair, paralyzed. After the first shocked moment, he slowly put out his cigarette, still held between his fingers. He snuffed it harshly in the large stone ashtray, as if, by this gesture, to free the anger and fury trapped within his heart.

He leaned back, and whispered to himself, "War! *Jihad*! War against the *Yahud*!"

The blood again surged through his temples like a drumbeat of battle. Yes, he was a Brazilian. But his blood brothers there, far away, were going out to war! Jairo, too, was a Brazilian. And yet, would his heart not be with the Jews of Israel, set for destruction as Allah willed? Paulo realized that cooperation between the two was now impossible. Their partnership was on the verge of dissolution. War! War would break out. The Arabs would win. The Russians would stand by their sides. His brothers would finally liberate Palestine!

His hand swiftly grabbed the telephone receiver. He dialed frantically.

"Hello? Hotel Ipiranga? I must speak urgently with Mr. Von Dorfman, of GAC."

Eduardo returned to the editorial offices of *Estado de Sao Paulo*, his spirits heavy. He entered his office and, as military correspondent, began to prepare material on the war that seemed, in all likelihood, to be about to break out in the Middle East. But his thoughts were on other matters. He tried to solve the riddle of his mother's strange behavior. It disturbed him greatly. He suddenly felt that nothing was clear. The secret of the safe, that he had not even known about an hour ago, just added more confusion. What was she hiding from him? From him, who, after his father's death should have become the one she leaned upon? What was she hiding? What had she planned on showing him, and why had she changed her mind? Why was she so afraid of the police investigation? He suddenly thought of the day of the murder and of the funeral. Why was she so certain that Jews had killed his father? What did she want of Jairo? What had he done to her? He, certainly, was no killer. Why were Nazis there openly during the funeral? Then, in his pain and grief, he hadn't thought clearly of these things. He had believed his mother's explanations, that they were not actually Nazis but rather collaborators who felt this to be a final honor for his father. And that the Jews had killed him, had threatened him more than once. Now, however, he was certain of nothing. Doubts coursed through him: Who was his father? What was his father?

The telephone rang.

"Yes?" he answered, distractedly.

It was his mother, Regina. Her voice was frigid. Her anger had not yet dissipated.

"Eduardo, he is coming."

"Who?"

"The lieutenant."

Eduardo felt his mother's hysteria.

"Mother, you're making too much of this. So he'll come. Tell him everything and that will be an end to it!"

"Come here now."

Eduardo felt his breath quicken.

"Mother, I can't. There's war in the Middle East! I have to get ready for tomorrow's paper. I'm already late. They'll fire me!"

"So you're not coming?"

"Mother," he said impatiently, "why can't you understand, I cannot come! I'm sorry."

There was a long moment of silence. Then he heard words he'd never heard before from her. Words that were cold, cold as steel, sharp as metal. Words that came slowly, slowly from his mother.

"You'll be sorry for this. Soon!"

22

Tel Aviv, Israel
6 Iyar 5727

The patrons of the library were excited. The IDF spokesman's announcement had removed them from the tranquility that reigned in the world of books. They began to whisper between themselves of the new war that was expected. The talk brought them closer together, with the kind of closeness that bonds people sharing a common danger.

But Yitzchak Austerlitz and the man in the cap sat quietly together.

Finally, Austerlitz broke the heavy silence. "When will you call your brother?" he asked the man sitting near him.

The man raised his head in surprise. At first, he didn't understand what Yitzchak had said. Thoughts of the war that might break out quite soon had transported him to Poland in the days before World War II. But in a flash he left those painful thoughts for the present, for the strange apparition sitting near him, in the shape of Yitzchak Austerlitz.

"Do I know? I'll write him today, if it's that important to you."

"Yes! It's vital. But not a letter. Please, phone him."

The man nodded his head in dissent. "I can't. It costs a lot of money."

"So come with me to my house and call from there. It won't cost you anything. Please, do me this favor."

"What's bothering you so? You've waited for so many years, wait another two weeks! Why the rush? And I'm not even sure my brother can help you."

"Any possibility of finding another detail on the man who murdered my family is important to me, particularly today," Austerlitz said, his fraying nerves becoming more and more apparent. "I'm asking you to do me a favor. A favor, that's all. I want you to call today. Before a state of emergency is called, heaven forbid. I don't know why, but I feel a deep fear within me. I feel that something terrible will happen to me. Something connected with this Heinz Krantz."

Yitzchak grabbed the man's hands and added, beseechingly, "Have mercy on me! Help me!"

The man stared at Austerlitz uncomprehendingly. It was clear that something had happened to this religious Jew, whose beard was quivering with tension. Austerlitz's gaze frightened him. Those eyes moved back and forth, back and forth.

The man slowly pulled his hands away from Austerlitz's steel grasp. After a minute he held his arms out in a gesture of surrender, as if to say, "What can I do?"

"*Nu*, okay. You really want this? Okay, I'll do you the favor. Where do you live?"

"Bnei Brak."

"And I, in Ramat Gan. Good, it's not so far. No big deal."

"When can you come?"

"This evening. Late."

"No. I want you to come with me right now."

The man began to laugh. "Right now, it's the middle of the night in Brazil! I won't wake up my brother to ask for his help in finding some cursed Nazi named Heinz Krantz. Do you understand?"

"Yes, I do."

After a moment he added, "I thank you very much, that you're willing to help a Jew such as me. You were sent to me from Heaven."

"Good."

Yitzchak Austerlitz left the library and walked in the direction of bus #54, that would take him home. Suddenly, he remembered that he'd never asked the man for his name. Nor for the name of his brother in Brazil ...

Sao Paulo, Brazil
May 16, 1967

Police Officer Roberto Nunes gave a thin, ironical smile. His eyes carefully and professionally swept over Jairo's features, still pale. In his hand he held the telegram that he'd received a few hours ago from the Interior Ministry in Brasilia that Jairo, after a quick perusal, had returned to him.

"No," he said pleasantly to Jairo, "I don't suspect you of anything. But I have the right to know what is being referred to."

Jairo remained silent. He couldn't find the right words. He realized that saying the wrong thing would be dangerous. Very dangerous. In an involuntary gesture, the fingers of his left hand tapped nervously on the desk. With a swift glance, Roberto took note of the movement. Suddenly, the ghost of a smile played on Jairo's face. He turned his face towards Roberto standing across from him and lifted his chin defiantly. "Helping a friend, that's what happened! I was impressed with Alberto Hunkes and I decided to help solve his problem."

The police officer slowly folded the telegram and thrust it into his inner pocket. The scorn in his voice was obvious. "I'm very moved, Jairo. It's always lovely to help a friend."

After a moment, he added, "And now you see whom you helped!"

Jairo felt a surge of anger in his breast. The thought that the investigation that his friend Roberto was carrying on in the matter of Hunkes's death might involve him was not a pleasant one. He immediately responded. "Nothing is certain yet, Roberto. I don't know Hunkes's identity. Maybe we've suspected him falsely. And I say this despite the widow's disgusting conduct and the awful things I saw at the funeral."

Roberto sat on the edge of the desk and said quietly, "Yes, but still, you went too far. To forge information in an official document? Imagine what would have happened if another police officer would have found out, and not me."

Jairo moved his eyes back and forth, studiously avoiding Roberto's steel-grey piercing gaze.

"I understand, Roberto. But there were circumstances … I couldn't do anything else."

"Why?"

Roberto's voice was so quiet and pleasant, and his question asked in such an off-hand manner, one might have thought he had little interest in the answer. But Jairo, as an attorney, knew all the tricks of police investigators, and knew how to be wary of them. Even so, he chose to walk into the trap.

"Look, Roberto, this man put a very large sum of money on my desk, offering it to me if I could take care of the matter. I don't know if you would refuse such an appealing offer. Maybe you would have. But the president of our republic would have done what I was asked to do, and for a smaller sum!"

Jairo knew these last words would intrigue Roberto. Police officers loved money.

Roberto, still sitting on the edge of the desk, was quiet. His gaze seemed glued to the wall. One leg moved back and forth, back and forth ... Finally he turned back to Jairo and asked, "How much money are you talking about? If I may be permitted to know? I won't tell the tax people."

Jairo grinned. He already understood where his friend, the seeker of justice, was headed. Clearly, the amount would tell Roberto just how much he could demand of Jairo, in return for a private investigation into the question of who, exactly, Alberto Hunkes was. He knew that he could not reveal the true amount of money — $25,000! It would cost him too much; the seeker of justice would demand his fair share. He understood, too, that he could not come up with too low a price, or the lieutenant would suspect him of concealing something and that would be the end of their friendship. Money had destroyed many unbreakable bonds.

"We're talking about $10,000. A lot of money!" he answered.

Roberto thought for a minute, not moving from his spot. Finally he stood up, walked around the office, and returned to Jairo's desk.

"Look, Jairo. I'm here not as a police officer obligated to worry about people breaking the law. At this moment — and this is not always true — I'm not interested in the law. At this moment I'm only interested in who was the real Alberto Hunkes. I admit, I'm impressed by your stories and I'd like to help you. But you've got to help me too. Tell me everything. Everything you know about him, and particularly all you did for him."

Jairo lit up a cigarette: an action that would give him a moment to organize his thoughts. But before he could begin, the door opened and Francisco burst through.

"Jairo, have you heard? The Arabs are gearing up for war on your country!"

Before he'd even digested the news, he noticed how even his good friend, the gentile Francisco, did not see him as a true Brazilian. *Your country*. He referred thus to Israel, a place Jairo had never even visited. A place that barely interested him. Though he knew that Francisco meant nothing by it, he saw that in a moment of emotional turmoil Francisco had revealed his true feelings for him. For Jairo, the young Brazilian Jew who wanted so badly to be a *real* Brazilian. Another thing to discuss and argue over with his father, one of these days, soon …

Suddenly Francisco noticed Roberto. He backed away. "Oh, excuse me. I didn't know anyone was with you."

Jairo waved his hand. "Come in and meet each other. This is my partner, Francisco Machado, and this is my good friend, Police Officer Roberto Nunes."

The two shook hands and polite smiles appeared on their faces.

Jairo turned to Francisco. "What war are you talking about?"

"Haven't you heard? The radio is full of it! News bulletins are coming from there without stop. Nasser has declared a state of emergency. He's advancing military units in Sinai and the Gaza Strip. He's demanded that the U.N. remove its forces that are guarding the Straits of Tiran. Commentators all over the world believe that he's planning a naval blockade of Israel. They think that this time it's serious and not just a show of strength. There's panic in Tel Aviv. The residents are terrified of what's going to happen. Some people are remembering the days of the Holocaust."

Jairo suddenly felt a hardness in his chest. Anxiety crept into his heart, wormlike; he could feel it begin to take over. This was the first time events in the Middle East had captured his attention. Why? He had no idea. Perhaps he'd caught some of Francisco's obvious excitement. Maybe. And maybe, just maybe, he had Alberto Hunkes to thank for this. For hadn't it been Alberto's mysterious death, and all that had happened afterwards, that had made him sense his Jewish identity awakening within him! Jairo didn't understand, nor did he know the source of the change.

In the meantime he realized, with grim satisfaction, that Francisco's interruption had saved him, for now, from the minor investigation of his friend Roberto. News of the great war that might break out in the Middle East had rescued him from a small, private war with the police officer ...

"Roberto," Jairo turned to him, "I'm just too excited now. We'll speak again. Go and talk to Regina Hunkes. Believe me, that's more important than interrogating me."

23

Sao Paulo, Brazil
May 16, 1967

Regina Hunkes let the receiver fall from her hand. She leaned weakly on the nearby wall. She ran a hand over her brow in an almost unconscious gesture. She gazed, unseeing, at her spacious living room. After a moment, she put her face in her hands. The harsh words she'd exchanged with Eduardo, the danger of the police officer, set to arrive in a short time in order to question her, made it clear: The moment of truth had arrived. She had feared this moment all of her life. She suddenly realized that her hands were moist. Were these tears? Regina, who never cried? Whose father, a Prussian, had taught her, so harshly, that one never showed emotion?

From the safety of the kitchen, Celia, the new maid, followed her mistress's movements with close attention. The door was opened just a little bit: Even from the crack, she could easily see Regina's anxiety. Celia hadn't managed to connect the instrument she'd been given to listen in on phone conversations; thus, she hadn't heard exactly what Eduardo had said that had so angered his mother. But from what she'd heard, she understood that the police officer was to arrive, despite everything. Schmidt would be very unhappy with this news. Still, she was obligated to let him know about this new development. In the few hours that she'd been in the Hunkes home, she hadn't had the opportunity to go into the bedroom, though she knew, now, that the safe that so interested Schmidt was located there. How to tell him? She couldn't call him directly; her mistress was too close and too nervous. She might find out ...

Celia entered the living room. "*Senhora*," she asked in a gentle, kind voice, "can I help you with anything?"

Regina lifted her face and bestowed a harsh and frigid look on her young maid.

"I have no need of your help, nor your offers of help. Go back to the kitchen quickly! You've got enough work there."

Celia stood humbly before her and answered quietly, "*Si, Senhora*."

Celia was satisfied. She'd managed to see Regina's face, her eyes reddened with tears. She now tried to discern what lay hidden behind them. Her mission was to report on everything happening in this house. To give a detailed description of everyone who came to visit. To keep track of who called on the phone. To investigate the possibility of a safe. And, particularly, to find out the plans of the lady of the house. She'd been promised a hefty sum of money if successful, a sum that would enable her to return to the village of her birth, near the city of

Blumenau in the southern state of Santa Catarina, and get married. She would finish her mission, at all costs. She must continue to speak with her mistress.

Thus Celia stood her ground, not moving from her place, as she asked, with childish astonishment, "*Senhora,* are you angry with me?"

Regina was surprised. At first, she didn't know what to say. It was hard to be angry with such naiveté! And yet, her fury burst forth:

"I don't know! And I'm not really interested! It may be that I don't need you anymore. Do you understand?"

Celia acted perplexed. "But why?" she asked, with a pretense of fear. "Try me out for at least one full workday! Give me the chance to clean up the house. The entire house. And you'll see how well I'll do. Okay? Please, good missus? Do you want me to clean the bedroom, perhaps?"

Regina stood up angrily and approached her in a threatening manner.

"Get out of here and get back to the kitchen now! Did you hear? In another hour I'll know if I need you at all or not. I may be going away. Do you hear? Going abroad — forever! Forever! Now do you understand what I'm saying?"

Celia trembled. She must let Schmidt know about this immediately. She couldn't call from the house. She burst into tears:

"I don't understand why you have to lose your temper and insult me! I really want to be a good maid. Why are you shouting at me? It hurts me!"

Celia hurried back to the kitchen. Regina felt she'd gone too far. Still, she was glad to see that the foolish maid hadn't seemed to understand the meaning of her last statement, which had accidentally erupted from her. She didn't want anyone to know of her desire to flee Brazil. No one! Not even Eduardo!

"Celia," she called after her into the kitchen, in a more gentle voice, "I didn't mean to offend you. I'm just upset over a phone call I made. So upset, I lost control."

Celia continued to sob. "I need some air. Can I go out for a little while, to calm down? I don't understand why you did this to me. What did I do?"

Regina gave an impatient wave of her hand. For her part, she'd be happy if this one left permanently. Thoughts of flight had begun to brew within her even during the funeral service. They had grown as soon as the police officer had said he wanted to question her. Why couldn't they let the investigation go? Dead, dead! What did they have to investigate? That was what frightened her. And now, within the hour, the lieutenant would arrive …

"Celia!" she called, suddenly noticing the unwonted stillness in the kitchen. "Celia? Where are you?"

But there was no answer. She went into the kitchen and saw the door facing the service elevator was open. Celia had fled.

Regina hurried to Celia's room. Her belongings were all there, lying in the confused heap in which she'd left them when she'd arrived, a few hours before. Apparently, she'd gone down to get a bit of air, as she'd announced.

Regina poured herself a cup of coffee. From the time of Alberto's death, as she'd distanced herself from all others, she'd gotten into the habit of doing things for herself. She'd cooked, she'd cleaned. On that very day she'd sent away her faithful and dedicated maid, who'd worked for them since their arrival in Sao Paulo five years before. It was no big deal for her, to make herself a cup of coffee. She took the cup in her two hands, trying to enjoy its warmth. Afterwards she returned to the living room and looked for the most comfortable chair. She took a few small sips even as her hard thoughts bit at her with their sharp fangs. She was exhausted. The decisions she had to make were too great for her. She stood up and began to restlessly pace the length of the living room. She reached the large window facing the street. As always, the street below was busy. From the height of eight stories everything down below looked so small. Small and unimportant. But looking at the people passing by, at the cars driving this way and that, calmed her somewhat. It was like looking at a tank in which the fish moved elegantly, in deep silence. The noise of the street didn't reach her.

Suddenly, her glance froze. Her eyes were riveted on the telephone booth across the street. She felt tension overwhelm her, dissipating the weakness of the past moments. Yes. There was no doubt: It was she! It was Celia, speaking excitedly on the phone, sending suspicious looks across the street …

Regina took a deep breath. She didn't move her eyes from the sight. With the intuition of a trapped beast she sensed a heavy warning signal. It seemed that this maid wasn't as innocent as she'd made herself out to be. Regina saw the excited manner in which Celia was speaking on the phone. Celia kept looking around her, making certain no one was paying her any attention. She cast many hurried glances in the direction of the living room. It seemed clear that Celia was afraid of being followed. Who? And why? Could it be that this Celia was actually shadowing her, Regina! Shadowing the Hunkes family! If so, who had sent her? Her husband's killers?

Or others? What did they still want? In an instant, it seemed to her that she knew. Her thoughts went to the safe. No! It couldn't be! No one knew of its existence, of what was hidden there. Could it be? How could anyone know? She must be careful. Very careful. A red warning light had lit up in her heart; years of experience had taught her to see danger signals ahead. It was true in Europe, it was true in Argentina, and — she couldn't hide it from herself — it was true in Sao Paulo as well.

Celia finished her call but didn't rush out of the phone booth. After a moment's hesitation she left. Regina saw that Celia's first look was directed upwards, towards the living room window of the Hunkes apartment. That was it! An inner voice whispered to Regina that Celia was working for someone else, not for her. In her heart she searched for a small measure of revenge that she could prepare as a parting gift for her delightful maid. A wicked smile appeared on her thin lips. The idea that she'd come up with seemed to her particularly refreshing. Just so that little demon with the innocent face, whose name Regina was no longer certain was Celia, would not think that she'd succeeded in deceiving her ...

Celia had sneaked away from the house the moment she thought her mistress wouldn't notice. The elevator had brought her down to the street. She ran swiftly to the nearest phone booth. From Mrs. Hunkes's behavior, she realized that her mistress was on the verge of dramatic decisions. If Regina ran away too quickly, Schmidt wouldn't pay her, Celia, what he'd promised. She must tell him immediately of these new developments. Schmidt must also know of Regina's conversation with her son, and of her extreme anxiety.

And, of course, that she'd threatened to leave, to flee. She would tell him also of the police officer who was planning to arrive soon to interrogate Regina.

She dialed quickly. Her wary glances searched ceaselessly around her. No, no one was following her. She recognized the voice of the man who'd recruited her for this mission. Celia swiftly reported all that she'd learned. Schmidt remained silent throughout. Finally, he said one word, "Thanks," and hung up. Celia replaced the receiver, paused for a moment and left the glass booth. She must rush back to the apartment, before Mrs. Hunkes noticed that she'd vanished, so that she wouldn't besiege her with unnecessary questions. She waited at the curb for the chance to race across. Without thinking, she sent a look towards the apartment. An arrow of fear shot through her heart. It seemed to her that she'd seen the image of Regina disappear from behind the window at the moment that she had looked up. Celia stood frozen. Did Mrs. Hunkes suspect her? Had she found something out? She felt a surge of panic. Had Mrs. Hunkes, in her absence, searched through her possessions and found the listening device that she'd gotten from Schmidt?

She crossed the street with slow steps. Approached the house. Suddenly, she halted. To flee or put herself in danger? To go up or not to go up …

The grey-haired man continued to hold the receiver tightly. Two of his colleagues sitting with him stared at him in impatient silence.

"The bird," he said in a quiet, calm voice, "feels endangered."

Silence.

"I think," he said, in the same tone, "that plans must be changed. We must act immediately. Immediately — before she leaves the cage."

The two others continued to sit in silence.

Bnei Brak, Israel
6 Iyar 5727

Yitzchak Austerlitz returned from *davening Ma'ariv*, happy and content. It had been a long while since his wife had seen him in such good spirits. She rejoiced inwardly, and added a small prayer that this situation should continue. She was very curious as to what had brought about the change, but didn't dare ask. She knew that questions might destroy everything. After dinner, they spoke of the latest news, of the increasing tension on the Egyptian border, of the heavy atmosphere all around them.

"I haven't the strength for another war," Rivka, herself a survivor of the camps, sighed. But she immediately regretted her words: Perhaps they would revive her husband's melancholy. To her astonishment, her husband answered in a restrained manner. "G-d will help. We're in *Eretz Yisrael*. Not over there!"

Something's happened to him, Rivka thought to herself. Optimism was certainly not characteristic of her husband. *What could it have been?*

Suddenly, she heard an unexpected announcement from her husband that returned her to reality and showed her that her joy was, perhaps, premature.

"I'm not going to the *daf Yomi shiur* today. I'm staying home."

Rivka was shocked. "Why?"

"Someone is coming to visit."

"Who?"

Yitzchak didn't rush to answer. Rivka again asked, "Who?"

"A man. I don't even know his name."

"What does he want?"

"He wants nothing. I'm the one who wants!"

Rivka felt her breath come and go. "What do you want from him?"

"That he make a call for me."

"What does that mean?"

"He'll make a call to Brazil for me."

Rivka felt her strength lapsing. Her husband, it seemed, was still in trouble. Why a call to Brazil? She spoke quietly, saving her energy, "What do you suddenly have to do in Brazil?"

Yitzchak Austerlitz stared at his wife with solemn eyes that showed a vein of decision within them. He realized that he was on the verge of a major turnaround in his life. Finally, he would tell his wife the reason for his strange behavior.

24

"Perhaps, in Brazil, lies the key to what has happened to me."

Silence descended upon Austerlitz and his wife. A tense silence, that filled the space in the small kitchen in which they sat.

"I think that the time has come to tell you everything. Perhaps Hashem will have mercy and you'll understand me."

Yitzchak said these words in a tranquil voice, vastly different from the tense, raised voice of the past few days. But for this very reason her own fears increased. Rivka didn't know what to expect. Her trembling fingers nervously grasped the edge of the plastic tablecloth; she hardly noticed that she was crushing it in her hand. She stole glances at her husband, whose thoughts had turned inward — glances in which there was obvious fear. *Perhaps*, the thought pressed through her mind, *perhaps, after this conversation life will return to the pleasant, comfortable pathways it had taken during the first years of marriage. Perhaps the good days will return, the days before the appearance of the fury, the long silences, the depression.* As in a movie played too fast, she saw in those few seconds scenes of the difficult moments of the past few years, scenes in which she had occasionally considered running away from home, as life became unbearable. She very much wanted this conversation with her husband. And yet, she was afraid of it as well. She was afraid of what he would tell her. Who knew, perhaps there would be things which would just make matters worse, Heaven forbid. Her thoughts were in disarray; she couldn't concentrate on anything.

Still, Yitzchak Austerlitz sat silent. He stared at his watch with deliberate concentration. Rivka saw how his ears were tensed and ready to hear any voices outside their door. Was that the sound of footsteps making their way towards them? The footfalls came nearer to their door. Yitzchak held his breath for a moment. But the footsteps continued and grew more faint. Someone must be going up to the neighbor who lived above them. The shadow of disappointment crossed Yitzchak's face.

Rivka waited to see what would happen.

Yitzchak stared at the ceiling; he didn't have the strength to meet her eyes. He looked for the right words with which to begin his story. Finally, he burst out, "Eichmann is the reason for everything!"

Rivka didn't react to these strange words. Her eyes remained lowered, staring at her hands, which were still playing with the edge of the tablecloth.

"I mean, Eichmann's trial."

Yitzchak realized that his story was coming out in pieces; that his introduction hadn't been successful; that he was trying to heal a rift that he'd created between them. In these past years he had done a terrible disservice to his wife, herself a Holocaust survivor. From the time of Eichmann's judgment, he hadn't treated her properly. His deep depression had poisoned the atmosphere of their home. This realization only added to his pain and melancholy. It was hard for him to control his emotions. They seemed to be choking him. With all this, he continued.

"I remember the day that Ben Gurion announced it from the Knesset podium. 'I hereby announce to the nation living in Zion that the arch-killer Adolph Eichmann, who was in charge of Hitler's death camps, is in our hands in prison in Israel.'

"I remember the day. The minute! The second!"

Yitzchak's breath came in gasps. He looked at his watch again, in the vague hope that the man with the cap would come at this very minute and allow him to put off this conversation, this impossible conversation, for another time.

"I was standing," he continued abruptly, "on Achad Ha'am Street, corner of Nachalat Binyamin. I was drinking a glass of seltzer in a *kiosk* and listening to the news. And then — an atom bomb fell upon me."

Rivka lifted her eyes in fright. She didn't understand to what he was referring. But Yitzchak didn't see her. It seemed that he'd returned to that Tel Aviv street.

"I don't remember anything of what happened at the moment I heard the incredible news on the radio. People said I fainted. That they wanted to take me to the hospital. That I came to and screamed, like a crazy man, 'No! Not to the hospital!' "

Yitzchak threw his hands out and added, "But I don't remember anything."

After a moment he continued, in a quieter voice, "I thought my last day on earth had come. At that exact minute, when I again stood on my feet, I knew that I had returned to there, to my village, to my home."

Yitzchak stared with anguished eyes at his wife and added, "And … to my wife. My children."

A short, quiet cry burst forth from him. "I've never told you of that moment in Tel Aviv. I know. I ask your forgiveness. Today. Now."

Rivka said, "Yitzchak, you don't have to tell me, if it's too hard for you. I forgive you. You know that I'm aware that you're going through a very hard time."

"Yes, I know."

"I spill enough tears before Hashem, that He should give you the strength to bear it. This is the test of our generation, and we must pass it. Really, you don't have to tell me more now. Or ever, if it's too hard for you."

She, too, felt the tears choking her …

"No. This time I've begun to tell you, and I'll finish. Perhaps, in this way I'll be free of what has been oppressing me. I know very well how much you've suffered from my behavior. And with all my suffering and torture I am hurt, also, because I'm destroying your life as well, in my own private *gehinnom*."

A terrible sigh escaped him.

"Where was I? Oh, yes. Good, helpful people picked me up. They asked if I was all right. I remember laughing like a madman. I remember shouting at them, 'There's something wrong with you if you think that I can be all right!' I was still confused, but I saw very clearly the looks that they were giving me, looks that absolutely showed what they thought of me during those moments when I was almost insane."

Yitzchak lapsed into silence. He began to cough lightly, giving him a chance to recover from the emotions that held him in their harsh grip.

"Someone brought me a cup of water. I drank. Someone else asked if I wanted to go home. I remember that I answered 'no' very firmly.

"I remember an angry and impatient voice asking, 'Hey, so tell us what we should do with you. Decide, already!'

"I lifted my eyes and saw before me a young, handsome sabra staring at me, clearly impatient. His eyes, sabra eyes that seemed to feel they knew everything, showed his disdain for the diaspora, for a diaspora Jew such as me. At first I felt like screaming at him, 'I'm from Auschwitz! Do you know what that is?' But at that moment a great fear came upon me. For the first time I understood what I should have realized years before: He and I and all like him are two nations! Two completely different nations! I belong to the nation that was there, and he to the nation that was not there. Do you understand? Two different people! Nothing can ever unite them ...

"I remember being quiet for a minute. Finally, I asked, 'Help me get to a synagogue. To the main synagogue on Allenby, on the corner of Achad Ha'am."

Yitzchak Austerlitz left the kitchen and went to the porch that faced the street. Rivka didn't disturb the silence. She understood his impatience, his desire to somehow hasten the anonymous stranger's arrival by watching for him. Could looking for him help? No! But she, too, would stand in the same way and hurry her son, Yaakov Yehoshua, home, when she expected him for Shabbos.

After a moment, Yitzchak returned to the small living room. He opened the door leading out of the apartment. Opened it, shut it. Stood next to the door and listened. Opened it and shut it again.

With heavy steps he returned to the kitchen. His weary face seemed to whisper the question, "Why hasn't he come yet?"

Like an echo, Rivka answered, "If he said he'll come, he'll come."

And she waited for him to continue his story ...

Sao Paulo, Brazil
May 16, 1967

Paulo Chilo waited patiently, the receiver in his hand. The Ipiranga Hotel was a large one; the operators were undoubtedly very busy. Surely they were looking for Von Dorfman.

The line came to life. "*Senhor?*"

"*Si?*"

"*Senhor* Von Dorfman left the hotel unexpectedly this morning."

Paulo felt dizzy. "He left? Without leaving an address?"

"No, sir. I'm sorry."

His anger began to stir. "How can it be? I was to speak with him!"

There was silence on the other end of the line. His outpouring of fury, it seemed, left the operator unmoved.

Hoping for an answer, he spoke in a quieter voice. "Hello?"

"*Si?*"

"What can this mean?"

"I'm sorry, sir, we're a hotel, not a security service."

Paulo realized that he'd gone too far. "I beg your pardon."

"That's all right."

The operator quickly brought the conversation to an end. Paulo was left, the receiver dangling from his hand. He whispered into it, in a wounded voice, surprise and confusion mixed together, "What can this mean?"

"Do you have a cigarette?"

Jairo was exhausted. The tension caused by the police officer, with his unexpected questions, destroyed whatever vestiges of tranquility were left within his heart. And now Francisco had bombarded him with these stories of war in the Middle East.

Francisco pulled a Minister cigarette out of its package. Before Jairo had placed it between his lips, he saw the flash of a flame from Francisco's golden lighter.

"Thanks."

Jairo took a few slow puffs.

"Sit down." It was partly a request, partly a demand.

"What have you heard?" Jairo added, when Francisco had acquiesced.

Francisco was surprised that Jairo hadn't heard the news, news that had taken over all the airwaves.

"You didn't know? Meanwhile, there's not much more than what I've told you. Nasser is advancing troops towards the border with Israel. He's threatening to have the U.N. troops in Sharm-el-Sheikh and the Straits of Tiran removed. That is, to form a naval blockade on Israel from Eilat. And in Tel Aviv, everyone's panicking. Reports coming out of there say there's a lot of confusion and indecision."

Jairo was quiet. A few more short puffs on the cigarette that seemed to be burning more rapidly than usual, and the next question:

"Is that all?"

"Just about. In Cairo the mob is dancing in the street, and hundreds of thousands calling for *jihad* and demonstrating in support of their master, Gamal Abdul Nasser."

"Is that all?"

Francisco felt uncomfortable. This monotonous repetition in a dry, distant voice seemed strange. His eyes ran swiftly over Jairo's face: It was as unreadable as that of the Egyptian Sphinx. What was happening to him? Was this more of the mischief that they'd seen in the past few days?

"What's wrong, Jairo?"

Jairo seemed to awaken from a distant dream. "Why do you think something's wrong? I'm just a bit worried about what I've heard from you."

Francisco didn't answer. With his sixth sense he knew that something deeper, more mysterious was behind this "worry." Was it connected with what they'd seen at the cemetery that last cursed Friday?

"Francisco?"

"Yes, Jairo?"

Jairo straightened in his executive chair. He folded his arms and looked Francisco straight in the eye. With a pleasant smile, he said, "Do me a favor. Leave me alone now. Okay?"

Francisco gave an answering grin. He understood that the storm of emotions roused in his Jewish friend had not yet diminished. The news from the Middle East undoubtedly had added to the hurricane.

"I'm going, but stay calm, *amigo*. Brazil is a large place."

As he stood by the door Jairo's voice suddenly reached him.

"Do you know where Paulo is?"

Francisco stopped. He whirled around and looked closely at Jairo.

"No. I don't know. I think he's in his office."

"Thanks."

"One minute! Why'd you ask?"

"No real reason."

Francisco nodded his head gently.

"Do you want him to leave the office, based on the news from Egypt? Have you suddenly remembered that he's an Arab?"

"Heavens, no. Why do you think so?"

"So why did you suddenly ask about him?"

"I told you, no real reason. That is, I don't even know myself."

Francisco closed the door behind him. He stood next to it for another minute, one hand holding the knob, the other gently stroking his forehead. The thoughts racing through his brain were giving him a headache. After a moment he turned into his own office and shut the door. It seemed to him that it gave a loud slam …

Eduardo was stunned and flabbergasted. His mother's cold words: "You'll be sorry," falling upon him like icicles, had upset him considerably. He bit his lip. Even as he was hurriedly reading the text of the column that he'd prepared on the developments in the Middle East his brain was working on trying to understand what was hidden in his mother's harsh words. He understood that something very serious lay behind the story of his father's murder. Behind the murder, and his mother's strange fears. He absent-mindedly continued to type his column on Middle East tensions.

The telephone rang. Eduardo lifted the receiver.

"Eduardo?"

"*Si.*"

It was the personal secretary to the editor of his newspaper, the *Estado de Sao Paulo, Senhor* Julio Mesquita.

"The editor wants to see you. Urgently!"

Eduardo felt his heart miss a beat.

"Me?"

He was nothing more than a young reporter. Except for the day he'd been hired, two years earlier, he had never had a conversation with the editor of South America's largest newspaper. What had happened that was so urgent?

"Are you coming?" asked the secretary.

"Of course."

"Right now!"

25

Sao Paulo, Brazil
May 16, 1967

Regina swiftly left the window and turned towards the kitchen. After a moment she returned to the living room. She paced back and forth, her nerves frayed, pursued by her wild, frenzied thoughts. Trapped. She felt trapped. What to do? Someone, it seemed, had planted a spy in her household. Who was this "someone"? What did he want from her? Did he know her secret, the secret she'd shared only with her husband? Impossible. Simply impossible, unbelievable. Was this little nobody returning from the street an agent of her husband's murderers? Who knew? How could one know?

Regina felt ill. She searched for her cigarettes but couldn't find them. She'd left them in the living room! Who had taken them? That wicked little fiend, perhaps, who called herself Celia? What could she do? She couldn't trust anyone!

Weakly she collapsed into one of the soft chairs that graced the four corners of the large, elegant living room. Her left hand, trembling slightly, stroked her cheek. What could she do?

Oh yes. She'd completely forgotten. Any minute now the police officer might turn up. Why were these thoughts torturing her ceaselessly? Why should the policeman insist on interrogating her despite the promise she'd received from GAC that the file would be closed? What was he looking for, this policeman? Was he, too, one of the murderers? Anything was possible in Brazil! It all depended on the price: how much you could pay and to whom. Why hadn't GAC opened its coffers? They could deduct the bribe money from her pension if they wanted! How could they leave her defenseless, at the mercy of the police?

Tears appeared in her eyes; she didn't wipe them away. She felt them roll down her cheeks, moistening them. How alone she was! And just at this time, Eduardo had left her! How much she'd put into that ... And this, this was the result! She had never asked him anything without him taking care of it immediately. And suddenly ... Perhaps, the thought flew through her head, perhaps he, too, knows more than he's saying. What could she do?

Making a sudden decision, she ran quickly to the bedroom and grabbed the purse where she kept her ready cash. With frenzied swiftness she pulled on the first coat she grabbed out of the closet and rushed to the door. She'd avoid this interrogation no matter what! The police officer wouldn't question her! She'd go directly to GAC and confront them! She hadn't the strength to face an investigation and she suspected she'd say things she oughtn't. That cursed Eduardo was forcing her to run away from the police. If he'd stood by her, as she'd asked him, she would have been calmer.

In a flash she closed the door behind her. She called the elevator, which brought her down to the ground floor. With quick steps she reached the building's entrance and faced the doorman. She noticed a man whom she didn't recognize speaking with him, but couldn't hear what he'd asked. But the doorman's answer came to her, loud and clear:

"Here she is. That's Mrs. Hunkes, Lieutenant."

Regina froze in her place. She wouldn't turn around. Her heart seemed to stop beating; she couldn't feel a thing. And yet, she clearly sensed the police officer approach her slowly, patiently …

Jairo was left alone in his office. He could hear Francisco's door give a slam. No doubt about it, Francisco was angry. But there was no choice. He needed a little time by himself now — a few minutes in which he could quietly organize his thoughts. Too many things had fallen upon him at once, this last hour. First there was Nunes's bursting in with the young man who'd collided with his car. Perhaps, perhaps Nunes was right? Was that young man sent by "them"? Afterwards, the pressure of Nunes's questioning in the matter of the document he'd forged for Alberto Hunkes, enabling Hunkes to stay in Brazil. Jairo hoped Nunes wouldn't make much of it. Jairo knew that it would cost him, to the tune of some hundreds of dollars deposited in the police officer's bank account. With that, he believed, the matter would end. And finally, there was Francisco's news of the war that was expected in the Middle East.

Jairo stood up from his chair, pushed it back a bit, and circled his wide desk. With slow steps, that were swallowed up in the deep pile of his wall-to-wall carpet, he walked towards the wall that held a map of the Middle East. In its center: Israel. No, Jairo was not a Zionist. He'd never even visited Israel. He spent his vacations in Europe or America, and, more frequently, in Argentina. He'd bought the map one night at a fundraiser of the Unificada, the city's Zionist umbrella organization, that he'd somehow wound up attending. He'd never paid much attention to what was going on there. But now, something pulled him towards the map. So small, that country! What did everyone want from it? For that matter, what did everyone want from the Jews? Why did they hate them so? Why should he, Jairo the Brazilian, feel so pressured because of some hate-ridden widow and a Nazi buried in the earth? Why was he so upset at the thought of a war that might break out in a country that had never really interested him? A country far, far away from his own, and even farther from his thoughts?

Jairo felt his depression growing. Abstractedly, he walked slowly back to his desk. He'd call his father, tell him he wanted to visit this evening. He felt he must speak with him about their Jewishness. Suddenly it was important to him, pressing his very being. He knew it would be a sharp discussion. He didn't know if his father would be happy with such talk. But he had no choice. Perhaps the conversation would help him understand why he, Jairo, was reacting as he was.

Jairo reached out towards the telephone. But before he could begin dialing, he was stopped by a shrill jangle.

"*Senhor* Silverman?" a harsh voice on the other end asked.

"Yes," he answered, after a slight pause.

"So, you've won, *Senhor* Jairo Silverman!"

There was hostility in the way the mysterious stranger emphasized the name.

Jairo was uncomfortable. "Who are you? And what do you want from me?"

"Who I am is not important. The main thing is, you've succeeded in overpowering us. You didn't listen to our warnings. Lieutenant Roberto Nunes is at this moment questioning Mrs. Hunkes. It's an accomplishment; absolutely, an accomplishment. But *Senhor* Silverman, your success is only temporary. Do you understand?"

The voice was menacing. Jairo was overtaken by a real, honest fear.

"Who are you?"

"For your own good, *Senhor*, you must call Mrs. Hunkes's home immediately, and ask to speak with the policeman you sent to her. We know that you sent him. Do you remember the driver that collided with the police officer's car? The one Nunes brought back to your office? Before he succeeded in fleeing, he used his many talents to gather information on you and your office. Do what I've asked. Phone the woman, ask for Roberto Nunes, explain to him that he, like you, is in danger, if this interrogation causes the woman to run away. We still need her. Do you understand?"

"Who are you? Who is 'we'?"

"You think you're so smart, *Senhor* Jairo. But you are making the mistake of your life."

Jairo, feeling strangely obstinate, didn't let up.

"Yes, but who are you?"

"Have you heard of the Spider organization?"

"No."

"Would you like to hear about it now?"

"No! Just tell me who you are!"

Jairo could clearly hear the deep breathing of the mystery man on the line.

"My young friend, you're showing too much courage. It's not courage that stems from wisdom; it's rooted in ignorance. Perhaps, in this case, in plain foolishness. You would seem to want to meet us personally. Such a meeting will be particularly unpleasant for you. In order to avoid more problems, quickly do what I've asked. Understand? Call your lieutenant now. Before it's too late. Too late for all of us. Including you!"

"I'll call the police!"

"For my part you can call the police or you can call the president. Do whatever you want. But remember what you must do first. And don't forget, you still don't know if Lieutenant Roberto Nunes is working for you — or against you."

The anonymous caller hung up the phone. From the receiver that Jairo gripped in his right hand, he could hear the dial tone. It sounded to him like an air raid siren.

Paulo Chilo hung up the receiver. After a moment, he picked it up once more. He began to dial, stopped, and lightly threw the receiver from hand to hand, his eyes riveted on it.

With a sudden harsh thrust he hung up the phone. He stood up with a firm and decisive movement, grabbed his jacket, and scrupulously straightened his tie. He took the file with the GAC documents and left the office with an energetic step. He knew now what he must do …

Eduardo decided not to use the elevator. He walked up the steps towards the office of the editor-in-chief.

He felt a certain tension. This sudden summons had come as a surprise. He was consumed by curiosity. What could the editor-in-chief want from him? Was he going to be fired for some reason? Or was it connected with the war between the Jews and the Arabs in Palestine? Eduardo had no idea of what to think.

With care and fear that he sought to conceal, he opened the door. The editor met him with a wide smile that had an immediate effect: Eduardo calmed down. It seemed that he wouldn't be fired after all.

"*Senhor* Hunkes," the editor got right to the point, "I am terribly sorry about the death of your father."

Eduardo bent his head politely.

"Thank you."

The editor slowly put the pungent Havana cigar that rested between his lips into the large elephant-shaped ashtray. He gave a short hoarse cough, the lot of all heavy smokers, and stared deeply into the eyes of the young man sitting opposite him.

"I've been following your work. You've shown a great deal of talent, with remarkable analytical ability. Good for you!"

It seemed to Eduardo that he was blushing. He could certainly feel his face burning. "Thank you very much," he said modestly.

"Eduardo, I want to give you an extraordinary opportunity."

Eduardo didn't answer. He waited for what would come next.

"You know, of course, that there is a distinct possibility that war will break out in the Middle East within days."

"Yes."

"What do you think about going to Israel as our military correspondent? To investigate what's going on in the Jewish state?"

Eduardo felt the shock choking him.

"It's … it's … it's a great honor for me."

"You won't be going by yourself. Sergio Gimarainz, who has more seniority than you, will also be leaving in two day's time. You'll cover the military aspect of the events on the Israeli side while he will take care of the political end of the crisis. You can begin to make your preparations for the trip. My secretary, *Dona* Daisy, will brief you on all the details you need."

The editor stood up, put his hand out and added warmly, "I wish you luck. *Chau.*"

Eduardo left the office, thunderstruck. This would be his first professional trip out of the country's borders. Strange that he, who had been raised in his home on hatred of the Jews, would actually travel to the aggressive little country of theirs in the Middle East. But it was certainly a major promotion for him in his newspaper career, and he wouldn't give up this chance. His heart was full.

There was only one person with whom he wanted to share his news: his mother. When he returned to his office he swiftly dialed. But when he heard her frigid voice saying hello, he quickly hung up without a word. Her parting words to him — You'll be sorry! — suddenly flew into his head. He couldn't speak to her. Yet.

26

The grey-haired man gently hung up the phone. He tendered a piercing glance at his two colleagues, who had sat quietly listening to their superior's conversation.

"I have the impression," Hermann Schmidt said, "that this time he's running scared, as he should be, this young hero of ours, the Jewish attorney, Jairo Silverman."

One of the men seated in the room put his cigarette into the ashtray that lay on the small table and said, "You think he'll call the widow? And really stop the police officer?"

Schmidt shrugged his shoulders. "Nothing is certain. We'll know better in a few minutes."

They lapsed into thoughtful silence.

"And if he doesn't call? If he's not frightened by our threats?"

Though he didn't show it, this sentence angered the grey-haired man.

"That's why you're sitting here. To help think, to make plans. One thing I know, this business has suddenly become urgent and serious. The operational squad is arriving tomorrow morning."

The two men momentarily raised their heads in surprise. This was news to them; it put the pressure on them. Neither said a word.

The grey-haired man looked at his watch. Close to 10 minutes had passed since his conversation with Jairo. He decided to try again.

"Hello, my young friend."

He heard Jairo's surprised voice on the other end of the line.

"What do you want from me? Leave me alone already!"

Schmidt spoke quietly. His Portuguese was perfect, though the heavy German accent was obvious.

"I want nothing of you. Just call the widow of your German friend, and tell the police officer who is there now the things I told you to tell him. That's all!"

The grey-haired man made a slight grimace. He'd succeeded in infuriating Jairo, who shouted into the phone, "Who told you Hunkes was a German? What are you trying to hide by stopping me from finding out who my friend was?"

Schmidt laughed. "So you've given up on your office work and become a detective instead."

After a pause he added, in a quiet, friendly voice, "Jairo, listen to me. Leave it alone. Call your friend, tell him not to do anything foolish in this unnecessary investigation. If she disappears from the city, it will not be good for you. You have no idea of our power."

The two men sitting with him heard Jairo's shout. "I won't! I'm not calling!" The phone slammed down.

Schmidt spread his arms, as if to say, "What can one do?" After a moment he turned to his men and said, "Stay here. I'm going to the GAC office."

Schmidt left the hideout on Gabriel Monteiro da Silva Street. He locked the door behind him and entered his GAC Clipper. He turned left onto Estados Unidos Avenue, moving as quickly as he could, until he reached the corner of the broad Reboucas Boulevard. He turned right there, speeding up even more, and climbed up to the Paulista, the elegant boulevard that bisected the large city center. Before he had cruised down the Consolacao, across from the Praca da Republica, he stopped and left the car. He found a small cafe and bolted down a *cafejinho,* in an effort to collect his thoughts.

He knew he was close to his mission's end. But the sudden murder of Alberto Hunkes had disrupted the plans. What bothered him most was that GAC had begun to panic. The murder worried them enough that they'd decided to call on Von Dorfman, one of the heads of GAC International. With great effort, Schmidt had managed to have him sent home this morning. After trying many tactics, he'd convinced Von Dorfman that he could trust him, Schmidt, the company's Brazilian representative, to find the golden mean, the way to deal with all the ramifications of Hunkes's death. He knew that he would only relax after seeing Von Dorfman safely off on the Lufthansa Boeing jet. Just now, Von Dorfman was the last person he needed here in Sao Paulo. Just when the professionals, from the hand-picked squad, were about to come from Europe …

The cafe was empty at that hour. Schmidt gulped down the *cafejinho,* paid a few hundred *cruzeros,* and without waiting for his change walked out with hasty footsteps towards his red Clipper. He came to a sudden halt. A man whose face he didn't recognize was carefully inspecting his automobile from all sides ...

Bnei Brak
6 Iyar 5727

Yitzchak Austerlitz gave his wife a sorrowful glance. "I truly hope he'll come. He must come! I was so overwrought in the library, I forgot to ask his name or address. I don't know what I'll do if he doesn't come! Where can I find him?"

"Hashem will send you help from somewhere else," Rivka answered. She spoke soothingly, hoping to calm him down, though she hadn't the faintest idea what he was talking about. She wanted to hear the story's end, the tale of what had happened to her husband on that Tel Aviv street when he'd found out that Eichmann was in jail in Israel. Perhaps now she'd understand the meaning of his strange behavior these past months.

Yitzchak returned, unwillingly, to his chair in the kitchen. For another minute he listened for some sound. But no! There was nothing. He must have been mistaken. After a few seconds he quieted down.

"So what were we talking about?"

"You fainted, and wouldn't let them take you home."

Yitzchak smiled. It had been a long time since Rivka had seen a smile on his face.

"No! No! Not like that! I don't want you to misunderstand me. It wasn't that I didn't want to come home. Heaven forbid! But at that moment I needed a *shul*. I wanted to be alone with the Master of the Universe. Can't you understand? The news had shocked me. It was too much for me to bear. I felt I couldn't stand the emotion. My heart was simply ready to burst. At that minute, as I was drinking that seltzer, holding the glass in my hand, I returned — to Auschwitz. I returned to Galicia, to my home, my family. At that moment I wanted to be close to G-d, to …"

Yitzchak couldn't continue. His breath came with difficulty, and for long minutes he simply couldn't speak. Rivka began to fear the consequences of his confession.

"Maybe you want to rest? We'll continue to speak another time."

Yitzchak waved her off. With a clear effort of will, he managed to finish the sentence he'd begun.

"I needed a few minutes of prayer. To pour my heart out before the Creator. To cry. Particularly, to cry.

"They, the men in the street, brought me to the *shul* … It was empty. Empty and dark. On top of the *aron kodesh* a small red light burned, like a memorial candle. The silence that enveloped the sanctuary penetrated my heart. I can't remember what my lips murmured during those few minutes. Perhaps I was silent, a silence that was like the most awful cry, the most horrible cry that had ever been heard on this earth. And then I spoke and spoke. I spoke aloud. I spoke to the Creator from beneath the sea of tears that flooded my face."

He leaned his face on his hand.

"Rivka, I haven't the strength to repeat my conversation, in the great, empty *shul* in Tel Aviv. I'll just tell you this, that I begged and beseeched: 'Please, Hashem, save my soul!' I remembered the commentary of the Sefas Emes on the *pasuk* of *Tehillim* that I had learned while still a youth in Poland that explains that King David is asking of G-d that even if 'I am surrounded by the bonds of death' and even if 'the narrow confines of the grave find me and I encounter trouble and sorrow' still 'save my soul,' that is, let my soul, at the very least, remain whole and untouched: Let my faith not be damaged by the strict justice that has been wrought upon me."

Again, silence fell.

"I don't know why, but it seems that I didn't merit that my prayer be answered. From that day on I have had no peace."

Silence.

"I don't know how long I was in the *shul*. What I do know was that when I left I was no longer the same Yitzchak Austerlitz that I had been that morning. I was not the Yitzchak Austerlitz who held the pain of losing his family in his heart, but who lived in Israel. I felt clearly that I was no longer in Tel Aviv; I was in Auschwitz-Birkenau. The houses of Rechov Allenby that stood before me had the brown color of the shacks that had been built there, in *gehinnom*. The passersby were all under sentence of death, wearing the striped pajamas of the inmates."

He held his face in his hands.

"It's hard for me, Rivka. Even today, it's hard. Why did they have to bring Eichmann here? Why? Why did they open all the wounds once again? What was the good of it? The voices came back to me. Everything came back."

He tried to smile, but couldn't.

"The nights are the hardest. Hour after hour I can't sleep. And when I finally do fall asleep, I dream … "

"I know," Rivka whispered.

"Wild dreams … Dreams that rob me of all peace . that madden me … Dreams that provoke in me the sane desire to meet the Nazi who murdered my wife and children … In my dream I see a long, white arm that …

A sharp ring of the bell shook Yitzchak from his place. He jumped to the doorway; to his great joy, the man with the cap stood before him.

"Good evening. I'm so glad you've come."

The man with the cap rubbed his head gently and gave him an indifferent look.

"Well, I promised, so I'm here. I'm a simple man. Not a politician who says one thing and intends another."

Yitzchak led him into the living room, while Rivka remained in the kitchen.

The man with the cap pulled a small notebook out of his pocket and dialed the international operator.

"Hello, I'd like to speak to Brazil. That's right. With whom? What kind of question is that? With my brother! Yes, I understand. You want to know his name? Yes, I know. Certainly. Yaakov. Yaakov Kleinbaum. His phone number? Certainly. 805-142. Yes, he lives in Sao Paulo. Haddock Lobo Street. You need his address? Okay. 1498. I don't know what neighborhood. It's in Sao Paulo. Yes, thank you, I'll wait."

The tension in the room was almost unbearable. Yitzchak felt his heart beating like the drums at a wedding party. He realized he was mumbling something aloud; when he listened he heard himself repeating, over and over, "Please, Hashem, help me, please. Please, Hashem, please." At that moment he felt like one of the Nazi hunters that he'd read about in the papers.

His guest's body stiffened somewhat. With a gesture, he silenced Yitzchak. He blinked hard, as if to hear better the ringing of the phone in his brother's home.

"Hello?"

"Yaakov, can you hear me?"

"Who's speaking?" a voice said in Yiddish.

"Yankel, it's Moishe," his brother said in the same language. "Your brother, Moishe!"

"*Oy vey*! What's happened? Is everything still all right with you there?"

"Yankel, what's the matter? Why do you ask if everything is still okay? What's all this *oy vey* about?"

"What's the matter with you? Don't you know that war is about to break out there? The radio and television here are telling terrible stories on what's going to happen in Israel. And you act like you know nothing! The Jews here are devastated. Do you want to come join us here, until it's all over?"

"Yankel, everything here is fine. Yes, it's a bit tense. But it'll be okay."

There was silence on the line. "Ask him already," Yitzchak hissed.

"Moishe," the man with the cap heard his brother's voice, "if everything is all right, as you say, why are you suddenly calling?"

"I'm trying to do another Jew here a favor. He's looking for some Nazi."

"What! Are you crazy? We have time now to hunt Nazis? What do you want from me anyway? Me, look for Nazis? Leave me alone with this!"

"Yankel, I'm not asking that you search for him. Just find out if anyone's heard of him."

"I simply don't understand you. The country is chock full of Nazis. They're dangerous people. They've already murdered Jews who've searched for them. I don't have enough *tzurris* without this?"

"Yes, but there's a Jew here who just wants to know

if you happened to hear or read about a Nazi by the name of Heinz Krantz."

The man with the cap listened to his brother Yankel's laughter on the other end of the line. "Are you and that man so innocent to think that Nazis who live here call themselves by their real names? They're wicked men, may their names and memories be erased, but they're not fools! Do you understand, or not? You want me to search in Sao Paulo, a city of almost 10 million, for some Nazi by the name of ... what was the name?"

"Heinz Krantz."

"Okay, Heinz Krantz. A little sense, my dear brother."

"But maybe someone knows something about him? Do you know any police officers? Do me this favor. It's vital to this Jew to find out something about this Nazi."

"Moishe, don't make me crazy! Tell this Jew of yours that's it's impossible. Besides, it's very, very dangerous. Anyone who just begins asking too many questions on this subject puts his life in jeopardy. Believe me, I know what I'm talking about. I've read about this more than once in our papers. Tell him to forget about it."

"Well, if you hear about a Nazi called Heinz Krantz, let me know. It seems that he fled to South America."

"What? You know him too?"

"No, just from reading in the papers."

"And it said there that he'd come to Brazil?"

"No, to South America. I thought it possible that it was to your country."

"We should all just be healthy. If I hear something, I'll let you know. If my answer does the Jew any good, terrific. And if not, find something else to tell him. Stay well."

The man with the cap picked up his hands. "It's not likely my brother can do anything. He said it's impossible."

Yitzchak Austerlitz felt his world grow black.

27

Sao Paulo, Brazil
May 16, 1967

Celia nervously fingered the button summoning the service elevator. No multistoried building in Brazil was without one, intended for the use of the maids working within the various apartments. The button blinked on and off as the elevator began its descent to the ground floor where Celia was standing. Her palms felt wet and sweaty; she realized she was panicking. She was, after all, just a young girl, and she'd never faced such a difficult, frightening, and dangerous decision as she did at this moment. Why had she agreed to the greyhaired man's request? Why had she been prepared to come to the Hunkes's home? What did she need this adventure for? She had no idea if she'd get safely disentangled from it! Celia felt like crying. Suddenly she remembered her mother, living in a small village near Blumenau in the state of Santa Catarina in southern

Brazil. Her mother, her wise mother, had warned her not to move to such a large metropolis. "It's a city full of sinners, dangers, and risks," she'd said, "and a young girl without family can get into deep trouble, without even knowing how to beware of it." But Celia had so wanted to try the exciting life of the big city. And now, standing before the elevator, the warnings rang anew in her ears.

She opened the elevator door but hesitated: Should she go up, or should she flee? A voice whispered within her that the mistress of the house had already discovered that she was no mere maidservant concerned only with housekeeping, dishwashing, and dusting the furniture. The furtive, quick manner in which Regina Hunkes had hidden behind the living room window at the moment that she, Celia, had lifted her eyes from the street to the apartment had confirmed this. Who knew what that woman was capable of doing? Perhaps she'd try to murder her! Schmidt had warned her to exercise extreme caution, as the woman was very dangerous. If so, who knew what would happen to her if she went up and encountered an angry and terrifying Regina Hunkes in the apartment!

Celia made a sudden decision: With a quick step she entered the elevator. She just had to go up! All of her belongings were still in the apartment, including her listening device, portable phone, and the list of addresses and telephone numbers that she was to contact in the event of a problem or for urgent help. And particularly, her identity cards — both forged and authentic. That's all she needed, that the mistress of the house should find them! She would undoubtedly hand them over the police. And they —they would find her with no problem, and she'd be in terrible trouble. Schmidt had warned her that if she were captured he could not help her. No one would come. But he'd promised her a reward of 5,000 *cruzeiros* if she was successful. A full year's salary for a maidservant in Brazil! She had no choice. She must put herself into danger and go up, try to get the pocketbook that she'd left open in the maid's room.

The elevator stopped at the eighth floor. Warily, Celia walked out, tiptoeing. Perhaps she'd manage to get to her room, grab the purse and disappear, without Mrs. Hunkes being the wiser. Perhaps.

Celia cautiously opened the back door that led into the kitchen. She tried to hear voices in the living room. Silence. Quietly, ever so quietly, she came inside, walking towards the back porch that opened up into the small maid's room.

The purse was there where she'd left it. No one had touched it. Celia took a deep breath. Wildly she threw her few possessions inside, snapped it shut and, with quick steps headed back to the service elevator. As a gift for Schmidt, she kept the key to the apartment's back door. It would be easy for him to get in, should he so desire.

She stood still for a moment. Before closing the door behind her she tried once again to hear what was happening in the living room. Nothing. The silence was complete. The telephone rang, again and again, for some minutes; no one answered it. No door slammed; no footsteps tapped on the floor. There were no voices. Celia's every instinct announced that the apartment was empty. Could it be that Mrs. Hunkes was no longer there? Impossible. Celia discarded that foolish thought. Hadn't Mrs. Hunkes stood before the living room window not five minutes earlier, gazing at her, Celia, as she spoke to Schmidt? What was going on here?

Celia felt her curiosity growing stronger. What could it be? Was it possible that while Celia had been standing, undecided whether or not to ascend, Mrs. Hunkes had left the house? Who knew?

Celia decided to investigate. First, she made certain that the elevator was there on her floor, ready for her should she have to flee. She left her purse next to the elevator and, with swift and careful steps, made her way back to the kitchen. She knew she was endangering herself, but her curiosity overpowered her. She carefully opened the kitchen door and peeked into the living room. Mrs. Hunkes was not there. The living room was a mess: the afternoon paper draped sloppily over the sofa, the pillowcases creased as if someone had just slept on them. The recliner, which normally stood next to the picture window overlooking the street, had been moved, and the carpet pushed away. From this corner, then, the mistress of the house had watched her maidservant make a phone call …

Celia walked hesitantly into the living room.

"*Senhora* Hunkes?"

What had she done! The words had come out of her mouth as if by their own accord. A trembling fear came upon her. Why had she done it? Too late now. If the lady of the house should appear in answer to her call, Celia would have to offer an explanation right then and there. Why had she suddenly gone down to call? She would tell her she'd called her hometown, and that her uncle had informed her that Celia's mother was very ill and that she, Celia, had to return home immediately. She would, of course, explain that she was very sorry to leave such a warm, pleasant home. She would promise to return if only she could. And naturally, she would tell everyone in the village what a delightful woman Mrs. Hunkes was, a Brazilian who spoke German as they did.

But there was no answer. Celia began to calm down somewhat. It appeared that the woman had left the house through the main elevator. Celia left the living room and walked down the hallway towards the bedroom. She stood by the door. With shaky hands she grabbed the doorknob and pressed it slowly. The door opened. Celia waited. No sound. She opened the door a crack, peeked through into the room. It was empty. Regina Hunkes was not inside. Celia suddenly tensed; she felt that she was suffocating. She bit her lower lip and, with sudden decision, entered the room, ignoring the danger. Her heart beat wildly. Maybe she would manage to quickly locate the safe that so interested Schmidt, for whatever reason. She knew it was somewhere in the bedroom. If she could find it she would have completed the mission that had sent her to this house, and would earn the 5,000 *cruzeiros* that Schmidt had promised her.

Celia left the bedroom door open just a little, so that she could hear any noise or voice in the hallway. Without waiting, she began to search the room. Her nervous hands ran over the walls. She moved the dresser, looked underneath the heavy chair that stood in one corner. After a few minutes, she acknowledged defeat. Not a sign of a safe. She felt a surge of anger. Still, she wouldn't put herself in more danger. She'd give up the search. Enough. She must leave the apartment quickly. She returned to the bedroom door and opened it wide. Suddenly, she froze.

She could hear a key turning in the apartment's front door. After a moment it was opened and her ears could clearly take in the sound of Regina Hunkes's voice answering the questions put to her by the man who'd accompanied her …

Celia, stunned, trapped like a wild beast, hastily hid beneath the bed. She cursed the moment when she'd decided to go back to the apartment instead of running away. How would she get out of here? The mistress of the house would undoubtedly find her here! Celia curled up beneath the mattress, trembling with fear. She shifted her body, trying to rest more easily. After a few moments, she felt the reason for her discomfort: Half of her body was lying in a depression in the floor. Her hand ran over the floor; she felt bulges and cracks that she couldn't account for. Suddenly, a mad idea flashed through her mind. This was it! The safe! Still, because of the carpeting, she couldn't be certain. She'd have to report this to Schmidt. A frightening thought went through her: *if I get out of this alive.*

Celia tried not to move, tried not to breathe. All her attention was focused on what was going on in the living room.

"No, that's not true!"

It was her mistress's voice, answering a question.

"And yet," a man's voice said, "what do you say to this document?"

It was, apparently, the police officer.

After a moment's silence, she heard Regina answer. "I don't know. It must be a mistake."

Regina's voice trembled slightly. Celia could hear the police officer's voice. "We're talking here of the Copenhagen police, and the Interior Ministry of

Denmark! They don't know what they're talking about? Neither recognize your name."

A long minute of quiet. The police officer continued. "Would the lady be prepared to tell me where she's come from?"

"I told you! From Denmark! We're Danes! Today, we have Brazilian citizenship."

Again, the policeman's voice. "Who got you that citizenship? Who took care of it?"

The woman answered hurriedly. "A Jewish lawyer by the name of Jairo Silverman."

"Interesting," the policeman replied.

A heavy silence fell on the room. Celia took a deep breath, squeezed her eyes shut in order to concentrate on hearing. She couldn't afford to miss one word of this fascinating conversation.

The policeman spoke again. "I met with him."

"With whom?"

"The lawyer. Silverman."

The trembling in Regina Hunkes's voice was now apparent.

"How did you get to him? What did you want from him?"

"For now, I'm the one asking the questions, *Senhora*. One doesn't ask a police officer for his sources of information."

"What did he tell you? He hates me!"

"Interesting. Why do you think so?"

Regina Hunkes wouldn't answer. "What did he tell you?"

"Oh, nothing much. I discussed various documents with him. I wanted to find out how he'd obtained documents from the Danish Interior Ministry showing you to be Danish citizens, while

Denmark absolutely insists that no man by the name of Alberto Hunkes was ever a citizen, and he never flew from the Copenhagen airport to any destination in the world."

Celia clearly heard Mrs. Hunkes's voice weaken.

"And what … did he … say …"

"Jairo Silverman has confessed that he forged the document on your behalf."

The woman began to cry hysterically. "I told you he hates us! He's decided to lie about us, that Jew."

The police officer asked slowly, "That Jew?"

"Excuse me, I meant no anti-Semitism. Heavens no. The Danish are not anti-Semites."

"I understand," the police officer said. "Okay, see here, *Senhora* Hunkes. This is not what interests me. I just want to know why you are so against investigating the death, that is, the murder, of your husband. Don't you want us to capture his killers?"

"I don't know what I want. I've been so confused since the murder. I just want quiet. Yes, that's all I want … quiet."

"And if I return again in a few days, will you give me more honest answers than you've given me now?"

"I don't understand. Why are you insulting me? I've done you no harm. Why are you calling me a liar?"

"Forgive me."

"I will not forgive."

Her voice was steely hard.

The police officer asked, "Would you allow me to speak with you again in a few days? By that time I'll have received information that I need, particularly from the Argentinian police. As I understand it, you lived in Buenos Aires for a few years."

Celia heard a noise in the living room. The police officer, it seemed, had stood up.

"At the end of the week," he said, "I'll be back. We can't leave a file open like this. In the meantime, you must stay in Sao Paulo and not leave the city."

After a few moments, the police officer spoke again, in an almost offhand manner.

"You understand, ma'am, that we suspect the hand of Nazis in this."

Regina Hunkes spoke hurriedly. "Where did you get that crazy idea? What connection could we possibly have with the Nazis?"

"That's what I'm asking," the police officer replied coldly. "That's what interests me, in this investigation of ours."

The two walked to the main entrance. Now, this was her chance to flee as quickly as she could to the kitchen, and from there to the elevator … Celia stood up and dashed to the doorway. From there she sped through the hallway like a cyclone. She hoped her mistress would escort the police officer to the main elevator, and in that instant Celia would race out.

But she didn't make it.

28

Regina Hunkes grabbed Celia just as she passed by the main entrance. She began to rain blows upon her, pull her by the hair.

"You thief, you little spy, who sent you here to me?" Regina screamed, as one insane. She held her in strong arms. Suddenly, she gave her a ringing blow on the cheek. Celia felt her face burning. The pain and her anger transformed her; she became a wild thing. She knew she was fighting for her life. She kicked Regina's ankle mercilessly, trying to get out of her iron grasp. Both women breathed deeply during the fight, groaning from the pain each inflicted upon the other. Celia's one free hand managed to grab Regina Hunkes's throat. Regina gave a startled yelp of agony. Somehow Celia managed to free herself. Without a moment's hesitation she flew into the kitchen, like an arrow shot from a quiver, slamming the door behind her. Regina, enraged, raced after her, charging into the door that had been shut in her face. She opened it in a fury, and swiftly followed her quarry through the kitchen to the service elevator. Too late: Celia had bolted. She had grabbed her purse, still resting on the floor, and managed to press the button. With blazing eyes, Regina saw the elevator descend. Celia could still hear Regina's fist beating on the elevator's steel door. Celia leaned weakly against the wall. In another moment she knew she would burst into tears — tears of freedom and liberation. Suddenly, to her consternation, she heard Regina shriek into the intercom, "*Senhor zelador*, help! My maid is running away in the service elevator! She's stolen my jewelry and my money! Stop her when she gets to the lobby! Call the police! Now! I'm coming down!"

"*Si, Senhora.*"

Celia paled, engulfed in despair. She hadn't dreamed she'd be trapped like this. But she quickly recovered. She pressed the button to the second floor, left the elevator, and descended via the emergency stairwell that circled the building and let out directly into the street. She rather enjoyed the thought of the building's security man waiting for her, ready for battle, near the elevator door. Celia quickly crossed the street and threw her arm out. A taxi halted in response.

"Please," she said excitedly to the driver of the GAC which had screeched to a stop near the curb, "please take me as quickly as possible to Gabriel Monteiro da Silva Street. Number 12. That's right, via Reboucas Boulevard."

Celia hoped with all her heart that she'd find Schmidt there, or one of his assistants at least. And next time, she swore to herself, she wouldn't agree to such dangerous adventures. Not for all the money in the world …

Jairo's entire body trembled. He had just hung up the phone, after having refused the order that the mysterious caller had given him. Again, fear of an unknown enemy overtook him. He could feel himself faltering. The man's threats had the ring of truth. What would happen to his wife, his children, if the Nazi murderers reached him? His fear was paralyzing: He sat, motionless, in his office, staring mindlessly at the ceiling. He had no idea how much time passed. Suddenly, he saw the skies outside darken as a pounding rain began to fall. It must be 5 o'clock, Jairo realized, the hour that Sao Paulo more or less regularly enjoyed its refreshing shower from heaven, a shower that washed away the day's dust and grime. It must be late, then.

Jairo stood up heavily. His legs were barely responding, he noted. He felt a deep weariness in his entire body. Perhaps he should ask for police protection? Jairo gave a cold, silent laugh. He knew exactly how much that protection was worth in the face of such threats. What to do? Again, he made his characteristic gesture of impatience and frustration: His left hand balled up into a hard fist, slamming into his right hand.

What to do? What to do?

Jairo lifted the telephone receiver, without a clue as to whom he would call. After a second, he replaced it on the hook. He walked over to the small aquarium in a corner of the office, stared at the tiny fish swimming leisurely and peacefully to and fro. His nerves were frayed. For no reason at all he shook the aquarium. The fish, terrified, began to swim quickly and nervously from side to side, as if trying to hang onto the walls. Jairo stared in at them. *Like me*, he thought, *panicking and frightened by something they can't understand.* He gave the aquarium one more wicked shake. *Actually, they're like all the Jews — particularly those who went through the Holocaust!*

And so he came back, without knowing it, to the thought of the Nazis. Infuriating, how much they had managed to infiltrate into his quiet, serene life here. They were threatening him here in Sao Paulo, more than 25 years after the Holocaust had ended, thousands of kilometers from his father's Buchenwald. How naive his good father had been, thinking that here in Brazil, at the end of the world, far, far from Europe, he could free himself and his son from the Jewish destiny, from hatred. What innocence!

Jairo walked over to the large window that looked down on the teeming center of the city. The rain was still coming down hard. From his high-rise office he could see the people, looking so small on the Viaduto do Cha, the city's famed bridge, running for shelter from the downpour. They ran here and there like ants, easily crushed beneath the gigantic heel of a man — just like the fish in his aquarium. "Here is all of Jewish history," he said quietly, as he held his face to the window, his eyes following the people downstairs. "To run back and forth. Always, to run. To look for shelter after shelter. Never to find peace. Thousands of years, never to find peace. And there's no end! It still hasn't ended! Perhaps it will never end! Despite the hopes. Despite the dreams. Here again, in *terra sancta*, the Holy Land, a new war threatens the Jews. Again, the Arabs are choking the land. What's the reason for this Jewish lot that one cannot escape, not in the farthest reaches of the earth? Why the Jews?"

His despair deepened. He was a Jew. He felt like a Jew. "But what is it? Is it biological? Because I was born that way? Because ... because ... what's happening to me? Should I be afraid of the Nazis, as my father was afraid of them?" Jairo felt his fragmented thoughts begin to unite, to coalesce into one great feeling of fury. "Why should I have to be something that I don't understand or know?" This infuriated him more than anything else: He couldn't understand the fact of his being Jewish. But another fact was glaring: His father had lost the battle, had been defeated! His son, Jairo, couldn't live in tranquility in the good land of Brazil, far removed from the memories of the death camps. Here, too, the Nazis were on his trail! How could he tell his father these things? And what would happen? Should he flee Brazil? To where? Wherever he went, these things could happen, for he was a Jew ...

He returned to his desk. His hand went to the phone; almost automatically, he dialed the number.

"Pa. It's Jairo. Is everything all right? *Gracas a Deus.* I'm still in the office. Why? That's how it is at times, at work. I'm coming to you directly from the office. No, nothing's happened. I want to talk about something. About the war in the Middle East. Does it worry you, Pa? Try to be calm, okay? That's right, I'm coming alone. *Chau.*"

Schmidt stood near the cafe, pondering his next step. He lit a cigarette in an effort to relax, covering his face with both hands in order to shelter the flame from the wind. The gesture also gave him the chance to cast a searching glance at the unknown man standing next to his car. The worst thing, from Schmidt's perspective, would be to give any indication that he suspected anything. He didn't recognize the man, though it seemed he'd seen him somewhere before. Had someone in the city found out his true identity and sent an agent to trail him? Not a very bright agent, it seemed. Schmidt couldn't be certain. Though that theory seemed a bit farfetched, Schmidt knew he must exercise extreme caution.

Schmidt took a few steps towards his automobile. His face was a mask of nonchalance, though his every sense was alert, carefully scrutinizing each move of the well-dressed man who leaned on his car. Schmidt could see the man's Middle Eastern features. An Arab, it seemed.

29

S chmidt bit his lip. Who was the Arab standing
next to his car?

He continued to walk, with calculated slow-
ness, along the sidewalk. Long years spent
living under forged identities on alien soil, far from his
homeland, had taught him well the rules of caution and
the many ways one could "lose" unwanted shadowers.
He plowed a way through the hordes of pedestrians
walking on Paulista Avenue. But instead of going directly to his car he changed direction and turned to the
crosswalk. He waited impatiently for the light to
change. And then he zoomed forward, together with
the others, to the sidewalk on the left.

There he stood before an attractively arranged shop
window looking, by all accounts, at the leather hand-
bags displayed there. Actually, he was carefully
scrutinizing the passersby, watching their reflections in

the window, that glittered like a mirror. His professional gaze searched for suspicious characters, for figures who might follow him as he approached the anonymous Arab who continued to stand next to his car. Again, it seemed to him that he'd seen him somewhere before. He searched his memory, to no avail. His sharp eyes and finely honed senses could see nothing untoward.

Schmidt walked over to a newsstand nearby and bought the evening paper, *Journal da Tarde*. Screaming headlines announced, "Danger of War in Middle East!" He then returned to the sidewalk near his car. He approached it, his head bent into the newspaper, concealed behind its large tabloid pages. One eye, though, looked searchingly at the Arab, waiting to see his reaction. Would the mysterious stranger recognize him or not? Nothing. The man didn't react at all. It seemed he was simply staring at the passersby, not looking for anyone in particular. What did it mean?

He would not take any risks, Schmidt decided. He approached his automobile. When he was face to face with the stranger he pulled his head out of the newspaper that concealed him and asked, in strict and authoritative tones, "Who are you? What are you doing next to my car?"

Standing so close to him, Schmidt knew, would make it impossible for the stranger to draw a gun, if he had such plans.

The unknown man was startled. The sudden, direct question surprised him.

"Excuse me," he said, "I saw you leave your car and quickly parked my own, in order to speak with you. But you disappeared into one of the cafes in the area, and by the time I caught up with you I couldn't find where you'd gone. I decided, therefore, to wait for you here."

Schmidt was not pleased with the response. His tension grew, and he drew even closer to the unknown man.

"Yes, but who are you?"

"Don't you remember me?"

"No, I don't. Give me an answer. Fast."

Schmidt's rough words angered the man. "I'm Paulo Chilo, from the office of Silverman, Machado, and Chilo. And even if you don't recognize me, this tone is not appropriate for you, a representative of GAC! You know me — we met yesterday in the restaurant on the Paulista. You GAC executives spoke with me and my partner, Francisco Machado. Don't you remember?"

Schmidt's tension eased; he suddenly felt lighter. He felt a surge of anger against himself: How could he have allowed himself to fall prey to vague fears and nebulous imaginings? He gave a big smile. "You're right. I ask your pardon. I didn't recognize you at first. I didn't like the way you were standing in front of my car."

"Sure, I understand. And I apologize."

"For nothing. And what would you like to speak about with me?"

Paulo hesitated, then said, "I've been looking for *Senhor* Von Dorfman, of Germany, for the past few hours."

Schmidt's face hardened. "What do you need him for?"

"In reference to the contract with GAC."

Schmidt opened the car door. "Forget about it, my friend. GAC is no longer interested in that contract."

Schmidt dropped down into the seat. But he didn't manage to get the door closed. Paulo Chilo grabbed his arm and cried, "One minute! I don't understand! What happened since our meeting yesterday?"

"Nothing happened. We are no longer interested in signing a contract with your firm."

"What do you mean, my firm? I'm no longer in partnership with the Jew Silverman! Where's Von Dorfman? He promised that if I came alone, I'd get the contract. I'm not giving it up!"

"So don't give it up. It will get you nowhere."

Schmidt attempted to free himself from the man who was rapidly becoming a pest. But Paulo grabbed the car door.

"Where's Von Dorfman?"

"Returned to Germany."

"When?"

"This morning."

Paulo grew silent, engulfed in despair. Inside, he cursed both Jews and Germans together. Because of the enmity between the two he was out an enormous amount of money! The injustice of it!

Schmidt felt Chilo's frustration. He looked for some words to calm him so that he would get his hands off the car and allow him to depart.

"Understand, *Senhor*," Schmidt said in a softer voice, "Von Dorfman has appointed me to deal with all GAC business. And I've told you the truth. We've already contacted another law firm."

"But why?" Paulo shouted. "What's wrong with us?"

Schmidt laughed. "You're more professional, perhaps, than the firm we contacted this morning. But they don't make trouble for us as you do."

Paulo didn't understand. "What kind of trouble?"

Schmidt gave a chilly smile. "Your Jew."

Paulo swallowed hard. "What do you care about him? I've come to you as an individual! I haven't yet told Jairo Silverman of my plans to leave the firm, but my mind is made up."

Schmidt made a dismissive gesture. "Fine. I understand. What has that to do with me, or with GAC?"

"It does! It does! Absolutely! You've got to help me. I too, like you, am against Jairo Silverman the Jew!"

Schmidt gave him a scornful glance. "Why are you accusing GAC of anti-Semitism?"

"Pardon me. Perhaps it's not anti-Semitism. But you've hinted quite broadly that you don't want him as your attorney."

Schmidt got out of his car and drew himself up to his full stature. He was a full head taller than Chilo. Now he'd make himself absolutely clear — and perhaps gain something from this curious conversation in the middle of the city.

"Pardon me, Mr. Attorney. We have no objection to a Jewish attorney. GAC is extremely careful not to show any form of discrimination on the basis of race or religion. Are you making an accusation against us in order to blackmail us into signing a contract?"

Paulo took a deep breath. He would give up the contract, but he wouldn't let Schmidt part, victorious, from this conversation.

"You can't deny that you insisted that Jairo Silverman no longer represent you as attorney! Von Dorfman clearly stated it! Give me his number in Germany, if you please."

"You won't get his number. Today, I am the official representative of GAC in Brazil. I haven't been told that I'm being transferred to Germany. With reference to your libelous statements in the affair of the Jewish attorney, you are acting as though you didn't know that Silverman is currently damaging the firm by the private investigation that he's carrying on. That is the problem, sir. Do you understand?"

"Do you refer to the fact that he wants to find out who was the Nazi from GAC who was murdered?"

Schmidt stood even straighter, and his eyes narrowed. He thrust his hands into his pockets, trying to control his growing rage. "I see another libel against GAC issuing from your office," he hissed quietly. "Why are you so sure that Alberto Hunkes was a Nazi? Has Jairo Silverman poisoned your mind too?"

Paulo didn't rush to respond. He looked over the man from head to toe. Yes, it was clear that the man was a German. His features proclaimed his origin. On his virile face, a face in which courage and authority were manifest, one could clearly see a scar. *Probably wounded in the Second World War*, the thought flashed through Chilo's brain. One could assume he had been a soldier in Hitler's army; otherwise, he would never have reached the heights of power in the German automobile company. Paulo tried to make a swift assessment of the situation. A quick evaluation showed him there was nothing more to be done. He'd lost the contract. Cutting himself away from Jairo Silverman wouldn't help him. He had nothing to lose; he could tell this German everything he knew and thought about him.

"Pardon me, my dear German friend. We are not talking about the silly imaginings of Jairo Silverman. My partner, Francisco Machado, testified that at Hunkes's funeral you, too, marched as a Nazi. I'm not certain, but I believe he heard you whisper the words 'Heil Hitler'!"

Paulo didn't take his eyes off the grey-haired man. He wanted to see how he'd react to this frontal attack. But Schmidt kept his cool, as he made an overture of peace.

"And you're telling me you've cut off your ties with Jairo Silverman?"

Schmidt held his hand out to Paulo and continued. "I think, *Senhor*, that the business connection between us is ended. You can begin them anew only in one way: if you can, today, succeed in silencing Jairo Silverman so that he gives up his investigation into Alberto Hunkes's identity. That's all. If you do so, I'll even forgive the insult of the behavior you attributed to me during the funeral of my friend Alberto."

Schmidt wheeled around and quickly got into his car. He could hear Paulo's surprised voice calling after him, "What do you want me to do? Kill him?"

Schmidt gave a smile and, from the car window, called out nonchalantly, "There are many ways, my young friend!"

The GAC car screeched away and was soon lost in the flow of traffic on the Consolacao.

Bnei Brak, Israel
6 Iyar 5727

Yitzchak Austerlitz quietly escorted the man in the cap to the door. The death of his hopes of uncovering Heinz Krantz had dealt him a devastating blow.

"I'm sorry," the man said, "maybe I'll try speaking to my brother again in a week."

He could clearly see the tears in Austerlitz's eyes.

"I don't know what happened to him, to my brother. He's always calmer than he was today, and always helps me out when I ask for something. I can't understand what happened. Maybe in Brazil they're portraying our situation here worse than it is."

After a moment's thought, he added, "We'll try again in a week."

The door closed behind him. Yitzchak Austerlitz listened as he descended the stairs heavily. Then Yitzchak walked slowly, very slowly, with a defeated tread, towards the kitchen. Rivka sat there, in the same position she'd been in when he'd left her to call Brazil. It seemed to him that he could see a spark of fear in her eyes. Yes, he realized, she was afraid of what would happen to him.

Sao Paulo, Brazil
May 16, 1967

Regina Hunkes hurried down in the main elevator to the ground floor. In her mind's eye she could see herself tearing her maidservant into pieces, the maid who'd captured her with her innocent smile, and who'd been revealed as a dangerous traitor. She would get out of her, even before the police would arrive, the name of the person who'd sent her to spy and snoop in Regina's house. A sudden fear overwhelmed her: Had the young woman paid special attention to the place where her safe was secreted?

On the ground floor Regina raced wildly to the service elevator. She hoped desperately that the security guard had managed to stop Celia and was holding on to her.

But the *zelador* stood before her empty handed.

"I'm sorry, ma'am, she didn't come out of the elevator. I've been standing here the entire time. The elevator came, but it was empty."

"Idiot! What do you mean, empty? Tell the truth! How much did she give you to let her go?"

The *zelador*'s eyes were beseeching. "I swear I didn't see her at all! She didn't give me a cent! I swear by all that's holy!"

"No one will accept such a stupid excuse. I'll see to it that you're fired, do you understand, you dumb Brazilian!"

Regina turned back to the elevator. The unfortunate *zelador* ran after her, and grabbed her by the hand.

"*Por favor, Senhora,*" he said, "have mercy on me. Truly, I'm not guilty! I didn't see her, and I have young children at home ..."

Regina pushed him away harshly. She walked into the elevator. She must flee, she knew, as soon as she could. Leave the city. The maid's treachery, the coming police investigation, all pushed her into the inescapable decision.

She walked into her apartment, pulled out a large valise, and began to haphazardly fling clothing into it. Then she moved the bed, pulled out her key ring, and pushed aside the carpet. Naturally, she'd take the entire contents of the safe with her ...

A sharp ring broke through the silence in the apartment. Regina jumped up. Should she answer or not? Who could it be? After a moment, her curiosity got the better of her, and she picked up the receiver.

"Good evening." She could hear the voice of her husband's grey-haired friend from GAC. "What's new? Is everything all right?"

Regina felt her strength leave her. She burst into tears. The grey-haired man was one of the friends they'd always been able to rely on.

"Hermann," she said. "Hermann Schmidt, is that you?"

"Yes, it's me. How are you?"

She was silent for a moment, and then whispered, "Hermann, I can't take any more! Can you come here now? I need help urgently."

Schmidt smiled to himself. Then he said, in a worried voice, "What's happened? Of course! I'll be right over."

30

Sao Paulo, Brazil
May 16, 1967

Jairo Silverman's Arrow-Willis drove slowly
through the Sao Paulo streets. The distance from
his office, in the center of town, in a skyscraper
near the famed Viaduto do Cha bridge, to his father's home on Julio Conceicao Street in the Bom
Retiro neighborhood was a short one. But the heavy
flow of traffic made progress slow. Finally, he
reached the jammed bridge that crossed the railroad
tracks, a bridge that acted as an unofficial borderline
between the center of the city and Bom Retiro. Here,
in this neighborhood, he'd spent his childhood
years. It was a Jewish area, with no particular beauty
or claim to fame, compared to others in Sao Paulo.
He'd first gone to the Renaissance School, a Jewish
institution whose principal, married to a non-Jew,
had preached intermarriage. The school had a tenu-
ous connection with Israel: There was a minor

celebration of Israel's Independence Day, with the blue and white flag waved during the ceremony. Jairo well remembered his father's anger over it: "I don't want," he had said in a fury, "for you to study in such a religious school, where they wave Israel's flag all day long!"

He'd transferred to the Dante Alighieri School, one of the best high schools in the city. Up until last week, Jairo had felt deep gratitude to his father for providing a top-notch education, an education that ensured his entry into the upper echelons of Brazilian life, where he now resided. But since the Hunkes affair, and the emotions that had swept over him these past few days, Jairo wasn't sure that he hadn't missed something by not studying in a Jewish school. At the moment of crisis, as he stood before the grave of his Danish (was he really Danish?) friend, near a Nazi ceremony taking place before his eyes, he had felt so weak, so powerless, so insignificant. He understood nothing. An inner voice whispered to him that if he knew more about being Jewish he would be able to bear it more easily. Perhaps a Jewish school, Jewish friends, would have given him the knowledge and the strength that were so lacking now. But perhaps not. What, after all, did his friends in the Renaissance School know of their Jewishness? Absolutely nothing!

Jairo parked the car near his father's house. He ran lightly up the wide staircase that reached the building's ornate entrance door, smiled in greeting to the guard who was hurrying to open the elevator door for him.

"Thanks," Jairo told the guard, who knew that such small favors endeared him to the building's residents.

The maid opened the door. Jairo gave her a nod and entered. His father was sitting in the living room, glued to the television.

"Good evening, Pa."

His father didn't answer, didn't even raise his head. He simply gestured to his son to sit down next to him. Jairo did as he was bid. His eyes, too, took in the images on the screen: long rows of soldiers marching in time. Then the smiling, satisfied face of the president of Egypt, Gamel Abdul Nasser. Again, rows of tanks in military exercises; warplanes zipping through the skies; the contented face of General Amar, head of the Egyptian army; and mobs in Cairo calling for *jihad*, holy war against the Jews. Difficult images to watch. Jairo felt his tension rising. No, this was more than tension: This was fear, fear of what might happen, there in the Middle East, there in Israel …

The two listened to the eager voice of the television commentator:

"The clouds of war are gathering in the Middle Eastern skies! The crisis grows deeper; the smell of gunpowder fills the air! The president of Egypt has demanded that the Secretary-General of the United Nation, U Thant, remove U.N. forces from the Sinai Desert and the Straits of Tiran. Political observers in the U.N. declare that tonight the Secretary-General will accede to the request. From Cairo, reports say that the next step will be to close the Straits to Israeli shipping in order to cut off the Port of Eilat. Jerusalem is in a panic, the Israeli government shocked and confused. The sound of saber-rattling can be heard throughout the Arab lands!"

Jairo looked at his father, saw him crying. It was at moments like these, Jairo thought, that his father returned, in his mind, to the death camps. For some reason Jairo remembered the Hunkes funeral.

His father stood up. With a slow step he walked to the television and shut it off. He returned and sat down in the soft armchair, fear in his eyes. The fear of the camps.

"What will be, Jairo?" he said, his voice cracking.

Jairo lit a cigarette. "I don't know."

"When will they let us live in peace?"

Jairo's father gave a deep sigh. Jairo inhaled; he remained quiet. The maid brought a tray bearing glasses and a few bottles — *guarana, agua tonica,* and Coca-Cola. For Jairo, who was a confirmed beer drinker, she included a bottle of *Brahma.*

Jairo poured his father a cup of *guarana,* and took Coke for himself. The beer could wait. They sipped in silence. The only sound in the apartment was that of the maid washing up in the kitchen. Finally Jairo spoke.

"Who?"

His father took another drink. "What do you mean, who?"

"You said, 'When will they let us live in peace?'. I'm asking who you meant."

His father placed his cup on the tray and gave his son a dark glance. He asked him, in Yiddish, "What's the matter with you? I meant the Jews in Israel!"

Jairo was quiet. He had to muster all his courage to continue. Finally he said, "And here in Brazil, here they let us live?"

His father's eyes showed his surprise. "What kind of question is that? You're comparing what's happening in Israel to our lives here in Brazil?"

Again, silence. But Jairo's father's instincts were awakened. He gave his son a searching glance. "Has something happened, Jairo?"

Jairo didn't rush to respond. He finished the Coke in his cup, placed his cigarette in the bronze ashtray that stood in the center of the coffee table.

"No," he said with attempted nonchalance, "no, nothing special has happened. Why do you think so?"

But his voice didn't ring true, not even to his own ears.

His father rubbed his forehead, licked his lips and nodded his head back and forth, trying to analyze his son's answer. Trying to understand what he'd said — and what he'd held back. He knew his son was hiding something …

Schmidt was satisfied. He'd waited for this moment a long time. Hurriedly he left the offices of GAC; despite the fact that he was no longer young, it took just a few minutes for him to reach his car in the huge company parking lot and roar off towards Piaui Street, to the home of Regina Hunkes.

He knew she was under pressure; it was up to him to ease that pressure and calm her down. Who knew what had happened during the police officer's interrogation? Just so that she shouldn't flee the city before he'd found the treasure he'd been seeking for so long.

Schmidt reached the beginning of the Angelica. If the traffic lights would only work for once, and the cursed traffic jam ease, he could be at her house in 10 minutes. Despite the friendship that had existed between him and her husband, Alberto, Schmidt had never been in the Hunkes apartment. The family guarded their privacy closely, and only infrequently invited colleagues over to their home. Surveillance of the Hunkes home during the year before Alberto's death had shown mysterious men sneaking into the

Hunkes's house, not during the hours normally fixed for social calls. Now, the opportunity was his — and he would grab it!

Schmidt rang the doorbell impatiently. Regina opened it quickly. Schmidt could see her eyes, puffy and red. Without waiting for a polite greeting, he cried, "What's happened? Tell me! Has someone harmed you? You know that GAC will stand by your side!"

"Hermann, I simply can't take anymore. I'm convinced they're following me. They've managed to get into my house!"

"Who?" Schmidt asked quickly.

"I wish I knew!"

Regina walked into the spacious living room and dropped down into a chair. She rested her cheek in her hand.

Schmidt clearly saw her despair. He leaned against the arm of one of the chairs, stooping towards her. "Can you tell me what happened? We can try to help."

"I had a maid here for a few hours...and she was a spy! I'm sure of it!"

Schmidt felt a thrill go through him, like an electric charge to the heart. It was Celia she was speaking of, Celia, whom he had sent to this very house. What had happened to Celia? Had she disobeyed her instructions? Where was she now?

He didn't dare ask the questions whose answers were so vital to him.

"You're being overly emotional, Regina."

"I wish you were right! After a small argument that cropped up between us, she asked to go down to the street to get some air. I didn't tell her a thing. I was worried about the police officer who was on his way here, and I strolled over to the window facing the street. And there she was, my maid, talking on the public phone. She was scared; she kept looking around her, particularly at my window, to see if anyone was paying attention to her."

Schmidt took a deep breath. He well remembered the conversation: Celia had been speaking to him.

"And what happened then?" Schmidt asked, worry edging his voice.

"At that moment I decided to run away! I was sure she was spying on me! Something inside told me so. Can you understand, Hermann?"

"Of course, certainly," he said, in a soft, sympathetic tone.

Where was Celia now, a voice repeated within him. *Just hope that Regina hadn't given her into the hands of the police!*

Schmidt stood up and began to pace the room. After a moment he returned to Regina.

"What happened to your maid, finally?"

"I told you I decided to run away. But the police officer met me in the lobby and made me come back here for his nasty, wicked questioning. When he finally left I grabbed her, the maid, leaving my bedroom. Do you understand that, Hermann — from my bedroom!"

"I think … I think I understand," he said in a quiet voice, although his tension was mounting by the second. "And … what happened then?"

"She managed to get away! She's disappeared!"

Schmidt looked up, startled. "That's terrible!" he said, after a moment of silence. Inside, he felt a great relief. Perhaps Celia had gathered information in the bedroom in the Hunkes home.

Regina stood up. Her face was hard and immovable. "Hermann, I've decided to run away now. To get out of Sao Paulo, that I've loved so well. I'm afraid that my end will be like that of my husband; I'm afraid of the lieutenant as well. Enough! I don't want any more of this! I'm going back to Germany!"

"Germany?"

"Yes, Germany! I don't care who knows. We're not Danes! Just help me. Alberto worked long and faithfully in the business; I deserve your help. I'm sure you'll stand by me, and get what's coming to me from the firm."

Schmidt made no reply. What should he do now? At all costs, he must prevent her escape!

"Why don't you answer me, Hermann? Won't you help me?"

"Of course, why do you think I won't do my best?" he stammered.

He hardly heard Regina's answer. He searched desperately for a trick, a scheme that would keep this woman in the city, at least for the next few days. Until the professionals could complete their work.

Suddenly, he had an idea ...

Bnei Brak, Israel
6 Iyar 5727

"Don't be afraid, Rivka. Nothing will happen to me."

Yitzchak Austerlitz said the words with his voice trembling. He stood in the kitchen next to his wife, who was sitting on one of the wooden stools wringing her hands.

"Don't worry," he continued, "perhaps tonight's attempt has healed me. I see I won't succeed. The failure of the phone call to Brazil has shown me that

I don't stand a chance. It was a stupid idea, to think that I could find the murderer of my wife and children! I can't understand how such an idea captured my brain, my soul, for such a long time. I admit defeat. I accept G-d's decree with all my heart. May His Name be blessed from now and eternally!"

He said the words with deep feeling, and then added, "I shall continue to mourn, though, in my heart."

Rivka didn't answer. Again, tears flowed down her face. She didn't know why she was crying; she only knew she couldn't stop.

And then she heard Yitzchak's voice, calmer now. "I will tell you everything. All that's happened to me ..."

31

Bnei Brak, Israel
6 Iyar 5727

Yitzchak pulled the stool over towards the small kitchen table and sat down. He looked intently into his wife's face, into her downcast eyes. He sighed and spoke.

"The dreams, the dreams caused it all."

His voice broke.

"Almost every night they came to me until there were nights when I begged G-d not to let me sleep. I could take no more."

Rivka listened carefully to the choppy sentences. Her husband, she saw, was speaking through tears.

"In all the dreams I returned to the village. I was standing next to my house. That's all I ever dreamed about. I never saw Auschwitz. I don't understand why not. Hadn't I seen the pit of *gehinnom* open there, day after day? And what's happened to me these past years has happened only because I thought I understood how to interpret my dream."

Yitzchak grew quiet. Rivka couldn't understand a word of what he'd said. She realized that after such a long time of being closed in upon himself, enveloped by his own self-imposed silence, he now felt the need to speak ceaselessly.

"I saw them every day, in a dream. They ... my young family. My wife ... my children ... I saw them standing, staring at me with beseeching eyes. Eyes that screamed, ' Save us!' I ran towards them ... but they grew further and further away and were gone ... I ran faster ... and they flew away from me ... from moment to moment they grew smaller ... until they were lost on the horizon and only their eyes ... their pleading eyes ... grew larger and larger with each moment, until they covered the entire sky ... I reached my arm out to them ... I called to them ... no, I didn't call ... I screamed like a wounded animal, 'Come to me! I am your father! I am Yitzchak Austerlitz ... your father ... father ... father ...' "

A heavy silence descended upon the kitchen. A thick silence, like the blackness of Egypt, that one could almost feel with one's hands. Rivka, whose tears lay wetly on her face, could hear her husband's labored breathing but she, too, was in the unshakeable grip of silence.

"And then — they disappeared into the sky, that had turned black ... Suddenly a hand appeared from among them, a white hand that grasped my finger ... a warm hand, a good hand, a tiny hand that held on so tightly to me. And in my dream, I saw myself say, ' This must be the hand of my Yaakov Yehoshua.' It was so good to hold that hand ...

"Suddenly — it disappeared. And I stood alone, in the doorway of the empty house. Above me, the sky filled with the face of the murderer. Today I finally know his name. Heinz Krantz. All the sky turned into the satanic face. A cruel face, staring at me and taunting me, in a voice that rolled through the sky like thunder ...

"And I would awaken ... drenched in sweat ... and perhaps tears ... I don't know ...

"This dream recurred tens of times. Returned again and again, with such power, as if it had actually happened ..."

Yitzchak stood up, approached the kitchen window that looked out onto the building's yard and opened it. He felt he must release himself from his oppression with a look at the heavens. He stared at the canopy of sky, dark now with the blackness of night, sown with twinkling summer stars. For a moment he felt his depression lift, but suddenly panic seized him. He pulled his eyes away from the deep sky and quickly slammed the window shut. The skies, in his dream, were always the skies of Heinz Krantz. No, he couldn't enjoy the vision.

"Hadn't you noticed how many nights I would get out of bed and restlessly pace the living room?"

Rivka didn't answer. Her head still was heavy with pain. But she nodded, as if to say yes.

"I couldn't find peace in my soul," he continued. "I didn't know what to do with myself. Even chapters of *Tehillim* which I recited during those late nights didn't calm me. And yet I felt G-d's closeness, knew that He was with me, even in the valley of death of my heart and soul. But peace and serenity would not return to me. ' Why?' I was tortured by the question. 'Why is this happening to me? What does this dream mean, this dream that returns so faithfully to haunt me?

What is it trying to tell me? Yaakov Yehoshua's hand clings to me. The murderer's face stares at me from the sky. What can it mean?' "

Another moment of heavy silence.

"I don't know when it happened. But one day I decided that it seemed that heaven wanted me to find the murderer. Just like Eichmann. I don't know why I got such a crazy idea. Truly — I don't know. It seems to me madness now. But from the minute it was fixed in my mind, it wouldn't leave me. I went to the Eichmann trial many times. I wanted to see for myself, prove that it was possible, possible to find the criminals and look them straight in their filthy eyes. I wanted to see my own personal Eichmann. I wanted to see my murderer standing there, as Eichmann did, standing before judgment. I believed that this was the reason for my wild nightly dreams. Only one thing I didn't understand …"

Yitzchak's breath seemed to come more heavily; he began to wheeze. Rivka lifted her head, startled.

"Yitzchak, what's the matter?"

Yitzchak didn't answer. He tried to continue his story.

"I didn't understand … I didn't understand …what it meant …the hand … the white hand … of Yaakov Yehoshua … my Yaakov Yehoshua …"

Rivka managed to catch him just as he fell to the floor, in a dead faint.

Sao Paulo, Brazil
May 16, 1967

Jairo pulled the cover off the bottle of beer. He poured it out slowly, watching the foamy head drip over the top of the glass and onto the saucer. His father didn't take his eyes off him.

Jairo took a long sip of the chilled beer. He licked his lower lip, grinned at his father. It seemed to his father, though, that there was bitterness in the smile.

"What's the matter, Jairo?" he repeated his question.

Wordlessly, Jairo gulped down another drink. He searched for the right words.

"*Nu*, speak already!" his father urged him with obvious impatience and increasing curiosity.

"Do you remember Alberto Hunkes?"

His father's eyes showed astonishment. "Of course. What kind of question is that?"

"He's dead."

"What does that mean: He's dead?"

"Exactly what I said. Dead. Actually, murdered."

Jairo's father shifted uncomfortably in his chair. He seemed agitated.

"I don't understand. Who murdered him?"

"It's not clear yet."

"I'm really sorry. He was a good man."

"No. He was a Nazi!"

His father looked at him, astonished. "What's the matter with you? He was so pleasant. And he was always interested in stories about Buchenwald and the Holocaust."

Jairo finally told his father everything: the ceremony in the cemetery, the mysterious phone calls that had been coming this past week.

Jairo finished the bottle of beer. He looked at his father with interest. It didn't seem that the news of Hunkes's Nazi past had disturbed him overmuch.

"Do you understand, Pa? Everything came back to me!"

"What do you mean?"

"I feel like a Jew. You wanted to keep it from me. But it was no use."

His father sat silent. Jairo added, trying to sound offhand, "But I don't know what a Jew is."

"What does that matter? A Jew is a Jew! That's all. That's the way it is. What's so important anyway?"

His son's interest worried him. In Brazil he had hoped to put it all behind him. If he was forced to carry the past in his heart, an open, unhealed wound, at the very least his son and grandchildren would live far, far from this terrible burden.

"Yet it seems to me that it is important," Jairo answered hurriedly. "If I knew … it … it would be easier for me to deal with Alberto's foul treachery. I think I would also feel stronger, better able to deal with the threats that the anti-Semites have been making these past few days. I don't know, that's just how I feel."

"Forget about Hunkes's identity and they'll let you alone. You yourself are causing these troubles! What are you, a lawyer or a detective?"

Jairo jumped up. "That's exactly the point, Pa. I can't stop! Something inside me, stronger than I am, is pushing me to continue. And it's clear to me that it springs from some search after my own identity. I never felt myself a Jew, not the way I've felt these past few days. What is it, Pa?"

His father made a gesture of dismissal. "Maybe you'll even wind up going to the synagogue! What would your mother, may she rest in peace, have said to these strange ideas that have suddenly come into your head?"

"I never thought of such a thing. The synagogue? What are you talking about? But in any case, what are you so afraid of? Didn't your father, your grandfather go to synagogue?"

"Enough, already!"

"No, Pa, it's not enough. For the first time in my life, I've really felt anti-Semitism. I've felt what it's like to be a Jew, pursued by those who hate me. It's terrible! But what makes it even more terrible is the fact that I don't know why anti-Semites hate us. I want to understand why."

After a moment's thought, he added, "And you see, it's the same thing again in Israel. Again, we're pursued. Again, they want to kill Jews. Again, declarations of war. Why should you be so shocked that I want to understand it?"

His father had lost his patience, and spoke in a way which infuriated Jairo.

"I'm not a philosopher. I want things to go well with you. That you shouldn't go through what I did."

"I, too, want things to be good. And because of that, I think it's important for me to know, to understand. Only knowledge will give me strength against these Nazis."

His father flung out his hands and said, "I haven't got the solution to your problems."

Schmidt gave Regina Hunkes a smile. "I agree that it would be a good idea to leave the country. To go somewhere in the world where you're wanted. Let it be Germany, Denmark. But — wait a few days."

"But Hermann, why not now? What do I have to do here in Sao Paulo? I'm sure you can send me my pension anywhere."

"Of course we will. GAC doesn't abandon its employees and their families. But understand, your Alberto was not just another worker. Correct? Alberto was responsible for all marketing and we owe him, in part at least, for the success of our South American operation. GAC has decided to hold a memorial ceremony for him in the Teatro Municipal. You're familiar with that lovely hall?"

Regina nodded.

"Everyone who's anyone in the city will be there. The mayor, senators, and others. How can you miss it? Patience, Regina. Just a few more days ...And afterwards, you can go wherever you want. We'll be sorry if you leave, of course, but we'll respect your wishes. Is that okay?"

Regina didn't react. The desire to honor her husband was strong within her. But her fear of the police, and of the mysterious others who'd sent Celia after her, was greater.

"I understand, Hermann. But I'm afraid ... "

Schmidt laughed. "You have nothing to hide, have you? You or Alberto?"

Regina felt a twinge of panic, which she tried frantically to hide under a mask of nonchalance.

"No, of course not. Our lives were clean slates. But I feel something happening around me. I don't understand it, but I know it's there."

"It's clear to me that this is all coming from an overactive imagination. The trauma you've been through is causing fantasy to conquer your reason. But I have an idea. Come with me now, I'll take you to the Excelsior Hotel on Ipiranga Street. On GAC's bill, of course. I'll deal with the bookkeeping department. You've got nothing to worry about. Will you come?"

Regina didn't answer. The veiled pressure behind his smooth words roused nebulous suspicions within her.

"Hermann, do you have a cigarette?"

Schmidt quickly passed her one and lit it for her. Regina inhaled deeply, immersed in thought, her eyes glued to the wall.

Schmidt looked at her tranquilly, working hard to hide his tension as he awaited her answer …

Eduardo had travel fever. This would be his first overseas trip as a journalist, his first to a trouble spot. He was excited. His apartment was a mess: suits, shirts, pants scattered on the bed, ready to be folded with military precision into his suitcase. He mustn't forget his Olivetti portable typewriter that went everywhere with him. And of course he couldn't leave behind the books on Israel that he'd bought on his way home from the office in one of the bookstores on Avinida Sao Luis. This trip, he was sure, would considerably enhance his prestige in the paper. He felt the joy of action, of adventure that might even be dangerous, if war should break out. As it looked now, there was a good chance of it. The trip had come as a complete surprise. Who knew what other surprises awaited him?

In two hours he was to be at the Congonhas Airport. From there he'd travel via Rio de Janeiro on Varig's night flight to Paris. After a short layover, he'd board an El Al flight to Tel Aviv. He had chosen to use an Israeli company; perhaps even on board he'd be able to sense the feelings of the besieged country and its citizens.

Oh yes, despite everything, he must call his mother. Despite his anger, he must say goodbye. Otherwise …

Eduardo dialed. This time there was no answer.

32

Sao Paulo, Brazil
May 16, 1967

Jairo stared at his father, baffled. He thought of the words his father had just said, tried to figure out their meaning and what lay behind them. *I don't have the solution to your problem.* What was he saying? Until now he'd thought that after the Holocaust his father had come to a carefully considered decision to abandon his Judaism. But if his father had no answers, if he became so nervous just hearing about his son being persecuted as a Jew, it seemed that his father was merely a coward, running away from battle. If the Jew hadn't managed to escape his destiny for thousands of years then, with all due respect to that up-and-coming young attorney, Jairo Silverman of Sao Paulo, there was no reason why he, particularly, should be able to do so. That he, and only he, should be able to loosen those mysterious ties that he had felt so strongly this past week. So what if his father gets nervous at the thought of his going to synagogue? He wouldn't go! He, Jairo, knew well that his feet wouldn't cross the threshold of a synagogue. But what had that to do with this? Yes, synagogue; no, synagogue. What did that have to do with the answer that he needed so badly? Why should the fact that he saw Nazis in action make him feel so … so Jewish?

Jairo didn't say a word. He stood up and began to pace back and forth through the living room, deep in thought. His father wouldn't look at him, Jairo saw: He was evading him. It seemed that his father felt he hadn't succeeded in giving his only son the complete gift of life, a life of serenity without the memories of the Jewish past, far from the terrible days, far from the anti-Semitism and terror …

Jairo's father jumped up. Jairo turned a searching glance on him, wondering what he would do next. Suddenly, Jairo laughed to himself, a bitter laugh. He saw his father walk slowly towards the television and turn it on. *That's what he has to suggest to me at this time?* Another evasive tactic: This was how his father proposed to silence the turmoil in Jairo's soul? With the noise of some stupid entertainer?

His father had disappointed him. He wasn't even searching for an answer. Because he'd been in Buchenwald for a short time, because he'd escaped as a penniless refugee right before the gates had slammed shut, because he'd shared a destiny with his fellow Jews, a fate that none had ever faced before, he was obligated to try and understand what had happened to him, to his nation. And now it was happening, at least a little bit, to his son. Could it be that his father was afraid of the answer?

His father returned to his armchair. He sat tensely, his torso bent forward, his concentration entirely on the flickering images dancing on the screen before him. Or was he just pretending to pay such close attention? Jairo couldn't tell. Were all survivors of the Holocaust, who had withstood so heroically the most unspeakable trials that one could imagine, still afraid, as his father was, of confronting their own destiny? Jairo couldn't be sure.

Jairo was the first to shatter the silence.

"Pa, when is your meeting?"

"What meeting? Meeting with whom?"

"*Nu*, the meeting of the survivors."

His father looked at him in surprise. "Tomorrow night. At the Hebraica Club. Why are you asking?"

"Nothing. I'd like to come with you."

His father grimaced. Clearly, he wasn't happy with his son's request.

"What do you need that for? A meeting of a group of old Europeans? Be a Brazilian, already!"

"I just want to ask them the questions that you won't answer!"

Regina Hunkes's moment of indecision seemed to Hermann Schmidt to last an eternity. He managed to keep his composure, but his feverish brain was already busy with schemes and plans of how to keep her in the city and yet get her out of her house for a few days, in the event that she would refuse to accompany him now. And yet he smoked calmly, as if he had all the time in the world.

"Hermann, do you know what?"

His breath shortened somewhat. What would the lady say now?

"Yes?"

"I'll do it!"

Schmidt closed his eyes for a fraction of a second. He felt a vast relief.

"Good," he said quickly, trying to inject a note of urgency into the matter, "why not go get packed? And we'll go to the hotel. Immediately."

Regina went swiftly to the bedroom and began to gather together her clothing for the temporary departure. She worked quickly, her tension and nervousness apparent. Clothing and other things that got into her way, that she didn't want to pack, flew to the floor or in a pile on the bed. A chair that blocked her way to the closet was flung angrily away and overturned. The closet doors remained opened. In a few minutes she stood in the living room next to Schmidt, a small suitcase in her hand and another hanging from her shoulder.

"I'm ready," she said in a wooden voice.

Schmidt, always a gentleman, took the suitcases from her and turned to the door. Regina walked behind him. She locked the apartment as Schmidt summoned the elevator. Schmidt had already entered and put the suitcases down, when he heard Regina's voice. "Oh, I've forgotten something in the house!"

She turned from the elevator and quickly opened her apartment door. The elevator doors closed and before Schmidt could do anything, he was on his way down.

"What are you doing, Regina?" he called loudly.

"I'm coming in a minute!" He heard Regina's voice, as if echoing from the end of the world. Schmidt burned with fury, but he was trapped in the descending elevator. He couldn't believe it, he thought impatiently. Had Regina planned this?

The elevator reached the ground floor. Schmidt banged wildly against the button that would bring the elevator back to the eighth floor. He must return to the apartment immediately. After a few minutes he was there. The apartment door was open wide. He hastened inside. And the sight before him was exactly what he'd been afraid he'd find ...

Eduardo dialed yet another time. Again, no one answered in his mother's house. What could this mean? Should he worry? Not necessarily. No, he wasn't worried. But tense? Absolutely. After having quarreled with her, he couldn't possibly fly away without saying goodbye. Eduardo continued with his preparations. His suitcases were already packed. He took care to leave his bachelor apartment neat and clean. He had no idea how much time he would be spending in the Middle East. At this time, despite the increasing tension between Egypt and Israel, there was no way of knowing if war would actually break out, or if Israel would capitulate to the new situation that had been created.

He made a snap decision: He wouldn't take a taxi to the airport. He'd take his own car to his mother's house, usually a 10 minute ride. He'd park in his reserved space and grab a cab from there. Eduardo hurried; time was growing short.

It took him 15 minutes to reach Piaui Street.

Francisco Machado was already asleep when the sharp ring of the telephone broke through the fog of his slumbers.

"Yes?" he said in an impatient, sleepy voice.

"Hello, Francisco?"

"Yes, who's this? Oh, Paulo. I didn't recognize your voice at first."

"We haven't spoken for four whole hours."

"Okay, okay. What's happened now? Have they given you GAC as a present?"

On the other end of the line Paulo Chilo burned with anger at his partner's feeble joke.

"No! We've lost everything!"

"What's that?"

"I met one of the executives of the firm, who'd been with us in the Cafe Fazano."

"And ..."

"He said that they are no longer interested in us at all."

A moment of silence. Finally, Francisco asked, "All because of Jairo?"

"Yes, all because of Jairo!"

Suddenly, Francisco remembered something. "Did you meet them behind our backs? Without telling us?"

Paulo gave a hollow laugh. "Not behind your back! I went there independently. I'd decided to leave the office. You understand, it's going to be difficult to work together. Particularly because I'm an Arab and he's a Jew."

"Paulo, have you gone completely out of your mind?"

"Not at all. Can't you see that Jairo may destroy us completely? He's a Jew! A fine man, but a Jew! It's hard for me now, when there's a *jihad* going on in the Middle East."

"I don't understand. What's going on in the Middle East?"

"*Jihad*. A holy war against the Jews."

Francisco, shocked, was quiet for a moment. "And you, as a Brazilian, agree with this?"

"Don't ask me things like that now, okay? Remember that I'm an Arab too!"

Again, silence. And Paulo added, "And Jairo is a Jew."

After a moment, Paulo continued. "They don't want to work with me either. Even as an independent party. They want me to silence Jairo first."

Francisco grew frightened. "What's that mean, to silence him?"

"He said to me, 'There are many ways.' "

"What are you planning to do?" Francisco said in a cold, controlled voice.

Paulo laughed. "Don't worry. I'm not going to murder Jairo. But I'm leaving the office. This partnership is damaging to me."

"I think you're making a mistake," Francisco said quietly.

"Perhaps. But I've made up my mind. We're breaking up."

"Okay. Do whatever you think best."

"*Chau,*" Paulo said quickly. "I hope we can remain friends."

"*Chau.* I hope so too."

The conversation came to an end. Francisco held the phone in his hand for some time …

Police Officer Roberto Nunes was preoccupied. Despite the fact that darkness had fallen upon the city, he was still in his office. He'd returned from his interrogation of Mrs. Hunkes with even more questions that needed answers. The widow had, it seemed, given him satisfactory replies. And yet, he couldn't get away from her obvious nervousness. As an experienced police officer, he could always tell when one of his "victims" was hiding something: Regina Hunkes was undoubtedly practicing concealment. But what was the "something" that she was hiding?

Roberto took another look at the pile of documents pertaining to the Hunkes file. One thing was clear: Alberto's country of origin was hidden in a murky fog. He'd used forged documents to obtain Brazilian citizenship. Jairo had helped him; Roberto would deal with that another time. But the fact remained, glaring: This respected family had something to hide. Oh, yes. And the mysterious murder added spice to the affair. It seemed to Roberto that the answer to the mystery lay somewhere in those stories of Jairo's, tales of anonymous callers. Roberto added to the calls the high-handed "visit" that they had paid to his own office …

He was on edge. The fact that he'd met Regina Hunkes as she was leaving the building, about to flee from him, reinforced his belief that she was about to leave the city. He had to stop that at all costs!

His hand seemed to take on a life of its own, as it reached out for the phone.

"Good evening, is this the Interpol switchboard? Good. Is *Hidalagado* George Vinicio still there? You'll check. I'll wait, and thank you very much."

Two minutes passed. "Hello, is that you, George? Good. I'm sorry about the late hour, but I need a favor from you. Get me an international restraining order against Mrs. Regina Hunkes. I'll explain another time. It's entirely possible that you people down at Interpol will also be involved. What's important now is for you to get hold of an identifying photo of her from the Population Registry. The woman may try to flee the country with a forged passport. It seems that she's got strong forces behind her. Don't ask me questions now. I'm in a rush. What I'm asking is for you to have instructions prohibiting her leaving sent to all the airports, and to land and sea-based border stations. Okay? Thanks a lot, *amigo*!"

Roberto hung up and quickly dialed the Hunkes number. He wanted to speak to her again. This time, he'd openly ask her about her husband's wartime acivities.

Suddenly, with the passing of an instant, he realized that the telephone was no use. His call might well send her fleeing. He must go with all speed to Piaui Street and surprise her.

Roberto shut the lights in his office and galloped down the steps towards the parking lot. In seconds he was on his way to Regina's house ...

Bnei Brak, Israel
6 Iyar 5727

Rivka managed to get her husband onto the couch. His eyes were opened wide, but they rolled from side to side. She was paralyzed with fright. It was clear that he was lost in that other world. He was sweating, trembling, mumbling to himself. She let him alone for a few minutes; then, as he showed signs of recovering, she gently placed damp cloths on his fevered brow. Bending over him, she could hear disjointed words: "Yaakov Yehoshua ... the white hand ... it will not be ... just a dream ... no Heinz Krantz ...Eichmann ... G-d's will ... where is the white hand ... G-d's will ... I am healed ... healed ..."

He fell into a deep sleep. Rivka left him alone.

33

Sao Paulo, Brazil
May 16, 1967

The blood raced through Schmidt's head. He felt himself losing control. He knew he must keep his cool: That was one of the secrets of his profession. And yet he couldn't hold himself back.

"What are you doing, Regina? We must leave now!" he yelled wildly.

In the bedroom Regina was trying to do precisely what Schmidt had been determined to avoid at all costs. She lay sprawled on the floor, the bed pushed slightly out of place, the carpet folded in one corner. In her hand she held a set of keys.

When she saw the grey-haired man standing in the doorway shouting, she felt true panic. With a quick gesture she attempted to hide the keys behind her, even as she pulled the carpet back to its original place. She knew she was too late. Hermann Schmidt of GAC could clearly see it: She was lying next to a safe …

"I forgot something in the house," she excused herself lamely, trying to stand up.

"And I apologize for shouting. But I'm afraid we'll be too late. I have a feeling that the police lieutenant may return any minute now, before we've managed to get away. I'm convinced he's going to want to interrogate you tonight. Do me a favor, leave everything now and come!"

"Why do you think he may return?"

"He's no fool. He's certainly going to realize you may try to get away. He may even have agents watching the house."

"But he said he would be back in a couple of days!"

Schmidt gave an impatient stamp of his foot. Every moment was precious, and here she was, wasting time with all her foolishness.

"He wanted to lull you! To let you feel you had enough time to make your preparations! They know how to work on their 'clients'!"

Schmidt knew he was frightening her without having any real facts to go on. But he had no choice. His prime objective was to get her away, far away, far from the safe. How much time had he put into uncovering the existence of this safe! The death of Alberto Hunkes had made the mission even more difficult. But events had come to a surprising, almost unimaginable pass — for here he was, staring at the safe with his own eyes. Regina must not be allowed to destroy everything now. "They" in Europe, were curious, very curious. They were waiting eagerly for his report on the safe's contents. And the professionals were arriving this very evening …

Regina stood up and stared him straight in the eyes. Her look, Schmidt saw, was cold and calculating.

"Hermann," she said in a tense voice, a voice radiating authority, "there is a limit! You will leave me now! I'm locking the door! Taking whatever I like. And afterwards, I'll come. It won't be more than a minute or two. Don't worry, I'm not planning suicide, if that's what you thought."

Schmidt grabbed her arm roughly. "Now that you've admitted to me that you are German, your danger is even greater. I am certain that the police are well aware of your identity. That is, they know that you've lived here on forged documents, as innocent Danes, when you actually are — Germans. You know, *Senhora*, that since the Eichmann trial, and all that was said of him, Latin America has no love for — Nazis. Particularly those embroiled in a murder case."

Regina's eyes blazed, but she made no reply. Schmidt could see a flash of fear, too, in her eyes.

"Don't worry, *Senhora*," he continued in a commanding voice, "the door will be locked. No one will enter. Don't worry!"

Without waiting for an answer, he pulled her out of the apartment. The key was firmly turned in the door and they descended to the ground floor. They raced through the lobby and, in seconds, the two were standing next to Schmidt's car, parked nearby. He opened the door for her. As Regina bent into the car, she heard a shocked cry: "Mother!"

For a millisecond she hesitated. She knew that voice well. Eduardo. Reflexively, she turned towards the sound. But Schmidt was determined. Gently but firmly he pushed her into the car, slammed the door behind her with a bang that rocked the small GAC. He jumped swiftly into the driver's seat and turned on the ignition. In his rear-view mirror he could see young Eduardo racing towards him. But Schmidt didn't hesitate for a moment.

"Phone him from the hotel. You don't have to tell him where you've gone. He knows what you've been through these past days. You'll see, he'll understand. Okay?"

"Okay."

Schmidt could hear the silent weeping in her voice.

Eduardo screeched to a halt, shaken and breathless. His gaze was riveted on the street before him, on the quickly vanishing red GAC. There was no point in trying to follow it on foot. For a moment he considered returning to his car to speed after his mother and the unknown man, but he immediately rejected the idea as impractical. There was no hope of catching up to them, not in the turbulent whirlpools of Sao Paulo traffic. Worst of all, because of the darkness he hadn't managed to get the car's license number. With that, he would have had the thread to begin a police investigation, though the car was undoubtedly stolen, and the Sao Paulo police had long since abandoned hope of controlling auto theft. Still, he would use all of his contacts at the paper in order to pressure the police to make an intensive investigation of his mother's kidnaping. Surely the police would be impressed by a newspaper of the stature of the *Estado de Sao Paulo*. But with all this he knew that the chances of success were minimal. He felt a cold sweat overcome him as the thought raced through his brain: his mother, kidnaped! That was the only explanation for what he'd just witnessed. She hadn't gone of her own free will. He had clearly seen how the mysterious man, whom he couldn't identify because of the night's dimness, had pulled his mother forcibly into the car. Eduardo was terrified. What to do?

First, he decided, he would go up to her apartment. Perhaps there he would find some sign of what had happened, some indication of the identity of her abductor. He turned towards his parents' home. The elevator brought him up to their apartment. He turned his key and entered. His eyes glanced rapidly in every corner. He didn't like what he saw. The confusion in the living room and bedroom showed him that his mother had fought desperately, if unsuccessfully, against her kidnaper. Who was he? Eduardo didn't have the faintest clue. Perhaps he'd been sent by the Jews who, according to his mother, had murdered his father?

Eduardo disconsolately sat down in one of the armchairs. He lit a cigarette. What to do now? Call the police? His hand went towards the telephone. After a brief moment of hesitation, it returned to the side of the chair. What could he tell them? Didn't he know that the police suspected his mother of — of what? But he knew they were watching her. He was no fool. The fear in her eyes told its own story. He felt his mother was concealing something. Her nervousness over the police interrogation was enough to send his own suspicions soaring. He balled his fingers into a fist, licked his lips nervously. What to do?

A sharp, shrill ring of the doorbell startled him, breaking into his thoughts. He opened the door. A man he didn't know was standing there. "Yes?" Eduardo asked politely.

The man, who seemed surprised to see Eduardo, quickly introduced himself.

"I am Roberto Nunes, an investigating officer with the Sao Paulo police."

Roberto, in his civilian clothing, quickly pulled out his identification card and showed it to Eduardo. Eduardo looked at it silently.

"May I come in?"

Eduardo gestured him inside. Roberto entered. His professional glance immediately saw that something had happened in the apartment. His eyes flashed a question at Eduardo, looking for an explanation. He didn't know who this young man was and what he was doing here, in Regina Hunkes's home.

"My mother isn't home," Eduardo said, as if reading Roberto's mind.

Roberto didn't react. He walked slowly through the living room, his eyes scanning every corner.

"Kidnaped!" Eduardo added.

Roberto stopped his pacing. In a few seconds he was beside Eduardo.

"What did you say?"

"I said — kidnaped."

Roberto's breath came unevenly. He could feel the tension rising within him. The story was becoming even more complex …

"How do you know?"

"I know. I saw the abduction with my own eyes."

Roberto then heard a complete report from Eduardo. The police officer didn't know whether or not to believe this son of Regina Hunkes. It was possible, after all, that Eduardo was covering up for his fleeing mother, helping her avoid a legal investigation. He was surprised he hadn't thought of it himself: A kidnaping was an extremely effective way of avoiding police scrutiny. But he also had to accept the possibility that Eduardo was not lying, that he was, in fact, telling the truth. In either case, he saw the money his friend Jairo Silverman had promised him disappearing before his eyes. And that was undoubtedly infuriating!

"May I make a call?" Roberto asked, with almost exaggerated courtesy.

Eduardo took a deep drag on the cigarette burning low between his fingers. He exhaled slowly and asked, "To whom?"

The police officer gave a frosty smile. He wasn't accustomed to civilians asking him the questions.

"You don't seem unduly disturbed by the fact that your mother has been kidnaped. Kidnaped, that is, according to you."

Eduardo certainly felt the sarcasm. He realized that the police officer probably did not believe his story.

"You don't trust me?"

The policeman gave a small, slightly forced cough. "I've just got to be very cautious."

Now that Roberto had made it clear that the police might not believe him, this insolent young man should be cautious with regard to his behavior.

"May I make a call?" he asked again. The challenge in his voice was obvious.

Eduardo nodded his head in assent, without looking at the police officer.

"Hello, operator? *Boa noite*. This is *Delegado* Roberto Nunes. Connect me with the duty officer."

A moment's wait followed, with Roberto holding the line, and then his voice could again be heard in the Hunkes' living room.

"Hello? Is that the duty officer? Oh, hi! Listen, Pedro. About an hour ago I asked that a restraining order be issued against a woman who is known as Regina Hunkes. I asked that it be sent to all land and sea-based border stations, including airports. I had her picture sent to Santos and Rio de Janeiro. Understand? I'm not certain if she'll be using a forged passport. Check it out for me, please. Oh, and wait a minute. Please add something. Make an official police announcement to all radio and television stations. I'll dictate it. Are you writing this down? Okay, thanks. Here it is: *The police requests the public's help in locating a German woman who carries a forged Danish passport in the name Regina Hunkes. She disappeared from her home on Piaui Street, Sao Paulo. The woman is about 47 years old, a meter 75 in height, blonde hair, blue eyes. Anyone who knows anything of her whereabouts is requested to contact the nearest police station. A reward will be given for information.*

"That's the notice, Pedro. The most important thing is to circulate her picture as soon as possible. Okay. And fill out the proper forms for the commissioner for tomorrow. Okay? *Chau!*"

The conversation ended. Pedro had hung up, but Roberto, wishing to give Eduardo one more small lesson in order to put him even more off balance, spoke into the receiver. "What's that, Pedro? You want to know who we're talking about? That's right, it's Alberto Hunkes's widow. Yes, the one who was murdered. Yes, it's true, he was a Nazi who lived here under false documents. Who was he? We don't know. That is, we don't know yet. But it's clear he was a Nazi, and he had something to hide. Otherwise, he wouldn't have had a false identity."

Roberto whispered another *chau* into the silent receiver. He slowly, patiently hung up the receiver. Despite his impassive countenance, he looked with great interest at Eduardo, seeking his reactions to the information he'd just imparted.

The young reporter, Eduardo Hunkes, felt he would explode. Before him stood a police officer who had chosen, it seemed, to destroy his career as a journalist. If he would continue to publicize that lie, that his, Eduardo's, father, Alberto Hunkes, had been a Nazi living in Brazil under an alias — a war criminal who'd fled justice in Germany or another European country — then it wouldn't take much time, days perhaps, for him to be called to the editor's office. His editor, Julio Mesquita, was known to be fond of the Jews. He would have nothing to do with a Nazi or, for that matter, the son of a Nazi. Eduardo felt that he must settle this account with the police officer. Now!

"What's this, Lieutenant? You're announcing on television that my mother has fled when I saw with my own eyes that she was abducted? And on what basis are you slandering her publicly, while the investigation against her hasn't been completed? And what's this story that my father was a Nazi whose documents were forged? You'd better be careful, Lieutenant!"

Eduardo was upset. How did this police officer, this Roberto Nunes, know that his Danish father had links with the Nazis? Who had told him what had gone on at the funeral? Was it Jairo Silverman, that cursed Jew? Who knew?

Meanwhile, Roberto stood nearby, leaning on a buffet, calmly smoking his pipe. It seemed to Eduardo that the police officer was smiling a little to himself. Finally, Roberto moved slightly towards Eduardo and said to him, in friendly tones, "Very well, young Hunkes. I think it's time we had a little chat."

34

Sao Paulo, Brazil
May 16, 1967

Eduardo sent the police officer a look of loathing. The officer continued to smile. He was used to such responses. This conversation, he hoped, would help advance the investigation into the burning question: Who, exactly, was Alberto Hunkes? He put the pipe down on the buffet, pulled a cigarette box out of his jacket pocket, and turned to Eduardo.

"Smoke?"

"No thanks," Eduardo answered shortly, though he was, in fact, a heavy smoker.

"Am I now part of a police investigation?" Eduardo asked, openly defiant, while Roberto lit up a cigarette.

"No," Roberto answered mildly, "you are not being investigated. This is nothing more than a conversation with the police."

Eduardo played dumb. "Is there a difference?"

Roberto laughed. "You're a journalist, my boy?

Do you live here in Sao Paulo? It seems that you don't! Otherwise, you'd know the difference. You're lucky you've fallen into my hands, and not into those of Captain Nemo of the Navy or one of the Air Force interrogators! Ah, you've heard of them?"

Yes, Eduardo had certainly heard of them. He had heard of this Captain Nemo, the tough interrogator of the Navy police. Fearful rumors of his interrogation methods abounded. He went after the Communist underground with raging anger and often tortured enemies of the regime. A harsh military junta ruled Brazil, Eduardo knew. It would be best, he decided, to remain silent …

Sao Paulo, Brazil
May 17, 1967

In the GAC offices, Hermann Schmidt burned with rage. It was this evening, the day after he'd escorted Regina Hunkes to her refuge in the Excelsior Hotel, that he'd heard the police force's televised announcement regarding her disappearance. All that day he'd been busy with preparations for the memorial evening in honor of Alberto Hunkes in the Municipal Theater — and with making the clandestine arrangements for the squad that had come from Europe and was now housed in the very same hotel, in a way that would not arouse the suspicions of the police. They had arrived, one at a time, each on a different flight and from a different country, with at least two hours between them. In all, four men. And now, after all that, to have this advertised throughout the country!

He was furious with himself. How hadn't he realized that the disappearance of Regina Hunkes would become public knowledge? He'd lost an entire day.

And the searches, undoubtedly, had begun. What if one of the hotel staff recognized her? And then …

What to do?

First, he put through a call to the Excelsior Hotel. "Hello, Regina. How are you?"

"Thank G-d, fine."

"Good. Have you told Eduardo that everything is okay?"

"I called the newspaper. They promised to give him the message."

"Excellent. I'll be over later to see how you're doing. *Chau.*"

After several stormy minutes spent wrestling with his thoughts, he came to a decision. He'd have to be firm: It was time to open his hand and reveal the cards. He had to ensure that this police investigation was terminated once and for all. What he needed more than anything was a few days of quiet. He must not fail, not when he was this close to the finish line. These announcements in the media must stop! This very night!

Schmidt nervously gnawed at his fingernails. It had been a long, long time since he'd felt such mounting tension, such doubts about themission's conclusion. Only one man could stop this circus that the police force was running. Jairo. Jairo Silverman, the young Jewish lawyer who had suddenly chosen to become a Nazi hunter. It was almost 10 at night. He would certainly not be in his office at this late hour. Determinedly, he dialed Jairo's home number.

Jairo drove in silence, his father beside him in the car. Their conversation of the previous night still hovered over them like a thick, threatening cloud. Jairo's father had hoped his son would forget about this meeting of survivors, scheduled to take place in the Jewish club, Hebraica. But Jairo had not forgotten. At exactly 8 o'clock he had arrived at his father's Bom Retiro home. "Pa, I've come to take you to Hebraica," he told the astonished man.

His father hadn't said a word. He slowly pulled on his suit jacket, straightened his tie, gave a quick glance at the mirror to see if his hair was combed properly. As he approached the door he remembered something he'd forgotten and went back to get it. Jairo didn't ask questions. He allowed the old man complete freedom of action. After a minute, Jairo's father came out of the bedroom. Jairo saw his father jam a large black *yarmulke* into his pants pocket. Strange. Jairo couldn't understand why his father would suddenly need this religious symbol. But he asked no questions.

The car slid down Pineros Boulevard. Like waves in a stormy sea, the beam of thousands of headlights flowed back and forth. The pale lights of the cars washed over Jairo's face, alternating with the garish reflection of neon flashing on the huge buildings that stood on either side of the wide boulevard, creating a strange symphony of color. Here was the pulsing heart of the dynamic, throbbing city, a city that knew nothing of the fears that consumed him. How far he was, at this moment, from the tempo of life in Sao Paulo, the city he so loved!

Jairo snatched a quick glance at his father sitting next to him, deep in his own thoughts. Jairo respected his silence and continued to drive without saying a word. Another few minutes and they'd reach the well-known Jewish club. Jairo, as a respected member, was there almost every Sunday. Sundays, that is, which he didn't spend in the Eldorado, on the ranch that his father had acquired at a bargain price years ago. At the club, Jairo would play a set of tennis, or take a swim, chat with his friends or run after his children, occasionally glancing at his watch to see if he could finally call a stop to all this nonsense and return home. But this was the first time he was coming to this place to take part in this gathering of the elderly, who were reliving the nightmare of the concentration camps on these serene lawns and luxurious rooms.

Jairo helped his father out of the car. His father was still hale and hearty, but Jairo had noticed over the years that somehow, on the days before this reunion, a weakness would set in. This time Jairo saw him actually grow more frail as he came closer and closer to the club. And now, here at the entrance gate, his father obviously needed his help ...

They were among the first to arrive. In the lavish club, everything was ready. Jairo's eyes looked over the food and drink laid out on a table. The evening's agenda was tacked up on the door. They would begin with the *Yizkor* and *Kel malei rachamim* prayers. Now Jairo understood the reason for the *yarmulke*. Afterwards, Dr. Efraim Green, cultural attaché in the Israeli consulate in Argentina, would lecture on the ramifications of the Eichmann abduction to Israel on the German community in South America. This sounded interesting. At the end of the lecture, there would be various announcements by the head of the organization, followed by light refreshments. *If not for the subject matter*, thought Jairo, *it could be quite a pleasant evening.*

Jairo waited impatiently for the program to begin. Slowly, more and more people arrived. It was obvious how much the participants needed such meetings: Jairo could see their faces light up as survivors met their friends, who were generally scattered throughout this great city. It seemed that these hours spent together dissipated just a little of their loneliness within the well of bitter memories that enveloped them every day. Jairo knew how his father relived Buchenwald every day, every hour, though he'd had a relatively short stay in that camp before bribing his way out to freedom. He remembered, with a sinking feeling, how his father would sit for hours and tell Alberto Hunkes what had happened to him before the war. Meetings such as these somehow helped lessen the pain.

He recognized only a few of the participants. Most were middle aged, old before their time. His father, who'd early on appropriated one of the most comfortable armchairs, nodded here and there, with the ghost of a smile, to people entering the room. He was completely removed from Jairo. The ceremony began half an hour late. Everyone stood up as the *chazzan*, a guest from Israel, recited *Yizkor* and *Kel malei rachamim* in a beautiful voice filled with emotion. The entire group wore *yarmulkes* in honor of these moments. Jairo, embarrassed, held his right hand over his bare head. Why hadn't his father taken a *yarmulke* for him too? Perhaps, after those awkward questions he'd asked the other night, his father was afraid of what would happen, should his son hold a *yarmulke* in his hand. Jairo smiled inwardly. And yet, he remembered his father's frigid words: Maybe you'll wind up going to the synagogue!

The *chazzan* ended with a flourish. The assembled stood, their heads bowed. No one was crying, Jairo noticed. No tear ran down a cheek, no sobs racked any of the almost 100 people filling the club. No doubt, there were no tears left in their haunted souls ...

The lecture that followed was a fascinating one. The speaker talked of the renewal of anti-Semitism following the Eichmann trial, a renewal sparked, in Argentina at least, by Nazis who had fled after the war. Though living deep underground, they managed to lend assistance to the local populace that resented the Jews. *Interesting,* thought Jairo, *to do a study of this phenomenon in Brazil.* He himself felt like a victim of this trend ...

But despite his interest in the topic, the evening did not strike a chord in Jairo. He stared at the wizened, inflexible faces of the audience and couldn't believe that he would find among them the answer to his question, the question of the Jewish destiny that so disturbed him. It seemed to him that these people cursed their destiny that had brought them, on one bright, sunny day in Eastern Europe, to the very edge of hell. Jairo understood them, as he understood his father. But he knew that it was not the anger, nor the fury, nor the flight of his father and his father's friends that would help him at this moment.

The lecture ended. The participants hurried towards the table laden with food. A few individuals stood near the lecturer, hoping to clarify one point or the other. Jairo's father remained in his armchair, silent. Jairo brought him a cup of coffee and a piece of cake and sat beside him. Two older men strayed towards them, and gave them a smile.

"Yankel, what's doing?" one of them said in Yiddish. "Why are you sitting on the sidelines?"

Yankel, Jairo's father, answered the smile. "We're not getting any younger."

"This you have to tell us?" the two answered almost simultaneously.

The two friends stared at Jairo. The older of them asked, "Who's the youngster, Yankel?"

"This is my son, Jairo."

Jairo smiled at the two men and gave their hands a warm shake. Jairo's father added, "He's an attorney. A successful attorney."

"Fine! You must have *nachas* from him! So what's new, Yankel?"

"Nothing special."

"Except, of course," the younger of the two friends said, as he sipped his coffee, "for the frightening news coming from there, from Israel. Who knows what they're going through over there? Particularly the ones who came from Auschwitz and Treblinka — the ones like us. Again, the fear of death. Again, the nightmares. Who has the strength to bear it anymore? It's too much!"

The older of the two men gave a flick of his wrist. "It seems they have no idea of how much trouble they're in!"

"Why do you say so?"

"I spoke to my brother who lives in Ramat Gan yesterday."

"*Nu?*"

"Forget it! You think he's worried? Not at all! He called on behalf of someone else, some *meshugener*."

"What do you mean?"

"I was so worried, hearing his voice on the phone. I asked him, my heart beating, "What's the matter?" Turns out he's looking for Nazis in Brazil! A lunatic!"

Jairo's ears perked up. His father spoke. "What do you mean, looking for Nazis in Brazil? He doesn't have enough problems back home?"

"That's exactly what I told him! You don't have enough *tzurris*? It seems he's doing some kind of favor for a Jew who's looking for a Nazi, the one who killed his wife and kids in Galicia. A *meshugener*!"

"But why in Brazil?"

"*Nu*, they told him that the Nazi fled to Brazil. Simon Wiesenthal told him. No, actually he read it in some newspaper."

"What was the name of this cursed one, may his name be blotted out?"

The man didn't answer.

"*Nu*?" Jairo's father pressed him. In his heart, Jairo, too, willed the man to speak.

"One second," the friend said. "You think I remember? Oh, wait a minute. His name was ... it was ... that's right. Heinz Krantz! Yes, Heinz Krantz. A lunatic! To think he could find him in Brazil! I'm going to make myself another cup of coffee. Anyone want some?"

"One minute! Don't you remember Heinz Krantz?" It was the other man speaking, clearly agitated.

"No."

"I remember that murderer!" Yankel Silverman's friend continued excitedly, "And I'd recognize him anywhere! He was around for a while with the S.S. officer Amon Gett, may his name be blotted out. He was also in the ghetto of Plaszow, near Cracow, for a week. Don't you remember?"

"No."

The man seemed disappointed. He turned to make himself a cup of coffee. Suddenly, the microphone barked an announcement. "*Senhor* Jairo Silverman, please come to the office. Your wife is on the telephone."

Jairo jumped from his place and hurried to the office. "Yes, what's the matter?" he said quietly.

"Jairo, the man who called that night, he's looking for you."

Jairo paled. "What did he want?"

"He wouldn't say. He just said he must meet with you tonight. And that you shouldn't dare avoid him."

Jairo's heart began to pound heavily. He could feel a deep fear begin to overcome him. Suddenly, he realized how well he fit in with the Jews sitting in the auditorium next door. He, too, was persecuted, just as they were! Persecuted! Here, in the heart of Sao Paulo, he felt the fear of Auschwitz ...

He heard his wife's voice. "What will you do?"

"I don't know. If I don't sleep at home tonight, don't worry. Maybe I'll leave town for a few days. I'm afraid, Paulina."

He could hear his wife's fear-filled voice cry his name, but he quickly hung up and returned to the hall.

35

Bnei Brak
7 Iyar 5727

Yitzchak … Yitzchak! Wake up! It's late! It's almost past *zeman krias shema*!"

Rivka stood near her husband's bed, trying to awaken him. She wanted desperately to know how he felt after what he'd undergone last night. She wouldn't ask him directly, for she didn't want to reawaken the stormy and painful emotions that had overcome him. She would only watch him, watch his movements. These would tell her the full story.

Yitzchak showed no signs of awaking. Her fear began to take on a dimension of panic. She shook him and yelled his name.

Yitzchak suddenly opened his eyes. "Wha—"

"It's late!"

"What? What late?"

"It's late! Late! You've got to *daven*! Quickly!"

Sluggishly, listlessly, Yitzchak Austerlitz got out of bed. Mechanically he washed his hands, rinsed his face, put on his *tallis* and *tefillin* and began to *daven* quietly. When he was done he flicked on the radio.

> *Kol Yisrael, Jerusalem. This is the news:*
> *The Secretary-General of the U.N., U Thant, has surrendered to the ultimatum given by Egypt and decided to evacuate the U.N. forces in Sharm-el-Sheikh and the Israeli-Egyptian border. Cairo is exultant and Israel is furious. The government has entered in emergency session to discuss the U.N. secretary's capitulation and its repercussions. One of the decisions that sources say will be taken is full mobilization of all IDF forces. The head of the opposition, Menachem Begin, has proposed that David Ben Gurion be installed as Prime Minister in order to prepare for a war that cannot be avoided, and to form a national unity government as quickly as possible. Prime Minister Levi Eshkol is completely opposed to these ideas, and Golda Meir supports his position. "We don't need partners in victory," she said. Mapai opposes the demand that Moshe Dayan be appointed Minister of Defense. In the Jewish world anxiety for the welfare of Israel is growing, as it is suddenly under mortal threat. And …*

Yitzchak didn't listen to more. With a weary, trembling hand he switched off the radio. To his wife's surprise, he returned to bed, as if he'd forgotten that he must dress for work.

"What's this? Yitzchak, what's the matter with you?"

Yitzchak didn't answer. But she didn't give up. She pulled at his blanket, "Yitzchak, don't you feel well? Don't do this!"

Yitzchak merely curled up more tightly in the bedclothes, without a response.

"But why?"

Her despairing cry finally elicited a reply. "I can't take it anymore! I give up! Another war? More fears and terrors? More Jews in danger? More Jews, Heaven forbid, dying? I can't take it! I just can't! No, I don't want to!"

He pulled the blanket over his head, as if his quilt sheltered him from what was looming over his land ...

Rivka was confused and shattered. Last night it seemed that her husband was recovering from his nightmares. He'd even told her that his hurts were healing. And now, this relapse.

Suddenly, with uncontrolled urgency, Rivka left everything behind — her house, her husband, still curled up beneath the blankets — and raced to the home of his *chavrusah*, Rabbi Yitzchak Mandelkorn. Perhaps he'd still be home.

Sao Paulo, Brazil
May 16, 1967

Eduardo waited nervously for what would come next. With his eyes, he carefully gauged the police officer's reactions. He was furious with the uncouth behavior of this, this representative of his government, who had, without asking permission, helped himself to the contents of the living room bar and then flung himself into a recliner, a glass of Chivas Regal in his hand. Well, let's see how much he likes my write-up about him, in the *Estado's* police blotter, edited by Eduardo's friend Julio Guimaraes. That would wipe off the stupid smile that was painted on his overconfident face.

"A little nervous, are you?" Eduardo heard the police officer's slightly amused voice. At the same moment, Roberto downed the contents of the glass with professional zeal.

"No. Absolutely not. Why do you think so, *Senhor* Lieutenant?"

Roberto gave an airy wave of his hand. It seemed he had all the time in the world. What was he planning, Eduardo wondered.

"But, Lieutenant, I am in a hurry. If you've got something to ask me, ask it!"

Roberto shifted in his chair. He didn't like Eduardo's tone of voice. Not at all.

"Oh, you're in a hurry. Very good. Where are you hurrying to? To your mother?"

Eduardo bit his lower lip. It would not be a good idea, he knew, to lose his temper.

"You know I won't go to my mother. You'll be following me."

Roberto laughed. No fool, this boy. And not especially frightened of the police. That's right, he was a journalist. They liked to think they had immunity from the law. Let him think so …

Roberto was standing now, standing close to Eduardo.

"I, my young friend, am in no hurry. I'm waiting here in this room for a phone call from Headquarters. Maybe they'll have good news about your mother. By the way, if you're not going to your mother, where are you rushing off to?"

Eduardo hesitated for a moment and then spoke.

"I'm flying abroad."

The police officer raised an eyebrow and gave Eduardo a searching glance. "Oh. I understand."

After a moment's pause, he continued. "Just out of curiosity: Where?"

For some reason, Eduardo felt that he was now in control of the conversation. "In one-and-a-half hours I'm leaving from Congonhas Airport, on a Varig flight. We'll have a short layover in Rio de Janeiro, fly on to

Orly near Paris, and then, after a few hours, I'll board an El Al flight to Tel Aviv."

The police officer gave a thin smile. "A full report. Bravo!"

"As a good citizen," Eduardo said, with a show of nonchalance, "I give full cooperation to the police."

Roberto ignored the sarcasm. "And you travel …alone?"

"If you're referring to my mother, then yes, I'm traveling alone. I'm sorry that you're not taking my report of her abduction seriously."

Roberto decided to cross swords with the journalist. "If it were my mother that had been kidnaped, I'd surely cancel my travel plans. Do you understand me?"

"I understand, *Senhor* Lieutenant. I was just about to take care of that very point. If not for your 'investigation' I would have already called my newspaper to tell them of my sudden change of plans. May I call the offices of *Estado de Sao Paulo*?"

Roberto put his hand on the telephone. "I'll dial. Okay?"

Eduardo nodded in assent. *He doesn't believe me*, he thought.

The lieutenant pulled a small pad out of his shirt pocket and skimmed through it until he found the number he was looking for.

"Hello. Good evening. Is this the *Estado*? Good, may I speak with …"

Roberto turned to Eduardo, gesturing his question.

"Let them call *Dona* Silvia."

Roberto spoke. "May I speak with *Dona* Silvia, please. Who's this? This is Eduardo. Eduardo Hunkes. Yes. Yes. Thank you."

Two minutes passed.

"Is this *Dona* Silvia?"

Roberto swiftly handed the receiver over to Eduardo.

"Hello, *Dona* Silvia, good evening. See here, Silvia, I've got a problem. My mother's disappeared from her house; it seems she's been abducted. What? What did you say? She called! When? What did she say?"

Roberto saw that Eduardo was sincerely stirred. It seemed, then, that he had told the truth, and he had honestly seen a stranger taking his mother away. An important point, that changed the tenor of the questions he would be asking the young journalist ...

Sao Paulo, Brazil
May 17, 1967

In the Excelsior Hotel on Ipiranga Boulevard, Regina put out the lights and went to bed. This was her second night away from home. Hermann Schmidt had told her that tomorrow night, following the memorial evening in honor of her husband, she would fly out of the country, and if the police should search for her ... he would arrange everything.

In another wing of the hotel, in three separate rooms, three men went to sleep. The grey-haired man had told them even before dawn they would go out on their first trip ...

Jairo's father clearly saw the fear that had overcome his son. The way his son hastily returned to the auditorium hinted that he had received unpleasant news in the conversation with his wife. Jairo's father's friends, Yankel Kleinbaum and Reuven Greenspan, too, sensed a change in Jairo, and were curious as to its cause.

His father straightened in his armchair. His thick brows knit together, partially obscuring his eyes. "Has something happened?"

"Yes. I can't talk about it now. Pa, you'll have to go home with one of your friends. I must leave now."

His father didn't answer. His wise eyes, experienced with troubles, looked wearily at his son. "Them?" he asked shortly.

Jairo saw that his father, despite everything, believed all that he'd told him last night about the mysterious phone calls and the threatening pursuit. That meant that deep in his heart his father, too, knew that "they" were in Brazil — and that the Jewish destiny, even here, was identical to that of Jews throughout the world.

He looked at his father with deep pity. Tears appeared in his eyes. "Yes. It's them."

Jairo's father gave a deep sigh. His friends stared at father and son with obvious concern mingled with burning curiosity. But neither spoke. They were too uncomfortable to voice the questions they so longed to have answered.

Jairo recovered somewhat. "Is that all right, Pa? You'll go home with someone else. *Chau.*"

Jairo hurried out of the Hebraica Club and without a thought made his way to his car. Suddenly, he stopped. Perhaps they were already on his trail. Jairo lifted up his hand in a quick gesture to hail a taxi. A GAC pulled up next to him with a squeal of brakes. The black driver opened the door and, with a wide smile that showed pearly white against his dark face, said loudly, "Come in, *Senhor*, but what's the rush? Are you running after someone?"

Jairo disappeared into the taxi. "Not exactly. Me, I've got no one to run after!"

"Very good! Very good!" the driver answered cheerfully. An unflattering assessment of the driver's mental abilities flashed through Jairo's mind.

"So where are you going, *Senhor?*"

"First just go, and quickly! I'll tell you where in a moment."

The driver turned off the engine. Jairo thought he would explode. The man turned to his passenger. "Oh, no, sir. I want to give you good service, and you make fun of me?"

Jairo, the ground burning beneath him, felt that he would suffocate. He searched for a way to extricate himself from the mess he'd gotten himself into.

"Excuse me, *Senhor,*" he said in gentle tones, "I meant nothing by my words. I simply have several stops that I've got to make this evening. I hadn't decided which would be first. That's all. It will be worth your while to drive with me."

Even in the darkness the driver could see his passenger wink: a gesture that meant a hefty tip at the end of the road.

The driver switched on the engine and zoomed towards the city center. Jairo's brain raced with ideas, as he searched for a solution to his problem. His driver, staring in the mirror above his window, could clearly see the passenger's nervous gestures. Occasionally the driver would shrug, as if to say, "What do I care? So long as I get paid at the end!"

"I'm getting on the Nove de Julio, *Senhor.* Have you decided where to go yet?"

Jairo answered quickly, "Drive towards the Sao Juao."

"Okay."

The car slid towards the city, its lights mingling with thousands of others. Even now, close to midnight, the streets teemed with life. Jairo knew he must decide in these next few minutes what he would do. It was clear to him he couldn't return home. They would undoubtedly be waiting for him there. To look for Roberto, thus getting the police involved, would be foolishness. "They" were faster and more effective than the police. If not for the lateness of the hour he could have traveled to Rio de Janeiro, to Porto Alegre or Bello Horizonte. Perhaps if they'd lose sight of him for a few days, they would leave him alone. Or should he leave Brazil entirely, as it had become too dangerous for him to stay here? He felt his heart catch at the thought. Where would he go? To Israel? Jairo flinched. Again, the Jewish destiny held him in its inescapable grip — until he could even entertain the thought of going to Israel! When had he ever thought about Israel! What was happening to him? Jairo felt trapped.

The driver was pleasant. "*Senhor*, we're on the Ipiranga. Where are we going?"

The situation was growing ridiculous. He must decide what to do!

"Stop here, near the Excelsior Hotel. I've got a meeting there."

"Should I wait?"

"No, that won't be necessary."

The man grinned as Jairo handed him a generous payment.

Jairo looked around him with eyes grown suspicious and tense. After a moment, he bounded across the wide street and entered the lobby of the Excelsior Hotel. He'd stay the night here, and then decide what he would do.

36

Sao Paulo, Brazil
May 16, 1967

Police officer Roberto Nunes shifted in his chair. He had listened alertly to Eduardo's conversation with his office. Now he waited for Eduardo to hang up the receiver. With typical Brazilian patience he gave Eduardo another moment to recover from his surprise. Then he shot the unavoidable question: "Where is your mother?"

If he could have done so, Eduardo would have gone after the police officer with his bare hands. It was driving him to a frenzy, the knowledge that Nunes didn't believe a word he said. It wasn't the words the police officer used: It was the tone in which he spoke. Such things were impossible to hide. But there was no choice: Eduardo would have to control himself. Answer the questions politely. The main objective was to get rid of Nunes as soon as possible, so that he wouldn't miss his plane.

Despite his best efforts, though, Eduardo couldn't quite keep the fury out of his voice:

"Lieutenant, my mother has disappeared! It appears that the police are more interested in wasting their time with me than with trying to find out where she is! I apologize if I haven't been as polite as I should; I am simply showing my disappointment with the keepers of law and order who are supposed to be protecting our security."

Roberto smiled. He leaned his head back further in the comfortable chair; his eyes drifted to the ceiling. He understood the young man. In fact, he had no desire to be so tough on him. But there was the possibility that, in the course of their conversation, some crumb of information might fall, some kind of key that would unlock this mystery, one that meant little to the Sao Paulo police force, and much to his friend Jairo. And he was working, right now, for Jairo.

"I'm sorry, Eduardo," Roberto suddenly straightened. His voice grew pleasant. "Let's concentrate on what's important. I'll be happy if you will help me."

"Okay."

Eduardo took a quick glance at his watch. "I'd appreciate it if you'd keep it short. I've got a plane to catch in an hour and a half."

"If you're in a hurry, I can drive you to the airport. We can talk along the way."

Eduardo liked the idea. A conversation in a moving automobile was always less tense than one in the living room of a locked house. Besides, when his flight would depart, the investigation would come to an abrupt end. Thus, he saw no reason to resist the suggestion.

Eduardo parked his car in his parents' parking lot. He transferred his luggage to the police officer's automobile.

"Excuse my interfering in your personal life, but what did they tell you your mother said?"

"Not to worry about her. And not to cancel my travel plans. That she's disappeared of her own accord and will return home in a few days."

"Interesting."

Eduardo sent a glance at the policeman, who was driving with stoical calm. And if he noticed Eduardo's look in his mirror, he made no sign.

"What's so interesting?" Eduardo asked.

The police officer gave a hearty laugh. "If my mother had been abducted, and had managed to call me, she would no doubt have asked me to stay in the city and do all I could to find her. Not to go flying around the world."

The officer was silent for a moment, then flung out the sentence. "But perhaps German mothers are different."

Without a second thought, Eduardo spoke. "My mother isn't German, Lieutenant!" he said hotly. "She's a Dane! And you know that well enough!"

Roberto didn't rush to respond. He imagined Eduardo's face, when the truth was revealed to him. He pulled into the right lane, slowing down somewhat.

"My young friend, I'm sorry to disappoint you, but your mother is 100 percent German! German! She specifically admitted it to me, in person! Let me tell you something else: I have the clear impression that she's planning on returning to Germany! Trust the instincts of a veteran police officer. Is that news to you?"

Eduardo didn't answer. The policeman's words had startled him. He didn't know whether or not to believe him. Perhaps Nunes was trying to trap him. And yet, there was something in his words that hurt, hurt badly. He asked quietly, almost in a whisper: "And according to the Sao Paulo police my father … was a German?"

Roberto was pleased with the way the conversation was developing. "Yes. We know this for a fact. Your parents reached Brazil from Argentina with German documents, probably forged. Here in Brazil they received new forged documents listing them as Danish citizens."

Eduardo's senses were on the alert. He tried desperately to understand what lay behind the words that Roberto Nunes had flung at him with the strength of two balled fists.

"How do you know?"

"When the police investigate, the police find out!"

"Tell me anyway."

The policeman waited for a moment. Then came the next blow: "We checked with Brasilia's Interior Ministry. We found forged documents. And we found one other interesting thing."

Roberto lapsed into silence. He enjoyed the atmosphere of mystery, the tiny drama he was directing. He was curious where this conversation would lead, and if this young man would, finally, begin to talk.

"What was so interesting?" Eduardo asked in a slightly shaky voice.

"Truly, interesting! Would you like to know who forged the documents for them? Who saw to it that the bureaucrats in Brasilia wouldn't cause too much trouble, so that your parents could live peacefully in Brazil? You won't believe it! A lawyer. A Jewish lawyer. A lawyer whose name was … was …"

Roberto hesitated, acted as if he couldn't remember for a moment. Eduardo felt ready to explode.

"Oh, yes. I remember! Jairo Silverman! Do you know him?"

Eduardo's head began to ache. The blood pressed in his temples, beating like the tom-toms of the natives during *Carnivale*. This was too much! If this were true, his parents had concealed their past from him. And if so, it was undoubtedly a Nazi past that they'd kept so well hidden. The fact of their Nazi activities didn't disturb him overmuch. But why hadn't they revealed it to him? And what did Jairo have to do with all this? It wasn't possible!

"Surprised, Eduardo?"

"Oh … yes. One can say, yes."

"Really?"

"Why do you doubt me?"

"Weren't you at your father's funeral?"

"Of course."

"So you saw the Nazi ceremony when he was buried. You saw his comrades 'Heil Hitler.' Oh, Eduardo! And now you claim to be surprised at what I've told you?"

Eduardo straightened in his passenger seat. He felt that the confrontation could no longer be avoided.

"Tell me, Lieutenant, what do you want from me? What have I done to you? This isn't a police conversation and it isn't a police investigation. It's a police slander!"

The police officer took his time before answering. His eyes were riveted on the busy road before him. Suddenly, he sped up.

"You're wrong, Eduardo. There is some mystery that is connected to the Hunkes family. Forged documents. A quiet, respected man suddenly murdered. Attempts to stop the police investigation. A funeral with Nazi symbols. Doesn't it raise questions within you, you, who knew with certainty that your parents were Danes?"

The policeman was essentially correct, that much Eduardo admitted to himself. The questions had arisen during the funeral itself, a funeral whose nature had shocked him even then. But he'd told himself that it was because his father had been a collaborator with the Nazi-installed regime in Denmark, as his father had always claimed. And so others like his father had arranged a funeral service that was acceptable to them. The murder itself, Eduardo knew, raised additional questions, questions that had no answer as yet. What particularly shocked him was the fact that his mother, immediately upon receiving notification of his father's death, announced that it was murder, and that the killers were Jews. How did she know that he'd been poisoned even before the police had ever entertained such an idea, even before the autopsy had revealed the truth! Her firm belief in the killing had left him shaken. Her hatred and enmity for Jairo, too, had seemed overdone. Even then he'd suspected that something deep and mysterious lay concealed behind the shocking events that had befallen his family five days ago. He had to admit it. His mother's disappearance had further deepened the mystery.

Roberto was the first to break the silence. He knew he had to hurry. He had just turned onto the direct road to the airport. On the horizon he could see planes flying low, in preparation for landing.

"Eduardo, do you hate Jews?"

Eduardo looked at the police officer. "Yes. Why do you ask?"

"Were you taught to hate them in your house?"

"Yes. Absolutely. But why do you ask?"

"Just for my own information. By the way, what sort of people would visit your house?"

Eduardo raised his hands. "Nobody special."

"No particular friends, different from the rest?"

"No, Lieutenant. No."

"Did your parents travel a lot?"

"Not particularly. Once every few weeks they'd go to Curitiba. One of their friends has a ranch there. They'd go for a long weekend and then return."

"Did you ever go there with them?"

"No."

"Why not?"

"They wanted to be by themselves. I remember I came to Curitiba once, for an article. I called, and my father was very angry with me for even coming while he was there. I didn't understand why. He absolutely refused my offer to come visit them there. He demanded that I return to Sao Paulo and not be in the area when my mother and he were there."

"Interesting. And that says nothing to you?"

Eduardo shrugged. "I don't know."

Roberto couldn't let Eduardo know that he, Eduardo, had just furnished him with a piece of vital information. He hoped to continue to get further details. He was absolutely convinced of it: Alberto Hunkes had been a Nazi. There had been many rumors of Nazi gatherings held on far-out farms. Curitiba was in the state of Parana in southern Brazil, which reportedly was crawling with war criminals of every ilk: Germans, Lithuanians, Ukranians, Poles and others. It seemed clear that this was what lay behind those long weekends, those vacations that Alberto Hunkes and his wife enjoyed, vacations which were out of bounds to their son. Roberto would have to check out what was going on there, in the southern part of his country, while not neglecting his search for Eduardo's mother, of course, the mysterious *Senhora* Regina Hunkes. He had something important to ask her.

Roberto's car stopped in front of the terminal. With a vast feeling of relief Eduardo stepped out. He grinned at the policeman, who returned the smile.

"I'll be seeing you, Lieutenant. I can't say it's been a pleasure meeting you. What can one do? That's life."

"I understand, and I'm not angry with you. I hope that your flight, following our conversation, will be a more interesting one. You've got a lot to think about."

"I don't think that I can thank you for it, though."

"It's okay, my young journalist friend. Life is still ahead of you. Try to get the most you can from whatever happens to you."

"I'm grateful to you, Lieutenant. And I'm proud of my country, where the policemen are also philosophers and teachers."

Eduardo hurried to the Varig counter. Within the half-hour he would be on his way to Paris, and then on to Tel Aviv …

Bnei Brak
7 Iyar 5727

Rabbi Yitzchak Mandelkorn stood next to Yitzchak Austerlitz's bed. He had immediately acceded to Rivka's request that he come. Austerlitz was bundled beneath the blanket; even his head was covered. It was hard for Mandelkorn to talk to a blanket. He knew that he wouldn't be able to persuade his friend to listen to him; instead, he merely spoke, hoping Yitzchak would catch something of his words:

"Can you hear me, Reb Yitzchak? The *pasuk* says: 'G-d is good to all, and His mercy is on all His creations.' The meaning is simple: 'All that the Merciful One does He does for good.' There is no bad in the world. Everything is good. There is good that is pleasant, and good that is less pleasant. That's what we ask in prayer: 'He bestows good kindnesses.' We know that all that comes from G-d is kindness — we merely ask that it be good, that is, that we perceive it as good. Can you hear me, Reb Yitzchak? All is His mercy and His goodness. There are those who, after a short while, merit seeing His good, even when it is concealed in the terrible things that befall them. Others have to wait longer. And yet others only recognize His goodness when they have left this world for the World of Truth. This is man's test: He must strengthen himself and believe that all comes from G-d. Everything comes from Him, with exacting Providence, for man's benefit. Reb Yitzchak!"

Rabbi Mandelkorn took a deep breath. He continued once again:

"Can you hear me, Reb Yitzchak? The *Midrash* says: 'Happy is the man who withstands his test, for there is no one whom the Holy One, Blessed is He, does not test. He tests the wealthy man to see if he will be generous to the poor. He tests the poor man, to see if he can accept his tribulations without anger.' Do you hear? Each has his own personal test! And if we realize that all that happens to us is merely a test, it becomes easy! If man stands erect in the face of his challenge he builds up his character, changes his strengths from potential to reality, as the Torah wills. Every person, Reb Yitzchak! You too, Reb Yitzchak! Do you hear me? Rabbi Elchanan Wasserman, a *talmid* of the Chafetz Chaim, told his congregation, at the moment he was being led out to be killed during the days of the Holocaust, that 'we must be very important and great in Heaven, if they believed that we could overcome such pain!' Be strong, Reb Yitzchak! You're greater than you think you are!"

There was no answer. Rabbi Mandelkorn grew quiet. He lifted his hands in a gesture of despair: What to do?

Before he left, he turned to Rivka. "I'll be back in the evening to see how he is. *Shalom*."

Rabbi Mandelkorn had not yet opened the door when a shrill, loud ring pulsed through the living room. In the doorway that was flung open stood a bareheaded man, no longer young, who handed Rivka a brown military envelope.

"Is your husband here?" he asked.

"Yes. He's here. But he can't come now."

"Good. This is Military Command #8. Tell him that he must come, immediately, to his unit's meeting point on Modi'in Street. Let him bring warm clothing ... "

"Because of the situation?" Rivka asked anxiously.

"That's right. This is a general mobilization. He won't be far from his home. All indications are that our unit is securing Lod Airport."

37

Sao Paulo, Brazil
May 16, 1967

Eduardo stretched out in his seat on the plane. He buckled his seatbelt in preparation for takeoff. He felt the joy of liberation course through his veins. Just boarding the plane had taken him from the pressure cooker of those dramatic events that had overtaken his family these past few days: his father's death, his mother's fears, her sudden disappearance — a disappearance shrouded in mystery. If his mother hadn't called the office and assured him that she was well he would undoubtedly have delayed his flight. Now he could breathe deeply of the scent of far places, a scent refreshing as a cool breeze.

And yet, with all this, he was anxious. His conversation with the police officer, Roberto Nunes, had captured his imagination.

"Good evening," he heard the quiet voice on the intercom, "my name is Silvio de Melo and I'm captain of this Varig DC 10. We hope to reach Paris at 10 a.m. local time. Our flight should be a quiet one. The cabin crew is at your service and will do everything possible to make this flight a pleasant one. Thank you and please prepare for takeoff."

Eduardo closed his eyes. He always felt a bit nervous during takeoff. But now the images that flew before his eyes were directly connected with his father and mother. And particularly, with Roberto Nunes's revelations about them. Nunes was right. He would have an interesting flight. He had a lot to think about ...

Bnei Brak
7 Iyar 5727

Yitzchak Austerlitz heard the conversation between his wife and his unit's courier. A few years earlier, he'd been transferred to *Hagah*, the Civil Defense Force, as a result of ill health. Yitzchak suddenly got out of bed and without a word began to gather his possessions and prepare to leave for the Reserves. *Tallis* and *tefillin*; *Siddur* and *Tehillim*; *Mishnayos Moed* and *Meseches Bava Kamma*. He added a washing cup, a small towel, and the like into his bag. His wife watched him silently. She was satisfied. Perhaps a few days away from the house would lighten his mood. Perhaps. And G-d would help and the military situation would ease and everything would be back to normal.

"Do you want a sweater also?" she asked tentatively.

"Yes," he said gently. It appeared that he, too, felt a few days away would be of help.

He reached the gathering point on Rechov Modi'in, corner Avraham Street. One by one the men arrived. By late afternoon the unit was complete. A bit later they arrived at a military base where they completed their enlistment procedures, received uniforms, Czech rifles, and Uzi submachine guns. They boarded trucks; half an hour's ride took them to Lod Airport.

By nightfall Yitzchak Austerlitz, soldier, was already on guard duty in the Arrivals Terminal, his *Sefer Tehillim* in his hand …

Sao Paulo, Brazil
May 17, 1967

The grey-haired man, Hermann Schmidt, sat in his office waiting for a phone call. Anxiously, he stole a glance at his watch. Almost midnight. Why hadn't they called? He couldn't imagine what could have caused the delay.

Schmidt stood up, began to pace the small office, back and forth, back and forth, with no real destination. On rare occasions he would lose his cool — like now, for example. The rigors of World War II, which he'd spent in Germany, and the difficulties he'd endured, had toughened his spirit, forged it into steel. And yet this evening he felt a finger of fear touch his heart, putting a doubt within him as to the mission's ultimate success. Only natural, he tried to assure himself, but his quiet reassurances were only partially successful. He well knew that luck would play a large role tomorrow night, more, perhaps, than the talent of the men who had arrived from Europe. All the preparations made until now seemed sufficient, at least at first glance. But who could know their outcome?

The preparations for the memorial service in honor of Alberto Hunkes were almost complete. He'd put a lot of work into them. The ceremony itself would be held in the lovely hall of the Municipal Theater in the center of the city. The mayor of Sao Paulo had already expressed his intention to participate. The Minister of the Treasury would also be there, in a show of respect, not to mention the politicians and military figures who had felt privileged to take part in the evening. After all, GAC was a gigantic concern, wielding enormous economic clout, that had brought major benefits to the Brazilian market. The fact that the son, Eduardo Hunkes, was no longer in Sao Paulo might raise a few eyebrows, yet his departure would make his, Schmidt's, mission in the Hunkes house easier to carry off. The young man wouldn't be there to get in the way.

What else was there to do? He had to carefully organize the entrance into the apartment, so that all would go smoothly. Schmidt was convinced that their plans were faultless. What bothered him was the ruckus being raised by Jairo Silverman and his police officer. These announcements on television and radio, requests for help in the search for Mrs. Hunkes, could arouse the attention of certain unwanted elements just at the time when he needed silence the most. Was this the reason for the pit that had settled in his stomach? Schmidt didn't know. Again, he looked at his watch. Why didn't they call?

The grey-haired man pulled a silver case from his pants pocket and took out a cigarette. He lit it, let a cloud of smoke out of his mouth. Smoking sometimes helped him gather his thoughts. But now it didn't seem to do any good. His gaze again returned to his watch, and then moved longingly to the telephone resting upon a nearby table, silent as the night.

He returned to his armchair, settled himself into it and thought about the following day. Tomorrow night, if all would go as planned, he would see his life's ambition fulfilled, the culmination of months of unbelievable effort. All the tension would disappear at once. Perhaps this was the reason for the nerves, the fears, that had begun to beset him from every side — the thought that he was about to close an important circle in his life?

The phone rang. Suddenly, it was difficult for the grey-haired man to lift the receiver. He was terrified of disappointment. But what was this madness, he thought angrily to himself.

The telephone continued its shrill ringing. Schmidt lifted the receiver.

"*Si.*"

For a few minutes the grey-haired man listened quietly to what was being said on the other side. A wide smile split his face, that still wore a look of solid determination.

In a firm, quiet tone he whispered into the receiver: "I'm coming immediately!"

By midnight, the three professionals had returned to the Excelsior Hotel. They came separately, at half-hour intervals. Each one went up to his room without encountering his comrades: The need for secrecy and confidentiality made this absolutely necessary. In the afternoon, in the apartment on Gabriel Monteiro da Silva Street, they'd had a working meeting in which they'd learned of their mission and reviewed the plans. They had also gone to familiarize themselves with their territory: Piaui Street. And they'd met with the grey-haired man, with the short man and the thin one. Now, it was time to sleep.

But after half an hour, they were hurriedly awoken …

Jairo went up the elevator to the room that he'd been assigned by the clerk at the reception counter. He walked through the long, dimly lit hallway with hesitating steps, his eyes jumping to and fro. He tried walking on his tiptoes, though the deep-pile carpet seemed to devour the sound of his footsteps. He was thoroughly frightened, he couldn't deny it. For some reason, he remembered the eyes of children during the Holocaust that he'd seen in pictures found in an album in his father's house. Again, the Jewish destiny! Every door that opened in the long corridor hammered into his heart. His ears, sharpened by fear, tried to make out any muffled sounds that came from behind closed doors. After what seemed a long, arduous trip, that took an entire minute and a half, he reached his room. His nervous hand, trying to hurriedly open the door, couldn't get the key into the lock. His lack of success made him impatient; in another minute, he was afraid he'd burst out crying. He simply didn't recognize himself! What had happened to him?

Another attempt and the door opened. Jairo entered, turned on the light and carefully looked all around him. The enemy could be waiting in ambush even here, in his hotel room. He left the door open. Who knew? He opened the door to the bathroom. Empty. He bent down and peered under the beds. Nothing! With a careful motion he opened the closet door, ready to flee if … But there was nothing there either. Jairo took a deep breath. He was embarrassed by the fears that had consumed him. He quickly locked the door, turning the key twice for added protection.

He turned to the telephone. Although it was after midnight, he called his wife.

"Paulina?"

"Yes."

"Have you gone to sleep?"

"How could I?"

It seemed to Jairo that she'd been crying.

"Look, Paulina. I'm at the Excelsior, on the Ipiranga."

"Yes."

"I'll sleep here tonight. Tomorrow morning I'll see what I'll do."

"What can I say?"

"Now, Paulina, tell me exactly what 'they' told you."

"Nothing special. They said that you knew who they were, and they must meet with you, face to face, as soon as possible. It was urgent, and they wanted to see you tonight. And that this time it was serious, and you shouldn't dare avoid it. I told him you weren't home. He asked where you were. I said, you'd gone to the Hebraica."

Jairo suddenly felt a tremendous pain in his temples. His vision grew clouded. He grabbed the receiver in trembling hands and cried in fury, "What have you done? Don't you understand, you've put me into their hands! You've made it possible for them to follow me anywhere! I'm certain they know I'm here in the Excelsior!"

He heard her burst out crying. From amidst her tears, she said brokenly, "Believe me, Jairo, I don't know what I understand and what I don't anymore! It just came out! I don't know why. What could I do?"

"Now — I'm lost. I'd better get out of the hotel now, and find myself some other place."

And after a moment, he added, in tones of sheer fright, "If it will help at all …"

Jairo was silent, and Paulina didn't say a word. Suddenly, she heard her husband's voice once again, a hysterical voice whispering in panic:

"Paulina! Paulina! I think they've come! They're knocking on my door … they're knocking louder … I'm hanging up … I don't know what I'll do … Call the police immediately. And the hotel, the reception area … tell them to come right now! I don't know what to do … quickly, Paulina, quickly!"

The conversation ended. The knocking at the door didn't stop. It grew louder and louder …

38

An airplane above the Atlantic Ocean
May 16, 1967

Eduardo couldn't sleep. A few hours had passed since the Varig flight had taken off from Rio de Janeiro after a short stop there. Now he was flying over the Atlantic Ocean, on his way to Paris. In the airplane all was silent. The food trays, empty of all but a few remaining leftovers, had been taken away by the stewardesses. The passengers curled up in the thin blankets. The lights were extinguished, and with them the quiet conversations of the passengers. The hum of the engine splitting the skies above was the one sound that disturbed the evening slumber that had overtaken all. All, that is, but Eduardo. It was a difficult hour for him: In the deep silence his thoughts came sharp and clear.

Eduardo unfastened his seat belt. He rose and began walking up the narrow aisle. In his slow journey he finally reached the end of the airplane. Why? He had no idea. Maybe to kill some time before going back to his seat. But finally, he returned. He sat down, carefully trying not to wake his snoring seatmate. He pushed him slightly, cautiously, in order to regain the seat he'd vacated. The man didn't stir.

Now, far from home, his perspective had returned. It seemed quite likely that his father hadn't been merely a Danish collaborator, but a full-fledged Nazi. A Nazi who'd escaped judgment in Europe. A war criminal, as defined by the criteria accepted by the world today. Eduardo tried to understand what difference this would make to his own life. Did he care? He, too, hated Jews, though not with the bitter vindictiveness his parents had displayed to that cursed people. True, they'd taught him to loathe Jews: The house had been full of that. But here, high above the ocean, he was forced to admit that their education hadn't succeeded, that they hadn't managed to infect him with the virus of hatred to the degree they'd wanted. His Brazilian education, liberal and open to all manner of people, had somehow negated the hatred in his heart. With such a background, he wasn't really pleased with the idea of his parents as Nazis …

A tiny doubt flashed through his brain. Why hadn't they allowed him to visit them at that ranch, near the Vila Velha, not far from Curitiba? Was there clandestine Nazi activity going on there in which his father took part? He had read in the papers of secret Nazi convocations in Paraguay and Argentina. And perhaps as a result his father had been murdered by Jews! It was clear that his mother knew something, if she'd been so certain even before the police had announced it, that his father had been murdered. Now his journalistic curiosity was aroused. He made a mental note: When he returned from the Middle East, he would investigate the affair.

A sleepy stewardess happened to pass.

"Excuse me."

She stopped and answered politely. "Yes?"

"Can I get a cup of cola?"

"Certainly, sir."

"With ice, please."

"Absolutely, sir."

"And some aspirin. For a headache."

"Okay, *Senhor*."

Eduardo swallowed the cold drink. His father, a Nazi. What a pleasant thought. A Nazi? What was the inescapable conclusion? Had his father taken part in murders, particularly the killing of Jews? The thought disturbed him. Maybe he was just a low-echelon Nazi, a junior officer in the S.S. or Gestapo. It wasn't possible that his father had stained his hands with blood. One didn't have to love the Jews to feel disgusted by Hitler's mass murder. Eduardo couldn't believe it of his father. But if not, why had he fled? Why had he hidden under a forged identity, as the police officer, the unsympathetic Roberto Nunes, had claimed?

Eduardo shifted the armrest, crossed his legs, and moved about nervously. But his father had been good to him! Humane, caring. Though he had occasionally felt a frigid, almost Siberian coldness, emanating from him. There were moments when he felt that the man simply hated him. There was a mysterious hardness within him that puzzled Eduardo. But the feeling would vanish almost instantly. The clouds that darkened his father's personality for short periods would quickly scatter in the sunshine of the warm smile that lit up his face. He had been a good father. Impossible for him to have been a Nazi, in the classical under-standing of the phrase. And in any case, why had his parents hidden their past from him? He remembered how his mother had wished to show him something from her vault, and how, in the last minute, she'd re-frained. Why? And still another mysterious, inexplicable point: his father's friendship with Jairo Silverman — the Jew. How could he explain the con-tradictions? And why had his mother disappeared? Despite her reassurances that she would return, there was the scent of mystery emanating from the whole business! Eduardo didn't know, couldn't see, didn't understand. But these were the facts. And they would give him no rest. He wouldn't be able to sleep. Despite all, though, he closed his eyes ...

Sao Paulo, Brazil
May 17, 1967

The skeleton key slipped smoothly into the key-hole. The door to Jairo's room suddenly burst open. Three men filled the entrance. Jairo immediately iden-tified the oldest of them, standing in the center, as the grey-haired man, GAC's power behind-the-scenes. The flickering image of the man giving the Nazi salute before the grave of Alberto Hunkes raced through Jairo's brain. The crushing thought pierced him like an arrow: They've got me!

Jairo raced wildly towards the window. If he had to, he would jump. But he didn't make it: One of the men made a swift bound and blocked his way.

Jairo stood, petrified and hopeless. His eyes jumped wildly from one man to the next.

"Jairo," the grey-haired man began to speak, "*Senhor* Jairo Silverman, I apologize for this uninvited intrusion. I'm aware that after midnight is not the usual time for a friendly visit. But what can one do? And you did bring this upon yourself, you know."

The grey-haired man was still for a fraction of a second, attempting to catch his breath. Then he continued.

"I heard you yelling at your wife to call the police. With this, *Senhor* Silverman, you've made a complicated situation even more complex. We wanted to talk to you here in your room. But the police may be here soon, depending on what tone your wife uses with the station chief. You must understand that we have to find a more amenable place in which to hold a friendly chat."

He motioned to the two men to approach Jairo, who stood paralyzed in the center of the room. He had no strength left to fight, no will to resist. He accepted his fate. The frightening thought went through his tortured brain: *So must the Jews been led towards the gas chambers!*

"So, Jairo, you've got to come with us. I would be very pleased if you avoided making a fuss, and came quietly. Okay?"

Jairo didn't answer. In his heart he bid a tearful goodbye to his wife and children. He was sure this was the end. His wife had been right: He should have left the whole thing alone. Should have abandoned his search for Alberto Hunkes's true identity. If he had, "they" would not have come after him. And now, he was caught in a trap he'd laid for himself. During one of those mysterious phone calls (had it been the grey-haired man on the other end?) someone had mentioned the Spider organization. Was he now caught in some sinister web of theirs? Jairo didn't know. Terror held him in its steely grip. He understood that he had no choice: He must follow their instructions.

The grey-haired man opened the door. With a strong motion of his arm, he invited Jairo out into the hallway. Jairo followed wordlessly. The two others walked behind him, like bodyguards following a president. They turned towards the elevator. Its doors opened, and the four of them disappeared inside. Jairo hung onto the hope that the reception clerk and the hotel guard might realize he was being kidnaped. Perhaps he could begin to scream, in order to get their attention. He was endangering himself, he knew, but it would be his last chance.

With a start, Jairo saw the grey-haired man push the elevator button for the hotel's underground parking lot. It seemed he was giving the lobby a wide berth. The grey-haired man smiled, as if he could read the chagrin in Jairo's heart.

A car was waiting for them, its engine running, a driver sitting behind the steering wheel. So the grey-haired man had lied, Jairo thought, when he'd claimed they had to leave only because he, Jairo, had warned his wife to call the police. Not that it made any difference at this point.

The car door opened. The grey-haired man's eyes showed Jairo what he was to do. Jairo hesitated.

"Get in already!" the grey-haired man shouted, his voice echoing eerily in the silent parking lot. "Do you think I want to meet the Sao Paulo police department here in this hole?"

Jairo surrendered to his fate. *My own personal train to Auschwitz*, his heart wept. He entered, sat down in the back, flanked on both sides by his silent "bodyguards." The grey-haired man sat down next to the driver, who sped down the Ipiranga Boulevard.

The roads of Sao Paulo, even at this hour, were full. Jairo stole a glance at the lit-up streets as the car hurried past. This was the last time he would see them. A sharp pain stabbed him like a knife flung through his heart. Had the Jews of Germany or Poland felt like this as they walked for the last time through the streets of Berlin, Warsaw, Cracow, Lodz? Perhaps! Jairo felt that he was suffocating. His breath came in uneven gasps. The two musclemen gave him impervious looks. He couldn't figure out their nationality. German? They didn't look it. But the grey-haired man — most definitely a German. Even his fluent Portuguese was spoken by a tongue accustomed to the German language. Oh, why had the Jewish destiny overtaken him, even here, in the free, open city of Sao Paulo? What would his father say to this awful moment, after he'd hoped that the assimilationist education he'd given his son would save him from the Jewish fate?

They were leaving the city, Jairo noticed, traveling onto the road that led to the forests surrounding the Pico de Jaragua, the High Mountain. What were they going to do with him? So, too, were the Jews brought to the forests of Poland during the *aktions* … Jairo couldn't take anymore. The trembling that began in his legs spread over his entire body. He wanted to pray so badly — but he didn't know what to say. He didn't know a word of Hebrew. Suddenly, from the depths of his despair, the Hebrew words that he'd learned so long ago in the Jewish school, the Renaissance, came back to him. Over and over, he said them to himself: "*Mah nishtanah halailah hazeh mi'kol haleilos*, Why is this night different from all other nights?" He felt his heart begging his G-d to hear his prayer …

The car sped on …

Lod Airport, Israel
8 Iyar 5727

A new dawn illuminated Lod Airport. Yitzchak Austerlitz had completed his guard duty. Before he went to bed, he wrapped himself in his *tallis,* put on his *tefillin*, and *davened.* There was no *minyan* here for him: He was practically the only religious soldier in the unit. Prayers, in this quiet corner in the terminal, were subdued. The mournful, melancholy spirit that had conquered his every action had overtaken his *davening* as well.

Yitzchak stood for the *Shemoneh Esrei* prayer. He reached the words of the *tefillah*, "Mainstay and Assurance of the righteous." Something stopped him, made it impossible for him to go on. He shut his eyes and remembered an explanation he'd once heard for the words. There are moments when a person is in complete despair. G-d's concealment is so great that he sees no possibility of salvation. He has no "assurance," and this feeling begins to impinge upon his faith in G-d. Then it is that G-d sends him a "mainstay" — some kind of heavenly sign that enables him to continue to believe that all is from G-d and that salvation will come — in its time.

Austerlitz remembered, too, the example that the commentator (he thought it was the Gaon of Vilna, though he wasn't certain) had given to illustrate the point. The decrees of Haman and Achashveirosh had dimmed the eyes of a generation of Jews. They had no idea from where their salvation would come. Their faith began to waver. It was then that G-d sent them Haman leading Mordechai on a royal horse. When the Jews saw this it was like a ray of sunlight breaking through the lowering clouds that had obscured it before. This, then, was the "mainstay" that strengthened them, enabled them to continue to have faith in their ultimate salvation ...

Yitzchak realized that his cheeks were moist. In his heart, he heard the question: Where is my "mainstay?" Where is my sign?

He opened his eyes to quiet the incessant question that he'd been asking. He could hear Rabbi Mandelkorn's voice, the words he'd spoken as he, Yitzchak Austerlitz, had lain cowering beneath his blanket: There is none whom G-d does not test. Praised is he who passes his test!

And he, Yitzchak Austerlitz, was being tested, as Heaven refused him even his "mainstay." Or so he felt. Each man, with his own personal test ...

39

Paris, France
May 17, 1967

The Varig DC 10 landed at Orly Airport, near Paris, at precisely 10 in the morning. Eduardo, bone weary, stood among the long line of travelers waiting for passport checks and the arrival of their luggage. Eduardo yawned unashamedly: He was exhausted from his sleepless night.

An excellent idea, not traveling to Tel Aviv until tomorrow. In no more than an hour he would be sleeping deeply in the room he'd reserved for himself in the Chibnai Hotel. The hotel was centrally located, not far from the Eiffel Tower, the lovely Champs Élysées, and the Arc de Triomphe. A tranquil day of touring in this wonderful city would help ease the pressure of these past few days in Sao Paulo. His father's mysterious death, his mother's voluntary disappearance (why?), the curious police officer had all taken their toll on him. Not to mention the suspicions he now harbored of secret Nazi activity …

Paris, France
May 18, 1967

Eduardo reached the terminal in Orly at 3 o'clock, somewhat calmer, though still tense as he prepared to embark on the last leg of his journey to Israel.

As he walked towards the El Al counter he noticed a disturbance of some kind. There was a crowd of Jews, or Israelis — in his eyes they were one and the same. There wasn't the semblance of order, as large numbers of young people pushed and shoved, ignoring the pleas of the hapless staffers, in futile attempts to get to the head of the line. The uncouth shouting stood in sharp contrast to the quiet, civil atmosphere that surrounded the non-Jewish counters. Was this barbarism, this uncivilized behavior taking place in front of his eyes part and parcel of the Jewish race? What was going on?

Eduardo approached the center of the tumult. He didn't understand a word of the Hebrew that most were speaking — that is, shouting — with great fervor and obvious emotion. In seemed that some were on the verge of fistfights. These inflamed passions would, it appeared certain, degenerate into a full-fledged brawl. The argument was somehow connected with the purchase of tickets. Didn't they believe in advance sales here? He stood silently at the edge of the fracas; in the meantime, he wouldn't push forward. His reservation, made in Sao Paulo, would be intact, he hoped, and not forcibly taken from him by one of these wild men. At some point he would have to contact one of the overwhelmed staffers: He had no desire to miss the Middle East war and lose the opportunity to prove his journalistic mettle.

An English reporter stood near him, also watching the fray.

"Do you understand them?" he asked Eduardo.

"No. I suppose that's just the way their people are. The Jewish people, that is."

The Englishman cast an astonished gaze upon him. "Are you an anti-Semite?"

Eduardo looked all innocence. "Not at all. Why do you think so?"

"It sounded like it, no less."

A young Israeli standing near them had also heard the short dialogue. He didn't shout, but his fury was clear in his words.

"You're looking at young Israeli Jews who desire to return to their land, at any price, to fight for their homes, and you don't like it? Is that it? You like Jews only when they stand, quiet and terrified, in orderly rows, with the S.S. shooting them down. Yes? That's it! Here, everyone shouts: We want to go home! The political and military situation grows worse and worse. War is inevitable. A difficult war. And you laugh at men hurrying to protect their homeland?"

The English journalist was chastened. "I'm sorry. I didn't say anything about them."

His eyes darted back to Eduardo, as if to say, he was the guilty one in the conversation. Eduardo stood, unmoved, a thin, frigid smile on his lips, hardly listening to the words of the young Israeli.

Who knew what other Jews, who called themselves Israelis, he would meet in the next few weeks, from the time he landed in Tel Aviv, this very night?

Lod Airport, Israel
8 Iyar 5727

It was 1 in the afternoon. Yitzchak Austerlitz had been on guard duty for a full hour already. He'd been posted at the entry gate for passengers arriving from abroad. His job was to inspect the passengers, looking for anything unusual among them. Arab terror could also board airplanes bound for Israel.

A Civil Defense officer passed by. "*Nu*, Reb Yitzchak, what's happening?"

"Thank G-d, everything's fine," he answered offhandedly.

"You have everything you need?"

"Thank G-d."

After a moment, he added, "It's impossible for a man to have everything. But — it's enough."

The officer approached him. He had known Austerlitz for several years, since he'd joined the unit — a quiet man, Austerlitz, who obeyed his orders without demur or complaint, not like some others. He stood out among the soldiers, the only one with beard and *payos*, and the one shrouded always, even in rare moments when he'd smiled, in deep melancholy. He never spoke of it, and no one ever brought it up. All realized that this was his secret, that no one had the right to probe too deeply.

The officer felt it would be appropriate to give a few encouraging words. "What are you missing? If I can, I'll see to it that you get it," he said in fatherly tones.

Austerlitz lifted his head towards the officer, a mournful smile on his face. He shifted the Czech rifle resting on his knees and answered, never raising his voice: "Nothing, sir. Nothing's missing."

The office put his arm gently on Austerlitz's shoulder. "Stick with it, Yitzchak. We'll need a lot of strength in the next few days."

The officer began to walk on, when Austerlitz's voice stopped him. "Excuse me, sir."

The officer turned and waited.

"Perhaps you could relieve me now. I'm not feeling very well. I've got a headache ... "

For a moment there was no answer. Austerlitz continued, "I'll take the night shift. All night."

It seemed a good idea. Soon another soldier appeared to relieve him. Austerlitz went to bed.

Until nightfall ...

Sao Paulo, Brazil
May 17, 1967

The car stopped in the depths of the forest. The blackness surrounding them was complete. In the darkness Jairo couldn't make out his captors' faces. He accepted his fate.

The grey-haired man lit a small flashlight. Jairo could see him smiling at him, the exultation of success. In his heart he cursed the man with every epithet known to him in Portuguese.

"Attorney Jairo Silverman," the man began quietly, "I am truly sorry that I had to frighten you so this past week. But the fault lies entirely with you."

This is it, Jairo thought. *Judgment*. He had no thought of fleeing: The two bodyguards flanking him held him tightly. One blow from either of those wild men and he would be in a better world immediately.

The grey-haired man continued. "We asked you not to interfere in things that didn't concern you. And you laughed at us. The question is: Why?"

Jairo didn't answer. There was nothing to say. And no reason to speak. He closed his eyes. Once again, he sought refuge in thoughts of prayer, of pleas, of beseeching ... Did the forest, the trees surrounding him, know what they were going to do to him? He had often read of men who disappeared in this huge country, not leaving a trace behind. He had never thought it could happen to him. Though he felt as if he were crying, no tears came …

The grey-haired man continued.

"You almost destroyed a project that had been years in the inception. Hunkes's sudden death was the first problem; you, the second."

Jairo, his body trembling uncontrollably, didn't understand a word the man was saying.

The grey-haired man lit himself a cigarette. He offered one to Jairo. "Smoke?"

Jairo quickly shook his head, no.

"I couldn't immediately reveal to you who I am," the grey-haired man said. "I should not do so as long as I am in Brazil. It's too dangerous. Very dangerous. For me, and for the work that I'm doing. Do you see? Even now, it is difficult for me to specify exactly what we're talking about. I can't tell what you would do with the information."

The grey-haired man inhaled deeply, then gently exhaled the fragrant smoke. The tension in the small, crowded car was unbearable. Unbearable, that is, for Jairo, who had no idea how this nightmare would end.

"Jairo." He suddenly heard the authoritative tones of the grey-haired man. "I have no choice but to be open with you. But I'm warning you now: If you reveal one word of what I tell you — your blood is on your head! Is that understood?"

Jairo nodded in assent. Without understanding.

The grey-haired man leaned back, his breath coming with difficulty. For a moment he remained silent. Finally, with a determined gesture, he said quietly, the hint of a quaver in his voice: "I have spent my life hunting after Nazis. I am a Jew, a survivor of the Holocaust. A German Jew, educated in Buchenwald."

Jairo felt his vision grow dim. He didn't believe a word he was hearing. The man was a Nazi: Jairo had seen him shout 'Heil Hitler' near Alberto Hunkes's grave. What was the point of this play-acting, here in the forest near the Pico de Jaragua?

The grey-haired man continued.

"Is it hard for you to believe me? Hey? I don't care, and I'm really not interested. I need just one thing from you. Silence! You must tell your friend, the energetic police officer, to stop arousing everyone in search of Mrs. Hunkes. And after I finish my mission, then he …"

The grey-haired man hesitated for a minute. With a decisive nod of the head, he continued.

"*Senhor* Silverman, I'm going to take a gamble. But I have no choice. Your friend, Alberto Hunkes, was one of the leaders of the Nazis in South America. Do you hear me? Regina, his wife, is no less a criminal. Do you understand?"

Jairo didn't react.

"He, Alberto Hunkes, had the keys to the plans of the Spider. Aren't you interested in what that is?"

Jairo wanted to know. Wanted desperately to know. But fear paralyzed him. He couldn't understand what kind of trap this grey-haired German was laying for him. And why, if he planned on executing him, did he reveal forbidden secrets? What was going on here?

"I'll tell you, *Senhor*. The Spider was the means by which people in the Catholic Church enabled tens of thousands of Nazis to evade justice and the hangman's noose. Thousands! Do you hear? They gave them money, refuge in monasteries, forged documents and the help of churches in the countries to which they fled until the pursuit had ended. These Nazis are scattered all over the world, but the majority came to this continent, to Latin America. Did you know of this, my young attorney?"

This time, Jairo managed a weak nod of assent.

To Jairo's complete astonishment, the grey-haired man turned to the two thugs sitting on either side of him and said something to them in Hebrew. Jairo didn't understand a word of what he'd said, but the sound of the language was familiar. Very familiar. Now he was completely confused. Perhaps the grey-haired man was telling the truth after all?

The two men and the driver, obviously in response to their employer's words, left the car. Jairo was now alone with the grey-haired man. Despite all that had happened, Jairo was still deeply suspicious.

"*Senhor* Silverman, ask me questions. I've given you a few facts, and now I have no choice but to share everything with you. The mission is contingent on absolute secrecy, and that's what I'm asking of you. As strange as it may seem: I'm now in your hands!"

The voice was pleasant and it seemed to Jairo that there was the hint of entreaty behind it.

Incredible, the thought flashed through Jairo's brain. It was difficult for him to grow used to the sudden change in his situation. He was still not completely convinced. And yet, there existed the possibility that he was not doomed to die. He would return home. See his wife. His children. His father, his friends — everything! His heart pounded, felt as if it would burst.

"What do you want me to ask you?" Jairo finally spoke.

"Everything! It will make it easier for me to explain what's happening. I am convinced that as a Jew you will not betray me, a Jew like you."

"A Jew like me." Jairo's voice was filled with emotion. "A Jew like me, standing next to the grave of Alberto Hunkes giving the Nazi salute? That's my first question. I haven't yet forgotten the image of that awful scene!"

The grey-haired man smiled. "I'm a Jew. I was born in Berlin. My name, in my youth, was Bruno Meinhoff. I discarded the name after the Holocaust, when I came to Israel. Today, my name is Reuven Morag."

The grey-haired man held out another cigarette. This time, Jairo accepted his offer. The man, Jairo saw, was very moved.

"You want to know why I made the Nazi salute? I belong to a Jewish group called The Avengers. It is an organization whose goal is not merely to root out hidden Nazis and turn them over to the governments of the countries in which they have hidden, as Wiesenthal does. No! Our organization has taken it upon ourselves to find Nazis — and execute them! Yes! Yes! To kill them! We will never reveal how many of that devil's brood we've murdered! But our work is not yet done. In my pursuit of them, I penetrated a Nazi organization in South America, in order to discover who headed the gang, who had the information on the Nazis living in this country."

Jairo took a deep breath. He asked the question, though deep in his heart he knew the answer to it.

"And did you find out?"

"Yes! I found him in GAC! I followed him there, after years of bitter toil. And do you know what his name was?"

The men gazed into each other's eyes. Neither mentioned Alberto Hunkes.

Jairo had another question. "Who killed him?"

"We did. Accidentally. Or rather, because we had no choice."

"What do you mean?"

"He had found us out. He knew we were following him. A man from Israel's Mossad who had come from Europe to meet with him realized that the fiend intended to kill him. It seemed from all his words and actions that he had uncovered our plans. He had to die, before he could set up any precautions."

There was a minute of silence. "Now, do you understand why I had to make the Nazi salute on his grave?"

"Yes," Jairo answered weakly.

"And now, *Senhor* Silverman. We are aware that Hunkes was in possession of the lists that we've been searching for many years. We've reached the point of knowing exactly where they are hidden. We've managed to get his wife away from his house. But your police officer is making noise, drawing the curious eyes of the police force to that apartment on Piaui Street. First it was you making an uproar. We were afraid the widow would flee, taking the lists with her."

"What are you planning?"

"The Mossad has sent three professionals who will enter Mrs. Hunkes's home tonight, and break into her safe. It was my luck that they were staying at the Excelsior, the hotel you chose when fleeing from me. As a result, it was easy for me to bring you here. Do you understand? Now, for the next two days I ask only one thing of you: that police officer Roberto Nunes end all investigations, put a lid on the newspapers and television. Afterwards, do whatever you want. Can I rely on you?"

The two exchanged a firm handshake; their eyes exchanged meaningful glances.

The grey-haired man called to his three cronies: "Come!"

"By the way," Jairo asked the grey-haired man, as the others entered the car, "what was Alberto Hunkes's real name? The name I knew him under was undoubtedly an alias."

"You're right," the grey-haired man answered, his voice drowned out in the roar of the engine, as the car began its return to the city. "We know his real name. It was Heinz Krantz."

40

E duardo sat, preoccupied, in the jam-packed El
Al plane. The noise and tumult of the passengers made sleep impossible. He looked
around him. He'd never seen such a great
concentration of Jews in one place. He felt repelled by
them. He couldn't understand a word of their loud,
angry chatter. He could see that all were excited and
nervous. Most were young. Few could sit still: They
pranced about the plane as if it were a seaside promenade. From the words of the young Israeli who'd been
so insulted in Orly he understood that they were returning to their land in order to join their army units,
which had been called to defend their flag.

His seatmate, who'd been dozing, suddenly turned
to him and spoke in Hebrew. Eduardo smiled. "I don't
understand," he said, in heavily accented English.

The Israeli youth straightened up, as if seeing one
of the wonders of the world.

"You're not Jewish?" he asked, surprised, as if to say: What is a non-Jew doing here at this time, flying towards war?

"No. No, I'm not a Jew," Eduardo swiftly said. *That's all that's missing,* he thought to himself, *to be a Jew.*

The Israeli didn't give up. "So why are you traveling to Israel now? Don't you know that war may break out any minute?"

"That's why I'm going."

"What do you mean?"

"I'm a journalist."

"Oh, a journalist. From where?"

"Brazil. Sao Paulo."

"Oh, Brazil! Are they interested in Israel there too?"

"You see for yourself."

After a moment's silence, the young man asked, "Will you be writing for us or against us?"

"Not for and not against. I'm a reporter, a military correspondent. I write what I see."

The Israeli wrinkled his nose, as if he'd heard some foul word.

"All over the world reporters write what they see, but it always comes out against us, even as they claim objectivity. What can you do? People can't give up their preconceived notions. A person sees facts through his own beliefs. The anti-Semite will always write against us, no matter what. He has a theory, and he won't let facts get in the way."

Eduardo agreed inwardly: The boy was right.

The young man smiled. "But you're Brazilian, and no anti-Semite. I've heard that the Brazilians don't hate Jews. Is that true?"

"It is," Eduardo reluctantly agreed. At that moment, his father, Alberto Hunkes, came to mind.

"Do you think we'll win?" the young man asked the reporter, who undoubtedly knew what would happen.

"Time will tell," he answered diplomatically.

The young man grabbed his hand. Eduardo felt slightly nauseated. *What's this Jew touching me for, anyway?*

But the young man wouldn't let up. "We'll win, do you hear! The holocaust will never touch our land! They, the Arabs, will not slaughter us, as the Nazis, may their names be erased, did. G-d will never allow it! Do you hear! And I tell you, and I don't know who you are, that it's worth your while to write well of us! Because you'll be on the side of the victors!"

"That's well and good," Eduardo said, losing his patience, "but would you mind letting go of my hand?" Eduardo felt sick. He remembered conversations he'd had with his father about Jews. His first report of his experiences in Israel began to take shape in his head.

The young man let go and sat still in his chair. He saw he'd gone too far.

"Excuse me," he said apologetically, "you must try to understand how I feel today, having to end my studies in the Sorbonne in Paris in order to fly home to protect my home, my parents' home!"

"Okay, okay," Eduardo made it clear that, at least in his eyes, the conversation had come to an end.

At least the talk had made the time pass by quickly. From the window he could see that night had already fallen. The lights of the coastal city of Tel Aviv winked in the darkness. The captain announced that it was time to prepare for landing. Seat belts were fastened. Eduardo closed his eyes, feeling somewhat nervous. Who knew what adventures lay before him, here in the land of the Jews, his father's sworn enemies, for whom he, too, had no love?

Fifteen minutes later, the plane had landed.

Lod Airport
8 Iyar 5727

Yitzchak Austerlitz tensed up. He could see the El Al plane landing. Now it would be his job to scrutinize the passengers. It was his right to stop and search anyone suspicious. Until today, he'd never had to do so. But he was prepared for anything. He peered into the darkness outside the terminal, and saw passengers begin to descend from the plane …

Sao Paulo, Brazil
May 18, 1967

The grey-haired man, a.k.a. Hermann Schmidt, a.k.a. Reuven Morag, brought Jairo Silverman to the center of the city. The giant metropolis was beginning to awaken from its nighttime slumbers. The sun, that could just be spotted rising over the horizon, painted the tops of the skyscrapers a deep purple. Here and there one could see early risers on their way to work. A few bars were open, and one or two stores selling bread. As Jairo left the car, the grey-haired man reminded him of what he was to do now:

"Send your friend Roberto Nunes away on vacation, for at least one day. Call him now! I'm sure your wife got him out of bed to search for you. I hope I can count on you. I apologize for having frightened you so. When I get back to Israel I'll send you a postcard with my address. You're welcome to visit me there. Goodbye."

The car disappeared in the city's quiet, sleepy streets.

Jairo entered the first bar he passed. "*Bom dia*. May I make a call?"

Impatiently he dialed the number, not noticing the young bartender watching his every move. Someone picked up the phone.

"Hello?" He heard the voice of his wife, to whom he'd bid a final goodbye just a few hours earlier.

He took a deep breath and said in a soft voice, "Hello, Paulina. It's me, Jairo."

He had expected the reaction. "Jairo!" his wife shrieked hysterically, "Where are you? Where are you calling from? Are you all right? They're searching for you throughout the city!"

"Shhh … shhh … don't shout. Everything is fine. In another hour I'll be home. I hope the nightmare is over. Now do me a favor. Do your best, and find Roberto Nunes for me. Let him come to me, right now!"

"Okay. But where are you?"

"Libero Badaro Street. He'll see me right away. Let him come alone. Tell him not to worry. Everything is okay. Do it at once. All right?"

She answered with difficulty. He could hear her sobbing on the other end of the line.

Jairo swiftly hung up the phone. He paid the young man and went out to the street, to await the police officer.

Jairo paced back and forth on the hard pavement, glancing nervously at his watch every few minutes. Why hadn't he come? The night's adventures had left him shaken up, particularly the shocking revelations of the grey-haired man. He believed the incredible story of the GAC executive, the man who'd caused Jairo's own personal crisis through his Nazi salute over Hunkes's grave. Hunkes, that vile Nazi, who had deceived him so brutally. Jairo felt a pang of self-loathing for having fallen for him, having helped that beast obtain his Brazilian citizenship. How he hated him now, the man who lay buried beneath the ground, this Heinz Krantz! If he'd meet that demon, Hunkes's wife, now, he would spit in her face. Yes, that's what he'd do.

He took another look at the watch. A quarter of an hour had passed since he'd called his wife, and there was no sign of Roberto. What did it mean?

He walked towards the bar. He would call home again. No, at the last minute he decided to wait a bit longer. Suddenly, he heard the sound of an approaching car. And before he could whirl around towards it, the car had shrieked to a stop next to him.

"Jairo!" Police officer Roberto Nunes leaped out of the car and enveloped Jairo in a Brazilian bear hug. "Where have you been?"

"Quiet! Stop yelling! I'll tell you everything! Let's get into the car and get out of here. That kid in the bar is already becoming too interested in me!"

They drove away and parked on a side street near the Praca Roosevelt.

"Okay, talk," Nunes said shortly.

"They want you to stop the investigation."

"Who is 'they'?"

" 'They!' You know who we're talking about."

Nunes looked deep into Jairo's eyes. "Nazis?"

Jairo nodded. "Yes."

"Did they hurt you?"

"No. But they wanted to prove to me that they could kidnap me, hide my body in the forest, and no one would ever find me. They took me as far as the Pico de Jaragua."

Nunes didn't speak.

"Roberto!" Jairo said, his voice beseeching. "I asked you to open the investigation. Now I'm asking you to close it. Okay?"

Roberto Nunes didn't answer.

Jairo continued. "I already know who Alberto Hunkes was. I don't need this investigation anymore. I'm satisfied. I'll pay you what I promised."

"Who's thinking about money now?" Roberto protested. He knew he was lying; he knew that Jairo was well aware of it. "What interests me," he continued, "is who he really was, this Alberto Hunkes."

"His name was Heinz Krantz. Have you ever heard of him? Is there anything on him in the police files?"

"I'll have to check. Who revealed his identity to you? 'They' themselves?"

"Yes."

"What? Are they crazy, to expose themselves like that?"

"They know I'll keep quiet. They know you'll keep quiet too — because they know you don't want me to be killed. And if you continue to investigate, that's what my fate will be. Do you understand? What does it bother them to reveal the identity of a dead man, a man beyond harming? They figured they'd calm me down by telling me, and I'll stop my involvement in Nazi activities. Understand?"

There was a long moment of silence in the street. Roberto leaned his head on the steering wheel. Jairo felt he could do no more: He dared not reveal the whole truth to his friend. He could not destroy the grey-haired man's mission. What did he care if Nunes believed he'd been captured by Nazis?

Jairo continued. "They also asked that you stop searching for that cursed widow. They've got her hidden, and you won't be able to find her. Why they've done so, I haven't the slightest idea. One thing is clear: They demand that you put an end to the announcements in the papers, radio, and television. From today on they want complete silence about the affair. I'm prepared to pay you for this service as well."

Roberto still gave no reply. He realized clearly that he would do as Jairo had requested, but he could not acquiesce immediately. Instead, he shrugged. "We'll see."

His answer calmed Jairo. He had known his friend the police officer for many years, and recognized his style.

"Take me home. For my part, it seems the nightmare is over."

The grey-haired man returned to the Excelsior Hotel. He sent his men to bed. He himself took a short rest, and by about 9 in the morning went up to Regina Hunkes's room.

"Good morning, Hermann," she greeted him.

"Good morning. I thought it would be a good idea," he added, with an obvious show of friendliness, "to let you know the program for this evening's memorial service."

Regina didn't answer, and her face was frigid.

"By the way," he continued, veering off the topic, "we tried to work things out with the police yesterday. We asked that they appoint someone other than Roberto Nunes to this investigation. That way, it will be simpler for us to get the file closed. In the meantime we haven't succeeded. We'll try again today, with the highest echelons."

After a short silence, he gave an embarrassed smile and said, "But let's get back to tonight. All of Sao

Paulo's political, economic and social leaders will be there to pay respect to our dear Alberto and to show honor to GAC. It's an honor for you as well, Regina. Tonight Roberto Nunes can't get anywhere near you. I hope that by this evening the file will be closed. And if not, I've made arrangements that will allow you to fly out quietly and safely to Germany. The GAC head office already has instructions to take care of you."

Regina didn't react. Schmidt handed her a beautifully printed program. He explained, "There will only be a few speakers: the head of GAC; the mayor; the head of the city's economic office; and perhaps a friend, though we haven't yet decided which one. Do you have any suggestions?"

Regina shook her head, no.

"After the speeches, you can see in the program, the Municipal Ballet Company will perform Rimsky-Korsakov's *Scheherezade*."

Regina continued to listen silently. She turned searching eyes upon Schmidt's face. It was hard for her to decide just what it was that was disturbing her so. His friendliness suddenly seemed exaggerated. A heavy suspicion blazed in her heart. Something was wrong ... but she didn't know what it was. Why did she suddenly feel so strange?

The grey-haired man stood up to leave. He had to hurry and awaken his henchmen for one last rehearsal, and then they would be off to break into the Hunkes apartment.

Schmidt was almost out of her room when he heard Regina's call.

"Hermann!"

"Yes?"

"I'm returning home — now!"

41

Sao Paulo, Brazil
May 18, 1967

The grey-haired man stood in his place, thunderstruck. He released his grip on the doorknob. His shock was complete. After a moment of paralysis he whirled around and slowly made his way into the room where Regina was sitting, ensconced on the sofa. She stared at him, her eyes inscrutable. He answered her glance with an expressionless one of his own. He lightly bit his lips and his left hand, in its pants pocket, balled up into a fist. When he was standing near her he asked, in a quiet voice that he managed to call upon from some inner recess of his soul: "What do you mean by that?"

She gave him a sullen glance. "I simply want to go home! I don't understand why you're so anxious to keep me away!"

His face took on an offended look. "You know your attitude is insulting."

"Perhaps, Hermann. But I've always been a woman who spoke her mind."

"Does this mean you actually suspect me of something?"

The grey-haired man was angry, and she knew it.

"Answer me," he demanded again, "do you suspect me of being up to something?"

Regina didn't respond immediately. After a moment of silence she threw her hands out and said nonchalantly, "I don't know exactly. Something like that."

The grey-haired man grew silent. He didn't remove his gaze from her, although his look revealed nothing. Quickly he sized up the situation. If she returned home now, his mission would fail. His henchmen would be unable to break in and take the documents that he needed so badly. There was, of course, the possibility of using violence: of breaking in, overpowering her, binding her and finally blowing up the vault in front of the terrified eyes of the prisoner — Regina Hunkes. But in that case the danger, to him and his colleagues, was greatly increased. Within a short time of their leaving the apartment all of Sao Paulo police would be on their trail. That was the last thing he needed now. And if even one of them was captured, there would no doubt be someone who would see to it that the State of Israel would be involved in the affair.

Reuven Morag's thought processes were lightning swift. How to keep Regina in the hotel? Suddenly an idea burst into his brain. He would stake everything on one wild gamble. A wide smile split his face. "Regina," he said in a gentle, friendly voice, "you're a free woman in a free country. If you want to go home — there's no one who'll stop you. But you'll be indicating that you've freed us at GAC of all responsibility for what happens to you in the course of the day. You understand what I'm referring to. Police investigations. Unpleasant conversations with that officer — what was his name? — oh, yes, Nunes. Our sympathy and personal friendship will last, I hope, for many years, but to help you, that will be very difficult indeed."

The room fell totally silent. Regina didn't answer. Her fingertips played with the cloth that covered the small table next to the couch. The grey-haired man took still another step. "Regina, I'm willing to cancel tonight's ceremonies that we've arranged to honor the memory of our dear Alberto. But tell me now, to give me the chance to inform the media that we've canceled it due to opposition from the widow, Mrs. Regina Hunkes."

The grey-haired man carefully enunciated the last few words, speaking slowly and clearly. Regina gave him a furious glance. That last sentence had wounded her like a poisoned dart. She saw in it an underhanded attempt to force her to give way before him. If not, he'd throw her before the public, intimating that she didn't care for the dear departed's memory. What did he want from her?

The grey-haired man continued to smile pleasantly. After a brief pause, when it became clear that her silence was a form of protest against him, he turned to the door and opened it.

"Regina, I'm leaving. You're free to do what you wish. You can leave me messages at the GAC offices. *Chau*. I hope you're not angry with me."

He left the room. But before closing the door behind him, he turned to her one more time.

"I forgot to tell you. Yesterday, when we were working on your problem with the police, they mentioned some kind of ranch. In the state of Parana, near Cortiba, that you visited regularly. They're investigating something in connection with it. Do you know what they're referring to?"

That was it! He'd won! He'd pushed the right button! Regina lifted her head wildly, her eyes flashing fiery sparks.

The grey-haired man, in his stubborn, relentless surveillance of the Hunkes family, had uncovered the Nazi's ranch headquarters in southern Brazil. The Hunkeses would appear there occasionally, generally about once a month. At that time there would be feverish activity, as black Mercedes automobiles with curtains obscuring their windows made their way there. Most came from Sao Paulo or from the southern state of Rio Grande de Sol. Morag's men, among them members of the Mossad, had discovered that some visitors came from as far as Asuncióan, capital of Paraguay. It was possible that Mengele, sadistic doctor of Auschwitz who'd made Paraguay his home, took part in the mysterious gatherings. The participants never arrived together, apparently so as not to arouse suspicions. Every hour, on the day appointed for the meeting, a car would veer off the main road onto a dirt path that led to the ranch, which was hidden in a thick forest. Two cars never, never arrived together. Now, with a lightning inspiration, the man called Hermann Schmidt knew that if he revealed knowledge of the matter, Regina Hunkes would be plunged into turmoil and confusion. Actually, as far as he knew, the police were completely unaware of the ranch's existence. But what did he care if she believed they were investigating in the area?

Regina sprang up from her place. She realized she'd made a terrible mistake. Her emotions had betrayed her. But it was too late. At that moment, she knew she was completely in the power of this smiling, grey-haired man. She walked towards the door where he was standing, quiet and relaxed.

"What does this mean? What did you just say? They want to accuse me of something again?"

"I don't know, Regina. That's what I heard. Maybe you want to explain what we're talking about?"

Regina took a deep breath. "I don't know what they're talking about either. It upsets me. Not enough they killed my husband, now they're examining our personal lives, as if we were criminals."

"You're right. But you must understand them. They want to find out the motive for the murder. So they're concentrating on your visits to the ranch. And on the guests who arrived there."

"Guests? What are you talking about?"

Regina Hunkes, the grey-haired man noted, was on the verge of hysteria.

"Relax, Regina, I don't think they were paying too much attention. They were just talking, that's all. They were dreaming that they, like the State of Israel, would all become Nazi hunters. The possibility of mysterious doings in some ranch in the south whet their imagination. That's it! Just talk. I don't understand why you're so nervous."

Regina didn't answer. Inside she cursed this man, who was playing with her feelings so expertly, in order to thwart her. She was confused. Maybe he was telling the truth? Perhaps they really did know, there in police headquarters, something of the skeletons in her closet? It was a distinct possibility. Otherwise, how had these details come to the attention of Hermann Schmidt, the grey-haired top executive at GAC? This was one of the family's most deeply held secrets.

"Do you want me to take you home?"

At that moment Regina wanted nothing but to murder him. That quiet, pleasant voice in which he asked his innocent question infuriated her. She knew it: He'd won. She would stay in the hotel. And tomorrow she would flee to Germany on the flight that he'd arranged.

Without answering she turned away and returned to her place on the couch. She faced the window, not favoring the grey-haired man with a single glance.

Her nemesis grinned. He stood beside her open door for another moment. He wanted to lay yet one more blow upon her head: He wanted to hint to her of the existence of one specific Nazi, a man by the name of Heinz Krantz. Just throw the name out nonchalantly. But he restrained himself. It wouldn't do to give her too great a dose of panic: It was impossible to be absolutely sure of her reaction.

He carefully closed the door and checked the long hallway. There was no one to be seen. He hurried to the elevator, descended two floors and went to the rooms of his comrades, still sleeping after their long vigil in the forests of Sao Paulo.

"*Chevrah*, wake up! We've got to go for one last tour of the area this evening."

Lod Airport
8 Iyar 5727

Eduardo felt a strange sensation course through him. His feet were treading upon the land of the Jews. He remembered well the taunts and contemptuous scorn of his father at the mention on television or radio of the Jewish State. Israel. And now he was here. Standing in the midst of a large crowd of young Jews, walking on the asphalt strip that led from the airplane to the airport terminal. Strange, what Destiny held for a man! That his first assignment abroad as a journalist would be in the midst of this contemptible people. Interesting to see what this strange experience would bring.

He noticed a certain military preparedness in the airport itself, with soldiers and armored cars to be seen here and there. At the entrance of the terminal Eduardo saw a truly strange-looking soldier: a man no longer young sitting on a chair, his uniform sloppy, an antiquated gun lying across his knees. The man caught Eduardo's attention. He bore no resemblance to the hordes of young Jews who'd been on the airplane with him. He reminded him more of the Jews who'd lived in Europe, the ones the Nazis had destroyed. During the Eichmann trial many pictures of those Jews had been published. A large *yarmulke* sat on the soldier's head; he had a long beard and rings of hair coming down from his temples. Eduardo stared for a moment at the Jew's nose; almost as a reflex, he looked to see if it resembled that of an eagle. How his father had laughed at such Jews!

Eduardo passed him. Their eyes held for a moment. Afterwards, as he lay on his bed in the Avia Hotel, the adventures of the past two days playing before his eyes like a movie in a cinema, he remembered the eyes of the strange soldier. Such melancholy eyes, Eduardo thought, and then he slept …

Sao Paulo, Brazil
May 18, 1967

The headache attacked Jairo when he passed over the threshold of his home. The clear realization that the nightmare was over caused the sharp, throbbing pain that almost paralyzed his right side, leaving his vision so blurry he could barely make out his joyous wife.

"Paulina, not now. I want to sleep. My head is exploding. I'll tell you everything afterwards. Call my father and tell him I've returned, alive and well. Call my office too and tell them that everything is all right."

With weak steps Jairo reached his bed. From the moment he fell upon it, drained and helpless, the battle for sleep began. He simply couldn't relax. Myriads of thoughts blazed through his brain, one after the other. He couldn't digest so many events, and particularly the incredible revelation that he hadn't been pursued by Nazis — except in his imagination. It was too much. He felt the tears begin to fall and made no effort to stop them.

These were moments of abnormal wakefulness, despite the heavy, heavy fatigue ... and finally ... he slept.

42

Jairo awoke in a panic. He muffled a scream that rose in his throat. Terrifying dreams had disturbed his sleep: He saw himself in Auschwitz. He stood there amidst a group of Jews who suddenly began to race wildly, confused and frightened, as Nazis screamed at their heels. Dread overwhelmed him. Vicious dogs chased him, and Jairo ran, fell, stood up and ran again. Where was he running? He didn't know. Suddenly, he felt a terrible blow to his back. The whip lashed at him. He turned towards the Nazi beating him and, beneath the Nazi helmet, the face of Alberto Hunkes laughed at him. Hunkes wore an S.S. uniform. Jairo stretched his arms towards him and begged for his life. "Alberto, Alberto Hunkes, what are you doing to me? I'm Jairo, Jairo Silverman. Because of me you live peacefully here in Brazil!"

Hunkes laughed. His eyes were frigid. In answer to Jairo's plea he aimed the relentless whip squarely at

Jairo's face. Jairo felt its stinging pain and a deep sense of humiliation. His face was wet: wet with blood.

At this point he woke up. His heart beat wildly. He sat up in bed. Indeed he was wet, not with blood, but with cold sweat. Where was he? He grabbed his head with both his hands. He was here, at home, in his room, his bed.

Jairo stood up. Outside, dusk was falling. Apparently he'd slept the entire day. He would have slept even longer, no doubt, if not for his fearful nightmare. He dressed quickly and went to the living room. No one home. His wife had apparently gone out to do her shopping. And the children? Jairo didn't know. Probably at friends. More than anything he longed to hug them. For almost a week he'd hardly paid attention to them. He felt that he himself was a refugee of the Holocaust, and not just the son of one.

He went into the kitchen to make himself a cup of coffee. The serenity and quiet of his home brought tears to his eyes. His heart was filled with gratitude. Just last night he was certain he was to be killed by Nazis and here he was, safe and secure in his house. If he knew how to pray, he would surely have done so now.

Jairo poured the boiling water onto the fragrant coffee. Was he actually safe in his house? Was he really secure? Physically, he was. But his soul had been shaken, shaken to the core. The trauma of this past week would not quickly vanish, he knew. He'd changed. He had become a different person.

Jairo returned to the living room. He dropped gently into the deep recliner and took small, slow sips of coffee as he reviewed the events of the past week. Why had this trouble descended upon him? What had he done wrong? Where had he sinned? Now that it was all over, he felt he must find the answer to the riddle.

He put the empty cup down on a small table next to him. His thoughts jumped from one idea to the next, without any pattern. Alberto Hunkes. His nemesis. The lying deceiver who'd caused him, Jairo, to lose all his faith in mankind. How could it be? How could he have been so mistaken about someone? Fine Alberto Hunkes, pleasant spoken and considerate, always so interested in every detail of his father's life in Nazi Germany. Was it nothing more than play-acting? And maybe, just maybe, the Nazi actually enjoyed the details of his father's torments? Who knew?

Jairo gave a sudden yell. Heinz Krantz! Where had he heard that name before? Hadn't someone mentioned it before the grey-haired man, Reuven Morag, had told him it was Hunkes's true identity? Where? Jairo scratched his head gently in an effort of memory. Where had he heard it? He knew that name! He knew it! But where? He couldn't remember.

Troubled by the stubborn refusal of his memory to cooperate, he began to pace the spacious living room. He stopped near the window, pulled open the drapes. He could see the city's skyline, already drifting into the darkness of night. Hundreds of thousands of pinpoints of light gleamed from dwelling in skyscrapers that reached almost to the heavens. He filled his lungs with the outdoors' breeze. Yes. Absolutely. Even amidst his confused thoughts, he felt a deep, inexpressible joy fill his being. He was home! He was free!

He drew the drapes and again turned to the recliner. No, he wouldn't switch on the lights: It was better to sit in the dark. Thoughts raced with more swiftness, more clarity, in the dimness. Yes, he was free. But he'd matured. He'd suddenly faced new depths within himself, fearful, inexplicable depths. He was a man with questions, questions he'd never before asked, and would never had thought to ask, if not for the events of the past week. Hard questions, inescapable ones. Could these feelings have occurred to, say, his partner, Francisco Machado? Would he have felt so terrified, so persecuted, if he'd found himself in the same situation? Jairo wasn't certain. Actually, he was certain that Francisco would have done no such thing. His, Jairo's, reactions were undoubtedly connected to the fact that he was a Jew. If so, what did it mean? His father couldn't answer him. Or, perhaps, didn't want to. But Jairo felt he must know.

Suddenly, he felt a flash of memory.

"Of course! I heard the name only a few hours before, from Pa's friend in the Hebraica! Amazing, what happens to people! What an incredible coincidence! Or, was this some form of Heavenly Providence?" The thought troubled Jairo.

He quickly dialed his father.

"Pa, hi, it's Jairo."

He could hear a deep sigh of relief on the other end of the line. "Thank G-d. How are you, Jairo? Paulina told me what happened. The main thing is it's ended well."

"I'm not sure, Pa, that it's ended yet."

"Why do you say that?"

"Because the questions you won't answer are important ones."

"You're starting again? The main thing is, you've called. I've been so worried."

"Pa, I didn't only call to say hello. I have something incredible to tell you."

"What's happened?! You're getting in trouble again, getting involved in things that don't concern you?"

"No. But I've learned that Alberto, our good friend, was really a Nazi."

"So what? A Nazi. Let him be a Nazi. The main thing is, he's dead."

"But I know his name also!"

"*Nu*, they didn't call him Adolf Hitler! And not Josef Mengele either. What difference does it make?"

"His name was Heinz Krantz."

"Oh."

"Pa, doesn't that remind you of anything?"

"*Nein*."

"Don't you remember last night at the Hebraica, before I ran away, one of your friends told you that his brother in Israel was searching for someone, a Nazi by the name of Krantz?"

A pause. "Yes. Yes! You're right!"

"*Nu*, here he is. Alberto Hunkes's real name was Heinz Krantz."

"How do you know?"

"They told me."

"They told you? The Nazis?"

Jairo hesitated. Finally, he blurted out, "Yes."

"Interesting."

"Just interesting? I think it's a lot more than that. I see this as an incredible coincidence. It's nothing less than Providence. Just two hours after I hear the name for the first time, I find out that he'd been my friend."

There was a long silence on the other end of the line. Jairo finally asked quietly, "Isn't that so, Pa?"

"Look, Jairo, I won't get into questions like that. I'm no philosopher. Don't even ask me."

"Okay, Pa. But call your friend, the one whose brother phoned from Israel, and tell him that Heinz

Krantz was murdered last Friday and was buried in a Nazi ceremony — in Sao Paulo."

"I see you can't get away from that funeral."

"That's right."

"Okay, Jairo, I'll tell him."

Jairo held the receiver in his hand for a long moment. He felt angry at his father. What had the Nazi ordeal done to these people? Nothing excited them. Nothing brought them joy. And nothing could even sadden them. Something had died in their souls. And he, Jairo, in his moment of truth, in the depths of his need, couldn't communicate with his father.

Suddenly, he decided to leave the house. To get a bit of air. To walk around a little. To feel the city around him once again. To stroll through its streets, without fear that someone was following him. To walk as he'd walked a week before, two weeks, a year, two years. To be a Brazilian, period. He took the elevator down to the parking lot, turned the key in the ignition, and went for a drive. To where? Nowhere, anywhere. He drove up Augusta Street, passed the wide Paulista Boulevard, went down one of the streets that wound down to the Nove de Julio. He reached the city center, the Sao Juao, the Brigaderio Luis Antonio, and purposely turned onto the Ipiranga, past the Excelsior Hotel, where he'd fled yesterday in a futile attempt to hide from his pursuers. The streets were heavy with traffic, the sidewalks teeming with pedestrians out for an evening promenade. Jairo took in the many images with joyful eyes. The din of the rumbling motors was like a soothing melody in his ears.

After an hour of wandering through the city streets he returned to the Jardim America neighborhood where he lived. He went down Haddock Lobo Street, crossed Tiete Avenue, and suddenly began to slow down. On his left he could see elderly Jews dressed in black leaving their synagogue. These images, truthfully, had always seemed peculiar to him. He'd never given them much thought. But at this moment a strange idea flashed through his brain. Perhaps they knew?

Jairo laughed to himself. These people? Refugees from the Middle Ages in a world strange to them would know the answer to the questions that so disturbed him? What did they know, these people, of what it was like to be a Jew in the modern world?

Jairo pulled over to the curb. He needed a minute to collect his thoughts. He stared at the old men, walking by slowly. They seemed to have a strength lacking in his father. And despite their repelling appearance, perhaps they actually represented authentic Judaism, more so than his father, more so than the other elderly men he'd met in the Hebraica. After all, this had been the way Jews had looked throughout the generations. But why did they remain so? Why didn't they assimilate into the modern world? Why didn't they care that their black, strange appearance caused anti-Semitism? What forced them to remain this way, apart, strange, cast out from all humanity?

Jairo lit up a cigarette. Something deep inside his heart whispered to him: Perhaps, just because of this, they knew. Perhaps they knew the reason for their Jewishness, a reason that eluded him, and this very reason caused them to refuse to change. His father didn't know; perhaps they did? When speaking to his father, he'd suddenly referred to Divine Providence. Was it not providential that he, without thought, had gone down Haddock Lobo, which was not really on the route from the center of the city to his home, had gone down just to see these *rabbinos* at the time they were returning from their synagogue?

Jairo put the cigarette out after a few puffs. He hesitated for a moment. Finally, he made his decision. He left the car, looked here and there, crossed the street with quick steps, and called towards the passing group, "Good evening, *senhores*, excuse me. I'd like to ask you something."

Lod Airport
9 Iyar 5727

Eduardo awoke with the dawn, roused from sleep by the roar of airplanes landing close to the hotel where he'd checked in. He went down to the lobby. The reception clerk handed him a file from the Government Press Office which included information that he needed during his stay, the location where press conferences would be held, the name of the government official who was to help him, and other such details.

First Eduardo put through an overseas call to his office. The international operator put him through.

"Hello, is that the newsroom? Good! I'm looking for Gorge Caetano, from the international desk."

A moment of silence.

"Hello, Gorge? Can you hear me? This is Eduardo, Eduardo Hunkes, speaking from Tel Aviv. It's morning here. I figured you'd be on the night shift there. What? Yes, the situation here seems quiet. There's a lot of tension in the air though. But nothing terrible. Listen, I wanted to ask you, have you heard anything new about my mother?"

"No, nothing new. Actually, yes. The police have requested that we stop reporting on the affair.

They've canceled the announcements offering a reward for information, and told us to stop running them. They didn't say why."

Eduardo was surprised.

"What do you think? What do they say there?"

"I haven't the slightest idea. It's all rather mysterious. I don't know. The guessing is that there've been new developments, which necessitate taking a different tack in the investigation. But other than that, there's nothing new. And you?"

"Me? As I told you. I haven't gotten settled in yet. Okay, thanks. I'll call again tomorrow."

Eduardo returned to the reception desk.

"Good morning," he said in his meager English, "how can I reach army officer Lipschitz? From the papers I've received from the Government Press Office and the Army Spokesman's office, it seems he's the officer who will escort me."

The clerk gave him a smile, even as she made a valiant attempt to understand his accented English. She dialed, spoke into the receiver, waited a few seconds and finally turned to Eduardo, answering him in fluent English. "Please wait there," she said, pointing to the comfortable lobby chairs, "and he'll arrive in 10 minutes. I wish you a pleasant stay in our country. The situation is a bit tense, but we hope that we will prevail."

Eduardo thanked her and turned to the lobby, almost empty at this early hour. He sat down and began to look around him, but there was nothing to hold his interest.

A young tall officer walked in through the main entrance and, as if they'd planned a rendezvous in advance, walked directly towards Eduardo, who jumped up out of his chair.

"*Bon dia, Senhor*," the man said in fluent Portuguese. Eduardo's eyes lit up.

"*Senhor e Brasileiro?*" he asked with unconcealed joy, his repugnance for these Jewish Israelis vanishing in an instant.

The officer smiled. "*Si*. I'm from Rio de Janeiro. My name is Ronny Lipschitz. In Brazil, they called me Gilberto. Gilberto Lipschitz."

The two exchanged a warm handshake. "I'm Eduardo Hunkes. And I think my assignment here will be a lot easier than I imagined, because of you. What a coincidence!"

"Absolutely not. The army assigns a Portuguese-speaking officer for the Brazilian correspondents, just as it pairs English-speakers with the Americans and Britons, and French-speakers with the Frenchmen. Okay, let's get down to business!"

Ronny spent the next hour explaining the country's political and military situation at that moment. He discussed the assessments of Egyptian military strength, the mobilization of the Israeli reserves, of his country's fear of a large-scale war. He mentioned their disappointment with the United Nations. He also described his professional relationship with Eduardo during the course of his stay.

Finally, Ronny asked, "Do you have any special requests?"

Eduardo collected the sheaf of papers that he'd spread out on a coffee table and began to slowly put them in his briefcase. He smiled at Ronny and said, "No, thanks. I'm grateful to you for the fascinating briefing."

The two stood up to say goodbye. Suddenly Eduardo had an idea. His eyes looked thoughtful. Ronny could sense a change in the young Brazilian journalist.

"Yes, actually I do have a request. Rather a strange one."

The officer's gaze encouraged him to speak further.

"You understand, I've got to supply my newspaper with good copy. Their appetite is enormous. When I landed last night, I noticed a strange soldier in the terminal. He had a long beard and a skullcap on his head. Sad eyes, I noticed. He didn't look at all like any of the Israelis I've seen here."

"Yes?"

"He looked … authentic. Could I interview him? It would be a good human interest story."

The officer laughed. "I'll check into it. I don't think there'll be any problem, though."

43

The religious Jews heard Jairo cry out to them. They turned towards him and looked at the young man who stood before them, meticulously, perhaps even elegantly dressed. They were used to these types, Jewish-born Brazilians who would come to them to clarify when they should say *Kaddish* or what day a *yahrzeit* came out on. That was the furthest their Judaism took them, these youngsters. One of the religious Jews, who answered to the name of Meir, the youngest of the group but one of the most experienced in such encounters, asked Jairo, "When did your father or mother die?"

Jairo was confused. "What does that have to do with this? I have something to ask you!"

Meir sensed that he'd made a mistake. His shortcut had caused him to offend where no offense was intended. His voice grew more friendly.

"Oh, excuse me. I meant nothing. I'll gladly answer anything you ask me."

"It's a bit involved. Could you give me few minutes?"

Meir thought for a moment. The others stared silently. The unpleasantness he'd unwittingly caused resulted in his assenting to Jairo's request. He took a swift glance at his watch and said with a smile, "Okay, *Senhor*."

The others went on their way. The two of them were left alone on the street. Jairo found it difficult to speak. His emotions had suddenly overcome him, blocking logical thought. He wished for a quiet spot where he would have the privacy and security necessary for conversation. Meir could feel the man wavering.

"Would you like to go into the synagogue?"

They opened the gate in the wall that surrounded the *shul*. This was Jairo's first visit here. They entered the small paved courtyard. A few short steps brought them to the synagogue itself. The light was still on within. In one corner a young man sat and learned in a quiet singsong, shaking back and forth over the large book opened before him. Jairo didn't know what the book was. He felt an eerie sensation, like that of one entering a mysterious and unexpected new world.

After they'd seated themselves on one of the wooden benches, Jairo told his story. He saw that the young bearded man didn't quite believe him. He understood the reaction: Even to himself, it sounded like a fantasy.

"Look, sir," Jairo finally finished, "I don't know you, and you don't know me. You can confirm my story with the partners in my law firm. Here's my card. Or you can call Roberto Nunes of the police force, who was somewhat involved in the investigation of Alberto Hunkes's death. You can ask him."

Meir made a gesture of dismissal.

"What for? Why shouldn't I believe you, *Senhor*? But what question has this terrifying story raised? What kind of question is it that you've decided only a Jew of my type can answer? I've never had any connection with the Nazis!"

"Yes, you're right. Let me explain."

Jairo lapsed into silence. It was clear he was searching for the right words. He crossed his legs and lit a cigarette.

"Oh, excuse me. May I smoke here?"

Meir nodded his head in assent. He could clearly see Jairo's internal struggle on the young man's face.

"My question is this," he finally said. "I simply want an explanation for the strange feeling, very strange, that attacked me, from the moment I stood in the cemetery. It was awakened within me, and has given me no rest since then. I don't want it, this emotion. It disturbs me. I want to thrust it out of my heart, and yet it grows even stronger. How can I express myself? Okay, here it is: I suddenly feel that I am a Jew. I feel a wall has grown up between myself and my gentile friends. I never felt such a separation before. Okay, I always knew I was Jewish. I even learned for a few years in a Jewish school — the Renaissance."

Jairo could see the scorn in Meir's eyes when he mentioned the school that he'd attended. Meir gave the school a dismissive wave, as if to say, "You call that school Jewish?"

Jairo continued. "But this knowledge of my Jewishness never influenced my life at all. It didn't cause me any discomfort. A Jew? Okay, I was a Jew, so what? Just like one was a Brazilian, another an Arab, or a Frenchman, or whatever you want. What did it matter, in the modern, open world in which we live today?"

Jairo was quiet. He took a deep breath. His emotions grew even stronger; he gave up trying to conceal them.

"And that's my problem. Why do I suddenly feel my Jewishness so deeply? Why am I pursued by these Jewish fears? Why wasn't I afraid of those phone calls as a person? Why as a Jew? What does it have to do with this? It's not logical! And I, despite all my efforts, haven't managed to free myself from this feeling. And even worse, as I told you before, from moment to moment it digs in deeper within me. What does it all mean?"

Jairo felt somehow lighter. He'd abridged his story, hadn't told the man sitting before him all the feelings that had overcome him in these past five days. Still he hoped he'd managed to pass on some of his concerns.

Meir was silent. First he gave Jairo an understanding smile. Then he closed his eyes. A gentle quiet pervaded the room. Jairo didn't take his eyes off Meir.

Suddenly Meir stood up and walked towards the bookcase. His eyes skimmed over the rows of books that filled the shelves. Finally he pulled a volume out and returned to sit next to Jairo. He gently leafed through the book until he reached the portion he was looking for. Jairo watched his every move.

"Understand, *Senhor*, I can only explain what happened to you on the basis of my faith. And I believe in this book — the Torah. I've opened it to the fifth portion, called *Devarim*."

Meir read the verses in Hebrew, immediately translating them into Portuguese. *And among these nations you will find no ease, and you will not find a resting-place for the soles of your feet. And G-d will give you there a trembling heart, longing eyes and a distressed soul. Your life will hang before you and you will be in terror night and*

*day, and have no confidence in your life. In the morning
you will say, Oh, that it were evening; in the evening you
will say, Oh, that it were morning, all from the terror which
fills your heart from the sights which your eyes will see.*

Meir folded a corner of the page and closed the
book, gently kissing the cover.

"These are verses of the Torah," he began to explain
in a quiet voice, "that seek to explain how Jewish life
will look over the course of thousands of years, as the
Jews wander among the nations of the world; that is,
during the years of the diaspora. Fear and insecurity
will be some of the most critical identifying features of
our lives as we live among the gentiles. It doesn't
happen every day. Many years can pass before it is
felt. But the earth beneath us trembles always.
Sometimes the seismographs, even the most sensitive,
fail to record any movement, even in the lowest por-
tions of the 'Jewish Richter scale.' But the trembling
exists. And occasionally the seismographs all but explode from the force of the great quakes — as
happened 25 years ago, in Europe. The laws of our
fear of the gentile, the laws of our being strangers
among the nations, these are immutable, unchange-
able laws. Like … like … like the law of gravity. It
doesn't mean the entire nation always feels it.
Sometimes, it comes to the attention of only one single
Jew. It's the law, my friend! Do you understand at all
what I'm trying to say?"

Jairo sat in stunned silence. He didn't know if he
quite comprehended what Meir had said. But somehow
the words moved him. He anxiously awaited more.

"And something even more interesting happened
to you, *Senhor*. This, too, is clearly written in the
Torah, this time in the Book of *Vayikra*, the third book.

You shall flee, and none shall pursue you. Do you hear? In the diaspora the situation can arise, our Torah tells us, in which a man flees imaginary terrors. He will believe he is being pursued and, ultimately, he will learn that it was nothing more than a dream. Do you understand, *Senhor* — "

"Jairo. Jairo Silverman."

"*Senhor* Silverman. According to what you've told me, that's exactly what happened to you! No one was after you! Your fears were, after all, false alarms. Misunderstandings. That, too, is one of the punishments of diaspora. It says so clearly: 'You shall flee, and none shall pursue you.' The fear in your heart is that which runs after you!"

Meir lapsed into silence. Jairo felt as if icy water had been flung into his face and he was losing his breath. He was confused, all out of ideas. He felt a sudden surge of self-pity. Suddenly, he heard Meir's voice once again, a voice quiet and somewhat apologetic.

"*Senhor*, I'm sorry if I've offended you. But I have no other answer."

Jairo didn't reply. He tried to digest all that he'd heard. Hard, it was so hard. He took the book in his hand, opened it to the folded page, but couldn't understand what was written within. He recognized the Hebrew letters, but had a difficult time reading them. He pushed the book away from him and his gaze rested, almost against his will, on the face of the man sitting opposite him. The tone of decision in which Meir had said his piece disturbed Jairo. What right had he to be so secure in his beliefs? Jairo felt a stabbing pressure in his chest. Finally he said, in a voice so quiet it could hardly be heard, "So you want to say that what happened to me is part of the Jewish destiny, something one cannot escape? That the fear lies hidden within me, because I belong to this race? And this fear will be hidden in my children after me?"

Meir well understood the distress of the young man, who until now had seen himself as a pure Brazilian, and suddenly ... Meir didn't answer. But the expression on his face told Jairo all.

A heavy silence descended upon the two of them. Jairo's eyes began to wander over the synagogue. The dimness within, despite the lighting, added to his melancholy. Everything was brown. The long rows of wooden benches and tables. The ark, the bookshelves filled with books ... books that, no doubt, expanded upon the words he'd just heard from this Jew. Clearly, nothing was as simple as it seemed.

Finally, a question escaped his lips. "But why? Why won't this book let the Jews live in peace?"

Meir answered quickly. "Because this is the only way, the only opportunity, to remind you of the fact that you are a Jew! That's the reality that you and others like you attempt to escape from! It's clear! Don't you see? What happened to you reminded you of this vital fact. Otherwise, would you ever have stopped in the street to speak to a Jew like me?"

Jairo knew Meir was right. That was the reality. Still, he continued.

"And is that justice? Such a holocaust, only to remind us that we're Jewish?"

Meir was impatient. "I'm not an expert on the Holocaust, nor in justice. I know only one thing. The Torah teaches us that a covenant exists between G-d and His nation, Israel. A covenant that will never be broken. Any attempt to break it brings about a reaction. Sometimes the reaction is greater, sometimes less. Go argue with a law. Do you know what? It was the prophet Yechezkel who explained this even more forcefully: *What enters your thoughts, it shall not be! That you say we will be like the nations and the families of the earth … As I live, the words of G-d, the Lord, I shall reign over you with a strong hand and outstretched arm and an outpouring of fury.* Do you understand, *Senhor*, what we're talking about here? G-d says you will not succeed in running away from Him to be like the other nations. Even if you want to do so, you'll never be a true Brazilian, *Senhor*. G-d says, 'I shall reign over you,' in all situations. That is, you'll remain a Jew whether you like it or not."

Meir stopped speaking. Jairo could feel Meir's emotions rising like a swell. A deep anguish could be heard in his voice, as he continued. "The Holocaust was 'an outpouring of fury.' What an outpouring of fury! And what happened to you this week was 'the strong hand.' Thank G-d, that He reminded you that you are a Jew, using a false alarm."

Jairo thought of his father, the poor unfortunate "graduate" of Buchenwald, who wanted at all costs to save him, Jairo, from the Jewish destiny. And yet he couldn't do it. "So you say anti-Semitism is an invention of G-d? A whip that He uses against us for the nation's spiritual purposes?"

Meir didn't hesitate for even a minute. "Yes. Absolutely! It is the law that guards the nation."

"And you can accept that? It doesn't seem terrible to you?"

Meir stood up and prepared to go. He didn't like the direction in which this conversation was headed.

"*Senhor* Silverman, you're making a fundamental error. You wanted to get our answer. You've gotten it!

I've shown it to you in black and white. What you're asking now is a philosophical question that has nothing to do with the facts. Think about it. If after you've done so you have more questions, you know where to find me! In the meantime, pay attention to one more thing: The things I've set before you were written down thousands of years ago. And the history of your nation, *Senhor*, has simply brought these words to life over the entire globe. And upon you — this week! Think about it! Could such things have happened, if not at the behest of G-d?"

Jairo didn't answer. With great difficulty he controlled the waves of emotion threatening to drown him. He felt dizzy. He stood up and left the synagogue together with Meir.

When they were standing outside together, Meir spoke. "Good night, *Senhor*. If you think about the last thing I told you, if you understand that G-d Himself said these things, your questions on whether this is 'terrible' and the justice of these things will have an entirely different perspective. I promise you. *Chau*."

Meir disappeared around the corner. Jairo sat in his car for a long while without the strength to turn on the engine and drive home …

Reuven Morag, the grey-haired man, was satisfied. In another half hour he would be on his way to the memorial service for Alberto Hunkes in the Municipal Theater. He had bought the afternoon papers and saw with satisfaction that the police notices regarding Regina Hunkes had disappeared. True, the announcement had appeared in *Estado de Sao Paulo*, the city's largest morning paper. But there was no mention at all in the *Journal de Trada*, the evening news. Even more important, the police car that had stood before the Hunkes home on Piaui Street since the night before had left at 9 this morning. His sentry had called him about half an hour before with the news that the area was "clean." The police presence hadn't returned at all during the day. It looked like the plan could be carried out without any trouble. Jairo had kept his word: He had silenced the policeman.

The grey-haired man reached for the phone and dialed. "Hello. Is this the Silverman family? May I speak with Jairo?"

Paulina felt a stab of fear. When she'd returned to the house she hadn't found her husband. Jairo had left a note saying he'd be back shortly. But who knew? And now here was that voice again, the voice that had so disturbed her in the past.

"Who are you, and what do you want from me?"

Morag tried to sound as reassuring as possible.

"Nothing, *Senhora* Silverman. Don't worry. Just tell Jairo thank you from me. He'll know what I'm talking about."

Morag quickly hung up the phone. He hurried to the Excelsior Hotel in order to bring Regina to the Municipal Theater. As the two drove off together, he handed her a ticket to Europe, on a Varig flight to Frankfurt. He also gave her the name of the GAC representative whom she should contact immediately upon arrival.

"I've arranged for the flight for tomorrow night rather than today, to give you a chance to pack. And I've got good news for you. The police have decided, in the meantime, to put a freeze on the investigation. They're waiting for a decision from their legal counsel. From our point of view that's just fine, right?"

He looked into the rear-view mirror in order to see her reaction. But she said nothing. Apparently, Regina was still angry at him over what had occurred that morning. The grey-haired man didn't particularly care.

The thin man reached the entrance of the Excelsior Hotel at exactly 8:30 in the evening. He was driving a taxi. Next to the doorway stood one of Morag's hired hands. He saw the flashing lights of the cab and turned directly towards it. He opened the door and disappeared inside. The thin man drove slowly until he reached an intersection. He saw a second man standing on the sidewalk, looking all around him. The thin man stopped nearby. The man, seeing his partner sitting in the cab, jumped in. The thin man then drove on, as planned, another 100 meters, and picked up the third of the party. From there he drove directly to the Angelica, and after a 15-minute drive reached Piaui Street. After ensuring that the surrounding area was "clean" he slowly approached the house ...

44

Sao Paulo, Brazil
May 18, 1967

The thin man was lucky: The parking space he wanted was free. He parked the cab near the entrance that led to the service elevator, used by maids, delivery boys, and the building's maintenance men.

"Wait in the car," the thin man whispered.

The others nodded.

"I'm going to talk to the *zelador*," he added. "When you see me lift my hand to cover a yawn leave the cab and go slowly behind the building. Go up in the service elevator to the eighth floor. The elevator will open right next to the door of the Hunkes's kitchen. Here's the key. Our agent got hold of it. When you get in, go as quickly as possible into the bedroom. Move the carpet beneath the bed and you'll find a safe, and then — to work! I'll keep the guard busy for exactly half an hour. That's the maximum time you have to do the job.

You have to finish the break-in and return to the car in that amount of time. Remember, don't open the door for anyone! You're mute workers for the neighborhood *Supermercado*. If there's a maid in the service elevator, or whatever, use sign language between yourselves. That way, no one will ask who you are or where you're going. I don't understand why you couldn't learn Portuguese today, now that you're in Brazil."

The men understood this as an attempt at humor. They chuckled weakly, as if they found it funny.

"I wish you luck."

The men nodded.

The thin man left the cab and turned to the front of the building. He walked up the five steps that led to the elegant entranceway, through the glass door that opened onto the opulent lobby in which the *zelador* was seated.

The guard sat beside a small table, his eyes glued to a television screen on which a soccer game was being played. He noticed the thin man approaching and hurriedly opened the door for him, with a small bow. "Good evening, *Senhor*."

"Good evening," the thin man answered.

"May I ask whom you are looking for?"

"They told me to go to Mrs ... Mrs ... one minute ... "

The thin man pulled a piece of paper from his pocket, one he'd prepared many days before. He opened it and read. "They told me to go to Mrs. Regina Hunkes, and take her to the airport."

The guard looked at him suspiciously. "*Senhora* Hunkes is not here."

The thin man gave him a surprised glance. "But they told me to come and pick her up!"

"Who told you?"

"I don't know. Some man. He said he worked for GAC. He paid me well."

The thin man pointed to a wad of bills in his hand. The guard's eyes seemed to pop out of their sockets, staring at the man's hands. The thin man yawned, and hurriedly raised his right hand to cover his mouth.

The men in the car saw the signal, and one by one silently left the taxi. They wore blue overalls, the uniform of a large supermarket chain. From the trunk they took out two cartons of vegetables, their tools hidden on the bottom. They turned towards the service elevator. They cast a quick glance through the building's main doorway. The security guard was deep in conversation with the thin man; he didn't notice them at all.

Luckily there was no one in the elevator. They reached the eighth floor without incident. They opened the door leading into the kitchen, pushing the two cartons of vegetables inside. They locked the door behind them. Their swift, practiced hands burrowed into the cartons, pulled out their tools. They raced into the bedroom.

The thin man walked into the lobby. The eyes of the security guard followed him closely, losing, as a result, sight of the entranceway. The thin man realized that his men had gone up in the elevator. Now he had to utilize all his talents to keep the security guard's attention riveted upon him. For half an hour.

"So what are you saying?" the thin man asked in obvious astonishment, "That she's not at home? When will she be back? I can wait for her here!"

The security guard, a pleasant Brazilian of about 50, waved his hand back and forth in a motion of dissent. His face was gloomy.

"*Senhora* Regina will not return. Bad men took her away two days ago."

The thin man came closer. He leaned his palm on the man's table, in a creditable display of bafflement.

"What are you saying? What do you mean, bad men took her? Where did they take her to? What? You want to tell me she's been kidnaped? So why did they tell me to pick her up from this building?"

"I don't know what they told you, *Senhor*. I know that she's not at home, and someone came and took her away."

A spark of satisfaction lit up the *zelador*'s eyes. He was flattered by the attention he was receiving, and by the impression his words were making on this cab driver who'd shown up here. At least a little of his boredom was eased. He gestured to the driver to come a bit closer. The thin man acceded to his silent request. The security guard put his hand near his mouth and whispered in the thin man's ear: "Do you know what? The police were here all day yesterday. Yes, yes! A police car and some officers. Interesting things must be happening here. Terrible things!"

The thin man sat himself down on a nearby chair without asking permission.

"What are you saying? What kind of terrible things could happen here?"

The security guard's heart melted like warm butter. Someone wanted to hear his opinion! His sense of self-importance grew sky high.

"Look, *Senhor*, the husband of Mrs. Hunkes was murdered last week."

"You don't say," the thin man cried out in shock, "so perhaps the ones that kidnaped her, murdered her husband also."

"I don't know."

The thin man came even closer. They were close friends now.

"And you, did you see them kidnap her?"

"Yes, I saw it. I didn't know it was a kidnaping. She went with a man. It seemed she went of her own free will. But it's true, he held her arm. It seemed that he was leading her, but not by force. I can't explain exactly. He, the man who took her, was about 50 years old. Not very tall. Grey-haired. If I would see him again," the *zelador* tapped his chest importantly, "I would certainly recognize him at once."

He watched for the reaction of his new-found friend, who gratified him by doing his all to show how much the guard's wisdom and alertness impressed him.

The guard added, "I even told the police! Yes, yes, I told them!"

The thin man filed that away: He would have to report it to the grey-haired man. Even a dimwit like this guard could pose a danger to them. He thought of the agents working in the apartment upstairs. He glanced at his watch. Fifteen minutes had already passed from the time he'd begun chatting with the guard, keeping his attention. The thin man hoped that everything was all right upstairs, there, in the apartment of Regina Hunkes …

The men found the safe, wedged within the floor, almost immediately. One of them banged gently with a hammer on each of the sides. It made a hard sound.

"It's poured concrete," he declared. "The demon did a thorough job. We won't be able to pull it out. We can't use a chisel; that will bring on all the neighbors. We've got no choice: We've got to cut through the safe."

They pulled out an acetylene torch and attached a special tip which would cut through hard steel. They turned it on. A blue, hissing flame shot out like a tongue of fire.

"Careful," one of the men said, "adjust the flame, so that it's not too hot. You don't want to burn the contents."

After a few minutes the steel began to give slightly. A small hole appeared. One of the men threaded in some fireproof material in order to protect the documents within. And the men continued cautiously to cut through the steel, until it began to bend before them, defeated …

The performance in the Municipal Theater was at its height. After a few short speeches, that lauded the contribution of GAC to the Brazilian economy and that praised the character of the dear departed Alberto Hunkes and his part in the development of the firm, the lights had dimmed. The theater's curtain had opened wide and the musical gala began with *Scheherezade*.

The grey-haired man, who'd organized the evening, sat at the edge of one of the front rows, close to an exit door. In the darkness his eyes searched for Regina, sitting in the center of the front row. He could see the head of Sao Paulo's Commerce Department sitting next to her, and the mayor himself as well. Nearby were top GAC executives. Let her feel important during these last hours before …

The light coming from the stage reflected on her face. The grey-haired man could see her, concentrating on what was happening onstage. With slow steps he left the auditorium and went to the office.

"Good evening," he said pleasantly. "May I make a call?"

"Why not?" answered the director, who recognized him as one of his contacts with GAC.

The grey-haired man lifted the receiver and dialed the Hunkes home. He heard it ring twice and hung up. He then dialed once again. Again, two rings; again, he hung up. Finally, he dialed and waited for an answer, having given the signal agreed upon between him and his men. By his calculations they should be there right this minute. Someone picked up on the other side. The grey-haired man spoke in German. "Hello, Fritz?"

The voice in the Hunkes home answered in the same language. "Yes, Franz."

"Are the vegetables in place?"

"Yes, Franz."

"Are they fresh?"

"It seems so. And they're nice looking too."

"*Auf Wiedersehen*, Fritz."

"*Danke*, Franz."

The grey-haired man quickly hung up the phone. He returned to the auditorium, well satisfied. The work in the Hunkes house, it seemed, was proceeding as planned.

"Listen," the thin man announced to the security guard, "you are a model citizen. The policemen no doubt said that to you when you told them you'd seen the kidnaper, eh?"

The *zelador* seemed depressed. "They didn't say it to me. But they probably thought so."

The thin man laughed. "Absolutely."

Again, he glanced at his watch. Twenty minutes gone. He'd give them an additional 10 minutes.

Would it be enough time? In the meantime, he had to continue talking.

"And tell me, what do the neighbors say?"

"About what?"

"You know, about the fact that they murdered some-one who lived in their house, and kidnaped his wife."

"What do you mean? They're acting like neighbors! One says it's terrible; the other doesn't care at all. And so on. Neighbors, you know, are not brothers."

The thin man continued. "What game are you watching there?"

"Palmango versus Santos."

"That must be a good game! Can I watch too?"

"Sure," the security guard said happily.

The hand that was thrust inside the hole in the safe rummaged through it, bringing out an envelope covered with crosses. A small Nazi flag, neatly folded, followed, and packages of pictures of Alberto Hunkes wearing an S.S. uniform, accompanied by other Nazis in various parts of Europe. There were also pictures of Hunkes and his wife. In all the photos he was smiling.

The men were disappointed. "We can buy this garbage in any store in Nuremberg, Dusseldorf, or Hamburg. For this we had to come all the way to Brazil?"

The hand again disappeared into the belly of the safe, searching, searching, until it found another pile of papers. The hand grabbed at it and pulled it out quickly ...

It was a thick cardboard file tied with a thin string. They quickly ripped it open. The documents were in German, neatly handwritten. There were also a number of letters. "For Eduardo Hunkes," read one of them.

"I think that's it, *chevrah*. We've got to get out of here, and quickly."

One of the men began to skim through the papers. "There's no time, Moshe. We've got to get out."

They didn't bother taking their equipment with them; everything was left as it was. There was no effort to conceal the break-in. They walked quickly through the kitchen exit, rang for the service elevator, and descended to the courtyard. Shielded by the darkness, they reached the cab safely.

With a farewell to his new-found friend, the thin man pulled himself away from the television. The taxi finally drove off …

On the way to Congonhas Airport, the men removed their blue overalls. When they left the cab they had once again become three solid citizens. One left an hour later on a Varig flight to Paris. A second took a direct flight to New York an hour after that. And the third man found himself in London some 12 hours later.

The thin man hurried to their hideout on Gabriel Monteiro da Silva Street. In the living room, beneath the buffet, he found a concealed drawer. He quickly opened it, placed the papers inside it, slammed it shut, and left the house.

The gala performance ended a few minutes before midnight. The crowd clapped enthusiastically; Regina Hunkes looked pleased.

The curtain dropped. The actors, musicians, and singers bowed politely. In the front rows the invited V.I.P.s shook Regina Hunkes's outstretched hand. The grey-haired man pushed through, trying to reach her.

Hermann Schmidt — Reuven Morag — had decided to escort Regina home. He deserved this sweet taste of revenge, this man who'd devoted his life to seeking Nazi war criminals. He gave her an easy smile, which she returned. The grey-haired man understood: The evening had done her good.

"Of course, I'll drive you home," he said pleasantly.

It took more than half an hour for them to leave the crowded auditorium and reach his car. They didn't speak on the way home. Regina felt liberated, and found herself laughing. The grey-haired man was tense. He hoped his gang had done their work well. And if not? Hitches were always possible. By all his reckonings, the three of them should be in the air now, on their way out of Brazil. And what if they weren't … He hoped, with all his heart, that they had taken care of what he'd planned to end this evening with. His *chevrah*, certainly they hadn't forgotten his special request to them, as they stood in the Hunkes home …

The car stopped in Piaui Street. Regina Hunkes, a broad smile on her face, thanked the grey-haired man one more time. "Hermann, I must admit that you've been wonderful to me."

The grey-haired man smiled. "I just did my duty, both as a GAC employee and as an old friend."

"I admit there were times when I was angry with you. Particularly yesterday, when you wouldn't let me go back home. But maybe you were right. In any case, many thanks for this wonderful evening you've given me. It was truly a lovely farewell gift. I'll never forget it."

The grey-haired man smiled happily. "Regina, have a good trip. We'll be taking care of your interests here in Brazil. In Germany, I've told you whom you should contact. And if you have a problem, I'm always here. It's just a shame that it should end so, and Alberto not here with us."

Regina didn't answer. She bit her lip. The mention of her husband's name tugged at her heart. The wound was still very fresh.

She left the car, her eyes moist. The grey-haired man gave a final farewell. "I wish you all the best. And time, you know, is the great healer. *Chau.*"

Again, she didn't answer. She waved her hand in a farewell gesture and went into the building. The grey-haired man waited for one more minute, watching her; he couldn't help but smile in anticipation. If he could have, he would have gone up with her. He would very much have liked to have seen her, when all was revealed. Particularly his small surprise to her ...

45

Regina went up in the elevator, feeling relieved. To be home again, at last! *But just temporarily,* the painful thought stabbed at her. This would be her last night in this house, in Sao Paulo. Now, as she stood next to the door, the name Hunkes inscribed upon it in golden letters, the awful reality hit her for the first time: She was leaving. Leaving forever. Leaving, with tragedy behind her. Her heart beat lightly within her. Goodbye, Sao Paulo! Goodbye, Brazil! It was hard to believe, that she would be returning to Germany alone, without her husband at her side. Though if Alberto were alive, she would never have been able to consider returning to the Fatherland. They were waiting there, for her Alberto. They would have arrested him immediately, and he would have been imprisoned as a Nazi war criminal. Now she could return — alone.

Her hands trembled slightly as she placed the key in the lock. She slowly turned it, as if to lengthen the time she would be spending here, in her home.

With a light motion she opened the door, but she didn't enter. Some sixth sense warned her suddenly to be careful, to keep her eyes open. She stood in the threshold. A heavy, though muffled, feeling weighed her down. Something wasn't right here. Her eyes darted back and forth over the living room, opening wider and wider. A lump grew in her throat, all but choking off her breath. *Someone's been here*, she whispered to herself. *Someone's been here*.

That much was clear. She could see the mess in the living room at a glance. The chairs had been moved around; one of the bar doors was open. An open bottle of whiskey stood on a small table, though she saw no glasses next to it. *Vandals*, she thought to herself, *barbarians! They drank directly from the bottle!* A dish-towel had been flung upon the sofa. It was soiled. Blackened. From a distance, it looked like it had been dipped in machine oil. What could it mean? *Thieves*, she thought. With short, cautious steps she entered the apartment. You never knew: Perhaps the burglars were still inside. Her heart thudded within her. One trouble seemed to follow another. This was it: She was done with Brazil. She felt a fierce longing to return to Germany, to her native home. She pulled the envelope bearing the ticket that Hermann had given her even closer to her.

Regina slowly approached the bedroom. She would take a nap, relax a little from the turmoil of the past few days. Tomorrow morning, when she began to pack, she would see what damage had been done. But when she opened the doorway she gave a horrified scream. Her hands traveled to her mouth, as if to try and silence it, to no avail. She screamed and screamed, as her eyes looked upon the devastation. Tragedy had beset her, escaping from the hole in the safe! Regina grabbed the sides of the bed; in another minute, she felt she would faint.

After the first moment of panic, she sat down on the bed, trembling. She was not yet prepared to believe what she was seeing. The secret was revealed! The great secret of their lives, of her husband and herself, was someone's property. Who knew what the unknown enemy would do with the information? Regina flung herself down on the bed in deep despair. She threw her head into the pillow, and bitter sobs wracked her entire body.

The scoundrels have succeeded, the frightening thought tore through her broken heart. *They heard on the radio, saw on television, read in the newspapers that I'd disappeared, that I'm no longer in my house, and took advantage of it. But how did they know where the safe was hidden?*

Regina felt a stab of impatience. Her world was destroyed. She didn't care what would happen to her anymore. She was furious with herself. Why hadn't she insisted on taking the contents of the safe with her, the night that Hermann Schmidt had drawn her away from the apartment? Everything would have been different! The night in the theater had given her a new lease on life, a feeling of relief, after the frightful week she'd lived through, since Alberto had been murdered. Now all was taken from her!

She jumped up in the bed. Could it be that all that Hermann had done for her had been nothing more than a plot to get her out of the house? To get her out in order to reach the safe in quiet and security, without interruption? Regina nodded her head vehemently back and forth: No. Hermann had nothing to do with this business. Impossible!

After a few hours she rose from the bed, completely exhausted. It was 4 in the morning. A frigid morning wind wailed through a crack near the window. Regina bent down towards the hole in the safe and thrust her hand inside. It was empty, with the exception of an envelope containing $20,000. They hadn't touched that. Regina understood the message: They were after the plans of the Spider, and nothing else. She nervously tapped her fingers together. What to do now?

On her way to the kitchen to get a drink she returned to the living room. For the first time she noticed a beautiful bouquet of roses filling a vase on the buffet. She didn't remember buying them. She saw an envelope dangling from one of the thorns. How was it that she hadn't noticed it when she'd come in? Regina walked over to examine the vase. The envelope had a name on it. A scream escaped her once again: It was addressed to Mrs. Regina Hunkes (Krantz).

A paralyzing fear overwhelmed her. Who knew their secret? And what did they want of her, now that Alberto was dead?

She turned the white envelope over in her hands, looking for a clue to the one who'd sent it. And suddenly, she felt as if struck by lightning. Her breath came in short gasps, her hands trembled wildly. The letter had been sent — by Hermann Schmidt, their pleasant grey-haired friend from GAC.

Regina took the letter and turned towards one of the armchairs. She sat down, leaning her weary head on her left hand. After a few minutes of silence, she carefully opened the envelope.

> *To my dear Regina:*
>
> *I have decided to prepare a small surprise for you before you leave us, to give you a small bouquet of roses as a farewell present, and to add a few warm words on the subject of thorns.*
>
> *Thorns, such as the thorn which holds this letter, have a lesson to teach us. The thorn is a silent object, not usually noticed. But if you touch it, it pricks.*
>
> *By the time you read this letter I will be far away from here, on my way back to my people and my land — Israel. With G-d's help I've completed my mission — to get my hands on the plans of the Spider. With the help of those papers, listing the whereabouts of Nazis hidden in South America, we will be able to continue to pursue those killers of my nation who managed to flee to that continent. To see to it that they are brought to justice and, if not, that they are killed by my organization's execution squads, which have not yet been satisfied, and still exult in the killing of any Nazi they happen upon. I've given more than two years of my life to this holy mission. Today I am satisfied that I have succeeded — with your help, my dear Regina. The nation of Israel shall never forget your help of the past few days. Help that allowed us to quietly break into your fortress and find those important lists that will give us all the information we need.*

Regina couldn't read further. From the first moment, she longed to tear the paper into a thousand tiny pieces, but she managed to overcome her fury. Hermann Schmidt! That blackhearted fiend! That cursed Jew! That traitorous scoundrel! *He will plant his thornbush on my grave. He ruined my life, and laughs at me! Where is Hitler? We need him today! Der Fuehrer! Why didn't he exterminate them completely, that accursed race?*

An overwhelming hatred of the Jews, such as she hadn't felt in many years, conquered her completely. If Hermann Schmidt should fall into her power, she would choke him to death — with her bare hands!

She continued reading.

> *I am imagining your face when you discover that your carefully hidden secret has been revealed. I am forbidden to do what I am doing now, forbidden by the rules of the game to reveal my true identity. But in order to heighten your humiliation, I tell you: I am in the Secret Service of the Jewish State, the State you loathe so bitterly. And I have a long personal reckoning with you, with the Nazis. You imprisoned me in Buchenwald, destroyed my entire family. And I? I was left alone in the world. There are not many in the world who can savor the enjoyment I feel at this moment, as I leave you bereft and, at the same time, grasp the documents of the Spider organization that you created. There is no punishment for the crimes committed by your husband, Heinz Krantz, and his cursed friends. But at the very least, let them not live in tranquility! At least, let them flee from one place to the next! Let them feel a tiny fraction of the fear that a Jewish child felt in the fearful ghettos and death camps that you established throughout Europe. I derive incredible joy from the*

> *feelings you must have as you realize that you have fallen into my power, in the power of a Jew, one whom you thought was a fellow German, one whom you turned to in times of trouble. Your fury is just a small part of my revenge. No, not revenge. There is no person who can avenge the murder of my nation, my family.*

Regina put the letter down. She ran trembling fingers through her hair. Wild thoughts raced through her head like runaway horses. At the first minute she thought of calling some of the heads of the Nazis in Brazil and Argentina, to warn them of the impending danger. Their secret list had been discovered; they must rush to change their homes, their identities. But on second thought she realized that she would be endangering herself through such an action. These harsh men would not forgive her for allowing the documents to be stolen from her home. She knew it for a fact: Sooner or later she would be executed. What could she do? Her journey to Germany was now a danger, not a solution.

She began to read once again:

> *Yes, Regina, there is one thing which pains me greatly. And that is that our dear Alberto is no longer alive. What to do? He has escaped a portion of the punishment he deserved. He will not have the taste of fleeing, the fear in the darkness of night of a visit by policemen or Jewish executioners. That fear will be with you eternally, cursed Nazis. But we had no choice. To our dismay he suspected what we wanted of him, and during that last fateful lunch he even hinted at it to our agent. We knew he might decide to flee the city and that two years of work — to locate the lists and ensure with-*

out a doubt that they were in your home — might have been in vain. We had no choice, Regina, but to see to it that he would enjoy a portion of poison that would bring him directly into the welcoming hands of the demons awaiting him in some deep portion of hell, if indeed even hell exists for such as he.

Regina, I will add just one more farewell word. You cannot fight against me in any way. By the time you read this, the lists will no longer be in my possession. The good men who, while you enjoyed the performance in honor of your husband, paid a cordial little visit to your apartment delivered, as agreed, the papers to me. And from me, immediately, they were delivered to addresses all over the world. I assume you need no more details, correct? You are intelligent enough to know who would be interested in them. Besides, it is worth your while to know: Some of the key men in your underground organization have been told that we have them in our sights and that you, Mrs. Hunkes, are responsible for handing us the information, that you leaked it out of anger at them for having abandoned you. I know that's not true. But this small lie comes to serve a great truth: a bit of panic, suspicion, and despair in your all-too-tranquil encampment.

That's it, Regina: I've finished. How you'll extricate yourself from the pit that you've gotten yourself in by accompanying me to the ridiculous performance in honor of your husband — I don't know. It is, frankly, not my problem. It's yours. In any case the Jewish nation, whose representative I am at this time, will follow your movements with interest, as you attempt to escape from the spider's web. Good luck, Regina.

"Hermann Schmidt"

Regina closed her eyes for a second, in a futile attempt to think clearly. After a moment she opened them again. Her eyes were riveted on the vase with its roses. With a wild motion she jumped out of the chair, grabbed the vase, and hurled it at the wall. She could hear it shatter. She walked over to the ruined vase, kicked furiously at a large shard of glass that flew into the air and landed embedded in the kitchen door. Regina knew she was losing control. She knew: She had little hope of escape. Hermann Schmidt, or whatever his name really was, had finished her off.

From outside the large living room window, the first traces of dawn could be seen. *The sun rises on Sao Paulo — but not for me*. Regina stood up and staggered drunkenly to the bedroom. Occasionally she would lean against the walls of the apartment to keep from falling. After an endless journey of about 10 minutes she reached her husband's bed and sat down heavily upon it. After she'd taken a few deep breaths she opened the night table nearby. She pulled out a Colt .45 revolver from within it, pulled out the safety catch. The revolver was loaded …

Lod Airport
9 Iyar 5727

Second Lieutenant Ronny Lipschitz returned from his phone conversation.

"The Army Spokesman has given its authorization. You may interview the soldier."

"Excellent."

The two of them, Ronny and Eduardo, entered the military jeep, that drove towards the airport. It was 10 in the morning. They reached the airport, going past one roadblock after another — but they saw no sign of the bearded soldier.

"Can you describe him?" the officer asked Eduardo.

Eduardo hesitated. "The characteristic that I noticed was his beard — and the skullcap on his head. What else do I know about him? Oh, yes, his eyes seemed very melancholy. They were noticeable. Though I know that's not an effective means of identifying him."

Second Lieutenant Lipschitz was silent for a moment. Then he said, "I'll do what I can. I'll try to find something out."

The army officer disappeared. Eduardo remained behind, in this Jewish airport, his eyes alertly following all that was happening. But not much *was* happening, really. Everything seemed normal, like an airport anywhere in the world. People going from one place to the next. Travelers leaving, travelers arriving. Goodbye hugs, tears of joy when people came together. Like anywhere in the world, like any nation. Yes, but with that, there was a difference. The thought wouldn't leave him: These were Jews! That was the difference! Why? Eduardo couldn't explain it rationally. He remembered Alberto Hunkes, his father. Would he have been willing to stand like this, like him, in Lod Airport, surrounded on all sides by free Jews?

The young officer returned, a look of victory on his face.

"I've managed to find him. He's the only religious soldier in this area. He'll be here in several minutes."

46

The grey-haired man — Reuven Morag — rapidly left the Hunkes home. A short ride brought him to the broad Estados Unidos Avenue. From there he took a sharp right turn to Gabriel Monteiro da Silva Street. He traveled in the wrong lane of traffic: He was in a hurry and at 1:30 in the morning, along the abandoned streets, traffic rules didn't matter. This way he could speed to his heart's content, with no one getting in the way.

He jumped out of his car, skipped lightly up the steps to the apartment. The door opened easily before him. He switched on the light and darted towards the buffet. He bent down under it and, with one hand propping up his body, pulled a hook that was hidden beneath it. Instantly, a drawer popped open wide. Reuven's heart beat wildly; he all but stopped breathing. Yes! There they were. The Spider file was in his hands!

Reuven shut his eyes. The blood thudded through his temples; at the same time, he felt a warm feeling of relief envelop his entire body. His lips whispered one wonderful word — thanks.

In his hand he held a thick cardboard file. The words "Spider Plans" were printed upon it. The documents inside the file were beautifully arranged, with the usual German penchant for efficiency. Yes, all the names were there. All the Nazis now hidden in South America. The war criminals whom the free world had given up on uncovering. Morag felt a surge of honest emotion. The documents included the real names, the false identities currently in use, and the addresses. Another document gave a detailed description of the Nazis' escape routes from Europe to South America. A third paper outlined the location of the riches in the Nazi's possession: vast amounts of money, gold, and diamonds stolen from the Jews of Europe during World War II. It was an incredible treasure that had fallen into his hands! From this day forward, the pursuit of Nazis in South America would wear a wholly different face. Who would have believed it? When he'd first been sent on this mission he hadn't the faintest idea of where to start and where it all would end. For months he'd stumbled through a black fog. And now — he'd succeeded.

His first instinct was to call home, to his wife. It had been more than two years since he'd seen her. He'd made a sort of vow not to return to Israel until his mission had been completed. But he thought better of it: One never knew what extra ear was listening to phone conversations.

Reuven looked at his watch. It was 2 in the morning. His thoughts flitted to Regina. How had she taken the final crushing blow that he'd given her? Had she read his "farewell" letter? Reuven grinned. He knew he shouldn't have done it. He knew that by his action he'd prematurely endangered his false identity. He had broken an iron-clad law of the world of spying. It had been a moment of weakness on his part, he admitted to himself. But he couldn't resist letting her know that she'd fallen into a snare laid by a Jew, who exulted in her downfall. He could vividly imagine the scene as she screamed and threw things, shattering them into pieces. During the time he'd gotten to know her he had learned much about Regina Hunkes, and he was convinced that she would react in that way. Most of all, he rejoiced in the knowledge that this proud and haughty woman felt helpless. To see a Nazi cast down into the depths — there was no greater pleasure in the universe.

Reuven took the precious file into the bedroom. He had to rest a little before his trip outside the city, outside the country. He knew he couldn't sleep: The dissipation of his tension, combined with his overwhelming curiosity about the contents of the file, overcame his fatigue.

He settled himself comfortably in a chair that stood in a corner of the room and began to skim through the papers. Only the soft glow of a nightlight illuminated the room. Drapes covered the windows.

Suddenly, he jumped up and walked towards the phone.

"Hello, Skinny?"

The thin man answered amidst a deep yawn. His superior had roused him from a deep, satisfying sleep.

"Yeah?"

"It's me. You recognize my voice?"

For a second there was silence. Then, "Oh, yeah."

"Good. I want to thank you for the valuable materials. Congratulations. Were there problems?"

"No. The mission was completed. The gang went to sleep long ago."

Reuven understood: They'd left the country.

"Look here, Skinny."

"Yeah?"

"Come quickly with your car. Switch to my car. The keys and registration are inside already. Leave me your car; put the registration in the mailbox. I don't want anyone to see my car near this house. Okay?"

"Okay."

The conversation came to an end.

Ten minutes passed. The grey-haired man listened contentedly to the sound of an approaching motor. An engine switched off. A car door banged. And another car roared off, driving further and further away ...

Lod Airport
9 Iyar 5727

Eduardo saw the religious soldier as he walked through the glass doors of the terminal. He gave him a professional glance, as a reporter looking for some local color for his paper. It seemed to him that a report on a soldier coming from such a background would clarify the contradictions that made up Israeli society to his Brazilian readers. And perhaps the man himself had a good story to tell, something that would touch the hearts of his readership ...

Yitzchak Austerlitz approached. He'd been told to find an officer by the name of Ronny Lipschitz, so he went to find him. After all, he was a disciplined soldier. He did what he was told, without asking questions.

"Are you Ronny Lipschitz?" he asked in his quiet voice.

"Yes? You are Yitzchak Austerlitz?"

"Yes. How can I help you?"

"Look, Yitzchak, this is a Brazilian reporter. His name is Eduardo Hunkes."

Yitzchak shook Eduardo's hand. Eduardo gave him the famous Brazilian grin. Yitzchak tried hard to respond with a smile of his own.

Yitzchak then lapsed into silence, waiting to see what would happen next.

"See here, Yitzchak, this journalist noticed you yesterday, when you were guarding the terminal entrance."

Austerlitz nodded.

"Something about you interested him. You're different from the other Israelis he's met here. He'd like to interview you for his newspaper, one of the most important in the world, the *Estado de Sao Paulo*. Do you understand?"

Ronny noticed signs of anger begin to darken Austerlitz's face. He spoke gently.

"Look, Yitzchak, I won't order you to be interviewed. But think a little bit about how necessary it is that we have a press sympathetic to us at this time. We're in a grave situation. War may break out. We need, we very much need the support of the world."

"What can he hear from me, an old religious Jew?"

"I don't know, Yitzchak. But he wants it!"

As he had done always in his life, Yitzchak gave in, defeated. The three turned to a distant corner of the departures terminal in order to speak without interruption. They found a few empty chairs near the KLM counter; the area itself seemed almost abandoned, with no travelers to be seen.

Eduardo pulled out his pad, turned a page, and began to scribble down some thoughts. Afterwards, he smiled at Yitzchak Austerlitz and said in Portuguese, turning to Ronny, "First of all, ask him his name."

A warm-up question, this, in order to get a conversation going. Eduardo wrote it down: Yitzchak Austerlitz. He realized that the old bearded Jew was quite unhappy about cooperating with him. Eduardo was quiet for a minute, as his brain searched for a more substantial question, a question that would get the interview rolling.

"I arrived yesterday in Israel for the very first time. I was in an airplane crowded with young Israelis. Here, too, I've seen some Israelis, almost all of them in uniform. You're different from them. Why?"

After a moment's silence, he added, "Also, I noticed your eyes. They seem so sad. Why is that?"

Yitzchak was not pleased with the question. Did he have to tell this young *goy* what he'd gone through, what tortured him even now? Could this Brazilian gentile ever understand? The thought of standing up and leaving flashed through his mind. He didn't need this! The army couldn't force him to take part in this difficult conversation. But suddenly a wild, mad idea took hold of him. This young man was a Brazilian journalist. Perhaps if he, Yitzchak, were to tell him all that he'd gone through, as the journalist desired, perhaps, if he listened to his story and understood why Yitzchak was so troubled, perhaps he could help him find Heinz Krantz in Brazil? Didn't journalists know everything?

Austerlitz suddenly felt his feelings towards Eduardo change. "I'm sad because I'm a Jew. Isn't that enough?"

Eduardo asked politely, though he didn't quite understand the man's tone of voice, "And the others aren't Jews?"

He waved his arm around as if to include the airport, and perhaps the entire country.

"Yes, the others are certainly Jewish. But they are not Jews of Auschwitz. Have you heard of that place, my dear young Brazilian journalist?"

"And what does that mean, to be a Jew of Auschwitz?"

Yitzchak Austerlitz raised his hand and brought it quickly down. "A Jew of Auschwitz is a Jew for whom the sun will never shine. A Jew of Auschwitz is a man who is lost among the pathways of life, like one wandering through a dark forest in the middle of the night. A Jew of Auschwitz never, ever knows true joy. Even vengeance against his killers will not give him the pleasure that he deserves. And I — I am a Jew of Auschwitz."

From here, the story took form. Nothing had disappeared from Yitzchak Austerlitz's memory. He was astonished at himself, at the way he revealed himself to this young stranger, a non-Jew who'd landed into his life from another planet, telling him all that had happened to him since that bitter hour when that cursed Nazi Heinz Krantz had burst into his house with fearful shouts.

Yitzchak could hardly believe himself. He revealed the innermost feelings of his heart to this Eduardo. He was carried away by the thought that the journalist could help him in his search for Krantz. Eduardo hardly had to ask him questions to keep the conversation going. Austerlitz told him of the child born to him after the war, who bore the name of the son who'd been carried to his death by Heinz Krantz. He told him of his irrational hopes that his son still lived. He knew it was foolishness on his part, thoughts that would lead nowhere. And yet ...

Eduardo listened carefully to Ronny Lipschitz's translation, and wrote and wrote without opening his mouth. Occasionally he would nod his head, in order to keep some kind of contact with Austerlitz. He was thrilled: Here was a tear-jerker of a story on a unique Israeli soldier. His readers would eat it up. The Brazilian public was a sentimental and emotional one and this story, told against the backdrop of an ever-increasingly tense situation in Israel, would surely touch them. Strange, he felt no animosity towards this Jew sitting near him. On the other hand, he felt no real empathy with the pain of this bearded religious Jew either.

Yitzchak suddenly stopped the flow of his narrative. For a few moments he was silent. He stared at the two men sitting near him as one suddenly roused from a dream. Finally, he asked with an appearance of cheerfulness, as if to cover up his embarrassment, "Does Brazil want to know anything else about me?"

Eduardo, satisfied, answered, "No. Thank you, sir. It was something special, meeting you."

The young officer seemed pleased; he'd done something positive for the public relations of his country.

"You see, Yitzchak, you've really contributed something. We're soldiers on many different fronts."

The two rose. But Yitzchak stopped them. "Ask him," he said, "ask him if he's willing to do something for me in Brazil."

Ronny was surprised. What could this Jew need in Brazil? But he asked Eduardo, who answered in the affirmative.

"I've done some investigating, and found out that 'my' Heinz Krantz is now in Brazil. I know it for a fact. Ask the young journalist if he'd be prepared to do me the favor of trying to find something out about him there. As a journalist he no doubt has a lot of connections."

Ronny, again, was surprised. Eduardo, too, was astonished by the request. Austerlitz could feel his hesitation.

"It's very, very important to me. It's a matter of life and death! I must know where he is! Can you help me?"

Eduardo didn't want to say yes. Though he never had approved of what the Nazis had done, still, to help Jews uncover their identities was unthinkable. Suddenly, for no apparent reason, he thought of the words of the police officer in Sao Paulo, Roberto Nunes, on their way to the airport, in which Roberto had claimed Eduardo's parents were Germans.

And yet, despite all this, he answered, "When I return to Sao Paulo, I'll try to find out if the police know anything of a Nazi named Heinz Krantz. Okay?"

Yitzchak was content. He smiled into his beard. A spark of hope lit up his eyes. Perhaps, he thought, it was Heaven that had arranged this meeting with the young journalist from Brazil, so that he could help him.

There was a sudden announcement on the airport public address system. "Reserve soldier Yitzchak Austerlitz, please come to the information desk for an urgent telephone call."

Austerlitz stood up. The others began to say their goodbyes.

"Excuse me, I have one more thing to ask of you. Just allow me to finish this call. I'm sorry."

Yitzchak hurried to the counter, with Ronny and Eduardo following behind him. Yitzchak took the receiver in his hands, listened with increasing tension to what was being said. Ronny Lipschitz was the first to notice: Yitzchak's eyes began to roll in their sockets, and his head lolled. The receiver fell from his hand. He made a terrible sound and fell onto the floor ...

Within seconds the army paramedic was there, checking Yitzchak's pulse, heart, reflexes. The few passengers in the terminal made a circle around the man lying there on the floor. Ronny hurried to pick up the abandoned telephone receiver to tell the unknown caller what had happened. He heard the hysterical voice of a woman screaming into the phone, "Yitzchak! What's happened, Yitzchak?"

"Relax, ma'am. Who are you?"

"I'm his wife. What's happened to him?"

"He fainted. We hope it's no more than that. The army doctor is already here, and he's called an ambulance."

Ronny could hear the terrible cry on the other end of the line.

"They're taking him, they've told me, to Tel Hashomer. The doctor doesn't seem overly worried. But what happened? What did you tell him?"

Ronny listened to the woman's story. Eduardo didn't take his eyes off the young second lieutenant's face, but he didn't see any reaction there. Finally, the conversation ended. Ronny slowly hung the phone up and stared at the stretcher being carried towards a military ambulance.

"What happened?" Eduardo asked quietly.

"It was his wife. She told him that an hour ago someone called from Brazil and told him that Heinz Krantz was dead. Murdered in Sao Paulo a week ago."

Eduardo could feel his blood freeze in his veins. His father had been murdered. A week ago. In Sao Paulo. After a moment he gave his head a powerful shake. "No," he said aloud, hardly realizing he was speaking. "It's a coincidence. That's all."

"What's a coincidence?" Ronny asked, interested.

"It's not important. Really, not important."

Ronny could see that Eduardo was disturbed. He didn't question him further. He brought him back to the Avia Hotel. On the way back, they hardly exchanged a word. At the entrance, Eduardo said goodbye.

"I want to get this written up quickly. The fainting at the end adds a terrific sense of drama. What do you think?"

"Absolutely," Ronny answered politely, though Eduardo's professional callousness repulsed him.

Eduardo smiled. *"Chau."*

At the counter, a message was waiting for him. "Mister Hunkes, your newspaper office called from Sao Paulo. It's urgent."

The reception clerk helped him with the connection to Brazil. "Hello? Who's this?"

"Soares. Who is speaking?"

"It's Eduardo. Eduardo Hunkes, calling from Tel Aviv. What's the matter?"

"Oh, Eduardo! I'm on morning duty here in the newsroom. They asked me to call you and tell you the news …"

"What news?" His nerves tensed up.

"I'm so sorry, Eduardo. It's your mother."

"What's happened to her!"

"Um … I'm sorry … They found her in her house. In the bedroom."

"Was she dead? Was she murdered?"

"It's not clear yet. The police haven't yet ruled out suicide."

There was a long silence. Finally, Eduardo whispered, "What do you say? Shall I return home?"

Soares didn't hurry with his reply. "If it had happened to my mother, I would come back from the end of the world. You know, a person has only one mother."

Eduardo didn't answer. He said only one word into the phone. *"Chau."*

And he went up to his room.

47

Reuven Morag woke up in a panic. For a moment he couldn't remember why he wasn't in his bed, why he was sitting in a chair, fully dressed, a night light giving off a thin beam of illumination. What was going on? Why hadn't he undressed and gone to bed? Had something happened?

After a moment, he calmed down. He saw the papers still in his hand and remembered. A wide grin spread on his face. Here were the documents of the Spider organization! His dream had come true! Apparently he'd fallen asleep while skimming through this incredible treasure. He glanced at his watch. Four in the morning. He must hurry, he knew. In an hour a car would pick him up and take him to Porto Allegre in the southern part of the country. From there he would fly to Santiago de Chile. He would spend two weeks there before returning to Europe — and then to Israel.

Morag needed a few more minutes to relax before getting up. Before he'd fallen asleep he'd been thinking of the huge number of addresses that he'd finally obtained of Nazi war criminals who'd disappeared from Europe with the war's end. At the moment, after waking from a deep sleep, he couldn't remember many of the names, but one stood out in his mind: Josef Schoemburger, known as the Mass Murderer of Poland, a name he'd earned as a captain in the S.S., when given the responsibility over the ghetto of Rosvadba and the Presmysyl labor camp. The eyewitness reports given in testimony against him were hair raising, describing a merciless killer who'd murdered hundreds with his bare hands ...

Morag remembered that this killer, who'd sent tens of thousands of Jews to their deaths in Auschwitz as well, had disappeared after the war. And here before him, Reuven Morag, were all the details! Schoemburger had been living in Argentina since 1949. He'd been jailed in 1945, as a result of information that Nazi hunters, working together with Simon Wiesenthal, had handed over to the occupation forces in Austria. But he'd managed to get out of the Austrian prison and, with the help of an Italian passport, to flee to Argentina. He'd been aided by various priests, together with agents of the American F.B.I. This last detail was news to Morag. This would cause a stir within the top brass, he knew. It seemed that this Schoemburger was living in the La Plata area, some 45 miles south of Buenos Aires, in the midst of a community with a significant number of Germans. Two years ago, in 1965, the Argentinian government had granted him citizenship.

According to the documents that Morag had read before falling asleep, Schoemburger had visited Brazil's Parana region a number of times. No doubt he'd been attending the Nazi conclaves in the ranch near the Vila Velha, the ones Heinz Krantz had traveled to. Now his address was known. It was possible that Schoemburger would soon learn of this breach of security and would disappear. Thus it was imperative that the material reach its goal as quickly as possible.

Morag yawned, flexed his muscles in order to ease the fatigue that still gripped him. He rose from his chair. The floor around him was covered with papers that had slipped from his fingers during his nap. He turned to the bathroom to rinse his face in the hopes of waking himself up. After a few minutes he returned to the bedroom and began to gather the papers together.

As he picked them up he glanced through them curiously. He didn't have much time, he knew: He really must hurry. But still … Here was the name of Josef Mengele, the bloody doctor of Auschwitz! Morag felt a thrill of excitement pulse through him. Unbelievable! Mengele had actually lived in Sao Paulo itself for a time, in the Pineros neighborhood, not too far from the apartment that he, Morag, was staying in at this very moment. All the world had searched for this fearful war criminal, without finding him! According to these lists, Mengele, too, had joined a convention in the ranch in Parana from Asunción, the capital of Paraguay. Morag noticed that Mengele's home address was in the city of Iguaso, located on the borders between Brazil, Paraguay, and Argentina, near a mighty waterfall. Apparently the lowdown murderer was hiding in a fortified area in the trackless jungle. Last year, Morag remembered, two bodies dressed in priests' vestments had been found floating in the Parana River, that bisected the jungle in that very area and emptied into the Iguaso waterfalls. After a time it became known that the dead men were actually Israeli agents on the heels of the Beast of Auschwitz.

And here, on still another paper, was the name Walter Kutzmann, a high-ranking Gestapo officer who'd murdered countless Jews. He was the top assistant to the commandant of the Druchovitz death camp in Poland. Today he lived in the Argentinian coastal town of Miramar under the name Pedro Ricardo Olamo.

Morag looked further. He could hardly believe it: Stengal! Stengal, commandant of Treblinka, living quietly in Sao Paulo! Remarkable! Stengal lived not far from Heinz Krantz's home. Incredible! How would they deal with all these war criminals, whose identities had now been discovered — by him! Would they have them extradited to the European countries that were searching for them or send Jewish vengeance squads to take care of them, as they had last year taken care of Zuckeros, the Lithuanian war criminal, who'd helped the Nazis in the extermination of Lithuanian Jewry? This Zuckeros, Morag remembered, had been persuaded by influential "businessmen" to leave Sao Paulo for an important business meeting in Montevideo, Uruguay — and had been executed there. Morag didn't know. But if it were up to him, he would choose the second option.

Morag's attention was suddenly drawn to an envelope that lay between the papers he'd picked up off the floor. It looked different from the other documents they'd gotten out of the Hunkes's safe. Somehow he'd overlooked it last night, as he'd first skimmed

through the papers. The envelope was addressed to
Eduardo Hunkes. He turned it over, and saw that the
sender was Eduardo's father: Alberto Hunkes. What
was this doing in the safe? Curiosity overcame him:
He quickly tore it open and read the contents.

Afterwards, he sat down on the recliner and read
the letter a second time. He stood up and hurried to
the kitchen, lit up the fire and placed a kettle of water
up to boil. He suddenly felt he must drink a cup of
coffee. He lit up a cigarette and read the letter through
a third time, this time out loud. He had to make certain he'd read it correctly. He sipped the steaming
brew slowly, his eyes staring blankly out the open
window at the grey skies of this pre-dawn hour ...

Avia Hotel
9 Iyar 5727

Eduardo locked the door of his room carefully behind him. The deep silence of the room, cut off from
the noises of the outside world, was bad for him: In
the quiet, he could hear the strange murmurs of his
brain, like the angry buzzing of a mosquito. No, he
wasn't dizzy, though he was forced to close his eyes
every few minutes. He was young, he was inexperi-
enced. Why were these troubles coming upon him?
His father, murdered a week before. No one knew
why. His mother, declaring it had been the work of the
Jews. Why had she thought so? A police officer raising
suspicions in his mind, suspicions that his father had
been an active Nazi. Was that true? Could it be? And
today — Mother! Had she died naturally? Had she
been murdered? Had she killed herself?

Eduardo grabbed his head in his hands. One second!
Soares had told him that she'd been found dead in her

home. When had she returned to her apartment? Perhaps the mysterious abductors, whom his mother had apparently trusted, had brought her back home and killed her? And then, in order to conceal their murderous deed, perhaps they'd made it look like suicide?

Eduardo was confused. He slowly sat down on the soft bed. His right hand gently rubbed his forehead. After a minute he stretched out on the bed. Here, his mother was dead, and he was thousands of kilometers away. Alone, abandoned. He had no one to speak to here. Officer Ronny Lipschitz? Yes, that was it! Absolutely! He was a nice guy, and there had been good chemistry between the two. But — how could he say this? — Lipschitz was a Jew. What to do now? Here in Israel, everything was growing more tense. The reserves had already been mobilized. The Arab states, particularly Egypt, were rattling their sabers noisily. The general opinion: War was imminent. The hotel was full of journalists from around the world. And he, Eduardo, wanted to stay here. He had found this land fascinating and wanted to see how it would deal with the coming battle. In the meantime, it was Nasser, Egypt's leader, who'd taken the initiative. The U.N. was evacuating its forces from the Straits of Tiran, according to Nasser's orders. Israel, it seemed, would be caught in a naval blockade. Things were hot here, very hot. And he wanted to be here, on the spot, where things were happening!

But — he couldn't get away from it. His mother! Some internal force was pushing him back to Sao Paulo. He would never forgive himself if he missed her funeral. Besides, he wanted badly to know what had happened. How had she died? Where had she been these past few days? His doubts, his fantasies were killing him. He must return to Sao Paulo, the sooner the better.

Eduardo stood up and approached the window. He pulled up the curtain and stared out at the airport. Planes took off, planes landed constantly. There was much more traffic than usual, as military transports kept the runways busy. Were they bringing soldiers? Equipment? Eduardo didn't know.

Eduardo heard Soares's words, whispered to him from thousands of kilometers away. They were repeated, again and again, in his brain: *If it had happened to my mother I would come back from the end of the world. You know, a person has only one mother.*

Only one mother. Only one. Though he had to admit he didn't feel any particular love for her, for this mother of his. More accurately, he had been afraid of her. A hard woman, she had been. And yet Soares was right: You only had one mother. And all things considered, she'd been a good mother to him.

There was no choice. He would return to Sao Paulo.

Tel Hashomer Hospital
9 Iyar 5727

Yitzchak Austerlitz lay unconscious in the Emergency Room. His wife, Rivka, arrived half an hour later. When she saw him she burst into silent tears. She had never thought that the news of Heinz Krantz would effect him so. Before she'd left Bnei Brak she'd made sure Yitzchak Mandelkorn knew what had happened. She hoped he, too, would arrive shortly. She needed someone near her now. She hadn't yet told her son, Yaakov Yehoshua. She first wanted to know exactly what the situation was.

The doctors who occasionally looked in on her husband were in no hurry to volunteer information.

"Doctor, I'm the patient's wife. Can you tell me what his condition is?"

The doctor muttered something and hurried away.

Fears battered at Rivka like a sledgehammer. What were they hiding from her? What had happened to him? Please, Hashem, help them!

After about half an hour two young male nurses, accompanied by a female nurse, walked over and carefully moved Yitzchak onto a gurney. Rivka followed them quietly. He was taken to one of the wards and again lifted onto a hospital bed. Now he was in the Internal Medicine department. Rivka looked brokenheartedly at her husband, lying there, unresponsive, not hearing her urgent whispers: "Yitzchak, it's me, Rivka! Yitzchak, answer me! Say something!"

An older doctor came by. "Are you Mrs. Austerlitz?" he said, without further pleasantries.

"Yes," she answered, feeling the pressure coming to a head.

"Look here, ma'am, your husband has had a stroke, possibly as a result of some tremendous emotion. We can't yet determine the extent of the damage. It seems that the event isn't over yet. I don't want to deceive you. We need a few days in order to see what kind of damage there is."

"But, Doctor, is there a chance he'll recover from it?"

"Look here, I can't promise anything now. In a few days we'll be able to give you a clearer picture."

Rivka's heart thudded, jumping like a bird as it approached its nest. Why had he needed that foolish pursuit of a cursed, rotten Nazi? And what would happen now?

"But Doctor, just one more question!"

But the doctor had already disappeared down the corridor. Rivka was left alone.

Sao Paulo, Brazil
May 19, 1967

Reuven Morag woke up from his daydreams with a start. He could clearly hear the sound of an engine downstairs. He was supposed to be waiting outside, in order to minimize the amount of time the car had to linger near the building. Morag didn't recognize the driver, and the driver didn't recognize him: That was important, in order to allow him to flee the country.

The grey-haired man quickly changed, grabbed the documents and some personal items, and raced down to the car.

"Good morning, sir," the young driver said courteously.

"Good morning," Morag replied. He gave the man a searching glance. No, he'd never seen him before. Excellent.

Morag got into the car. "Before we leave the city, please drive to Jardim America. To Almeda Franca Street. Okay?"

The driver looked anxiously at Morag. "Not really. I have express instructions not to spend any extra time in the city. I've got to get to Curitiba at a certain time, and it's a six-hour drive! They're waiting for you there, *Senhor*."

Morag knew that from Curitiba he would continue on with still another driver, and that this man had no idea of his ultimate destination.

"You're right, but there's been a slight change in our plans and I've got to give an important letter to someone there before leaving the city. Understand?"

Morag used his sternest decisive tone of voice, and the young man agreed, defeated. The car lurched forward. Schmidt gave a last look at his hideout, that he was now leaving forever. His driver was already speeding down Augusta Street, up to Franka. There, after a sharp left, he stopped near the house of Jairo Silverman. It was close to 6 in the morning. Morag jumped out of the car and went swiftly to the entrance of the building. He woke the *zelador*, who'd been napping.

"Good morning, *Senhor*," he whispered in the *zelador's* ears. "Please tell Jairo Silverman that *Senhor* Hermann Schmidt wants to see him urgently."

The *zelador* spoke into the intercom. The answer came swiftly. "You can go up."

Morag hurried to the elevator and ascended to Jairo's apartment. The door was already open for him. But when Jairo saw the man standing in front of him he quickly slammed it shut.

"Who are you?" he called from behind the closed door.

Morag burst out laughing. Jairo was right. Before leaving he'd removed the grey-haired wig that had concealed his bald pate. And he was now dressed in the clothing of a simple laborer.

"Jairo," he called, "It's all right! It's me! I've just taken off the wig that I wore to cover my lovely scalp. It's all right. Don't worry."

Jairo hesitantly opened the door. The fears that had beset him until now had clearly not disappeared. He stared at Morag for a long minute. Then a smile chased away the doubts that had attacked him.

"May I come in?" Morag asked him.

Jairo didn't answer. But he opened the door wide.

"*Senhor* Jairo, I have completed the dream of my life. The documents of the Spider are in my possession." He lifted his hand, which still clutched the file. "I thank you for your help. I'm now on my way out of the country. *Shalom.*"

The two shook hands without a word.

"But before I leave, I want to include you in an incredible adventure that happened to me this morning."

Morag handed Jairo the letter without explanation.

"Read it and do as you see fit. It's my farewell gift to you."

Jairo opened the letter and began to read. Morag could hear his breath rising and falling, faster and faster, as he took in the words. Jairo finished, carefully folded the page, and gently placed it back into the envelope. Finally, he asked, "And this letter was also in the safe?"

"Yes."

"Together with the Spider documents?"

"Yes."

"What do you think of it?"

"I don't know."

"And yet?"

Morag's eyes shifted uncomfortably. He said quickly, "*Shalom,* and I wish you all the best." Then he disappeared into the elevator.

Jairo held the letter in his hand for a long moment. He had so looked forward to a little peace, after the eventful week he'd gone through. And now here was a new and heavy burden on his shoulders ...

48

Jairo slowly shut the door of the apartment. He listened for the elevator as it descended to the ground floor. Then he hurried to the large living room window and stared outside. He could see Hermann Schmidt — Reuven Morag — hurry into the Transit that awaited him. He disappeared into the vehicle and left Jairo's life, forever.

Forever? Perhaps not.

Jairo cast a fearful glance at the envelope that he held in his frozen hand. This was the legacy that Morag had left him, and it would bind him, for who knew how long, to the dizzying chapter that he'd somehow gotten involved in, quite against his will. The nightmare, it seemed, was not quite over for him. He would remember this Jewish agent, who'd so disrupted his life, for a long, long time.

Jairo lifted his head. His glance fell on the lovely crystal chandelier that hung from the middle of the living room ceiling. *Disrupted my life? Truly? Was that what the grey-haired man had done? Or perhaps — the opposite? Perhaps he's opened new understandings in my heart? Am I not a new person today, different from who I was only one week ago?*

Jairo knew that he would never be able to escape from the knowledge of his Jewishness, knowledge awakened inside him by his perceived pursuit by Nazis.

He glanced at his watch. It was almost 7. His father would certainly be awake. He dialed.

"Hello, Pa?"

"Yes?"

"Good morning. How are you?"

"Nothing new here. But it doesn't look good in Israel."

"Did they say something on the news?"

"Yes. The U.N. has begun evacuating its forces. The Russians are sending arms to Egypt and Syria. The reporters say that the Israeli government is out of ideas. *Ess is nisht gut.* And what did you want from me, so early in the morning?"

"I want to read you a fascinating, and frightening, letter."

There was silence on the line. Then Jairo heard a muttered, *"Nu?"*

Jairo read Morag's parting gift to him.

"What do you say to it?" he asked his father carefully after he'd finished.

His father was in no hurry to respond. Finally, his words came out, a flowing waterfall.

"Jairo, maybe you should see Doctor Minsis? He'll recommend a good psychologist. I thought you'd calmed down from all your fantasies and dreams of the past week. Fantasies of Nazis running after you, of Nazi funerals for Alberto Hunkes, some Nazi named Heinz Krantz, other crazy stories. And now it seems it's still not over! It's still going on! Jairo, you need help! Now! It's nothing to be ashamed of, Jairo. It can be done in a way that no one will know of it. Not even Paulina."

Jairo could feel the blood pounding through his temples in a virtual flood.

"But Pa, it's true! All of it! The letter is true!"

"*Shoin*. I'll have to do something, I see, to make you stop this nonsense. Ha, the letter is true he says to me! Nonsense, do you hear me! Nonsense, nonsense! You're completely crazy! What's happened to you?"

And the phone went dead.

Avia Hotel
9 Iyar 5727

Eduardo got up from the bed. His weary hand moved towards the phone. He dialed the number that Ronny Lipschitz, the young officer, had given him.

"*Shalom*, may I speak with Ronny Lipschitz?" he said in halting English.

"Okay," came the reply on the other end of the line.

A long moment of silence, then, "Yes?"

Eduardo spoke in Portuguese. "Hello, is that Ronny? Ronny Lipschitz?"

"*Si*," came the answer.

"Ronny, this is Eduardo."

"Oh, Eduardo, how are you?"

"Not too good."

"What happened? Is it because of the soldier who fainted? Yitzchak Austerlitz, the one you interviewed?"

"Not exactly. But how is he?"

"I don't know. Like you, I saw them take him to the hospital. But what's happened to you?"

"I'm going back to Sao Paulo."

Silence.

"I have no choice, Ronny. I wanted to stay. I think important and exciting things will be happening here in your country soon. But I received bad news from home."

"What happened?"

"My mother died."

"Oh, I'm so sorry."

"I'm sorry too, Ronny. Maybe I'll come back here someday. In any case, it was a pleasure meeting you."

"Likewise."

"*Chau.*"

"*Chau*. And may we meet again."

> *Sao Paulo, Brazil*
> *May 20, 1967*

Eduardo landed in Sao Paulo the next day. From Lod he'd traveled on an El Al flight to Rome. After a few hours in Piaumiciano Airport he'd continued on an Alitalia plane to Viracopus Airport, a two-hour car ride from Sao Paulo. A taxi brought him to the city. At the outskirts he'd felt a rising tension almost suffocating him. He had no idea of what he was returning home to ...

"Hello, driver, kindly proceed to the *Estado de Sao Paulo* newsroom."

The driver turned to face Eduardo.

"Didn't you say you wanted Piaui Street?"

"Yes, I did want to go there. And now I don't want to. Take me to the *Estado*."

"It's all right. You're the boss."

True, his first thought had been to travel to his parents' home. But he couldn't find the courage to face the tragedy all at once. To stare grimly at the black reality that from this day forward he was all alone in the world. He wanted first to hear from his friends in the newsroom what had happened to his mother. They would give him an accurate description of what had occurred.

Eduardo reached the office at 9 in the morning. The first man he looked for was Soares, but he wasn't there. For a few minutes Eduardo wandered aimlessly down the corridors of the newsroom, seeking someone who could give him information about his mother's death.

Finally, he landed in the secretary's office.

"I'm sorry for disturbing you."

The secretary lifted her eyes and said in obvious surprise, "Eduardo! Is it you? When did you get back?"

"Just now. I came here straight from the airport."

"Oh … I understand."

Eduardo looked at her. "Could you … could you," he said, hesitating "could you tell me what exactly happened?"

"No one knows, Eduardo. Even the police. What's known for certain is that she returned to her home at about 1:30 in the morning. The *zelador* is ready to swear that the person who brought her back is the same man who abducted her two days earlier."

"And what happened then?"

"At 4 in the morning she called to the night watchman. When he picked up the phone he heard her say, in a terrified voice, 'This is Regina Hunkes! Help me!' "

"And what happened?"

"The watchman heard one shot immediately afterwards."

The secretary lifted her arms in a gesture of despair. "And … that was it."

After a moment's silence, Eduardo asked, "But why was I told that the police suspect suicide?"

"Because there was no one with her. The door was locked from the inside; they had to break it open. No one had entered or left the building at that time. I'm sorry, Eduardo."

Eduardo kept his eyes carefully down, staring at the desk.

"Has she been buried yet?"

"Yes. This morning. No one knew if you were coming back or not."

"Where?"

"Next to your father, Eduardo."

For a long moment Eduardo stood still. Finally, without saying goodbye, he turned and strode out of the room. As he was about to leave, the secretary's voice held him back.

"Eduardo."

He stopped, but didn't turn around to face her.

"This is for you. A letter from your mother."

Eduardo's face showed his surprise. He returned to the desk and took a letter from the secretary's outstretched hand. Eduardo opened the envelope slowly, and read the contents with a frozen face. He waited for a minute, scanning the lines one more time. The secretary watched Eduardo curiously. Before her astonished gaze, he tore the letter into tiny pieces with a cold, slow motion, discarding them in the glass ashtray on the desk.

And without a word, he left the room ...

Sao Paulo, Brazil
May 21, 1967

Jairo reached his office in the center of the city after an absence of several days. Today, Sunday, was not a workday, and yet he wanted to spend a bit of time there. He felt it necessary after the wild week he'd just lived through. He wanted to breathe in the air of the office, just sit there, the nightmare behind him, not feeling persecuted or followed. Just to be himself, Jairo Silverman, young, successful, self-confident attorney.

He took the elevator to the 33rd floor. With a firm grip and a deep sense of contentment he opened the office door, engraved with the proud words "Silverman, Machado, and Chilo, Attorneys-At-Law." He looked at the words for a minute, felt them give him new confidence and strength. "Silverman, Machado, and Chilo." Chilo? Paulo Chilo? Where was he? Hadn't Paulo planned on signing a contract with GAC behind his back? When had it happened? It seemed to Jairo that all that had taken place years ago. But — no. It had been only three, four days, since the affair had begun. But where was Chilo? Was he still a partner in the firm? Or had it all come apart? For some reason Jairo suddenly thought of the situation in the Middle East, the tension between Arabs and Jews. And what about Francisco Machado, his good friend? Had he, too, fled the office, after the past few days of madness? Jairo had no idea.

Jairo entered the office. He walked carefully, his footsteps muffled in the soft pile of the carpets. One could actually hear the deep silence. No one was there, it seemed, in any of the offices. Jairo entered his private office, sat down in the recliner, the same recliner in which he'd received news of Alberto Hunkes's death a week and a half earlier: news that had changed his life. After a few relaxing minutes, Jairo pulled the telephone receiver towards him and dialed.

"Francisco, it's Jairo. What's new?"

"Oh, it's you! Where are you?"

Jairo could clearly hear the coldness in the voice, though it tried hard to sound friendly.

"I'm in the office. It's been a while since I've worked. I decided to come in today and see what's going on. And what about you? Is everything all right?"

"Yes, Jairo. But are you okay?"

"Gracas a De-us. Now, everything is fine. I won't hide it from you: I've had a tough week. But that's it! It's over, I hope. I'm coming back to work."

"Excellent."

Jairo wasn't satisfied. Something felt wrong here. After a moment he said, "And you? Are you coming back to the office?"

Francisco sounded encouraging. "Of course, of course I'm coming back! Why not? But Jairo, we'll first have to sit down and talk. We can't just ignore what happened. Do you agree?"

"Yes," Jairo murmured, though he didn't.

"And what about Paulo?"

Francisco hesitated. "I don't know, Jairo. He said he's leaving. He wanted to sign with GAC on a personal basis. I don't think he succeeded. No one wanted to look at him there. I don't know what he's doing now. We'll have to talk about that too. Okay?"

The receiver was gently placed back on the hook. Jairo shook off the worrying thoughts that beset him during the conversation. He had to return to normal life as soon as possible. The troubles with Francisco — if there were any — would be overcome during their upcoming conversation. Jairo walked over to the cabinet to try and put some order in the files whose existence he'd more or less forgotten. He felt like a man who'd sustained brain damage, who had to learn everything anew. He had to study, read, try to remember all the cases that needed to be dealt with.

Suddenly the doorbell rang. Surprised, Jairo looked up from the file he was perusing. Must be a mistake, he thought. Who would know that he was in the office today? He listened again to see if there would be another ring. Yes, there it was: a longer, more determined sound than the first.

Jairo waited for a fraction of a second. Finally, he went to open the door. His shock was complete: Eduardo, Eduardo Hunkes stood before him.

The two men, separated by a deep chasm, stood across from each other. Jairo's eyes looked askance at Eduardo. He had known that this moment was inevitable, that he must one day confront Eduardo. But the suddenness of their meeting paralyzed him. The words froze on his lips.

Jairo had no idea how much time passed as they stood, rooted to the spot, in his office doorway. Finally, he roused himself, knowing that he must set the tone.

"Come in, please," he said in a dry, cool tone, in a voice which held no trace of the friendship that had existed between the two just a week and a half before — that is, before the death of Alberto Hunkes.

Eduardo quietly entered the office. He recognized it well, had visited it several times, just to chat with Jairo. In the past, they had shared a common bond. Now, he didn't know what to say. He couldn't even explain to himself why he'd decided to come here.

Jairo sat down in his place. Eduardo grabbed a chair opposite him. The silence was too heavy for either to bear.

"Yes?" Jairo shot the first groping word out.

"My mother is dead. Did you know that?"

Jairo nodded.

"I was in Israel when it happened. Did you know that too?"

The last sentence aroused Jairo's curiosity. What was Eduardo doing in Israel?

"No. I didn't know."

"I was sent by the *Estado*. You know, as a military correspondent. They're talking war over there. That you certainly know."

Jairo felt the sarcasm of the last words: You certainly know, because it concerns you Jews.

"How did you get back?"

"They called me."

Another silence. Neither could find the words to continue the conversation.

"I got back to Sao Paulo yesterday."

Jairo didn't answer and his eyes didn't meet Eduardo's.

"I got here after the funeral. That hurt."

Jairo pulled a Minister cigarette out from his jacket pocket. He offered the pack to Eduardo, who took one. Jairo lit it up for him with his lighter. At that moment the two men's faces came close together; their eyes met in a quick, confused glance.

"But it doesn't hurt any more."

Eduardo said the last words as he blew cigarette smoke through the office. Somehow, the action gave both of them the chance to hide their confusion.

"It doesn't hurt me that she died. Do you understand?"

No. Jairo didn't understand. He realized that the man was trying to tell him something, but he didn't know how to encourage him to speak. Jairo remained silent, trying by examining Eduardo's face to figure out what Eduardo wanted of him.

Eduardo's eyes were wounded and determined.

Eduardo continued to speak in short bursts.

"She left me a letter."

"Who?"

"My mother!"

"Oh … "

Another silence, a heavier one. It seemed to Jairo that he could hear Eduardo's heart beating, as the young man's emotions began to overpower him.

"She wrote to me …"

Eduardo took a long drag on the cigarette. Then he jumped up and began to pace the office floor. Finally, he took his seat once again.

"She wrote to me … a farewell letter. An accursed letter."

Jairo held himself back and didn't ask for more. He had to let Eduardo speak at his own pace. In his heart, Jairo had begun to suspect what the letter contained.

"She wrote to me that she was about to commit suicide. That I was responsible, because I had left her alone during her hardest hours. She said … she was cursing me in the last minutes before death."

Jairo stubbed out his cigarette in the stone ashtray that lay in one corner of his desk. He could feel his fingertips burn from the heat.

"But the main thing was her last line: 'Go, go to your Jairo Silverman.' "

Jairo felt the moment of truth had at last arrived. But he didn't have the courage.

Eduardo continued, "I listened to her. I came. Simply to ask you: What does it all mean?"

Jairo didn't answer. He opened the top drawer of his desk, searched through it quickly, and pulled out an envelope. He handed it to Eduardo.

"Perhaps this letter will explain a lot of things."

49

Eduardo stared suspiciously at Jairo's outstretched hand. For some reason he felt himself flinching, holding back. Some internal force warned him not to take the letter. Jairo's hand remained suspended in the air for some seconds. Finally, Eduardo surrendered; he slowly took the proferred letter. He immediately recognized his father's handwriting on the envelope. He stared, with growing wonderment, at the words "For Eduardo Hunkes." When had his father written this letter? Why hadn't he, Eduardo, received it prior to his mother's death? He lifted his head and stared at Jairo. His eyes asked the question: How did you get hold of this letter? Jairo saw the gaze but maintained his frigid stance, not giving away anything that was going on inside of him. He never took his eyes off Eduardo.

Eduardo opened the envelope and pulled out two pages covered with writing. He began to read.

To "my son," Eduardo:

He picked his head up from the letter in complete astonishment, assaulted by a wave of confusion. Those quotation marks on the words "my son" boded ill. He had no idea of what to expect. For a moment he felt the strong urge to fold the pages, thrust them back into their envelope and delay reading them until he was alone. But he simply couldn't. Jairo's eyes boring into him willed him to continue. Now.

Eduardo continued to read.

> *This letter is addressed to you. You are 15 years old today. But it's not to be given to you immediately; it will reach you only after I am dead. This, so you will not be able to use it against me. I know that the things I will tell you are not going to be pleasant for you, and will probably wound you terribly. For this reason, I am writing them. For even now I derive enormous satisfaction in the face of your suffering.*
>
> *And so, Eduardo, I have the pleasure of telling you that you are not my son at all. You are a Jew. A Jew I decided to protect, and not bring to the destiny that I, with my own hands, brought upon your mother, sister and brother. This was the destiny that we, the Nazis, prepared for your entire accursed race. Don't make a mistake. I didn't protect you from any feeling of mercy that may have been aroused in my heart upon seeing a poor, helpless Jewish infant. No! At the moment that you fell into my hands I decided to let you live in order to destroy your life. The dead don't suffer. And I, in my hatred of your people, decided to*

cause true torture even to living Jews. Your father, too, I didn't kill then. I left him alive,
lingering in the pain of his family's death. I don't
know if he survived the war or not. If he's alive or
dead. But on that day I "had mercy" on him. At
the moment that I shot your mother and family, I
had an original, a unique idea. I decided not to
take your wretched Jewish life; rather, to grant life
to you. A life that would, at a certain specific moment, turn into one of unbearable torture and
agony. I took you with me to Germany. I gave you
to my wife to raise. And during all your childhood
years we ingrained in you, in every possible way,
a hatred of Jews. We drilled into you our truth,
our belief that the Jewish race has no right to live
on this earth, that its destiny is destruction. After
the war, when the Third Reich fell as a result of
the treachery of international Jewry, I was forced
to conceal my German descent and my loyal service to the S.S. on behalf of my Fatherland and my
Fuehrer. I managed to hide it from you too. And
yet I worked ceaselessly to instill within you hatred of the Jewish people. Do you remember,
Eduardo? I think that I succeeded somewhat in
planting within your heart hatred for your own
race. Many times I received great pleasure from
you, as I saw your animosity towards Jews living
in Sao Paulo. What a wonderful game! A Jew,
bearing Nazi hatred towards the Jewish people!

But that wasn't my ultimate goal. It wasn't
enough that you would hate the Jews as much as
my education would make you hate them. I decided that after my death I would tell you the
entire truth of your miserable beginnings. Now,

faced with this unbearable reality, you wouldn't know who you were. You would perhaps feel a deep self-loathing, knowing that your destiny made you part of an accursed people. You will, perhaps, hate me too, for having caused this to you. This load of hatred will destroy you, and you will spend the rest of your days alone, without roots. You will never know who you are. I have stolen your identity from you. And you will not be able to bear the knowledge that you truly belong to those whom you've been brought up to despise. This is my small vengeance against the Jewish nation, which brought about the fall of the Third Reich. And now, go your own way. I would relish seeing you cope with the terrible burden I've just given you, Eduardo. No, No. Not Eduardo. That's too nice a name for a Jew such as you. Your real name, that I managed to squeeze out of your father, is Yaakov. Yaakov Austerlitz, if you truly want to know where you belong.

And with this, I hope you won't be completely furious with me. After all, I did save your life. You don't have to leave a bouquet of flowers on my grave. Neither should you leave a thornbush.

With the blessings of "Heil Hitler"
From Obersturmbannfuehrer
Heinz Krantz
whom you knew as Alberto Hunkes

Eduardo was silent. In his fevered brain he saw wild, frenzied pictures in deep, dark colors, heard confused sounds coming from a turbulent whirlpool. He was in the eye of a hurricane, being lashed from all sides, pushed here and there, his breath coming faster and faster. His head lolled as if he were asleep. Jairo could see Eduardo's hands trembling as they still held onto the pages of the demon's letter.

Jairo quietly took the receiver off the hook. He didn't want a chance call to break the deep silence that lay between the two like a heavy boulder. Jairo understood. This was an awesome moment. The moment of truth. The moment from which there was no escape. He knew that it was his obligation at this time to stand by Eduardo, who'd been hurled with such cruel suddenness into the lion's den.

Jairo stood up. He hesitantly approached Eduardo, who was sitting on the other side of the spacious desk. For a long moment he stood next to him without moving, looking down at the ruin sitting in the armchair. Carefully, with slow and gentle movements, he lay his arm on Eduardo's shoulder. Eduardo didn't react. Jairo didn't say a word, just stood there, his arm upon his shoulder. It seemed to Jairo that the shoulder was trembling ever so slightly.

"You want a drink?"

No answer.

Despite this, Jairo walked over to the small refrigerator in the corner and pulled out bottles of *guarana*, *agua tonica*, and Coca-Cola. He put them on the desk and set a clean glass out next to them.

"What do you want? Cola? *Guarana?*"

Eduardo picked up his hand in a gesture of refusal. Jairo was glad to see it. It told him that Eduardo wasn't totally cut off from reality.

"You've got to take something to help you recover."

No use. Jairo regretted having spoken of recovery: The time was not yet ripe.

Suddenly Eduardo put his face in his hands. His entire body was wracked by sobs. Jairo stood by, helpless. He stole a glance at his watch. Ten o'clock. His wife, in the house, was undoubtedly beginning to worry. He'd promised to return home early so that they could leave together to Santos before traffic became heavy. But what could he do? He couldn't leave Eduardo.

Jairo walked into the next room and dialed his home number.

"Paulina, I'm stuck here. No choice."

Her voice was concerned. "What's happened now?"

"Nothing special."

"So why don't you finish up and come home? Who's there with you?"

Silence. Paulina repeated the question. "Tell me, who's there?"

"Someone. It's not important."

"Tell me!"

Her voice was demanding. After all that she'd gone through this past week, Jairo didn't want to fray her nerves further.

"Eduardo. Eduardo Hunkes."

"What? Are you still involved in that? Leave him already! You promised me!"

"No. It's actually the end of the story. A fascinating and surprising end, hard to believe. Don't worry. I'll tell you everything on the way to Santos."

He quickly hung up and returned to his office. He saw that the bottle of *guarana* was empty. Jairo felt encouraged. Eduardo had used his absence to take a drink. Good.

Jairo gave him a smile. "How do you feel?"

A chilly, mocking smile answered him. "I feel wonderful! Couldn't be better! What do you think?"

Jairo swallowed his anger and took the taunt in stride. His brain searched feverishly for the right words, the words that would help him penetrate the shell that surrounded Eduardo's heart. Eduardo needed help. And he, Jairo, had to give it to him. That was destiny's decree. And perhaps, the fleeting thought raced through his brain, perhaps it wasn't destiny at all, but something greater, something truer. Jairo remembered the conversation he'd had last week with Meir in the synagogue on Haddock Lobo Street.

"I read the letter," Jairo said, sending it out as a trial balloon.

Eduardo wasn't surprised. Nothing could surprise him, not since the blow that had hit him squarely between the eyes. Not even the insolence of Jairo, who apparently read private mail. And yet, he answered, "What do you mean, 'I read the letter'?"

"They brought it to me here, so that I should read it."

"Who brought it? From where?"

"The one who brought it doesn't matter. From where? From your ... Have you been to the house on Piaui Street yet?"

Eduardo shifted in his chair. "No. Why?"

Jairo lit another cigarette. The look he cast upon Eduardo was sharp and clear.

"It was taken from the safe in your parents' bedroom. They broke into it a few hours before your mother's apparent suicide."

Eduardo was silent. He remembered that safe. He remembered how Regina had wanted to take something from it to show him; how she'd held back at the last moment. Had she planned on giving him this letter? Who knew?

"Who broke into it? And why?" Eduardo asked weakly.

"I don't know who. I found the letter in my mailbox, together with a note. The note hinted that documents found in the safe indicated that Alberto Hunkes was not as innocent as he liked to pretend to be. That the man whose name was Heinz Krantz, the man who, until half an hour ago, you called Father, was one of the central figures in the Spider. And that ..."

"Spider? What?"

"You never heard of the Spider organization?"

"No."

Jairo moved in his chair. He felt more relaxed, more capable of speaking openly.

" 'Spider' was an underground organization that was behind the flight of large numbers of Nazis, war criminals, who hid in countries around the world, among them Brazil. No doubt you'll find a lot of material about it in the *Estado* files."

After a moment, Jairo added, "This letter was together with the other documents. That's what the unknown man who left it wrote to me."

Eduardo looked at Jairo with weak eyes. He didn't believe that Jairo was unaware of the identity of the thieves. He didn't ask why the mysterious stranger had left it for Jairo, of all people. He wouldn't press the point. He remembered his mother's (his mother's!) declaration that the Jews had killed her husband. Then, he didn't understand her belief. Now — he understood all too well. Oh, how he understood!

Jairo poured another drink for Eduardo. Wordlessly, he drank it up. Jairo asked him, "Will you be able to bear the burden?"

Eduardo tightened his lips until they seemed like a scar across his face. His balled fist made contact with his right hand, pounding until it hurt. He moved his head back and forth and his face showed a deep wound, that gave off a soundless scream: It can't be! It can't be!

After a long moment in deep thought, he said, "I don't know."

Eduardo stood up and moved restlessly through the office. Occasionally he stood near the window that looked down upon the Viaduto do Cha. Then he would begin to pace again. Jairo didn't interfere. He sat quietly in his recliner, almost invisible. He didn't know, he simply didn't know what help he could offer in this terrifying affair. It needed greater powers than he possessed, perhaps greater than any man possessed. That cursed Nazi, who even from his grave could torture living Jews ...

Eduardo stood close by Jairo's chair. He leaned his palms on the desk; his body swayed near Jairo.

"You don't know the most incredible part of it, Jairo. And it — it's left me paralyzed."

Jairo didn't answer. The stage was Eduardo's. Eduardo straightened up, without explaining his cryptic words, and began to walk through the office again like a restless shade. His balled fist continued to smack at his hand. Occasionally he would say aloud, from the depths of a tortured soul, "It can't be! It can't be!"

And again he would return to Jairo's desk, staring deeply into his eyes. He spoke in a whisper, in a voice that could barely be heard.

"I came back from Israel yesterday. You didn't know that I'd gone there, right? My newspaper sent me as a military correspondent, to cover the battles — if they'd break out. At the airport I noticed a strange, a funny-looking soldier. An Orthodox Jew, with a beard and a skullcap. Not a Jew like you and like — "

Eduardo suddenly stopped. He stared at the palms of his hand with a look full of fear. "I ... a Jew? A Jew?"

He turned his hands over from side to side. Suddenly, he couldn't bear it any longer. He burst out crying, unashamed. He collapsed in an armchair and sobbed for a long while. Jairo again looked at his watch. It was noon. There'd be little time for a trip to Santos this week. How would he pacify Paulina?

A full 15 minutes passed before Eduardo calmed down somewhat. Slowly, slowly he became himself again. He pulled out a handkerchief from his pocket and wiped his eyes. He even tried to give Jairo a smile, with little success.

"You understand," Eduardo continued the conversation that his tears had interrupted, "I interviewed this soldier. I thought he'd be interesting to my readers. He told me about his life during the Second World War. Of his wife and children who'd been killed by a Nazi named Heinz Krantz."

Jairo's eyes lit up. "What an incredible coincidence!"

"Yes, but listen. During the interview he was called to the phone. Someone told him that Heinz Krantz had been murdered in Sao Paulo."

"Amazing."

Jairo realized that it was he who had actually passed on the information, via his father and his father's friend in the Hebraica. And Eduardo, of all people, had met this Jew. Absolutely unbelievable!

"Go on."

"The Jew was very affected by the news, and he fainted. He was taken to the hospital from the airport."

"Listen, Eduardo, that's a remarkable story. You could write a fascinating book about it, don't you think so?"

Eduardo felt a weakness overtake him. He looked at Jairo, at his enthusiasm, at his feeling that he was watching a new and exciting drama. He seemed to have forgotten one thing: This was his, Eduardo's, life they were talking about.

"Jairo, you don't know the entire story. It's frightening."

"What do you mean?"

Eduardo's voice was weak and broken. "The Jew's name was ... Austerlitz. Yitzchak Austerlitz."

Jairo leaped out of his chair. He stood open mouthed.

"That means ... that means ..." he tried to say the words but couldn't formulate them, couldn't put together a sentence. He collapsed back into his recliner, trying to take it all in.

"That means ... that you, Eduardo ... whatever your name is ... you met ... you happened to meet ... by coincidence ... absolute coincidence ... your ... your father? Your real father?"

Eduardo wearily nodded his head.

"So it seems."

Jairo wrung his hands in growing excitement. "Do you ... do you understand ... what happened to you?"

Eduardo closed his eyes. "No!"

50

Jairo jumped up from his seat and moved swiftly around the desk. With hurried steps he approached Eduardo, who was slouched in his chair, his head hanging low. Jairo's hands gripped Eduardo tightly and shook him wildly.

"Don't you understand what's happening here?" Jairo shouted the words, as if Eduardo were deaf.

"No!" Eduardo screamed, in a sudden burst of fury.

Jairo's grip eased. His fingers, that had held Eduardo's shoulders in a vise of steel, became soft and gentle. Slowly, slowly he left Eduardo and returned to his seat near the window. The two young men stared wearily at each other. They were exhausted from their emotions; they had run out of ideas. The heavy silence was finally broken by Jairo's quiet voice.

"You have no idea how much your life and mine are intertwined."

Eduardo stirred. Jairo's words disturbed him.

"What are you talking about?"

"Okay, maybe I exaggerated a little. Maybe not intertwined. But your destiny has certainly affected mine."

Eduardo felt a surge of impatience, almost of anger.

"Are you ready to explain?"

Jairo took a deep breath, put his legs up on the desk and crossed them. Somehow, it eased the tension of this difficult conversation.

"It all began at the funeral of your father. That is, excuse me, at the funeral of Alberto Hunkes."

Eduardo's eyes showed increasing curiosity.

"I mean," Jairo continued, "at the Nazi ceremony at the graveside. You know … the ceremony, with the Nazi salute and the cries of 'Heil Hitler.' "

Silence.

Jairo probed a bit. "Did you know he was a Nazi?"

"No."

"So how did you explain that terrible ceremony?"

"I asked my mother … that is, Regina, for an explanation. She told me that her husband hadn't been a Nazi, but that, during the war, in Denmark, he'd collaborated with them. Collaborated out of fear. Now, at his death, the Nazis living in Sao Paulo had decided to show their 'thanks.' This was the way they chose to do it."

"And you … accepted the explanation?"

"Yes I did. Why not?"

"Did you see how she insulted me at the graveyard? Me, who'd been such a good friend to Alberto and the entire family?"

"Yes."

"And what did you think of that?"

"You want the truth? I didn't think about it at all. They didn't love Jews; they hated them. I never quite understood their friendship with you. Now, with all that I know today, I understand it. They needed a good cover story. Friendship with a Jew would help them by keeping suspicion off them."

Eduardo lapsed into a thoughtful silence. Suddenly, he asked, "But what do you have to do with the affair? What interconnecting destiny are you talking about?"

This was it! Jairo knew. The difficult moment had arrived. Now he had to speak, explain, tie up the loose ends. He hesitated for a few minutes, looking desperately for the right words. Finally, he began to tell the story. The whole story. Of the grey-haired man, who was Hermann Schmidt, who was Reuven Morag. Morag was undoubtedly far away and couldn't be harmed by Jairo's revelations. During the next long hour Jairo told Eduardo all that had happened during the past week, from the moment he'd found out that Hunkes had been murdered. He told him of his shock at the cemetery. Of the awakening of Jewish feelings within him during that frightful time. Of the anonymous phone calls. Of his feelings of persecution. Of his nightmares. Of his incredible uncovering of the truth. Of the fraud and deceit of the man called Alberto Hunkes. Jairo told him also of his strange conversation with the Orthodox Jew named Meir in a synagogue on Haddock Lobo Street — a conversation that had left him in shock, a conversation that he couldn't forget or escape. And if that wasn't enough to shake up his world and change his reality forever — here was the grey-haired man coming and leaving him this letter that Alberto Hunkes had written to his "son."

Eduardo sat, open mouthed, listening intently to the strange tale. He didn't react, neither during Jairo's narrative nor after he'd finished.

"And now," Jairo shot out a final sentence, "you come with this story of your meeting in an airport in Tel Aviv. And I — I'm just drained emotionally."

"Why?"

Jairo didn't seem to hear the question. He followed the thread of his thoughts.

"Meir, the religious one, was right!"

"I don't understand."

"It's simple. Too many things have happened to me, all of them leading to the same place. I can't dismiss them all as coincidences. That's all. Do you understand?"

"No!"

Jairo's eyes looked wonderingly at Eduardo.

"What's so hard to understand? Eduardo! I can't figure you out! You are like me, Jairo Silverman, a happy Brazilian guy, without a care in the world, slowly building myself up a career in law. I see myself, first and foremost, as a Brazilian. I find the fact that I'm Jewish meaningless. Suddenly, one morning, I'm taken into a crazy new world that I don't recognize. One strange thing follows another, and together they draw up a picture of an entirely new world. And when I'm trapped helplessly in this new reality I bump into a Jew, Meir, who shows me that it is all written in the Bible. It's written, that this will happen. That it will always happen. In millions upon millions of variations, in all places and in all times where the Jew lives, when he says *chau* to his Jewish identity. You agree that it's madness to argue that no one had really run after me, that it was only my imagination that lent danger to the telephone calls and warnings not to go after Hunkes's identity, that it was only a mistake which aroused my Jewish consciousness? Finally, to see in the Bible itself, that this will always happen to Jews in the diaspora?"

Jairo picked up a Portuguese Bible that lay on his desk. A bookmark lay in the verse that he wished to emphasize. He read it aloud, emphasizing each word: "You shall flee, and none shall pursue you." He closed the volume and whispered, "And that — happened to me! To me, Jairo Silverman!"

Eduardo stirred uncomfortably in his chair.

"I'm sorry. I see your excitement, your emotions. But with all the desire to understand, I don't see what you're looking for. And what do you want from me?"

The last words burst forth from Eduardo in a voice of despair, a voice of one doomed to death.

Jairo suddenly pulled his legs off his desk. He jumped out of his chair like a lion pouncing on his prey and raced towards Eduardo. He bent down on his knees, so that his shining face was just opposite Eduardo. Eduardo could feel his breath. He averted his eyes: He couldn't face the sparks shooting from Jairo's eyes.

Jairo spoke with uncontrolled fervor. "Understand! I want nothing from you, Eduardo. I just want you to understand what you've caused me today! My feeling, from the time I had the conversation with the Jew in the synagogue, has been that coincidences show some kind of Heavenly Providence. It shows G-d, Eduardo! A G-d who is directly concerned with us! Nothing merely happens in this world, Eduardo! What happened to me was a signal from Heaven! Do you understand, Eduardo?"

Eduardo didn't say a word. He tried to move his head and distance himself a bit from Jairo, but he was unsuccessful. Jairo was still in his trance.

"And if I had any doubts, if I still felt misgivings — you have given me the final blow."

Eduardo managed to break into the flow of Jairo's words.

"What did I do to you?"

"That's it exactly, Eduardo. You didn't do anything! 'Someone' did it through you. 'Someone' brought you. You tried to figure out the situation in the State of Israel because your editor gave you the job. There, by a coincidence, you met a Jew — the first you saw who perhaps fit all your anti-Semitic stereotypes. Black beard, skullcap, maybe bent over with a hooked nose. I don't know. You decided to interview him, thinking it would be a good story for your readers. And now you come back home and learn — in a truly remarkable 'coincidence' — that the man is your father! You have to be a complete idiot not to see this as the hand of some Divine Providence. And I, after the insane week that I've just gone through, am no longer an idiot! Do you understand? What happened to you finally convinced me how to perceive all that's happened!"

Jairo straightened up. It seemed to Eduardo that he had calmed down somewhat. Eduardo himself felt strangely removed, as if he were watching an exciting action film that had nothing to do with him. He saw how Jairo began to walk wordlessly back and forth, like a sleepwalker. How much longer would this nightmare continue?

Jairo returned to the desk, picked up the Bible, and began to leaf through it. He smiled apologetically. "Since the day before yesterday, I've been skimming this. Believe me, I never thought I would do such a thing. But … that's it! And just by randomly reading through it I found the verses that set my heart racing. I keep imagining that Jews throughout the generations felt this way, when they read this book. I don't know why, but this particular verse … Where is it? … Oh, here: 'If your banished ones be at the end of the heavens, G-d will gather you from there, and take you from there.' "

Jairo lifted his eyes from the book and again approached Eduardo, who was still sitting in the same place, in the same position.

"I don't know what the verse actually means. I know what I felt when I first read it. Suddenly, like a crack of lightning in the middle of a dense fog, I understood that it was talking about me. I don't know why, but something within me explained the verse: If you are far, far away from the Jewish nation, actually at the end of the world from the point of view of Jewish identity, G-d will take you from there and bring you back to Him. How? Simple! This past week was a Heavenly exercise, to shake me up!"

Jairo suddenly burst out laughing. "If my father knew what I was doing now, he would kill me."

He grew serious and whispered to Eduardo, "And you, Eduardo, had the first part of your Heavenly exercise in Lod, and the second part here in my office, when you read that cursed letter. The two pieces came together for you — and for me, the puzzle is complete! What did I say, that cursed letter? Blessed is more like it!"

Jairo sent a searching glance towards Eduardo. "You have no choice, Eduardo."

Eduardo felt the pressure. He suddenly understood where Jairo was trying to take him. No. He wouldn't allow it. Let Jairo play these coincidence games as much as he wanted. But he, Eduardo? Never!

"Leave me alone, Jairo. Let me try to come to grips with this heavy boulder that you've placed on my shoulders. I suspect that I'll be carrying it, bent underneath it, all my life. Leave me!"

Jairo felt a surge of anger. He pulled the letter out from Eduardo's hands.

"So you've decided to fulfill the last wish of that Nazi, the one who destroyed you and murdered your family? You've decided to show him that he's managed to implement his devilish plan? To turn you eternally into a pathetic, miserable unfortunate? Has he defeated you even from the grave? Coward! What are you afraid of? Why not get vengeance on him, defeat his demonic schemes? You're still young, Eduardo! Don't destroy your life! Live it as you should!"

Eduardo was surprised. In his heart, he knew Jairo was right. But he wasn't the kind of man to admit it publicly. In a voice that was quiet but sure he hissed between clenched teeth, "Give me back that letter! Now!"

Jairo, his fury abated, hesitated. Eduardo repeated his request. "I demand that you give me back that letter. It's mine! "

Eduardo stuck out his hand. His eyes mirrored his determination. Jairo gave in before the force of the demand and returned it. His bafflement was obvious. What would happen now?

Eduardo continued. "Give me your lighter."

Jairo didn't understand.

"Your cigarette lighter, please!"

Jairo handed it over. Eduardo gave the letter one last look, flicked on the lighter and brought the bluish gas flame near the edge of the paper. The flames licked at the paper, hungrily devouring it. It spread rapidly, changed the color of the paper to an ashen brown, and finally to a charred heap of tiny black pieces that fell soundlessly down to the carpet. The letters of death had disappeared ...

Jairo stared as one hypnotized, as if looking at some ancient ritual.

Eduardo returned the lighter. A wide smile lit up his face.

"It's hard for me to admit it, but you're right. I must not fulfill this last wish. No, the opposite: I must take vengeance upon those 'parents' who adopted me, against my will. I must devote my entire life to such revenge. To love, instead of hating."

He grew silent and gave Jairo a dark look.

"But how? How?"

Jairo didn't answer. He remembered his doubts and struggles, the torments he'd undergone when he suddenly realized that the Jewish destiny had him in its grip, despite his feelings of being a Brazilian. He understood Eduardo and how he felt about his new situation. A non-Jew, an anti-Semite, suddenly finding out that he was, indeed, Jewish. No, Jairo had no answer. Each person had to find his own way. To deal with it by himself. And he, Jairo, still didn't know what his own lot would be.

Eduardo stood up.

"I've decided. I'm going."

"Where?"

"To Israel. I want to meet that Jew again. Tell him who I am. And then, disappear."

"But why?"

Eduardo's voice came out, almost a tortured scream. "Leave me alone! Don't ask me questions!"

Jairo closed his eyes for a moment. "Eduardo."

"Yes?"

"I'm coming with you."

Eduardo was shocked. "Why?"

"I don't know. Maybe it's still coincidences sending me there. I just don't know."

After a moment's hesitation he added, "And maybe I can help you."

They stood, the two of them, in the center of the office, staring at each other. Their eyes met; the two shook hands warmly. It was a firm handshake that underscored a new understanding between them ...

They stood to say goodbye. It was easy for them, though neither knew what the future would bring. The two stood next to the office door. Jairo, particularly, began to hurry. His mind whirled with thoughts on how to calm down his wife's perfectly justified anger.

Suddenly Jairo grabbed his head. "What fools we are!"

Eduardo spun around. "What's the matter?"

"How can you go? Do you think that anyone there, in Israel, will believe this crazy story? They'll laugh at you! You should have heard my father make fun of me when I read him the letter. He didn't believe a word of it. Maybe if he'd have seen the letter with his own eyes and recognized Alberto's handwriting, he would have felt differently. But now that you've burned the letter — what's left?"

Eduardo understood. "So what do we do now?"

"I ... I really don't know."

Tel Hashomer Hospital
9 Iyar 5727

Yitzchak Austerlitz had not yet awoken; from the time he'd been brought into the hospital he'd been wholly unconscious. The doctors wouldn't tell Rivka a thing, neither good nor bad. From the few things she'd managed to overhear she understood that the situation was critical. Very critical. They were talking about brain damage. Even if he lived, he would be paralyzed. His chances? One of the few doctors who would volunteer a tidbit of information merely threw up his hands as if to say, only Heaven knew. Rivka, in despair, decided to call her son, her Yaakov Yehoshua, from his yeshiva.

51

Jairo arrived at his office early in the morning. He'd scheduled a meeting for 10 to clarify matters with Francisco. It wouldn't hurt, he thought, to be prepared for the conference, one that could be crucial to the continued existence of their partnership. Today, Monday, he was feeling a little calmer than he'd been during the weekend. He'd been particularly worked up over his extraordinary conversation with Eduardo. Even now, after hours of deep thought, he felt he lacked the proper tools to evaluate and understand Eduardo's incredible story, and what position he should take with regards to it. It was undoubtedly, as they say, a story "larger than life," that placed everything that had happened to him, Jairo, in a different light.

The short vacation they'd had on Sunday in Santos and Sao Vicente had done him good. His wife and children had spent it on the beach while he, Jairo, had wandered in his car among the picturesque villages that dotted the Atlantic coastline. He had even taken a ferry to the magical island of Guaruja. Interesting, this was the first time he'd noticed the fact that many Brazilians called the island "Guarujalem," a word that sounded similar to the Portuguese pronunciation of Jerusalem. The large numbers of Jews who'd built themselves houses on the island, and who would come to vacation on its beautiful beaches, clearly disturbed some Brazilians. He'd never before noticed the latent anti-Semitism hidden in the phrase.

His lone rambles, with no one to disturb him, enabled him to think in peace about what had happened to him. And, particularly, on what would happen to him in the future. He knew, with crystal clarity, that his life was going to change. But he didn't know how, by how much, or when. The Jewish feelings that had been aroused within him would demand it of him, would give him no rest. They had grabbed him and would not let him fall once again solely into his career, his search for clients and cash. Could he explain these things to Francisco? To his wife, Paulina? To his father? These thoughts oppressed him, even during the quiet calmness of vacation. His chest would begin to feel tight; his emotions became a dark, turbulent whirlpool. At these moments he would pull the car over, jump out, and take a long look at the great blue ocean that ebbed and flowed towards him. His eyes would take in the horizon, so far away as to be almost indiscernible.

Jairo looked at his watch. 9:45. Another few minutes and Francisco would be here. Jairo didn't really know how much he could make his faithful friend, almost like a brother to him, share in his doubts and questions. For, despite everything, Francisco was not Jewish. A fine Brazilian gentile, with whom one could get along beautifully — but a gentile nevertheless. Could his friend understand what went on in a normal young brain when suddenly confronted with the inescapable fact of his Jewishness? Jairo didn't know. Obviously, he would say nothing of Eduardo, not even give a hint of it. For that matter, where was Eduardo now? He'd invited him to join the family in Santos, but Eduardo had declined. When they parted Eduardo explained that he felt a deep need to be alone, alone with his stormy thoughts. From then on, he'd given no indication that he was alive. Jairo was beginning to feel worried. After the meeting with Francisco, he would call the *Estado de Sao Paulo*. Perhaps they knew where Eduardo had gone ...

Francisco arrived at exactly 10 o'clock. A wide smile covered his face when he burst into the office, a smile that immediately dissipated all of Jairo's tension.

"Hello, how are you, Jairo?"

"*Gracas a De-us*, fine."

Francisco burst out laughing. "You look good! Of course, why not? At last you got smart. Santos, Sao Vicente, Guaruja. You finally realized that that's better for a man than running after Nazis, or running away from them, hey?"

He walked towards Jairo and gave him a friendly slap on the shoulder. Jairo bent slightly forward under the impact. Beneath his aching muscles he could sense a powerful feeling of friendship and amity.

"You're right," Jairo answered, "Santos is certainly better for someone who wants to relax and not learn anything about life or from life. This time, Santos was very different for me, after all I've been through. And I mean that in a positive sense."

After a moment's silence he added, "But let me not confuse you. From our point of view, and from the point of view of the office, at least, I hope that whatever happened — happened. A new day has begun! A new week! A new year!"

A smile appeared on Jairo's face as he ended his speech. "Okay?"

His smile is forced, came the unbidden thought into Francisco's head. *Why?*

"And why do you say it's a new day for the office? And what about you personally? Is it still yesterday for you? With Hunkes? With the Nazis?"

Jairo took a deep breath. "No, Francisco, even for me today is, it seems, a new day. But not a day completely unconnected with what happened, like the new day which I hope will begin in the office, if you want to continue our partnership. Today begins a new day for me because of the Hunkeses, the Nazi funeral, the pursuit that, by the way, has ended. They'll be leaving me alone."

Francisco crossed his legs and the fingers of his left hand tapped gently on the desk.

"I don't understand."

"What?"

"I suspect that you haven't yet freed yourself completely from the affair. Are you in contact with any doctors?"

Jairo gave Francisco an amused look of comprehension.

"Understand, Francisco, it's over! Finished! That's it! If you want we can turn over a new page in this office this very instant. And that's what's important to the two of us. If you see any changes in me that disturb our office work — as it did last week — I promise to see a doctor immediately. Okay?"

Francisco didn't answer. He listened quietly, thoughtfully, to Jairo's next words.

"I'm not crazy, Francisco. It's true, I've changed. Absolutely. But I'm all right. Totally. Maybe I was crazy before this."

"What does that mean?"

Jairo laughed heartily. "It's not important. Let's get on with business!"

Jairo thrust out a hand towards Francisco, as a sign of their newly agreed-upon commitment to each other. A short moment of hesitation, and the two were shaking hands. Francisco had never intended to break up their partnership. He would give it another try.

"And what about Paulo?" Jairo asked.

Francisco didn't hurry to answer.

"You can tell me everything. Today, I can take it."

"Okay. I'm not certain, but it's possible he's left the office."

"Why?"

No answer.

"Because I'm ... a Jew?"

Silence.

"Did the new outbreak of tensions in the Middle East arouse something in him?"

"Not exactly. But ... maybe a little." Francisco gave a distressed nod of his head. "I don't know."

"And—"

"The GAC affair angered him."

"And then?"

"He tried to get them to sign with him alone."

"And what happened?"

"One of the executives, Hermann Schmidt, made problems for him. He's the one who told us to persuade you to stop looking into Hunkes's identity."

Jairo gave an inward smile. He knew whom Francisco was talking about. The grey-haired man, Reuven Morag. But of course he kept silent.

"Okay, so we'll go on without Paulo. That's life."

The telephone rang. Francisco picked up the receiver. "Silverman, Machado, and Chi—"

At the last moment he stopped, not finishing the name of his former partner. "Good morning."

Francisco listened for a minute. His face grew gloomy. He handed the receiver over to Jairo and whispered, "It's a new Hunkes looking for you. Eduardo."

The enthusiasm that lit up Jairo's face when he heard the name of the caller did not please Francisco. Something told him his partner had not yet finished with this strange affair. But Jairo paid him no heed.

"Hello, Eduardo? Great, I was worried about you."

Jairo didn't notice Francisco leave the room. His attention was completely focused on Eduardo, on the other side of the line.

"Do you hear, Jairo? This morning I began to believe a little in your tales of all the 'coincidences.' "

"What happened?"

"Since we met yesterday I've been at home, in bed. I felt like a mountain had dropped onto me, and it was just too much for me. I couldn't lift it by myself. And I was furious with myself for having, in a moment of anger, burned the letter, the only testimony and proof of this crazy story. Do you hear?"

"Yes."

"I was completely depressed. Alberto Hunkes, it seemed, had beaten me. I felt that despite everything he'd gotten his wish. But this morning the newsroom called me. Can you hear me?"

"Yes. What did they want?"

"They told me that a notary by the name of Dr. Antonio Batista de Oliveira was looking for me. He wanted me to come to his office immediately."

"Yes?"

"And so I went. And it was worth it."

"Why? What did he want?"

"He opened an envelope containing the will of my cursed 'parents.' "

"And what did it say?"

"Give me a minute and I'll tell you!"

"Sorry."

"They again repeated all that Alberto Hunkes had written in the other letter. That I was not their son, that I am ... a Jew, son of someone named Austerlitz, from a village in Galicia. Believe me, Jairo, it's hard for me to relate to the word 'Jew'!"

There was a short silence on the line.

"And particularly," Eduardo continued, "it said that all their property, their apartment and its contents, their bank deposits and everything else does not belong to me and I have no rights to them. They appointed Dr. Batista de Oliveira the executor to sell all their property and give the proceeds to some relative in Germany. Believe me, I don't care who she is."

"What are you going to do about it? We're talking about a lot of money!"

"I'm not going to do anything! You don't seem to understand what I'm talking about. This legal declaration helped me free myself of them. That's it. I no longer feel myself a person by the name of Hunkes!"

"Instead—"

Again, silence. This time, the quiet seemed heavier, laden with tension.

"Instead?" Eduardo's quiet voice continued. "Instead? That is, indeed, the problem. I don't know yet. But it seems again that you've missed the point. Something happened here that you would no doubt call incredible. Don't you see?"

Jairo tried but failed. "No. What do you mean?"

"I received, from a completely unexpected source, an official notification that this story is true! This is worth more, much more than the letter that went up in smoke. This really fits your philosophy of 'coincidences.' Understand?"

Jairo felt a surge of satisfaction. "Yes, I do! And how I do!"

After a moment's thought, he added, "Great. So it's okay to travel to Israel."

"Don't jump to conclusions, Jairo."

Jairo's face evidenced surprise. "What's that mean? Have you changed your mind?"

"I don't know how to express this. But I thought, what do I need this for? Okay, I lost my parents. But I'm not so anxious to meet new ones. It's hard. They're not like me."

Jairo didn't rush to reply. He felt a sudden anger choking him. He couldn't understand why he cared so much about Eduardo's future life. But with that, he couldn't ignore the powerful desire to see Eduardo pick up the gauntlet that Hunkes-Krantz had flung at him. *It seems the Jew in me is working overtime*, he thought.

"Eduardo, are you listening to me?" he said authoritatively.

"Yes."

"Repeat after me. 'Heil Hitler!' 'Heil Alberto Hunkes!' They are the victors!"

Eduardo reeled from the blow. "What are you saying? Are you crazy?"

"No! But if you've decided to put into operation the personal Final Solution that the Nazi Krantz planned for you, at least do it with due ceremony. Give a salute and call out, 'Sieg Heil!' "

"What do you want from me?" Eduardo asked brokenly, on the edge of tears.

Jairo had no mercy. He continued to pound at him. "Your job now is to fight the Nazis! Not to do their will! Your war is clear: to destroy the plans of Alberto Hunkes; to act in the exact opposite manner from what he desired. So you must travel to Israel! Understand?"

Eduardo didn't answer. A flood of emotions had washed over him, like the torrential waters of the Iguasu waterfalls. He felt himself choking. He understood, logically, that Jairo was correct. And yet he couldn't follow the path that logic mandated. The emotional effort that such actions demanded was too much for him. It was impossible.

"Do you think they'll believe this fantastic tale? Do you think it will be easy for them, with a lost son suddenly turning up out of nowhere? Why not let the matter die on its own? Why make it harder for them? Enough, Jairo, that I have this unsolvable problem to deal with."

Jairo was silent. It was true: a problem. How to make the Austerlitz family believe that Eduardo was, truly, their son, reappearing from the ruins of the war? Suddenly, he had an idea.

"Eduardo?"

"*Si?*"

"Listen. I'll meet you at seven at the corner of Tiete and Haddock Lobo Streets."

"Why?"

"There's a synagogue there, where I met the religious man named Meir. I think that is the time they pray there. Maybe we'll meet him, and get his advice. Okay?"

In a weak and defeated voice, Eduardo gave his unwilling answer. "Okay."

Tel Hashomer Hospital
12 Iyar 5727

There was no change in Yitzchak Austerlitz's condition. This was the fourth day he lay unconscious, uncomprehending. Rivka anxiously watched the frequent visits of Yitzchak's friends. Perhaps they knew something she didn't? The doctors didn't talk. "We've got to wait," was their laconic reply to all her frenzied questions. Yitzchak Mandelkorn, faithful friend and *chavrusa,* was a daily visitor, assuring Rivka, "We are *davening* for his complete recovery. It's in G-d's hands."

Despair engulfed Rivka's heart. She wordlessly cursed this Heinz Krantz, this bestial Nazi, who had so wounded an innocent Jew 22 years after the war had ended ...

Sao Paulo, Brazil
May 22, 1967

Eduardo's and Jairo's cars reached the appointed spot in the luxurious Jardim America neighborhood at the same time. They both parked on Haddock Lobo, crossed the street and walked towards the synagogue. Jairo opened the small gate that led to the entranceway. There they stood.

Jairo's eyes searched for Meir among the congregants who were praying quietly. This was a difficult scene for Eduardo to watch. *These are my brothers,* came the frightening thought. He moved a trembling hand towards his face, as if to wipe off imaginary sweat. *It can't be!* His eyes closed, as if he desired to flee from the sight of the worshipers. But he knew: *too late*. There was no way back ...

The synagogue emptied. The congregants looked curiously at the strangers. Eduardo made a manly attempt not to meet the eyes of the passing men. Finally, only three of them remained in the synagogue. Eduardo, Jairo, and Meir ...

52

The three stood on the threshold of the synagogue. Meir, last of the worshipers, slowly switched off the lights, leaving only the bulb that illuminated the spot where they were standing. The dimness of the yard outside enveloped the synagogue itself. Eduardo stared curiously at the *aron kodesh*, at the *bimah* standing in the center of the room, at the rows of benches that reminded him of a church. His eyes moved slowly over the bookshelves that lined the walls, shelves laden with oversized volumes reminiscent of ancient lawbooks that he'd seen in libraries. Strange to see them in a place of prayer. His feeling of discomfort grew greater from minute to minute ...

Meir broke the silence. "How can I help you, *senhores*?"

Jairo spoke after a brief silence. Meir listened courteously and attentively to his words. He didn't believe a word of it, but he remained quiet. He remembered the strange story that Jairo had told him last week. And now he brought new fantasies with him. Jairo spoke quietly, with a voice heavy with emotion, glancing frequently towards Eduardo for confirmation. A passing thought flitted through Meir's mind: *Who knew what crazy tale the lawyer would bring next week?*

Suddenly, Meir's face changed. His cynical look disappeared, replaced by one of utmost seriousness. He held the notarized declaration that Eduardo, at Jairo's behest, had handed him. He squinted at the page in the dimness of the one bulb. His fingers gripped the paper tightly in his hand. It seemed that the story, that transformed a young Nazi into a Jew, was not a delusion. There was, at least, something in it. It was hard to deny such an official document. He knew Dr. Batista de Oliveira personally, knew him as an upright and honest man. He wouldn't endanger his professional standing with foolishness. The document certainly gave some confirmation of the unbelievable story. Meir gave Eduardo a searching look. He looked at his face, his gentile face, for a spark of Jewishness. He couldn't be sure if he saw any sign. Meir, confused, asked, "Why have you told me this story?"

"We need help."

Meir looked puzzled. "For what? Conversion?"

"No."

"So what?"

"Do you have any relatives or friends in Israel?"

"Yes. Why?"

"Are they religious?"

"Yes. Why do you ask? What do you want of them?"

"Maybe one of them knows this Austerlitz, his father?"

Jairo pointed towards Eduardo.

"It could be. So what?"

"Maybe you can do us a favor and ask him to tell Austerlitz what we've just told you."

Meir looked at them, uncomprehending.

"Why is that so important?"

Jairo and Eduardo exchanged a quick glance, one not lost on Meir.

"He," Jairo's arm rested on Eduardo's shoulder, "wants to go to Israel. He wants ... to meet him."

Meir's hand stroked his forehead, then traveled down to his wispy beard, as if he would find an answer there.

"Okay," he said after a long silence in which the tension in Jairo's heart grew, "I've got an idea. Call my house after midnight. I'll know then if I can help you. I'll call Israel at midnight. It will be early in the morning there. I've got relatives in Bnei Brak. It's a small city, mostly religious, near Tel Aviv. I'll speak with them and see."

Jairo called Meir at 1 in the morning. He was wide awake and it seemed to Jairo that his voice was excited. *Perhaps*, he thought, *perhaps he, too, feels the urgency of this incredible hour. Perhaps.*

"*Senhor* Silverman? It's all taken care of. My relatives were in total shock when I told them the story. Finally, I managed to persuade them. They don't know Yitzchak Austerlitz personally, but they know who he is, they've heard of him. A few minutes ago my cousin in Israel phoned me and told me the details of the story match with what is known over there. The fact that he is ill, and how he fell ill, also corroborate the story. He said that despite the early hour, the story is already going all around Bnei Brak."

"Thank you so much, *Senhor* Meir."

Meir hung up the phone. He prepared for bed. He skimmed through his *siddur*, searching for *Krias Shema*. Suddenly, he stopped. His eyes focused on the bookshelf that covered a wall in his living room. In the deep silence of the late hour, he could clearly feel the emotion that gripped him and overpowered his heart. Here he had been a tool in Providence's Hand. A tool to help bring, perhaps, a Jew that had been banished, back into the arms of Israel. Who knew? He'd become that tool involuntarily, without seeking the job. He was a necessary link in an involved chain. By coincidence ("coincidence?") he'd met with some confused Jewish attorney last week. That meeting began this evening's drama. Suddenly, Meir couldn't relax. He remembered, for some reason, the story of Yosef in *Sefer Bereishis*. What was written there? Yosef had gotten lost in the fields of Dosan. And it said, "A man found him." A "man" showed him the way to his brothers in Shechem. At that moment, without ever knowing it, that "man" changed the course of history of the Jewish people eternally. It seemed that this had been his fate, as well, this evening: a tool for some important and great matter, whose conclusion one couldn't know ...

Bnei Brak
13 Iyar 5727

Yitzchak Mandelkorn moved abstractedly across the *shul*. His *tallis* hung from one shoulder. It was hard for him to believe that he would manage to concentrate on his prayers this morning, not after the news that he'd heard, from reliable sources. He simply couldn't keep it to himself ...

Rabbi Mandelkorn sat down on the first bench that he passed. He paid no attention to the others who had begun to pray. His right hand slowly rubbed his temples, sliding down his face until the tip of his long beard. He suddenly remembered the conversation he'd had with Austerlitz last Shabbos after prayers, on Rechov Rabbi Akiva. Now, only now, could he truly understand Reb Yitzchak's words to him: "I still mourn my family, and particularly my son, Yaakov Yehoshua, may G-d avenge his blood."

Rabbi Mandelkorn remembered well how Reb Yitzchak had continued with the following words: "Like Yaakov mourned for 22 years for his son, Yosef."

Rabbi Mandelkorn lay his head down on the table. After a few seconds he moved restlessly. *How great and wondrous are the ways of Hashem! And so hidden from us! No man can understand them! It seems that Yitzchak Austerlitz was right! He was truly mourning, as did his forefather Yaakov Avinu, whose son, Yosef, was ultimately returned to him. Incredible are G-d's ways!*

Hot tears fell from his eyes like pearls. He knew: He must go immediately after *davening* to the hospital. He had the holy obligation to tell Yitzchak Austerlitz the news. To tell that good, tortured soul, lying in its defeated body, its unresponsive body, its unconscious body, the incredible news. Perhaps he would hear it, hear it and awaken. Things like that had happened in the past. Doctors constantly told the family to speak to the patient. Perhaps this would be how salvation would come? Who knew?

Sao Paulo, Brazil
May 23, 1967

Jairo left his home in the morning and drove straight to the office. He knew he couldn't back down now. They would be flying to Israel that very day. With every fiber of his being he felt that his destiny was linked with that of Eduardo. He felt, that as a result of the support that he, Jairo, had given Eduardo these past few days, he was involved in an effort that was binding him, Jairo himself, to the Jewish people.

He called his travel agent from the office, ordered two tickets to Paris with a direct transfer to Tel Aviv. He hurriedly let Eduardo know that he should be at the Congonhas Airport in the evening. They'd meet at the Varig counter at 8. He would tell his wife that business matters were taking him to Europe for a few days. He must conceal his true destination: The thought of him traveling to Israel would undoubtedly send her into a panic. The news coming out of the Middle East indicated that war was imminent. Consulates were already warning their citizens to leave the area of tensions. Yes, neither Paulina nor his partner, Francisco, must know where he was going.

Tel Hashomer Hospital
13 Iyar 5727

"Reb Yitzchak, can you hear me?"

Rabbi Yitzchak Mandelkorn leaned on the patient's bed. He stared at the body, lying unconscious, attached to various pieces of equipment, its breath labored and shallow. Rabbi Mandelkorn's heart thudded within him at the sight of his friend. That morning he'd done his best not to speak with Rivka. He was afraid of the surge of emotion that would beset her when she heard the incredible news. But when he arrived at the hospital he found she'd already heard rumors of the lost son who had suddenly been found. Rabbi Mandelkorn found her sitting quietly by her husband's bed, endlessly drying moist eyes with her handkerchief.

Rabbi Mandelkorn bent over the patient. "Reb Yitzchak! I've come with news today! G-d loves you very, very much! Something has happened to you that didn't happen to millions of Jews who died in Hitler's tortures. Your son, Yaakov Yehoshua, was not killed by Heinz Krantz! Can you hear me, Reb Yitzchak? He's alive! He's been found! I am speaking the truth, Reb Yitzchak!"

His voice was beseeching …

Rabbi Mandelkorn looked intensely at the frozen face of Yitzchak Austerlitz. Nothing. No reaction at all.

He glanced at Rivka, then looked immediately back at the still body on the bed. He took a deep breath, gathered all of his rapidly dissipating energies, and tried again.

"Did you hear me? Your son, Yaakov Yehoshua, who was born to you in Galicia — is alive! Alive! Alive! Do you hear me? He's in Brazil. He didn't even know he was Jewish. Can you hear me, Reb Yitzchak?"

Again, no reaction. Rabbi Mandelkorn raised his arm in a gesture of despair. *What a terrible situation*, he thought, *that just when the son is found, Yitzchak cannot rejoice with him! Please Hashem, help, please! Give us a good sign …*

Sao Paulo, Brazil
May 23, 1967

Jairo was content. Eduardo had come to the airport as they'd agreed. Up until the last minute, Jairo was afraid he'd disappear, that he would not be able to bear the thought of the difficult reunion that awaited him. But Eduardo didn't disappoint him. At least, not yet. Jairo was also pleased with the success of his deception: His wife hadn't asked many questions, despite her usual habit of interrogating him closely about his affairs. She simply accepted his reasons for the trip without inquiry. Francisco, too, was simpler to deal with than usual. He didn't ask, he didn't investigate. When the plane finally took off, the thought flashed through Jairo's head: *Again, this Divine Providence of Meir's is pushing me ahead, taking all obstacles out of my path*. The thought surprised Jairo, but left him with a feeling of contentment. He grinned at Eduardo, who sat quietly, somberly, deep within his own gloomy thoughts ...

> *Tel Hashomer Hospital*
> *13 Iyar 5727*

Rabbi Mandelkorn wouldn't give up. He gently took the sick man's hand and patted it. His voice was quiet and reassuring. "Reb Yitzchak, G-d's salvation comes in the blink of an eye. Just as your son has appeared from out of nowhere, so you will be cured quickly, suddenly. But Reb Yitzchak, the doctors say that much of your cure rests with you, with your will, with your faith. Now, Reb Yitzchak, prove it. G-didn't bring you this far so that you shouldn't live to see your son. Can you hear me, Reb Yitzchak?"

No. Nothing happened.

"Reb Yitzchak, I won't leave you, not until you give me a sign that you've heard me. Did you hear me? You must get better! Your son will need you very much. Who can help him become a Jew again, a good Jew, if not his father? Who will teach him to say *Krias Shema*, put on *tefillin*, keep Shabbos — except for you? Do you understand — it's not for your sake, but for his, that you must give us a sign of life!"

Yitzchak Austerlitz's labored breathing strengthened a little. Rabbi Mandelkorn gazed intently at him, in his heart a prayer. But after a minute everything returned as it had been before.

"Is there a patient here by the name of Austerlitz?"

Rabbi Mandelkorn and Rivka, the only ones in the room, looked up towards the speaker. Before them stood a young officer.

"Why?"

"I saw him collapse in the airport. He was actually talking with me."

They looked at the man wonderingly.

"I'm Second Lieutenant Ronny Lipschitz. I'm with the Army Spokesman's office. How is he?"

The looks of despair on their faces told the story only too well.

"Not good. He needs Heaven's mercy."

"So what's going to be?"

"What do you mean?"

"I don't know if you know. It happened during an interview with a Brazilian journalist."

"We know. It turns out to be his son."

"What?"

The word came out as a shout. It was clear that he didn't understand.

"It doesn't matter. That's our concern," Mandelkorn interjected quickly. "But what's brought you here?"

"I received a phone call from the journalist. He told me he's on his way here. He said he wanted to meet the Jew whom he'd interviewed that day in the airport. I came to see if he could speak with him. I see that his condition is serious. Should I phone him not to come?"

"No," Rabbi Mandelkorn shouted. "Don't do that! Let him come. Absolutely, let him come."

Ronny Lipschitz's gaze moved from the bearded rabbi to the woman who stood near him. *Something strange is happening here*, he thought. He left the room with hurried steps.

Rabbi Mandelkorn turned with new energy towards the patient.

"Did you hear, Reb Yitzchak, what the officer said? Your Yaakov Yehoshua is coming to Israel! Your Yaakov Yehoshua wants to meet you, his father! Your son is coming home! Will you greet him like this? Reb Yitzchak, it can't be!"

Rabbi Mandelkorn grabbed hold of Yitzchak's hand. Suddenly, he felt a movement in its fingers. They tensed up a little, and gently patted Rabbi Mandelkorn's hand. Rabbi Mandelkorn's heart began to beat wildly. "He heard me! He's giving me a sign!" Rabbi Mandelkorn gazed at Yitzchak's face. It seemed that one of the eyelids were twitching a little. He couldn't be certain. But that's what it looked like.

Rabbi Mandelkorn turned to Rivka, a wide smile on his face. "Call a nurse, a doctor, quickly."

The doctor heard Mandelkorn out. "If it's true, what you say, then we're at a crossroads. Good for you, for all of your efforts. Continue to inspire him with these stories."

Paris, France
May 24, 1967

The Varig D.C. 10 from Brazil landed at Orly Airport near Paris at 10 in the morning. Eduardo quietly followed Jairo towards the terminal. The night flight had passed in a long, deep, unbroken silence. Eduardo felt a rising tension. He had woken up several times during the flight. The ticking of his watch was like arrows shooting into his heart, reminding him of time passing, passing, bringing him ever closer to this impossible, inescapable reunion. At those moments he felt that he was suffocating. He shifted in his seat, and Jairo, awakened, asked, "What's happened?"

"Nothing. Everything's all right."

Jairo went back to sleep while he, Eduardo, lay with eyes wide open, listening to the hum of the plane's engines as it cut its way through the darkness ...

Jairo and Eduardo settled down in a corner of the giant airport. Their flight to Tel Aviv was at 5 p.m. They had almost seven hours to wait before the El Al jet would take off. Lost hours for Jairo. Difficult ones for Eduardo.

"Come, let's tour the city a little."

It was Jairo who made the suggestion.

"I don't feel like it. I'll be happy if you go on your own."

But Jairo stayed with him. He wouldn't leave Eduardo by himself. And so he sat and gazed vacantly for several hours, together with Eduardo, at the milling crowds that surged back and forth in the terminal. Their conversation was short and laden with emotion. Once, after long hours of silence, Eduardo spoke. "I feel like a 'kamikaze' pilot. He flew his suicide plane, saw his goal coming closer with incredible speed, dived into it and was blown to pieces."

"That's how you feel?"

A moment's hesitation. "Yes."

Jairo didn't agree. "It's not at all the same, Eduardo. The kamikaze's goal was to be destroyed. He wanted to blow himself up. And you — no! At least, I hope so."

Eduardo didn't answer. From moment to moment contrasting emotions surged through his heart. From the house of Alberto Hunkes to a connection with some anonymous Jew, whom he didn't know, whose way of life he didn't know. Finally, he burst out. "You don't understand me!"

"Eduardo, you're wrong. I'm in the same boat as you, just in a different place. I, too, was pulled into this strange world just recently. I, too, am in the middle of changing worlds. It's hard. It's wild. True. But why think in terms of destruction? Because the changes take their emotional toll? But isn't truth worth more?"

"What truth are you talking about?"

"For you — finding your true father. For me — finding my deep ties with the Jewish people."

Jairo handed Eduardo a cigarette. The two smoked in silence for a long, long while.

Tel Hashomer Hospital
13 Iyar 5727

Rabbi Mandelkorn felt encouraged. "See, G-d's salvation is near. He pressed my hand lightly. I'm sure of it. I felt his fingers tighten around mine. The doctor said that if I'm right, we may be at a breakthrough. Let us have faith in G-d — that this is, truly, a breakthrough."

He spoke quietly, pleasantly, with confidence. Rivka didn't answer. She merely nodded her head as a sign that she understood him.

"I have the impression," Rabbi Mandelkorn continued, "that the fact that his Yaakov Yehoshua is coming gave him a shock. I felt his fingers press on mine at that exact moment. We must use the opportunity. Maybe this is where the cure will begin."

Rivka still kept her silence. Rabbi Mandelkorn turned to leave.

"Call me the minute the Brazilian comes. It doesn't matter when, night or day. I want to be here when they meet. It's important. In a difficult meeting such as this, it's important that every word be appropriate. The smallest error can have grave consequences."

Rabbi Mandelkorn lapsed into silence. Finally, he took his leave of his unconscious friend. "*Shalom* and *refuah sheleimah*. I hope you've understood what I said to you."

Lod Airport
May 25, 1967

The El Al flight from Paris landed at 3 in the morning. There'd been a seven-hour delay at Orly. The plane was jammed with Israelis, who continued to flock back to their homeland as the tension on the Israeli-Egyptian border increased. In Paris they heard that the Egyptian president had decided to close the Straits of Tiran to Israeli shipping. War! the Parisian papers proclaimed. Jairo and Eduardo tried to lose themselves among the noisy passengers. After their exhausting day in the Paris airport, they couldn't get a moment's rest with all the noise and clamor on the plane. They reached Lod exhausted and drained. Eduardo noticed many changes since the week before. Security had been tightened; there were many more soldiers in the area. And the first signs of a blackout could be seen.

Ronny Lipschitz was waiting for Eduardo. They gave each other an exuberant Brazilian bear hug.

"Please meet my friend, attorney Jairo Silverman."

"Pleased to meet you."

There was a handshake and an exchange of smiles. Then they entered the military jeep that would take them to Tel Hashomer.

They reached the hospital at 4 in the morning. A thick fog hung over the ground, soon to be dissolved in the early morning chill. Ronny Lipschitz wandered through the paths of the hospital until he'd found the entrance to ward 24. He helped Eduardo jump from the jeep, noticing that the young man was trembling slightly. He didn't ask unnecessary questions. The strange sentence that had slipped out from the mouth of the rabbi in Austerlitz's room seemed to dance before his eyes: "It turns out to be his son." Ronny shrugged his shoulders and brought Eduardo and Jairo to the darkened room.

Eduardo stopped at the threshold. From this vantage point he stared at the bearded man who lay unconscious on his bed. A small bulb illuminated the room. Near the bed Eduardo could see a thin woman sitting on a chair, a scarf covering her head. At the same moment a tall young man with a dark beard entered the room. The scene in front of Eduardo seemed to have come from another world.

The bearded man turned to Second Lieutenant Lipschitz.

"Which of the two men is the journalist?"

The officer pointed to Eduardo.

The bearded man approached him and shook his hand warmly. Then he turned to the sickbed.

"Reb Yitzchak, come see. The miracle has happened! Your Yaakov Yehoshua is now standing here in the room. Yes, standing right next to me! The miracles of Providence! Show us a sign of life for his sake. Reb Yitzchak, please! He's come here, here, from a long and bitter exile that lasted tens of years, the exile of a

Jew among gentiles. Will you not leave your own exile now? For his sake, Reb Yitzchak, for your son."

Ronny Lipschitz whispered a Portuguese translation into Eduardo's ear. Eduardo leaned on Jairo's shoulder. He felt his entire body go weak. His knees trembled.

Rabbi Mandelkorn motioned to Eduardo to come closer. Eduardo approached the bed with slow, careful steps. Rabbi Mandelkorn took Eduardo's hand and put it into Yitzchak Austerlitz's lifeless one. Eduardo closed his eyes. He seemed to hear the echo of explosions in his mind.

"Reb Yitzchak, can you hear me? You are holding the hand of your son, your Yaakov Yehoshua, who was born to you in Galicia. Reb Yitzchak, have mercy on him and show him a sign of life."

A sudden trembling overcame Austerlitz's hand. His lips moved, for a breathless moment, without making a sound. Rabbi Mandelkorn leaned close to him; perhaps he would make out a word or two. Nothing. And yet he saw that Eduardo wanted to pull away, and could not. The sick man's hand had grasped his tightly; Eduardo surrendered.

But it was too hard. Eduardo felt he was suffocating; he could no longer bear it. He wanted to get away at any price. But the sick man wouldn't let him go. And so a battle raged between the two, a battle that reached its inevitable conclusion: Eduardo, the winner, broke away.

And then it happened! Yitzchak Austerlitz's body shifted. He slowly lifted a hand, as one looking for something to hold on to; after a moment the hand fell weakly back onto the bed.

No one said a word.

Suddenly, Yitzchak opened his eyes slightly. Rabbi Mandelkorn gripped the bedframe to stop his trembling. First Yitzchak gave a blank stare, the eyeballs moving sightlessly back and forth. But slowly, slowly his gaze grew clear. He stared at the people surrounding his bed in deep terror. Rabbi Mandelkorn understood. He grabbed Eduardo and said out loud, "Reb Yitzchak, this is your Yaakov Yehoshua. He is here. He isn't going."

The gaze shifted. Slowly, slowly the terror disappeared, and great tears flowed out, down his face, down his cheeks, vanishing into his beard. His eyes tried to focus on the face of the young man being held by Rabbi Mandelkorn, but his head kept falling backwards. With a great show of strength he opened his eyes again, lifted his hand. Lipschitz translated Rabbi Mandelkorn's urgent request: "Hold his hand, quickly!"

Eduardo acceded, as one bewitched. He grabbed the outstretched hand. The eyes of the sick man seemed to smile weakly, then closed. His head lolled on the pillow, his lips moved soundlessly. Austerlitz's body relaxed. Just the hand, the hand gripping that of Eduardo, remained firm and tight.

Rivka sat and wept. Rabbi Mandelkorn, too, could not contain the tears. Jairo put his arm around Eduardo, who remained rooted to the spot. Ronny Lipschitz watched the drama that he'd somehow become involved in, biting his nails nervously.

Rabbi Mandelkorn was the first to recover.

"Tell him," he turned to Lipschitz, "tell him that he just saved his father from certain death. Since the moment he was taken ill, this was the first time he showed a response like this. He's opened his eyes, moved his hand. He'll recover. And they will learn to live together. It will be hard, I know. But it will be, if G-d so wills it. But tell him, now, only that he saved his father's life."

Eduardo heard the words without reacting. He gently pulled his hand away from that of his father, and left the room.

The coolness of dawn whipped at his face. His tear-filled eyes stared at the dark sky. It was a darkness that contained no stars to illuminate it, the darkness before dawn. In the east, beyond the buildings of the hospital complex, he could see the purple sky heralding the sunrise. The darkness of night was slowly lifting the hem of its black robes and turning towards the light of day.

Eduardo knew: From the darkness, a new day would dawn.